THE DEVIL'S BANQUET

PHIL LECOMBER

TITAN BOOKS

The Devil's Banquet
Print edition ISBN: 9781835417317
E-book edition ISBN: 9781835417324

Published by Titan Books
A division of Titan Publishing Group Ltd
144 Southwark Street, London SE1 0UP
www.titanbooks.com

First edition: June 2026
10 9 8 7 6 5 4 3 2 1

This is a work of fiction. All of the characters, organizations, and events portrayed in this novel are either products of the author's imagination or are used fictitiously. Any resemblance to actual persons, living or dead (except for satirical purposes), is entirely coincidental.

A CIP catalogue record for this title is available from the British Library.

EU RP (for authorities only)
eucomply OÜ, Pärnu mnt. 139b-14, 11317 Tallinn, Estonia
hello@eucompliancepartner.com, +3375690241

Printed and bound by CPI Group (UK) Ltd, Croydon, CR0 4YY.

In that broad banquet hall, the fiends one and all
Regardless of shriek, and of squeak, and of squall,
From one to another were tossing that small,
Pretty, curly-wigg'd boy, as if playing at ball.

—Richard Harris Barham, 'The Lay of
St Cuthbert; or The Devil's Dinner-Party'

A glossary of slang is provided at the end of the
book for those that would find it useful.

1

G EORGE HARLEY GAZED down on the flurry of early-morning activity from the first-floor window of his newly acquired offices in Frith Street. With the janes and their ponces, the villains and the showgirls, all still sleeping it off in the dingy bedsits and boarding houses of the capital, this time of day presented a good opportunity to study the well-oiled machinery which kept that gaudy old fairground ride of Soho trundling around on its tracks every night: kitchen porters on their way back from Berwick Street market, weaving between the pedestrians with their sack-barrows stacked with crates of fruit and veg; Italian waiters – smouldering beneath a thin veneer of Britishness – emerging from newsagents with Art Deco packets of Nazionale cigarettes and copies of *Il Popolo d'Italia* under their arms; stoic-faced shopkeepers mopping away diligently at their doorsteps to remove the unsavoury evidence of the previous night's debauchery; and, blocking the narrow streets and alleyways at every turn, the ubiquitous delivery vans – some new and resplendent in the liveries of long-established grocers, others beaten-up jalopies, crewed by furtive-looking individuals with Woodbines stuck to their bottom lip and caps pulled down to mask their ever-vigilant eyes. And here, nestled in the heart of it all, was the new George Harley Detective Agency.

Harley knew this should have been a moment to relish. After all, he'd fought long and hard in the four years since his beloved fiancée, Cynthia, had been brutally murdered in retaliation for him apprehending the infamous child-killer Osbert Morkens; a daily battle with grief, remorse and that Black Dog of depression; a struggle as hard at times as anything he'd faced in the trenches. But somehow, he'd managed to turn it around. He'd finally cut down on the drinking and had (reluctantly) once again confined the exquisite silver-inlaid opium pipe to its secret compartment in the chinoiserie escritoire. Following a few weeks of vigorous physical training, he now felt in good enough shape to return to working the streets of the capital; and so he'd recently taken the plunge and invested the nest egg left to him by his Uncle Blake in this new premises in Frith Street. Granted, the timing might not have been perfect – with the country struggling with its own harrowing bout of depression, caught in the tight grip of the Great Slump: unemployment at an all-time high, hunger marches on the streets, and the ominous shadow of fascism creeping over from the Continent. But here he was regardless, back from the brink, looking to the future once more, rather than lashing himself to the mast of that sinking ship of remorse. A significant achievement, in anyone's books.

But this new buoyant mood of Harley's had been punctured the previous evening by a worrying glimpse of someone from his past; someone he thought he'd just caught sight of again, down there in the busy Soho street, in the gap between the back of a delivery van and a teetering stack of cardboard boxes; someone dressed in an astrakhan coat and a top hat.

But when the fellow finally emerged in the stretch of open pavement, Harley saw his hat was actually a Derby, and the coat a slightly shabby Ulster. And besides, the face was all wrong. This character had a toothbrush moustache and the ruddy, well-fed cheeks of a provincial grocer – not the haunted features of the criminally insane. No, his mind was playing tricks on him again; hardly surprising, considering all the abuse he'd given it over the last few years with the drink and the dope. It clearly wasn't that shicer Osbert Morkens. After all, how could it be? The Nursery Butcher was safely banged up in the high-security wing of Broadmoor Asylum.

But if Morkens were still under lock and key, who, then, had he seen the previous night, leering at him from the back of a taxicab in Piccadilly Circus? It had certainly looked like the infamous professor – doffing his top hat in salutation to reveal that bald dome, housing what more than one expert had testified to be a brain of rare and exceptional quality. The experience had lasted for only a few seconds before the cab disappeared into the traffic, but it had left the private detective with a nauseous feeling, the ghost of which was still haunting his gut this following morning.

* * *

At the same moment Harley was gazing out of his office window, Elizabeth Chatterton stood before the anonymous-looking front door, feeling decidedly out of place amid the cosmopolitan bustle of the Soho morning. She was doing her best to ignore the posters displayed on the shabby façade of the neighbouring theatre – which was proving rather difficult, unaccustomed as she was to such brazen advertisement of the naked female form.

As she stood there, two off-duty showgirls tumbled out of the theatre's entrance, pushing past her with a cavalcade of throaty laughter. She watched as the confident young women teetered off up the street and felt another little flurry of trepidation for what lay ahead. The environment seemed so alien to her; all these coarse, extravagant types. How on earth would she manage to pull it off? Surely, she'd immediately be exposed as an impostor.

She regarded her reflection in the grubby window, giving a timid pat to the back of her shingled blonde hair.

Come on now, that's all just rot. You're merely wavering a little. A flutter of nerves, that's all it is.

Positive thinking, that was the thing. If the job was still going, then she'd make sure she presented as the best candidate. That was all there was to it.

Having made this silent, defiant assertion, she checked the address against the printed card from the Labour Exchange, set a smile on her slightly tremulous lips, and pressed the bell above the brass plaque labelled *The George Harley Detective Agency*.

* * *

She gave another little nervous cough. Up until a little while ago, she'd manage to convince herself the interview had been going well, but her prospective new employer had been silently gazing out of the office window now for well beyond what could be considered a normal pause. She wondered what on earth she'd said to upset him.

'Is there anything wrong, Mr Harley?'

'What…? Oh, no,' he said, returning to his seat with an embarrassed grin. 'Sorry, I got a little distracted.' He reached for the packet of Gold Flake as he quickly scanned his notes. 'Well now, I think that just about wraps it up.'

'Really? I was expecting a jolly good grilling, given the nature of your business.'

'To be straight with you, Miss Chatterton—'

'You know, I'd really rather you didn't call me that, it

reminds me of school. It's Bunty. Well, Elizabeth actually, but nobody ever calls me Elizabeth – apart from Great-Aunt Maud. And I only see her once a year, at Christmas. Big sis calls me Betty every now and again, but for the most part it's Bunty. Bunty Chatterton.'

'Got it.' Harley couldn't help thinking, regardless of what might come before it, how apt the young woman's surname was.

'Oh dear, am I talking too much? I do apologise. I'm a little nervous, you see.'

'There's really no need to be.'

'Oh, but I am. You see, I really do need this job, and compared to the other meagre offerings on show, I'd say this is a wizard opportunity.'

Harley gave a sigh. 'The thing is, I'm not so sure this is the right kind of caper for… well, for a young woman of your sort to get mixed up in.'

'But you saw me at the typewriter. I can do sixty words per minute on a good day. Oh, I know some of those typing pool girls can trump that standing on their heads, but I'm sure I'll improve with practice. And you've seen my testimonials; they're acceptable, aren't they?'

'The testimonials were blinding. But this ain't some dusty clerks' office up in the City. My line of work can sometimes be—'

'Dangerous?' interjected Bunty, a little too eagerly for Harley's liking.

'To be honest with you – yeah, dangerous. People can get…' He took a pull at his cigarette. 'Well, people can get hurt in this game.'

'I bet you're alright though, Mr Harley. You don't seem like the sort of chap that bruises easily. I'd say you're of the type my father used to call the Bulldog Breed… Once had that said of me, you know,' she added, with a wistful smile. 'When I was fielding goal for the first eleven.'

'We're talking about a little bit more than just a hockey

stick to the shin here. Anyway, it's not just the risk of violence. I mean, some of the characters I knock about with… well, let's just say they're probably a bit more colourful than what you're used to. Even just travelling to and from the office might be a bit of an eye-opener. In the depths of Soho here it's sometimes a bit…' Harley gave a little grimace by way of explanation. 'Especially at night. A young lady needs to have her wits about her in this part of town.'

He noticed that Bunty had suddenly lost her enthusiastic grin.

'I'll have you know, I'm quite capable of holding my own in most situations. Father was in the diplomatic service and from a very early age we were constantly being whisked off to the far reaches of the globe. I've had to fend for myself in many places I'm sure most girls would find quite challenging. The souks of Morocco, the back streets of Singapore, downtown Rangoon – these aren't places for the faint-hearted, Mr Harley.'

'Now, don't get me wrong. What I was saying was—'

'Are you really going to discriminate against me just because of… of… Well, what is it, actually? My social standing?' Getting increasingly worked up, the young woman now leant forward with her arms firmly crossed. 'Well, I must say, that really is the limit.'

'Alright, alright,' said Harley, holding his hands up. 'Point taken. But tell me something: if your father was a diplomat – are you really so desperate for the work?'

'You shouldn't let appearances deceive you. I lost my parents in an accident last October.'

'I'm sorry to hear that.'

'Yes, well, the long and short of it is that, after the executors had settled my father's affairs, it turned out that the family wasn't quite as well off as we'd assumed. Not well off at all, in fact. I know it's rather distasteful to talk about money, but believe me, I really do need this job, just to make ends meet.'

'And there's no prospects of…'

'Of what?'

'Well, most girls, most *young ladies* of your age, are…' Harley regarded Bunty's rather severe glare and decided to change tack. 'What I'm trying to say is—'

'What you're trying to say is, why don't I just get myself married off to the first willing man who comes along and resign myself to being an obedient little housewife for the rest of my life. Really, Mr Harley, with your earlier comments on the state of modern politics, I took you for someone who'd want to encourage emancipation in the workplace. I mean, hasn't a young woman as much right as—'

'Listen, Bunty,' he interjected. 'Let's just calm it down a bit, shall we? Just give me a minute to think here.'

Harley stubbed out his cigarette in the ashtray and took a moment to thumb through the details of the previous candidates he'd seen that week. It made for sorry reading – an assortment of flotsam and jetsam from the labour market, the majority of whom were drab, broken-spirited clerks cast adrift due to the downturn in the City. None of them had shown anything like the passion of this young woman's recent outburst. Harley had to admit that, though she might appear a little too 'jolly hockey sticks', Bunty Chatterton had some bottle – though he guessed she'd probably describe it as *pluck*. She would present well to the clients, of course, add a little class to the establishment. She was bright, and it sounded like she really could do with the work.

'And you've got some foreign languages, you say?'

'Yes. Almost fluent in German, and my Italian and French are passable.'

'Alright,' he said, tossing the paperwork back onto the desk. 'We both might live to regret this, but congratulations, you've got the job.'

'I have? Really? Why, that's wizard!'

'Yeah, ain't it just. But let's start out on a trial basis, shall we? We'll give it a fortnight and if one of us wants to knock it on the head, then we'll shake hands and part company. Agreed?'

'Knock it on the head?'

'Give it up as a bad job.'

'Oh, rest assured, I shan't be doing that, Mr Harley – I need the money.'

'Call me George.'

'Not in front of the clients, though. That wouldn't do – gives the wrong impression, don't you think?'

'Alright, Bunty,' said Harley, laughing as he came out from behind his desk. 'Have it your own way. In front of the punters I'll be Mr Harley, but it's George when we're alone. Deal?'

'Deal,' said the young woman, giving the detective's hand a surprisingly vigorous shake.

'So, when can you start?' said Harley, returning to the window to scrutinise the pedestrians in the street below.

'Straight away, if needed.'

'Good. Then you'd better start making like an assistant. Looks like we've got ourselves a punter. Come and look… Down there, see? Early fifties, reasonably expensive suit – though not of the latest cut. From out of town I'd say, maybe from up North, or the Midlands… possibly foreign. Definitely no Londoner.'

'How can you tell?' asked Bunty, looking at the individual in question on the opposite side of the street.

'His complexion, for one – far too healthy. It only takes a few months of living in the Smoke for your skin to adopt that jellied-eel pallor. And look – that's a folded copy of the *Oracle* he's holding. He's checking the address in my advertisement against the number on the door and asking himself what kind of business would set itself up next to a dodgy variety house offering non-stop nude revues. Which was exactly what you did before you came up, by the way.'

'But,' said Bunty, with a frown now marring her own out-of-town complexion, 'how can that possibly tell you he's not from London?'

'It's that look of distaste on his face. Look at him studying those posters displaying the dubious delights on offer at the Rendezvous. Now, your native Londoner might well be shocked and dismayed by some of the sights hereabouts; some of the things they get up to around here would make Old Nick blush. But the difference is, they'd never show it. Surviving in this city is all about wearing a mask, you see? Adopting a neutral stare set somewhere between boredom and mild irritation. Anything else makes you stick out like a steamer.'

'A steamer?'

'A steam tug – a mug. Easy pickings… Right, look sharp – he's finally taken the plunge. My guess is it's a wayward wife or a missing person. Grab that notebook there and make out you know what you're doing.'

'Gosh, George, how exciting.'

'That's Mr Harley to you, Miss Chatterton.'

* * *

Five minutes later the new client was installed in Harley's office, sipping Bunty's rather weak version of tea from a cup hastily reclaimed from one of the many packing cases lining the newly rented rooms. So far, the interview had attested to Harley's astute observational skills on two counts: Mr Parker was a reasonably successful businessman from the outskirts of Dudley, and he was seeking to engage the private detective in the investigation of the disappearance of his elder daughter, Louise, who had run away from the family home some eighteen months previously.

'For a while we had absolutely no idea whether she was alive or dead; it was as though she'd simply vanished off the face of the earth. Her mother was distraught, of course, near hysterical – and, seeing this, our younger daughter eventually confessed that Louise had actually maintained regular contact with her by way of a series of letters.'

'That must have been quite a relief, Mr Parker,' said Bunty.

'Hardly,' said Parker, with a dismissive sniff. 'It was in reading through this cache of clandestine correspondence that I discovered, to my utter horror, that our elder daughter had abandoned the comfort and security of a respectable family home to pursue her dream of becoming a dancer in a chorus line.'

'I'd say it sounds rather romantic,' ventured Bunty, provoking an admonishing look from her new employer.

'Romantic?!' spluttered Parker, spilling some of his tea into the saucer. 'A decent, well-brought-up girl, purposefully exposing herself on stage to the wanton desires of crowds of lascivious older men? When there's not a week goes by without one reading in the Sunday papers of the nefarious machinations of the narcotic pedlars, white slavers and other such undesirables who frequent these nightclubs and variety theatres? No, Miss Chatterton, I'm afraid I do not find such a foolhardy, infantile ambition romantic; not in the slightest. Quite frankly, my wife and I are terrified of what might happen to our daughter in such company… or, indeed, what might have already happened to her. And, of course, those fears were hardly allayed when Louise wrote to her sister from Paris, announcing she'd been engaged by a dance company led by an infamous German cabaret artiste by the name of Ilse Blau.'

'Blau, did you say?' said Harley, jotting down the name in his notebook.

'Yes,' said the aggrieved father, placing his cup and saucer on the desk and beginning to fill his pipe from a small leather pouch. 'By all accounts, Fräulein Blau caused quite a stir a couple of years back in the clubland of Berlin. I have it on good authority, Harley, that the city became a viper's nest of deviants under the Weimar regime; a magnet for degenerates of all types, seeking satisfaction for their despicable perversions. By all accounts these National Socialist chaps have begun to clean the mess up a little, but still, I can hardly bear to think of my daughter mixing with such people. This Blau character revelled in it all, apparently, styling herself "the Queen of Depravity".'

'And where did you get this information on Ilse Blau? I don't remember reading anything about her over here.'

'From your predecessor. A local private detective I engaged, by the name of Charles Spender. Ex-Birmingham City Police. Good man – thorough, dogged. When we received the first letter from Paris, he was out there like a shot.'

'Sounds like a useful pair of hands. How do I contact him?'

'You can't, I'm afraid.' Parker let out a resigned puff of pipe smoke. 'You see, two days after arriving in Paris, the poor devil was pulled out of the Seine with his coat pockets full of rocks. I appealed to the British Consulate to get involved, but the authorities said his death was the result of his fraternising with the Parisian underworld. I tried to make them understand that Spender was just following certain lines of enquiry, but in the end, I had to give it up as a bad job.'

'Did Spender ever get any significant leads on Louise's whereabouts?'

'Unfortunately not. But we did get one further letter from her which I'd like to think represents a glimmer of hope. You see, Louise wrote to inform her sister that Blau's dance troupe was planning to travel to London.'

'And that's when you decided to look me up.'

'Indeed. I did a little digging – business contacts and such. You have a very respectable reputation in your line of work, Harley.'

'I don't think I've ever been called respectable before. I'm curious as to who these business contacts might have been.'

'Well, if you must know, it was someone with connections

to the Metropolitan Police Force. But I wouldn't want to divulge any more detail. It was all on a confidential basis, you understand. Suffice to say, the party in question convinced me that you have the requisite skills and experience needed to track down this Blau character and hopefully my daughter as well. So, what do you say? Are you willing to take on the case?'

'Of course. But what happens if I do manage to track Louise down, but she doesn't want you to know where she is? After all, she's over twenty-one.'

'In that case, I'd appeal to your better nature and encourage you to do the right thing. But we'll cross that bridge when we come to it, shall we?' Parker stood up and grabbed his hat from the desk. 'Here's my card. I'm travelling back home tomorrow, but I'll have my secretary contact you regarding your terms.'

'Right you are… There's just one more thing – do you have a recent photograph of Louise?'

'Oh yes, of course,' said Parker, producing a small photographic print from his wallet. 'That was in one of her letters; some promotional portrait they'd had done. That damned silly hairstyle is new of course, we'd never have countenanced that at home. Apparently this Blau character encourages all the girls to adopt the same look.'

The photograph was of an attractive young woman with a severe, angular bob.

'She's a good-looking girl.'

'Yes… unfortunately that's part of the problem.'

'And the letters Louise wrote to your younger daughter – do you have them with you?'

'I'm afraid not, Harley. My wife has formed a somewhat unhealthy attachment to them, you see. This whole sorry affair… Well, it's hit her rather badly. Her nerves, you understand. I could get the letters typed up for you, if you think it would help.'

'Yes, I do. But I'd also like to see the originals, if possible.'

'I'll see what I can do.' Parker checked his watch. 'I really must be off now. I'll be in touch.'

'Well, well,' said Bunty enthusiastically, after seeing the businessman out. 'My first case. A missing person. It's all jolly exciting, isn't it?'

2

WALTER SMETHWICK'S FINGER carefully traced the outline of the cherubic face in the photograph: his little Lorna, frozen in time, forever squinting against that glorious midday sun. Viking Bay, Broadstairs, summer of '28. A time before the Crash, before the morass of debt. A time when he'd still had pride in his reputation: a good father and husband, a respected landlord. A time before the accusatory stares, the whispered comments in the corridors. Before the drinking. A time before *that* night.

Smethwick gently caressed his daughter's favourite dolly, which lay nestled in his lap. Piecrust she'd named it. A silly name, they'd said – choose another. But she could be such a stubborn little thing when she wanted, so Piecrust it had remained. Some might have said that Piecrust had an ugly face, with her double chin and vacant eyes; but how Lorna had loved that doll. They were rarely apart. She'd even persuaded her mother to make her a frock to match the one Piecrust wore – a scarlet affair with a little stand-up collar and white polka dots. But that all seemed a lifetime ago now. And, of course, for Lorna it was.

He pushed aside the dirty dinner plate to stand the photo frame on the table. 'Little princess,' he mumbled. But, as he rubbed his palm against the four-day stubble, Smethwick's gaze had already drifted from the smile of his dead child to the level of gin left in the bottle. Just under a quarter full. If he were disciplined, he might just eke it out for the rest of the night. And tomorrow? Well, there'd be no money for gin tomorrow, not unless one of his lousy tenants coughed up what they owed, and there was slim chance of that happening. Nowadays it was almost impossible to confront any of the scoundrels face to face, they'd become so adept at avoiding him. If he did happen to hear the front door opening, by the time he'd summoned the energy to clamber up the basement stairs they'd already scuttled off to their rooms, just like the cockroaches that disappeared between the gaps in the scullery floorboards.

The majority of these elusive tenants were from the entertainment world: chorus girls and assorted 'dancers' from the shabbier grade of variety theatre. It had started with just one or two at the beginning, but then the word had spread – the word being that the landlord of the Sunny Side Boarding House was an easy touch – until almost all the rooms were being let to female performers of one sort or another. At first the beleaguered landlord thought this might lead to an easier life, that the girls might be less demanding than the travelling salesmen and impoverished drifters who had previously made up the majority of his clientele. But he soon came to the conclusion that many of these so-called 'dancers' were little more than common tarts, bringing back a stream of furtive-looking punters throughout the day. There were fights breaking out in the street; disgruntled suitors hammering on the front door; impromptu bottle parties in the early hours of

the morning; unwelcome visits from the local constabulary…
and to think that the Sunny Side had once been such a
respectable household. Whatever would Maureen make of
it all, if she were ever to come back? But, of course, that was
out of the question. Maureen would never be a part of his life
again, not after what had happened with little Lorna.

To quell the familiar surge of self-loathing, Smethwick
grabbed at the bottle and carefully measured out a sixth of the
remaining spirit. He was just savouring its harsh burn when
he became aware of movement on the landing above.

He cracked the door an inch or so and placed his ear to the
gap. Someone was using the telephone in the lobby.

After carefully replacing Piecrust among the other
mementos laid out in the little shrine on the Welsh dresser,
Smethwick slipped out of the kitchen and began to creep up
the basement steps, fumbling with the buttons on his grubby
cardigan. His heart was racing a little, the pulse thrumming
in his ears. After all, here was a definite opportunity. Most
of his tenants owed a considerable amount and he need only
squeeze a few shillings or so out of whoever it might be in
order to replenish his gin supply for the next few days.

But as he reached the ground floor, the landlord stopped in
his tracks. This was certainly not one of his tenants. The voice
was of a somewhat higher social standing than the typical
Sunny Side boarder. He might even have gone so far as to say
it sounded positively aristocratic.

Puzzled, Smethwick took a step into the corridor and
listened.

A man's voice. A little intoxicated. And somewhat
panicked.

'You simply must come, I tell you… Yes, I'm quite sure…
Well, I held a mirror to her mouth… No, of course I haven't
summoned a doctor, I'm not a complete imbecile… Frankly,
I can't see what relevance that has to— Yes, of course it was

a normal dose... Oh, you're being quite beastly, Simeon, really you are. Can't you just come and deal with the situation yourself? You know how difficult I find these things.'

Smethwick crept a little closer and peered through the balusters.

The caller was a porcine-looking individual decked out in white tie and tails; rather sweaty, with thinning sandy hair.

'What? You will? Oh, thank God! How long will you— Yes, of course, I understand, I shall go straight back up there now and— Alright, yes. But do hurry, won't you?'

The stranger hung up the receiver and pulled a handkerchief from his pocket to mop his brow. As he turned to go back upstairs, he caught sight of Smethwick lurking in the shadows.

'Who is that skulking around down there?'

Even though he was standing in the hallway of his own property, the landlord found himself shuffling nervously. He cleared his throat to answer. 'The name's Smethwick.'

'And hasn't anyone ever explained to you, Smethwick, that eavesdropping on someone's private conversation is incredibly rude?'

Having delivered this rebuke, the stranger began to stomp up the stairs.

'I say, one moment, please!'

'Well, what is it?'

'Might I ask who it is you're visiting?'

'I don't see what business that is of yours.'

'I'm the landlord here, you see, and—'

'Dark bob. Top floor. Calls herself Tallulah. Now, if you'll excuse me.'

Smethwick found the courage to climb a few stairs after the man. 'From what you were saying on the telephone... What I mean to say is – is everything alright? With Tallulah?'

'Perfectly fine, thank you. Goodnight!'

The confrontation left the landlord feeling humiliated.

He returned to his basement room in a blue funk and immediately poured out another measure of gin.

'Arrogant pig!' he grumbled into his glass. 'Speaking to me like that, in my own house. It's those confounded showgirls, dragging the place down into the gutter, continually flaunting themselves in the hallways.' He sucked greedily at the drink. 'Tallulah? Well, serves her right, I say.'

As he sat there brooding, Smethwick found the drink beginning to anaesthetise his cowardice. He recalled phrases from the eavesdropped conversation: *held a mirror to her mouth… summon a doctor.* And, as he speculated about the various potential medical outcomes for the unfortunate showgirl, another more pressing – if less altruistic – worry overtook him: the consequences of a second death on the premises. The interminable questioning at the police station; the packs of journalists hounding his every move; the taunts from strangers in the street… And what if the authorities pried into the unsavoury habits of his tenants? Under closer inspection wouldn't the Sunny Side Boarding House appear somewhat like a common brothel? And where would that leave him in the eyes of the local magistrate?

Downing the remaining gin in his glass, Smethwick stumbled over to the dresser to search out an ancient bottle of sal volatile, and then rushed up the four flights of stairs as fast as his unsteady and malnourished legs could carry him.

Reaching the top floor, he paused a moment to compose himself, then took a deep breath and hammered on the door – which was immediately flung open by the aristocratic individual he'd met in the hallway.

'Thank God! I thought you'd never—'

Realising his error, the stranger attempted to shove Smethwick back out into the corridor, but the landlord had wedged himself in the opening and now stood there, swaying a little as he took in the scene before him.

The dimly lit room was a confused mess of discarded clothing and overturned furniture. The grate held the last vestiges of a fire, the few remaining embers casting a faint glow over the cluster of empty bottles, spent syringes, and other paraphernalia scattered across the shabby hearthrug. A heavy pall of incense and cigar smoke hung around the gas fitting, adding to the overbearing odour pervading the room.

What was that odour? Burnt hair, perhaps?

The centrepiece of this decadent tableau lay strewn on the bed: there, stretched out on the crumpled sheets, with a worryingly morbid pallor, was the naked body of Tallulah.

Relinquishing his hold on the door, the stranger gave a dismissive sniff and strode across the room to retrieve a smouldering cigar from the mantelpiece.

The bewildered landlord reeled for a moment, steadying himself against the door frame. Then, having recovered from this sudden rush of vertigo – more intense than the usual gin spins – he somehow found himself at the bedside, gazing down at the motionless, naked young woman.

And, in the midst of that tawdry scene, like the return of a nagging toothache, Walter Smethwick became aware of a stirring.

Of course, he felt immediate self-disgust at such a transgression – just like those times holed up in the attic above the communal bathroom, his eye pressed hard to the knot hole as he spied on the lithe showgirls bathing below, rubbing himself like a dog against the rough floorboards, when he should have been watching over his little asthmatic daughter. But, as though witnessing the scene in a fevered dream, he found he couldn't resist, couldn't wrench himself away. Not until he'd drunk it all in: the contrast of areolae against the creamy white skin, the sculptural swell of the breast, the subtle clefts and hollows…

Then he caught sight of the angry wound that marred this

physical perfection, like a scrawl of graffiti on an Old Master – and the source of what he now realised was the nauseating smell of burnt skin.

He pointed at the circular symbol branded into the young woman's thigh.

'What is that?'

'What, indeed?' came the reply, but the voice was not the high-pitched drawl of the little porcine individual at the fireplace; this one had a rich, melodious quality, and was coming from directly behind him.

Before he could turn to discover its owner, Smethwick felt something small and hard thrust into his lower back.

'What you feel there, my dear chap, is the muzzle of an exquisite little pistol made by W. F. Mills, gunmaker to Queen Victoria. A stunning example of London gun-making at its finest. Rosewood and ivory. Superb… And, of course, quite deadly at such short range.'

The landlord froze as the mysterious newcomer leant over his shoulder to gaze at the body, bringing with him the complex floral bouquet of an expensive cologne.

'Hmm… I'm no medical man, but I believe we shouldn't hold out too much hope for this young lady.'

'But shouldn't we try to revive her?'

'Quite right. Yes, an exemplary display of civic duty, Mr…?'

'Smethwick. I'm the landlord here.'

'Ah yes. Well, rest assured, Smethwick, we shall do everything within our power to maintain any feeble life-force still extant in this delectable example of pulchritude. However, as I see it, the immediate concern is to contain the situation. After all, I would imagine the discovery of a tenant in such a condition in one's lodging house would present an inconvenience to any landlord at the best of times. But with your reputation, put together with such suspicious circumstances – the excess of alcohol, the lack of clothes, the drug paraphernalia, the *branded thigh…*' Here, the newcomer flashed a stern look at his associate, who was slumped in a sulk against the mantelpiece. 'Well, one can only imagine what a nuisance the authorities might make of themselves. So, I have a proposition for you. Would you care to hear it?'

3

IN THE HAZY morning sunshine, with its two open fanlights, blackened by city smuts, resembling the mascara-smudged lashes of a drunken showgirl, it was hard to see the Rendezvous Revue Bar as anything other than a shabby theatre which had seen better days. But for the initiated, this modest venue provided a temporary escape from the tedious grind of everyday life in 1930s Britain. Here – once he'd paid his 2/6 – a working man (for the punters were almost exclusively male) could forget, for an hour or so, just what a grey and bedraggled land his country had become under the Great Slump. At the Rendezvous, the talk wasn't of hunger marches and means testing, but of music and laughter, and *girls, girls, girls!*

'Continuous variety,' read Bunty from the poster beside the stage door. 'Come in when you like and leave when you like… that's a little unusual, isn't it, George?'

'It's the new thing, ain't it?' said Harley, sparking up a Gold Flake cigarette. 'Musical numbers, hoofers, a bit of comedy, the odd juggler. Though, most of the punters don't really come for all that.'

'No?'

'No. They're here for the *tableaux vivants*. Following Mrs Henderson's lead around the corner at the Windmill, these gaffs have cottoned on to a sure-fire way of getting bums on seats.'

'Which is?'

'Bramas in the all-together.'

'Sorry?'

'Nudes, Bunty, nudes. Each performance ends with a gaggle of beauties up on stage posing in the buff.'

'Gosh! Right next door to our office... And that's allowed, is it?'

'Somehow someone has convinced the Lord Chamberlain that, as long as the girls stay stock-still, posing like statues, then it's no different to a visit to the National Gallery. I'd imagine there's been a little lubrication involved.'

'Lubrication?'

'The oil of angels – a little bribe here and there. Right, come on. It's as good a place to start as any. Let's see if any of this lot have heard of the elusive Miss Parker.'

After a minute or so, Harley's persistent knocking was answered by the sound of bolts and chains being withdrawn on the inside of the theatre's front door.

'If you're after the girls, we ain't open yet. If you're trade, you need to be going round the back.'

This welcoming slogan was delivered by an ageing individual holding a mop in one hand and a half-eaten sausage roll in the other. Though the man's voluminous trousers and shabby jacket had a certain Chaplinesque quality, the clutch of medals adorning his left breast were polished to the highest shine.

'Oh, it's you, George.' The old-timer stood to attention, his mop held as a rifle. 'All present and correct, Corporal!'

'At ease, Private,' said Harley, laughing. 'Jimmy, this is Bunty Chatterton. Bunty, Jimmy.'

'Pleased to meet you,' said Bunty, offering a gloved hand.

The caretaker replied with a little comical curtsy. 'Pleasure's all mine, I'm sure… Right, in you come then,' he said, shutting the door on the bright sunshine and casting the foyer into gloom. ''Spect you're here to see Jerry. He's downstairs.' Jimmy jerked a thumb towards the floor. 'Auditions.'

'Actually, we're here to ask about a missing girl. Got that mugshot, Bunty…? There we go. Ring any bells? Her name's Louise.'

'Hold on a mo' – can't see a ruddy thing in this light.'

Jimmy stuffed the greasy remnant of his sausage roll into his pocket and started to paw at the wall by the door. 'Where was Moses when the lights went out, eh? Ah, there we go!'

The foyer was suddenly bathed in bright light from the ornate chandelier hanging above their heads.

'Right, let's have a look then.'

He studied the dancer's portrait, all the time working his tongue to get at the errant flakes of pastry which had become trapped in his beard. 'Very nice, very nice indeed… quite a doll, ain't she?'

'But do you recognise her at all?' asked Bunty. 'From one of the shows here, perhaps?'

'Sorry, dear.' He handed back the photo with a shake of his head. 'All these girls, they're in and out like a fiddler's elbow. And when I do get a chance to catch one of the performances, well… I'm not really paying much attention to their faces, am I? But the boss should be able to help you. There ain't much that gets past Jerry Paladino.'

* * *

Even though the late-morning sunshine was doing its best to brighten the grubby streets of Soho above them, the atmosphere in the Rendezvous' subterranean auditorium was decidedly damp and fusty. As well as adopting a Spartan approach to heating the draughty old Georgian building, the theatre's proprietor was adding to the chilly atmosphere with his own personal demeanour. For Tuesday morning was audition morning at the Rendezvous, a chance for the management to discover new talent to feed the show's never-ending demand for variety acts. Since taking over the business, Jerry Paladino had discovered his definition of talent was somewhat at odds with the majority of the hopefuls (or 'no-hopefuls', as he liked to call them) who'd recently been convinced by the dwindling opportunities in the job market to reinvent themselves as entertainers.

As Harley and Bunty made their way quietly down the aisle, the performer up on stage was just coming to the end of his routine. To the accompaniment of the house pianist – who wore a fixed expression of professional ennui – this 'musical comedy' act crooned the last line of his song and then violently slapped the face of the ventriloquist's dummy he was holding. He followed this by producing an oversized box of matches from a Gladstone bag and, after a number of abortive attempts, finally managed to set fire to his hat. Shuffling nervously to the front of the stage in the ensuing silence, he coughed once and then gave a brief bow to the empty theatre.

A few lonely claps could be heard emanating from behind the scenes.

'Don't clap him!' shouted Paladino, sitting in the stalls a few rows back from the now-smouldering performer. 'Why are you clapping him?'

'I'm his agent, Jerry,' said the eager-looking young man in the bow tie emerging from the wings.

'My sincere commiserations.'

All eyes turned to the increasingly nervous-looking

performer as the flames began to engulf his top hat.

'God help us!' exclaimed the exasperated club owner. 'Will somebody please put him out?'

With a face admirably expressing his current level of career fulfilment, the pianist grabbed the water jug from the top of the piano, sauntered over to the act, and gave him a good dousing.

'Say goodbye, Ernie,' Paladino said to the agent. 'And take Gertrude Lawrence here with you. I'm sure you'll be very happy together.'

'But I've still got one more act, Jerry. You've just got to see this one.'

'Not today I haven't. Scram! Call me when your brain's healed over.'

As the dispirited young man accompanied his bedraggled act to the exit, Harley introduced Bunty to Paladino.

'So, how's business, Jerry?'

'What can I tell you? They're breaking down the doors every night, George. Trouble is, it's to get out... But listen, Mori tells me we're neighbours now. You've rented next door for that sherlock agency of yours, right?'

'That's right.'

'And a glamorous assistant to boot. Going up in the world, eh? And I hear Solly and Marni have ended up with their feet under the table over at the Bag O'Nails.'

'That's right – Marni came into some money. Some rich uncle snuffed it or something.'

'Good luck to 'em, is what I say. Believe me, anyone trying to make a go of something in this recession needs all the luck they can get. So, neighbour, why the visit? You dropped in to borrow a cup of sugar?'

'As it happens,' said Harley, breaking out the Gold Flake, 'I want to pick your brains about something.'

'Well then, let's retire to my office. After suffering this

morning's parade of bedlamites, I could do with a little refreshment.'

* * *

Having fortified himself with a little brandy and soda, Paladino settled at his desk to listen to Harley's story of the missing showgirl – a tale he received with the detached air of a seasoned club owner who'd heard it all before. He made a quick study of the dancer's portrait and handed it back with an explanation that he'd seen dozens of girls like Louise Parker pass through his clubs over the years, many from 'decent' suburban homes, and a good proportion of whom had simply disappeared from the scene a few months later. And, he added, their stories didn't always have a happy ending. At this comment Harley had to dissuade his new assistant from interrogating the impresario on his apparent ambivalence towards the welfare of his female staff and instead steer the conversation towards the subject of the German cabaret act, Ilse Blau. At which stage Paladino suddenly become far more engaged.

'Oh, her,' he said, with a schoolboy twinkle in his eye. 'Yeah, she's in town alright. Only she's going by a different handle: "Astarte" is what she calls herself now.'

'You're sure it's the same character?'

'So I've been told. I've not actually seen her act yet, but I've heard all about it. And, by all accounts, it's a real piece of work. I'd go into details, but I wouldn't want to offend Bunty.'

'I wish everyone would stop assuming I'm some kind of delicate flower.'

'Go on, Jerry,' said Harley, giving Bunty an old-fashioned look.

'Well, as I say, I've not seen the act; but I have seen the lady herself. Though, I'm not too sure you'd describe her as a lady. It was a couple of weeks ago. I was out with our band leader from the Cat's Whiskers.'

'Tyrone Stirling.'

'That's right. I'd forgotten you're a music lover, George. Well, we're on the lookout for a new singer for the All Stars at the moment, you see, so Tyrone had dragged me south of the river to listen to this girl at the Tinderbox in Woolwich. Not bad, either; had a touch of the Norma Shearers about her. Anyway, this brama was belting out some moody little number – had the crowd eating out of her hands – when suddenly, there's this big kerfuffle from the back of the house. Glass smashing, general sounds of drunkenness, the usual story.'

'A normal Saturday night at the Tinderbox.'

'Exactly. Anyway, the music stops, and we all crane our necks around to see what the fuss is about. Suddenly, out of the hush comes this deep, rasping voice, with a thick German accent: "Vot are you idiots lookin' at?" Like some lit-up Marlene Dietrich. The house lights go up and there she is, in all her glory – Astarte. 'Course, I didn't know her from Adam at the time, but Tyrone filled me in afterwards. She's quite something, I can tell you.'

'Attractive, you mean?' asked Bunty.

'I s'pose. But not in the normal way. I mean, I've been in this game for donkey's years and I thought I'd seen it all; but this Fräulein's something else. Picture it – she's sitting there, glaring at everyone in the club like she's about to murder us all. Her hair's the same severe cut as that doll in your mugshot, but dyed red, a bright copper red, see? Her eyebrows… well, they've been shaved right off and painted back on. She's wearing a monocle, smoking a big cigar, and her face is white; I mean deathly white – like it's made of wax. Oh, and hanging around her neck is a soddin' monkey.'

'What kind of monkey?' asked Harley.

'What am I, a zookeeper? What do I know about monkeys? A little furry one, with long arms. The point is, she had one around her bloody neck! This was in Woolwich, remember, not Kathmandu.'

'She sounds extraordinary,' said Bunty, taking out a little book to make some notes.

'Yeah. But that's not the best bit. You see, now that she's got our attention, Astarte clambers up onto her chair – and she's definitely one over the eight at this stage, so it's touch and go whether she'll make it in those high-heeled pumps. Once she's up there she balls out: "I'll give you all somethink to look at! Ja?" and promptly whips open her mink coat… under which she's starkers.'

'Naked?'

'As the day she was born.'

'Good grief.'

'And I got the feeling,' said Paladino, chuckling, 'that, if it wasn't for her mates pulling her down and bustling her out of the club, she'd have had a few more strokes to pull.'

'Who were the sidekicks?' asked Harley.

'Looked like a couple of swells, out slumming it for the night.'

'On safari?'

'That's the impression I got.'

Harley nodded and tapped out a smoke, lighting up while he pondered for a moment. 'So, if I wanted to experience the shocking Miss Astarte and her troupe of severe bobs, whose palm would I have to grease? I'd imagine she's had no problem finding a home for her act on the underground circuit?'

'Spot on. She's got herself a residency down at the Grimaldi Vaults. And a tidy little business they're making out of her too, by all accounts.'

'The Grimaldi Vaults?' said Harley, looking puzzled. 'Never heard of it.'

'Oh, you know these underground joints – they seem to just pop up overnight out of nowhere, like bleedin' toadstools.

This one's hosted under the Joseph Grimaldi pub, just off Rathbone Place – Gresse Street, I think it is. The building used to be an old vintner's; it's got a big complex of vaulted cellars. Not a bad venue, as it goes. Their schtick is the old Joey the Clown thing: all the waiters, the emcee, they're all done up in the Grimaldi face-paint. It's all a bit spooky, if you ask me, but the toffs love it, of course.'

'Can you get me in?'

'Uh-uh. Nothing doing, I'm afraid. I fell out with the bloke who runs it.'

'Who's that?'

'A stuck-up berk by the name of Simeon Dubois. Like his club, he popped up on the scene out of nowhere, about a year ago. Not sure what his connection is with the bogeys, but he's bound to have a tame one in tow, otherwise he'd have had his collar felt by now, with the reputation the place is getting. He's got a lot of high-class contacts, this Dubois, and a lot of dough behind him, as well.'

'Whose dough?'

'Wish I knew. If I did then I might be able to get Mori to apply a little pressure. This character has been rubbing everyone up the wrong way – paying the talent and the staff way over the going rates. Sure, he's only got this one underground club at the moment, but we're all worried he's gearing up to branch out into the mainstream.'

'So, you went round there to explain to him the error of his ways, eh?'

'No,' said Paladino. 'You know me, George – charming to a fault. I leave the heavy-handed stuff to my business partner, who has a certain knack for it, as I'm sure you're aware. No, I took round a bottle of cognac as a peace-offering. Suggested a pow-pow with some of the Soho club owners. But this posh shicer wasn't having any of it; sent me away with a flea in my ear. 'Course, I played it down a bit to Mori – after all, I don't want to start a civil war, it's bad for business. Anyway, now they've got this crazy act, Astarte, headlining, and suddenly the club's becoming a big noise in the upper echelons. I'm a little worried, I can tell you.'

'And you've no idea where her digs might be?'

'The German? No. Can't help you there at all, I'm afraid. But if I hear anything more about her, or your missing dancer, I'll be sure to get in touch.'

4

'**M**AY I HAVE the picture of Miss Parker?' asked Bunty, back at the office. 'For the file?'

'There you go,' said Harley. 'And you'll need to fill out one of these.'

'Index cards. Yes, a very efficient way of recording information.'

'I'm glad you approve.'

'You know, it's all quite intriguing. Don't you think?'

'What is?'

'Well, we have a glamorous missing dancer and that poor detective chap's body floating in the River Seine… I'd say it has all the makings of a good Agatha Christie.'

'You're a fan, then?'

'Of her books? Rather! I simply gobbled them up at school. You?'

'Well, I've read a few of 'em. They're entertaining enough, I s'pose. But it's all a bit too cosy for my liking.'

'Cosy?'

'Well, the murders are always so neat and tidy, aren't they? I mean, all those exquisite drawing rooms and well-mannered killers. Where are all the knocking shops and late-night spielers? All the maniacs wielding razors?'

'Razors?'

'Round this neck of the woods, rather than an antique duelling pistol or heirloom candlestick, it's your common or garden cut-throat razor that's the weapon of choice. And that ain't neat and tidy, I can tell you. If you were thinking this job might be something like those country-house whodunits, then I'm afraid you're in for a surprise.' Harley walked over to the hatstand, to grab his hat and coat. 'Now, what did you have planned for lunch?'

'Lunch? Well, up until yesterday I didn't have any guaranteed income, so lately I've been rather inclined to skip lunch. Which is doing wonders for the figure, of course. There aren't any cooking facilities in my lodgings, you see, so I've been having to take my supper at tea-shops – which is proving a little expensive.'

'Well, I don't want you fainting away at the desk. Where are these lodgings of yours?'

'The Elephant and Castle,' replied Bunty, a little sheepishly. 'Not knowing London, I thought it sounded rather exotic.'

'Exotic? That's one word for it. I take it we're not talking the Ritz, then?'

'Oh dear, no,' said Bunty, looking rather deflated. 'Actually, George, it's too awful to describe. Simply ghastly. I doubt whether it's seen any proper housekeeping in decades, and the sheets… I chose to sleep in my overcoat last night, which kept me warm at least. But that's not the worst of it. You see – and I know I'll sound rather silly saying this – but I really don't feel at all safe there. There's a simply dreadful man in the room next door. Inebriated most of the time. Last night… well, there was this thumping at my door, you see. And when I opened it, he…'

'He did what?' asked Harley, genuinely concerned now.

'Well, thankfully nothing; mainly because I emptied a glass of water over him and slammed the door in his face. But he had his *little man* out,' whispered Bunty, pointing to her crotch. 'Poking out of his grubby pyjamas.' She gave a little involuntary shudder.

'That settles it. You're not staying there another night,' said Harley, doing up his coat. 'We'll go around and pick your stuff up this afternoon.'

'But I'm paid up for the week. I can't afford rent anywhere else.'

'Not a problem. You can stay in my spare room, until we find you somewhere decent.'

Harley noted his assistant's wary look. 'Now, don't you worry, Miss Chatterton, your honour will remain intact. I'll sleep here on the couch.'

'All the same. I don't think it's quite appropriate, do you?'

'Look, I understand where you're coming from, Bunty, but I'm really not that kind of bloke. Still, if you'd rather stick it out in those delightful digs of yours, then…'

'Can I at least have time to think about it?'

'Of course you can. Now, get your coat – I'm taking you out for a spot of lunch.'

'Crumbs. You're quite forceful when you want to be, aren't you? Dare I ask where we're going?'

'Around the corner: the Bag O'Nails. My old mate Solly Rosen's just taken over as landlord. I've not paid my respects yet, so we'll be killing two birds with one stone.'

'The Bag O'Nails?' said Bunty, looking a little concerned. 'A public house?'

'Is that a problem?'

'No, I expect not. Only I've never really been into a pub before.'

'Get out of it!'

She wandered back to the window to gaze down on

Frith Street. 'Especially one in Soho… You know, this whole experience is turning out to be a rather thrilling adventure.'

'Come on, Miss Marple,' said Harley, chuckling. 'Let's get you some grub.'

'Oh, George, wait!' she said, catching sight of someone approaching the front door. 'It looks like we might have another client. Now, let me see if I can apply your technique. I'd say this fellow is rather well-off. Nice expensive-looking coat, rather good deportment… high-quality leather gloves. And a… oh, hold on… I think he's just posting a letter through our door… Yes, he's off again now.'

'Expensive coat?' Harley's face was pressed hard against the glass now. 'Where?'

'I don't know, I've lost him. I thought he was coming up to see us.'

'What kind of hat did he have on?'

'A dress hat, actually. Which is a bit odd at this time of day, wouldn't you say? He was an older chap, possibly early sixties. Smart. Were you expecting someone?'

But Harley was no longer at her side.

'Whatever is it?!' she called out, as she heard him thundering his way down the office stairs. 'George?!'

* * *

Five minutes later Harley returned, looking a little flustered.

'Did you find him?'

'No. He was long gone. He left this, though.' He dropped a small white envelope on the desk. 'Did he take his hat off when you were watching him? Could you see whether he was bald?'

'No. Why? Do you think you know who it was?'

Harley ignored the question. He went over to the filing cabinet and began to root through the drawers.

'Not here,' he muttered to himself.

'What isn't?'

'I wanted to show you a picture, to try to identify him. But the file's at home.'

'You do know who it was, then?'

'Possibly.'

Bunty picked up the envelope from the desk. 'As you've already opened this, do you mind if I…?'

'Hmm? No, help yourself.'

She removed a plain white postcard, which had on it one line of handwritten text:

Πρόσεχε τί ἐπιθυμεῖς

'Curious… Greek, isn't it?'

'That's what I thought,' said Harley, dragging a hand through his hair, obviously deep in thought. 'Didn't you say you had some foreign languages?'

'German, yes. And a little French and Italian. No Greek, I'm afraid.'

'Pity.'

'Is it from a potential client, do you think? A foreigner, without any English perhaps?'

Harley shook his head. 'No. He's trying to needle me. Get inside my head.'

'Who? The chap in the top hat?'

'Yeah, the chap in the top hat. Only, if it's who I think it is, he shouldn't be out there, walking the streets of Soho, posting notes through people's letterboxes. He should be safely banged up in a padded cell in the madhouse.'

'Who should?'

'Osbert Morkens.'

'Morkens? You mean that horrendous child-killer? What was it they called him? The Nursery Butcher?'

'Yeah, that's the fella.'

'Dear God, George!'

5

Broadmoor Criminal Lunatic Asylum

S AT AT A small deal table, surrounded by a teetering pile of books, the inmate paused for a moment in his studies as he became aware of the murmur of voices from beyond the reinforced door of his cell.

Out in the passageway, the principal attendant disengaged the inspection plate and took a step back.

'There he is, Bullen: Osbert Morkens. Professor of Ancient History, child-killer and – if you believe what you read in the *Daily Oracle* – the Devil incarnate.'

The bear-like Bullen stooped to peer through the grating.

'What, that old bald coot?' He hawked up a gobbet of phlegm and spat with contempt on the worn flagstones. 'He don't look all that to me.'

'Yes, that was Smythe's opinion as well, at first; and just look where it got him.'

They were interrupted by a frenzied jabbering from a nearby cell, which soon drew an accompaniment of shrieks and howls from further along the corridor.

'Cheese it, you dogs!' shouted Bullen. 'Don't you know this voice? Don't you know me, I say?!'

As the clamour tailed off to a half-hearted whimpering, the warder grinned, exposing a row of carious teeth. 'D'you see, sir? I have them in the palm of my hand.'

'That's all very well,' continued his superior, taking a pinch from a pewter snuffbox, 'but I think you'll find this particular patient somewhat less compliant. Underestimate him at your own peril. You know what he did to Smythe.'

'Smythe topped himself, didn't he? I don't see what his suicide has got to do with this old bookworm.'

'Now listen, Bullen – and I wouldn't wish this to go any further, you understand?' The principal leant in close to whisper. 'But the week before your unfortunate colleague's demise, he was found by the morning shift slumped here, outside Morkens' cell. The man could barely string a sentence together.'

'Yeah, well, old Smythe always was a little delicate.'

'Delicate? He'd been reduced to a dribbling imbecile, man!'

'By what, exactly?'

'Nobody knows.' Agitated, the principal dabbed a handkerchief to his tobacco-stained moustache. 'But according to the statements given by the night staff, Smythe had been observed on more than one occasion with his ear to the inspection grate, seemingly transfixed. When questioned, he explained that Morkens was helping him with some philosophical enquiries.'

'What does that mean, sir?'

'God only knows. What I do know is the day after he was found slumped outside this cell, Warder Smythe wrote a suicide note to his elderly mother, telling her how Professor Morkens had explained it all so clearly that he didn't really see the point in carrying on anymore. He then promptly knotted a bedsheet around his neck and jumped over the banister.'

Bullen sniffed. 'Not cut out for the work, if you ask me. But I can assure you, sir, Morkens will find me a rather different proposition.' He pushed his face up to the inspection grate. 'Oi, Teach! Listen up!'

The professor laid down his pen and turned towards the door. 'Is there something I can help you with?'

'*Is there something I can help you with?*' mimicked Bullen. 'Yeah, no doubt there will be… in good time. All you need to know now, though, Prof, is that I'm the new boss around here. And you can forget all about that old abracadabra mumbo-jumbo nonsense, 'cause that ain't going to wash with me. See, I ain't one of your milksop mummy's boys like old Smythe. You'll find that Beef Bullen is cut from quite a different cloth.'

'Ah yes, Mr Bullen,' said Morkens, with a thoughtful stroke to his aquiline nose. 'I do believe I've heard reports of your rather zealous approach.'

'Zealous, is it? *Zealous?!*' Bullen started fumbling with his large ring of keys. 'I'll show you ruddy zealous, you stuck-up berk!'

'Careful now, man,' said the principal, placing a restraining hand on his arm.

But Bullen pushed on, thrusting open the door, which clanged heavily against the wall. For a moment he loomed in the doorway, casting a long shadow into the cell, the tip of which fell across Morkens' desk.

With a thin smile forming on his rather sensuous, feminine lips, the professor extended one long-nailed finger to give the shadow head a slow caress.

Bullen strode over to the table.

'Good evening,' said Morkens in a measured tone, holding the warder's threatening stare. 'Delighted to make your acquaintance.'

After belching a sour memento of tripe and onions into Morkens' face, Bullen grabbed a book from the top of the pile.

'What's all this bollocks, then?'

'That? Let me see… Ah yes, *The Testament of Solomon*, a pseudepigraphic catalogue of the demons summoned by King Solomon.'

'Very interesting, I'm sure.' The tossed book hit the floor with a thump. 'And where exactly did you get all this old rubbish from, eh?'

Morkens paused a moment before answering, the serenity of his imposing face, with its hooded eyes and caprine tuft of white beard, suggesting he might have already acquired the measure of this new adversary. 'Why, these are all from my own private collection, Mr Bullen. Dr Andrews kindly arranged for them to be delivered here. He believes attendance to my former studies might be beneficial to my rehabilitation.'

The warder scoffed. 'Rehabilitation?'

'Indeed. After all, as the good doctor has pointed out on more than one occasion, this is a place of healing, not of punishment.'

Bullen's bellowed laugh resounded off the stone walls as he turned to address his superior, who was observing from a safe distance in the corridor. 'D'you hear that, sir? It's healing he's after.'

'That'll do, Bullen,' hissed the principal. 'For goodness' sake, leave it for when you're on night shift, won't you? You're being far too conspicuous, man.'

'Oh, I think just a few more minutes, don't you?' Bullen turned his attention back to Morkens. 'After all, we haven't quite got to know each other yet, have we? So this is your thing, is it? Your little hobby horse – all these mouldy old books?'

Morkens retained his beatific smile. 'Well, seeing as I held the Camden Professorship of Ancient History at Brasenose, I suppose one could say that, yes, this is *my thing*.'

'Professor of Ancient History, eh? But that's not what they call you now though, is it? Not since you had your filthy way with those little kiddies. Now you're the Beast of Brasenose, ain't you? Well, from where I'm standing, you don't look much like a beast; more like a mangy old cur.'

'I agree, it is a rather childish sobriquet.'

'Oh, listen to it. Think you're something special, don't you? With your big words and your college pals…' Bullen thrust his truncheon under Morkens' chin and bent down to growl in his ear. 'Well, let me give *you* a little lesson, Professor. Free of charge. You can forget all about that King Solomon of yours. The only king you need worry about now is the King of the Back Blocks, yours truly – Beef Bullen. See, I've been ruling these 'ere secure blocks for over ten years now. And if it turns out you're not a loyal subject, then you'll be paid a visit by my yeoman of the guard here.' Bullen smashed his truncheon down on the table, scattering papers and books across the cell floor. 'This here is Captain Hackum. Take a close look at 'im, I'm sure you'll become the best of pals over time.'

Holstering the weapon, Bullen now made his way back to the doorway, where he stood for a moment, arms akimbo. 'From now on I'm your god. I tell you when you eat, sleep and piss in your pot. And it'll be me who decides whether you continue to get your precious little books delivered. So, best you say your prayers. Understood?'

'Oh, I'd say you've put your case most succinctly, Mr Bullen.'

'Glad to hear it. Sweet dreams, then… for now.' The warder slammed the cell door behind him.

As he strode off down the corridor – closely followed by his nervous-looking superior – Bullen was feeling rather satisfied with himself. It would appear this so-called criminal genius had already heard of his reputation, so there'd probably be no need to raise a sweat beating the facts of life into him. And having now got the measure of the old duffer, it was obvious he'd be a pushover to handle. Then, of course, there was the added bonus of the professor's private income (Bullen had already done some digging with the boys in the admissions office); after all, if Morkens wanted to carry on receiving his books, there'd have to be some kind of administration charge. *Oh yes*, he thought, as he watched the principal disappear into his office, *stringing himself up with that bedsheet was the best thing milky old Smythe ever did.*

* * *

Having heard the decisive clang of the closing gates at the stairwell entrance, Morkens bent down to retrieve *The Testament of Solomon* from the cell floor. He trimmed the wick of the oil lamp before closing his eyelids for a moment, taking a few deep breaths to quieten the tumult of voices raging inside his head.

'Patience,' he whispered, then fished around for something in the depths of his pocket. Moving over to the bed, he sprinkled the crumbs of stale bread on the floor between his feet and waited.

The dark brown sewer rat emerged tentatively, investigating the scents about the floor before climbing onto Morkens' foot to devour the meagre offering.

'So, Elemauzer. You heard that oaf? Declaiming his command over my fate. A deluded fool. He'd do well to ponder his own fate.' A smile broke Morkens' black look. He reached down to gently caress the back of the rat's head with a long, ivory-coloured fingernail. 'The time is almost upon us, my little friend. As for this mooncalf, what was it he called himself? The King of the Back Blocks?'

Becoming suddenly agitated, Morkens jumped to his feet, sending the startled rodent scurrying back under the bed. He swept over to the door to shout through the open inspection hole. 'Know this, King of the Back Blocks! The glories of our blood and state are shadows, not substantial things; there is no armour against fate; Death lays his icy hand on kings!'

Having worked himself into a frenzy, Morkens clenched his fists and began to pummel the cell door. 'Sing it out, my children! Come now – surely, you've not forgotten your parts?'

The professor's command was immediately answered by a chorus of whoops and howls from the neighbouring cells. Before long the tumult had spread like a forest fire, alighting the whole block, a lunatic cacophony conducted by the chief lunatic himself – the Nursery Butcher, the Beast of Brasenose: Osbert Agamemnon Morkens.

6

O N THE THIRD floor of the Sunny Side Boarding House, the wide-boy Frankie Roscoe snapped down the brim of his fedora and regarded his reflection in the mirror. 'Be lucky, son,' he said, with a half-hearted wink. He tweaked the ends of his polka-dot bow tie – almost a badge of honour among the shadier racetrack punters – and completed the daily ritual by placing a matchstick in the corner of his mouth.

Luck. Yes, that's what was needed now. Because, for the past three months, Roscoe had been riding the tails of the most devastating losing streak of his career, a career forged through years of ducking and diving, petty crime and gambling. Mostly gambling.

He began to search through his pockets, discarding the spent betting slips from the previous night's trip to White City – a visit which had been prompted by a hot tip on a dog, from one of his cronies who worked at the kennels.

Hot tip? What a mug!

The plan had been to place the majority of his remaining

dough on the mutt and win back enough to at least meet that month's extortionate interest on the loan he taken out with the mobster Mori Adler. That had been the plan. But Roscoe had awoken that morning with a thick head, grumbling bowels and the grand sum of five shillings and sixpence in his trouser pocket. Now he'd have to go back on the lay, sniffing out any opportunity to make a few illicit shillings, enough to build up that stake money again, to have another scratch at that itch; all the time trying to dodge Adler's crew and his other creditors – including his landlord.

Which explained why the wide-boy now quietly closed the door behind him and began to tiptoe down the rickety staircase, doing his best to avoid the noisiest of the loose treads.

'Ah, there you are, Frank!' said Walter Smethwick, emerging from the first-floor bathroom, looking even more dishevelled than usual. 'I was going to knock, but I thought it might be too early.'

Roscoe tried to mask his disappointment at being so easily ambushed with his default grin. He decided to engage in a little verbal misdirection, while his brain ran through a number of possible escape tactics. 'Blimey, Walter! My word, you do look queer! What is it now, touch of the collywobbles? A lot of it about, I hear. You want to get yourself a little fresh air once in a while, bit of sunshine on your face. My old mum used to swear by it. Nature's tonic, that's what she called it; and the old bird knew a thing or two, I can tell you. Booked your holidays yet, have you?'

'Holidays? No, no... The thing is, I need to talk to you about—'

'Brighton, that's the place to be. I'm sure you've got a bit stashed away – am I right? Why not treat yourself to a weekend at the Royal Albion? That Harry Preston, he knows what he's about and no mistake. You could hobnob it with the best of them down there, Walter. They've got it all going on – motor yachts, tea dances. And those lovelies, in their bathing suits? Cor! You wouldn't get much change out of two thrupenny bits from those bramas, eh? After all, if it's good enough for the Prince of Wales – know what I mean?'

'No, I don't know what you mean,' said the bemused Smethwick, rubbing a hand across the back of his neck. 'Listen. I really do need to ask you—'

'Oh, hold on! You know, I'm glad I bumped into you. I've just remembered – I've got a little something for you.' Roscoe removed a rolled-up newspaper from his jacket pocket. 'All your talk about Brighton has just reminded me.'

'My talk? But—'

'No need to thank me. It's a horse, see – the nap at the two-thirty at Brighton, this Saturday.'

'Nap? What's a nap?'

'What do you think it is? Don't be a mug all your life, Walter. It's a tip, a sure-fire thing. I'm only giving you the winner of the two-thirty at Brighton, that's all.'

'Stop it!' Smethwick shouted. He grabbed the newspaper and threw it to the floor. 'Just stop talking for a moment, will you? I can't hear myself think… Listen. I need you to follow me downstairs. I must talk to you about something urgent.'

'Well, I'd love to stop and chat, Walter, but you see I've got this thing that I—'

'Oh, for God's sake! It's not about the damned rent. God knows, I don't expect miracles.' Smethwick slumped on the top step and held his head in his hands. 'I just need to talk to someone… about that poor girl.'

'Alright there, fella,' said Roscoe, hauling the now sobbing landlord to his feet and helping him down the stairs. 'I'm sure there's no need for waterworks. Let's go down to your rooms and you can tell Uncle Frankie all about it.'

* * *

Ten minutes later, Roscoe was lighting two cigarettes from the gas hob in Smethwick's kitchen, having just listened to the landlord's account of the discovery of his molested tenant.

'What was that about her thigh, again?' he said, placing one of the cigarettes between Smethwick's lips.

'Branded,' replied the exhausted Smethwick. 'As though she were livestock. Burnt with a hot iron. Something like a Star of David.'

'Star of David? These toffs, they weren't ikey-mos, were they?'

'I'm not sure. They were gentlemen, certainly. The one I caught on the phone had breeding. Though, when you think about what he'd done to that poor girl…'

Smethwick took a long pull on his cigarette and then began to search among a mess of empty bottles on the table, to see if he could muster enough gin from them for a small taste.

'Describe him to me.'

'Small… plumpish, with rather ruddy complexion. Sandy hair. Well-dressed, in white tails. His voice, his manner, was *aristocratic*, I'd say.'

'And the other one?' asked Roscoe, trying to sound nonchalant, but already sensing the whiff of opportunity in the landlord's bizarre tale.

'Rakish looking. Black hair. One of those Van Dyke beards. Looked a little like that actor chappie – Rathbone.'

'Handsome was he, then, this cove?'

'I wouldn't know about that. But I somehow got the impression he was in charge. The podgy one addressed him as Simeon.'

'Simeon?'

'Do you know them, Frank? After all, you knew that girl, Tallulah, didn't you? You're acquainted with quite a few of them here, it would seem.'

'Oh, I didn't really *know* her. Only to say hello to. You know me – sociable, ain't I? Can't help myself.'

'But these two men? Do you know who they might be?'

'Haven't a clue. But they sound like right cowsons to me. I mean, branding that poor girl like she was a haunch of beef at Smithfield Market. And there was dope, you say? Needles and suchlike? Did they leave anything behind, by way of evidence?'

'No. That Simeon character marched me down here. Told me to wait an hour before I came out again. The room was immaculate afterwards. As though nothing had happened.'

'But it did happen though, right? I mean, the old brain can play some funny tricks on a man when he's had a few.'

'Don't be ridiculous! Of course it happened. I only wish it hadn't.'

'Alright, son. I believe you. And the girl – there's no chance she was just sleeping it off, right?'

'No. She was deathly white. Still as a statue.'

'And in the buff, you say? Tallulah?' Roscoe gave a short whistle. 'That's some statue.'

'I keep wondering: should I have called the police?'

'Are you mad? Call the bogeys?! With half the girls in this place on the bash? Your feet wouldn't have touched the ground, my friend. They'd have banged you up for living off immoral earnings.'

'Immoral earnings? Most of them haven't paid a penny in rent in the last six months.'

'That's as may be, but the judge ain't going to see it like that, is he? I hate to mention it, Walter, but it's not the first unfortunate death in this place, is it? If the poor girl *is* dead, that is.'

Smethwick hauled himself up from the table and began to yank open the cupboards and drawers, desperately searching for a slug of spirit to take away the tremors. 'They had a gun,' he said, beginning to sob again, thrusting aside a nest of empty bottles. 'Threatened to frame me if I didn't comply. What else could I have done?'

'Nothing. You did exactly the right thing, pal. Don't you worry about that.' Roscoe coaxed the distraught landlord back into his seat. 'Now, you sit down there, take it easy. I'm guessing you want a little drop of sauce? Well, I'll go and see what the girls have – they've usually got a bottle or two knocking about. Why don't you make yourself another cuppa while you're waiting? Take your mind off things.'

'Where did it all go wrong?' asked Smethwick, with his head in his hands at the table.

'I often ask myself the same question. But I guess the likes of us have just got to make the best of a bad deal, right?'

And as Roscoe made his way upstairs to search out a pick-me-up for his troubled landlord, that's exactly what he was contemplating – how to make the best of this new hand of cards he'd just been dealt. Because, despite what he'd told the distraught Smethwick, he knew exactly who the two mysterious guests had been. After all, wasn't he the one who'd introduced them to Tallulah in the first place? Roscoe didn't like to think of it as *poncing* exactly – it wasn't as if he actually took a cut of the punters' fee – it just all went towards what he liked to think of as his 'favours account'. And the knowledge that these toffs might be responsible for the murder, or at least the serious assault, of a young woman, was potentially valuable information. An opportunity of blackmailing Simeon Dubois and the Honourable Hugo Fitz Corbet might just prove to be very profitable in the long run. Very profitable indeed.

7

'**O**H, GEORGE,' SAID Bunty, as they made their way through the lunchtime Soho crowds, on the way to Solly Rosen's new pub in Little Dean Street. 'Did you manage to get that note translated? You said you were going to show it to a waiter in that restaurant. What was it, now?'

'Kettner's,' said Harley. 'Yeah, I did.'

'And?'

'Well, at first Nikos was a little puzzled.'

'Why? Isn't it Greek, as we thought?'

'It is. But it's *Ancient* Greek. Like Homer and Aristotle, you know? He said if it had been a longer phrase, he might not have been able to translate it for us.'

'But presumably he did?'

'*Be careful what you wish for.*'

'Sorry?'

'That's what it says.'

'Oh… And does that mean anything to you at all?'

Harley took a long pull on his cigarette. He thought back to the last time he'd encountered Osbert Morkens: walking with John Franklin down that long, dismal corridor in Broadmoor, having just left the professor's claustrophobic cell, the lunatic's rant echoing off the walls: 'Be careful what you wish for, my friend!' Now, here it was, back to haunt him again, translated into a menacing whisper in some ancient tongue.

He blew a thin plume of smoke from the side of his mouth and shook his head.

'No. Means nothing. But it's in Ancient Greek, and that shicer Morkens was a Professor of Ancient History at Oxford, wasn't he? So, my theory still stands.'

'*Be careful what you wish for,*' repeated Bunty. 'You know, it puts me in mind of a terrifying story I read at school. About a chap who wishes for money on an old magical fetish, only to receive it in the form of compensation for his son's tragic accident, after he's caught in the machinery at the factory he works at. And so the chap wishes again, this time for his son to—'

'*The Monkey's Paw*, W. W. Jacobs.'

'That's the one! Bravo, George! You've read it, then?'

'Yeah. And enjoyed it. It's a creepy little tale. Uncanny. I like all that stuff. But I'm not sure how that's relevant to the case… Anyway, we're here now: the Bag O'Nails.'

'Fascinating.' Bunty tried to sound enthusiastic as she regarded the rather grubby exterior of the pub. 'You said your friend has just taken over as landlord?'

'Solly Rosen. Used to be a boxer. Pretty tasty in his day – British Middleweight Champion, 1924 to '25. The Yiddish Thunderbolt, they used to call him.'

'Yiddish? And you're close friends, are you?'

'Well, we've had our moments,' said Harley, with a smile. 'But, yeah, we're close. His heart's in the right place. But where his brain is at is sometimes hard to fathom. Still, his missus does her best to keep him in check. You'll like her – Marni. She's one in a million.'

'Was their previous hostelry in London?'

'No, this is the first boozer they've run. They came into a bit of money recently, so decided to invest it in this place.'

'Lucky things.'

Bunty looked up at the painted pub sign. 'If it's called the Bag O'Nails, why do they have a picture of the Devil up there?'

'It's supposed to be Bacchus. It's a very old boozer this, see. They reckon the name could come from a corruption of Bacchanals.'

'Those ancient drunken orgies? Well, there's a coincidence! They were Greek too, weren't they? Like our note.'

'Alright, Miss Marple. Don't get carried away. You can't start seeing connections in everything you stumble across. There's got to be some logic to it all.'

'No, of course,' said Bunty, looking a little embarrassed. 'Shall we, then? This door, is it?'

'No, that's the tap room – the public bar. It'll be a bit too *gorblimey* in there, even for your liberal outlook. This one's the saloon.'

The pub was beginning to thin out after the peak lunchtime trade. Harley led the way through the remaining cluster of customers towards a large figure seated at the bar, who was voraciously attacking a corned beef sandwich.

'Hard at it, I see.'

'Georgie boy!' said Solly Rosen, spinning around on his bar stool. 'And who's this, then?'

'This is the latest addition to the George Harley Detective Agency, Sol – Bunty Chatterton, my new assistant.'

Rosen jumped off his stool and grabbed Bunty's hand to deliver a quick kiss.

'Orp! Sorry about that, love.' He produced a handkerchief and began to dab clumsily at the bright-yellow smear of piccalilli he'd left on Bunty's skin.

'Gosh! No, erm… Think nothing of it, Mr Rosen.'

'I see you've met my oaf of a husband,' said the woman with the lustrous dark eyes serving at the beer engine. 'I'm Marni, dear.' She clasped Bunty's hand. 'So, you've joined the agency, have you? Well, I'm sure you'll get on just fine. George is a mensch... But this one?' She patted Rosen playfully on the cheek. 'Look at him. Like he hasn't seen food in a week. What is it, Sol? You weak from spinning all those yarns to the punters, eh?'

'I'll have you know I've just shifted ten crates of ale down into that cellar,' said Rosen in protest.

'Mazel tov! And I suppose the other five are going to grow legs and march down there themselves, are they? While you sit there stuffing your fat face?'

'Alright, alright. Stop coming on my ear'ole, wontcha? Sheez! It comes to something when a bloke can't have a bite of lunch in peace.'

Rosen stuffed in the remainder of his sandwich and wiped his mouth on the back of his hand. 'George – want to give me a hand with the rest of those crates?'

'How could I resist?' said Harley, hanging his jacket on a nearby hatstand. 'You'll be alright for a few minutes, Bunty?'

'Why wouldn't she be alright?' said Marni. 'Bunty, you sit yourself down there. I'll get you a drink. Gin and It, alright?'

'Lovely, thanks.'

Bunty surveyed the pub's clientele with a slight air of wonderment. 'Awfully colourful, isn't it?'

'Well, I haven't quite finished with the decoration yet, but we're getting there. You should have seen when we moved in – such schmutz!'

'I think she means the punters, Marn, not the decor,' said Harley, with a smile. 'It's the first time our Miss Chatterton has been in a pub.'

'Never!' said Solly, astonished.

'Straight up.'

'Oh, stop it, you two,' said Marni, giving Bunty her drink. 'You're making the poor girl blush. Just because she wasn't dragged up in the gin shops like you. Solomon, take your little friend off to play in the cellar. And don't get up to any mischief… Don't listen to them, dear. Get that down you and I'll organise a little bit of nosh. Well, boys? Something keeping you, is there?'

* * *

'Blimey!' said Harley, regarding the stack of crates and boxes cramming the cellar. 'You're a bit overstocked, aren't you?'

'It ain't all booze, is it?' said Rosen, with a wink.

'What d'you mean?'

'Well, let's see now, what d'you fancy…?' Rosen cracked his knuckles and pulled open the flaps of a cardboard box. 'Silk tie?' He moved to a stack of larger cartons by the stairs. 'Fur coat? Only mogs and coney fur, mind, not the good stuff… What's this here? Oh, yeah… tin of red salmon?'

'Knocked-off gear? Are you going for some kind of record? Trying to lose your licence in the same month it was granted? All you need is for your barmaid to blab to her boyfriend about the cheap stockings she's been offered at work and the place will be crawling with bogeys.'

'You worry too much, my son,' said Rosen, placing the canned fish in Harley's jacket pocket. 'Most of this stuff'll be moved on by the weekend. Besides, I ain't got to worry about the bogeys sniffing round here, have I? That's what the silent partner's for.'

'Silent partner? Hold on. Don't tell me – Mori?'

Rosen gave him a schoolboy grin.

'Solly,' said Harley with a sigh, pulling out his packet of Gold Flake. 'What are you up to? I thought this was an opportunity to start afresh. To finally escape the clutches of Moriel Adler.'

Rosen accepted the offered cigarette. 'I'll have you know Mori's been good to me over the years. Anyway, this is a new start, ain't it? I mean, I'm my own boss here, right?'

'I don't know – have you asked Marni?'

'You're a funny man. Seriously though, you're the one who wanted me to knock the strong-arm work on the head, get a job on civvy street. Well, here I am. What could be more respectable than your friendly local landlord?'

'Yeah right, dead respectable – with a cellar-full of stolen goods. I take it Sonny Gables is involved in this lot somehow,' said Harley, reasoning such a large haul of illicit merchandise must involve the notorious West End fence somewhere along the line. 'Judging by the amount of old tut you got here, this would keep Gables going at the Cally for months. Look at it all: babies' rattles… canned peaches… Hold on!' The logo stamped on a nearby crate had caught Harley's eye. He bent down and struck a match to better illuminate the design. 'What the bloody hell is this?!'

'Oh, that's nothing. Come away now, George. I get the message. As I say, most of it will be gone by the weekend. Now, listen, the reason I wanted to get you down here was—'

'Schtum!'

Harley hauled the top crate off the pile and manhandled it onto the floor in front of him.

'There!' He pointed to the insignia stamped onto the lid. 'Royal Army Ordnance Corps. What the fuck have you got yourself mixed up in here?'

'It's just something I'm holding for Mori.'

Harley grabbed a screwdriver from a selection of tools stashed in an old paint pot on the floor.

'That ain't your property, George. Don't you open that, now!'

Ignoring his friend's protests, the private detective prised the lid off the crate.

'Jesus Christ!' He stared incredulously at the stack of hand grenades packed into the straw. 'Are these live?'

''Course they're live,' said Rosen, sheepishly. 'They'd be no good to anyone if they weren't, would they? And keep your voice down. You'll have half of Scotland Yard down here with all your carry on.'

'Listen, mate. You do realise that if any of Mori's crew uses one of these Mills bombs to open a peter or to put the frighteners on a rival – or whatever else they intend to use them for – they're just going to end up killing someone. Now, don't get me wrong, I know that won't be a first for that lot, but there's a difference between the silent kiss of a cut-throat and a ruddy huge explosion from a fragmentation grenade. Not exactly subtle, is it? Bound to generate a lot of interest, that. And when that box of pineapples gets traced back to the respectable and friendly landlord of the Bag O'Nails, then, my old pal, it won't be too long before said landlord finds himself at Messrs Ketch & Sons getting fitted out for the old hemp necktie. You'd swing for it, Solly – and that's stone ginger.'

'No, it ain't, George.'

'It is.'

'That ain't going to happen.'

'Well, I'm glad you think you've got so much control over the notorious Mori the Hat.'

'It ain't going to happen because that box of Mills bombs ain't intended for Mori's crew.'

'Go on, then – who is it for?'

'This needs to be strictly *me and you*, Georgie boy.'

'Listen to yourself.'

'I mean it. If this gets out, I'm in real schtuk.'

'My lips are sealed,' said Harley, noticing with concern that his friend was beginning to look uncharacteristically nervous. 'What exactly is going on here?'

'*Zionists*,' whispered Rosen, leaning in close.

'What?'

'The Haganah; out in Palestine.'

'Jesus, Sol!' Harley sat down on the steps and put his head in his hands. 'This just gets better and better. So, let me get this straight – you're now telling me that, rather than just a bit of petty larceny, you're actually involved in some kind of international arms smuggling here. Is that it?'

Rosen shrugged his huge shoulders. 'If that's how you want to look at it.'

'Well, that's just how the soddin' judge will want to look at it.'

Harley got up and walked over to the stack of crates. 'Are these all grenades?'

'No, there's all sorts there.'

'And all pinched from the British Army? You got someone on the inside at Woolwich Arsenal?'

'I don't ask where they come from.'

'Well, it don't take a genius to work it out, does it? Not with the coat of arms stamped all over them. You should have ditched the crates. It's a dead giveaway.'

'Great minds think alike. That's exactly what they're doing here. When I'm through with them they'll look just like a consignment of—'

'Cheese it! I don't want to know any more details, thank you very much.'

Harley took a moment to fix Rosen with a long, black look.

'Tell me, Einstein – once they've been shipped out to Palestine, what's to stop these weapons being used against our own boys?'

'Nah. This Haganah mob aren't interested in the British, they just want to take the fight to the Arabs.'

'So, when did Solly Rosen become a card-carrying Zionist? It's a bit out of the blue, ain't it? That's some serious stuff you're getting involved in there, son. Have you thought about the possible repercussions for Marni and the girls?'

'That's who I'm doing it for. Have you not seen those Blackshirt bastards gathering in Whitechapel High Street every weekend? Sir Pelham fucking Saint Clair and his British Brotherhood of Fascists, dripping poison into everyone's ears. Only last night that shicer was on the radio, talking about the "Israelite" and his malign alien influence on Westminster. It's only going to get worse, George, I'm telling you. Some of those Jew-boys out there in Palestine are actually standing up for themselves. They're out to get what's been promised to them, and to defend it with a bit of strong-arm if necessary. I admire their stance.'

'Promised to them by whom? God?'

'Don't be daft – you know I don't go in for all that old bollocks. No, by the British government.'

'Well, I ain't so sure it was theirs to offer in the first place.'

'Yeah, well, I reckon those out there have got a right to defend themselves. 'Cause from what I've heard, our British Tommies ain't too concerned about doing it for them.'

'Heard from who?' asked Harley. 'Oh, hold on. Has this got anything to do with your new pals in that civic society you were talking about?'

'Well, yeah, I suppose you could say it's connected. But this gear we're sending out to Palestine ain't official Maccabean business. It's just that the main players behind it all are members; that's where me and Mori first met them.'

'Mori's in on this as well? I thought he didn't get involved in anything unless it was guaranteed to bring in a decent profit. I've never seen him as a political animal.'

'Well, he's seen the writing on the wall with those Blackshirt bastards. Someone's got to make a stand. Otherwise us Jew-boys are just going to wind up the victims again. Now, that might've been alright for my Uncle Nate's generation, poring over their books in their little garrets, meekly waiting for the next pogrom; but I won't be nobody's mug, see? And neither will Mori.'

Just then the door at the top of the cellar stairs burst open and a familiar voice bellowed out: 'George?! George Harley! Come up here this minute! I've got a bone to pick with you.'

'Who's the hell's that?' said Rosen, hurriedly grabbing an old decorating sheet from the cellar floor and throwing it over the stack of contraband munitions.

Harley sighed and extinguished his Gold Flake under his foot. 'Sounds to me like the dulcet tones of my next-door neighbour.'

'And what have you done to incur the wrath of Vi Coleridge?'

'God only knows. She spends most of her time nowadays trying to marry me off. Maybe I'm supposed to be at a registry office somewhere.'

'Come on,' said Rosen, laughing. 'Best you come and face the music, then.'

'Hold up. I want to ask you something first. This is going to sound a bit barmy, mind.'

Harley paused for a moment, contemplating the end of his cigarette.

'Come on, George,' said Rosen, puzzled by his friend's uncharacteristic reticence. 'Out with it.'

'It's Morkens.'

'That shicer? What about him?'

'You haven't heard anything about him recently, have you? Something you might be keeping from me, for my own good?'

'Like what, for instance?'

'Like he's gone over the wall, maybe?'

'Escaped from Broadmoor? Is that even doable? I always imagine him done up in a straitjacket, padded cell, the works.' Rosen shook his head. 'Not heard a dickie bird, George. It'd be in all the papers, wouldn't it? Why you asking?'

'It's nothing. Thought I saw something in the Dilly the other night, that's all. Probably just my eyes playing tricks on me.'

'Maybe Vi's got it right after all,' said Rosen, placing his bear-like arm around his friend. 'Maybe you do need a little looking after. Come on, let's see who she's got lined up for you. Of course, you never know, she might have her eye on you herself.'

'Get out of it!'

'You could do worse. She's turned a few heads in her time, has Vi Coleridge. And Eric must have been worth a few bob when he snuffed it. Nice rich widow, knows her way around. What's not to like, eh?'

* * *

Back up in the bar, Harley soon discovered that on this occasion it wasn't *his* marital status which the redoubtable Violet Coleridge was concerned with, but that of his new assistant.

'I mean, whatever were you thinking?' said Vi, hoisting her ample posterior onto the bar stool. 'Inviting a young innocent like Bunty here to kip at your place? A lady of Miss Chatterton's standing has a reputation to consider, George. You can't just treat her like one of those waifs and strays you always seem to have knocking about; all those tarts and irons and goodness knows what else.'

'But I told you, I'd be sleeping at the office,' said Harley. 'I was trying to do her a favour by getting her out of that fleapit she's in.'

'Yes, and sullying her honour into the bargain,' said Vi, pulling her fur stole around her and pursing her lips.

'Sullying her honour? She's lodging in a gaff where they walk around at night with their hamptons hanging out.'

'I won't hear another word on the subject. Bunty, you'll be staying at my place. It's a boarding house, dear. Number six is free at the moment. Naturally, there'll be a discount on the rent, seeing as you're an employee of George's.'

'I say, that's most kind of you, Mrs Coleridge.'

'You do know she's already paid up to the end of the week at the other gaff?' said Harley, with a wry smile.

'Well then,' said Vi, with a brief adjustment of her girdle, 'she won't have to start paying me until next week, will she? Now, stop trying to put the mockers on it. She'll not be staying at your place and that's final. You can fetch her stuff from the Elephant and bring it around later, after work.'

'Priceless,' murmured Harley. 'Any other part of my life you'd like to organise?'

'I think you know the answer to that already,' said Vi, with a meaningful glance at Bunty, who was making herself busy with her drink. She leant forward to continue in a whisper: 'And if you play your cards right, we might be making some strides forward on that account in the very near future. But we'll be doing it all above board, thank you very much. Oh, hold yer horses...' she said, nodding towards the entrance. 'Look what the cat's just dragged in.'

'Friends of yours, George?' asked Bunty, regarding the three individuals making their way towards the bar, one of whom – a commanding character in an expensive, if slightly garish-looking, suit – seemed to be causing quite a stir among the drinkers.

'Not exactly,' said Harley. 'That's Mori Adler.'

'The hoodlum chap you were telling me about? Gosh! How exciting. What should I do?'

'Do?' chipped in Vi. 'You needn't do anything, dear. You're not to worry about the likes of Moriel Adler, not with Violet Coleridge as your friend. That one owes most of what he has today to those who went before him – namely my late hubby, Eric. You just carry on enjoying your drink.'

'But for God's sake,' added Harley, 'don't agree to buy anything, or do anything... in fact, don't agree to anything at all.'

'Righto,' said Bunty. 'Got it.'

'Georgie boy!' bellowed Adler, showing a glint of gold in his smile. 'How's tricks?'

'Oh, mustn't grumble, Mori.'

'And Violet. I trust we find you in good health?'

'Blessed as I am with a robust constitution, you'll rarely find me with a complaint in that department, Moriel. Mrs Adler and the kiddies; all well I hope?'

'In vigorous health, thank you for asking, *vigorous*… Now, boys, where are your manners?'

Adler turned to his sidekicks, 'Big' Terry Lampton, and the small, wiry Benny Whelks. Contrary to first impressions, Whelks was the more dangerous of the two – a pasty-faced chiv-man, named for his penchant for pickled seafood, whose stammering speech was compensated for by his eloquence with a cut-throat razor. 'Pay your respects to Mrs Coleridge, please.'

'Mrs C,' said Lampton, nodding briefly at Vi before going back to checking his reflection in the looking glass behind the bar.

'Terence,' replied Vi. 'And where's your shadow today?'

'Shadow? D'you mean Pony Moore?'

'Who else? He's usually to be seen trotting along behind you, ain't he? As sure as night follows day… And how are you, Benjamin?' she asked, turning to Whelks.

'Very w-w-well, thanks, M-M-M-Mrs C.'

'Ooh, that stutter's no better, is it, dear? You'd think in this day and age, what with all their new-fangled contraptions… Still, if they can't cure the Duke of York, I don't suppose there's much hope for the likes of—'

'Mori,' interrupted Harley, thinking it best to change the subject, as he'd noticed a worrying increase in the frequency of Whelk's nervous tics. 'Let me introduce my new assistant: Bunty Chatterton. Bunty, Mori Adler.'

'Charmed, my dear,' said the villain, pulling the young woman's hand to his lips.

'Mr Adler.'

'Right,' said Vi, giving Adler a disapproving look before pulling her stole around her and shuffling off the bar stool. 'I can't stand around here chewing the fat all day. Bunty, I'll see you later. Make sure he doesn't work you too hard. Gentlemen…'

Adler stood aside with his hat in his hand to allow Vi to bustle out. Once she'd gone, he took the vacated seat next to Bunty at the bar.

'Now, my dear, would you care for another drink?'

'Oh, I don't think I should, Mr Adler. We've got to get back to work, you see.'

'Very professional,' said the mobster, giving the young woman an appraising look. 'So, George, an assistant already? And Solomon tells me you have premises now, for that sherlock business of yours.'

'That's right. Frith Street.'

'Yes. Next to the Rendezvous.' Adler traced the shape of a sign in the air. 'The George Harley Detective Agency. With a little brass plaque and everything.'

'As well-informed as ever, Mori,' said Harley, shooting Rosen a black look.

'Well, if the eyes don't see, the hands can't take,' said Adler, accepting a glass of brandy from Marni. 'And as you well know, my eyes are everywhere.'

'Frith Street?' asked Big Lampton, adding a melodramatic intake of breath. 'You might want to watch yourself around there.'

'Oh yes, and why's that then, Big?'

'A few months ago, the Elephant and Castle mob had a go at the Rendezvous – took the place apart.'

Adler produced a double corona cigar from a spring-loaded leather case. 'Unfortunately, Terence is correct there, George. Lucrative business, some of these variety halls. And with this Slump on… well, there's all sorts of pond life trying to muscle in on the action. It all got a bit too rich for the former management's blood, I'm afraid. They almost bit Jerry's hand off when he made an offer for the place. Of course, with Jerry and I being business partners… Well, let's just say the security of the establishment is now assured. But, as for other vulnerable businesses in the area…' The mobster held out his hands to illustrate this precarious state of affairs.

'I think what Mori is saying,' added Lampton, as he sparked up his lighter and held it to the end of his boss's cigar, 'is that you might want to think about taking out a little insurance. That is, if this sherlock lark of yours actually manages to take off. After all, there are a lot of nasty characters out there. I'm sure you wouldn't want the lovely Miss Chatterton here to witness any unsavouriness.'

'Alright, Big,' said Adler, lost for a moment in a haze of aromatic smoke. 'Ease off a little there. We don't want to upset the young lady.'

'If I didn't know better,' said Harley, grabbing his jacket from the hat stand, 'I'd say you were trying to squeeze a little grease out of me. But that can't be right, can it? I mean, we go back way too far for any of that kind of malarkey… Come on, Bunty – we've got work to do.'

'Georgie boy,' said Adler, with a look of mock surprise. 'What gives? We're all friends here, ain't we? Just a little advice, is all. Come, sit, have another drink. Bunty?'

'Thanks awfully, Mr Adler,' said Bunty, standing up and grabbing her bag from the counter. 'But George is right, we really should be heading off now. We've just picked up a new case, you see.'

'Oh yes? More graft for your pals at Scotland Yard, is it, George?'

'No, Mori,' said Harley, giving his assistant a disapproving glance. 'It's back to the small fry, I'm afraid. Just your common or garden missing persons.'

'Alright, then. But you will let me know if anything juicy comes your way, yes? After all,' Adler paused to punctuate his sentence with a smoke ring, 'it could be mutually beneficial to do so. If you understand my meaning.'

8

Hugo Fitz Corbet, the fifth Marquess of Clenham, struggled to a sitting position and attempted to focus on the figure standing in the doorway of the majestic Belgravia drawing room.

'S'at you, Simeon?' he slurred, smearing a line of pink spittle across his double chin.

'Good grief, Hugo! Would you please take a moment to attend to yourself. It's eleven in the morning, for goodness' sake. Where are the staff?'

'Gave them the night off. Had a little soiree with some friends.' The nobleman held up a large decanter and giggled as he peered at the remnants of the liquid inside. 'Rather underestimated the effects.'

'Oh yes, and what have we been guzzling this time?' asked Dubois, closing the doors behind him. 'You know, it's rather depressing to watch you swilling your way through that exquisite cellar of yours. To think of all those years your father spent putting it together, scouring the Continent for exemplars of vintage, laying them down for future generations… only for little Billy Bunter to try to polish it off in one sitting as soon as he got his hands on the keys to the tuck shop.'

'I say, stop being beastly! And anyway, if you must know, this isn't one of Pater's clarets. It's a little something I picked up on a recent trip to Limehouse. *Yen-shee suey* they call it – opium dissolved in wine. Packs quite a punch, I can tell you.'

'You're in serious danger of becoming a cliché, Hugo.'

After using the finial of his walking stick to clear a tangled nest of lacy underwear from a Louis Quinze armchair, Dubois sat down and fixed the hungover Fitz Corbet with a disapproving look.

'You might like to know that, while you were embraced in the arms of Morpheus, I was busy clearing up your mess for you.'

Fitz Corbet squirted soda water into a glass and quaffed it greedily. 'Sorry? I don't follow.'

'No? Then I shall set the scene for you. Imagine we're in the garret room of a seedy boarding house, in some godforsaken quarter of the city. On the unkempt bed lies a naked form – *une fille de joie*, once vivacious and comely, now the wretched victim of our lecherous villain; a man who, in place of his human brain, seems to have had transplanted the organ of a juvenile, priapic chimpanzee.'

'I shan't be spoken to like that, Simeon, do you hear?!' Fitz Corbet's usual rubicund complexion had now returned to his chubby visage. 'What happened to that chorus girl was an unfortunate accident.'

'An accident?' Dubois arched an eyebrow. 'And I suppose the branding was an accident as well, was it? What on earth were you thinking?'

Placing a hand to his throbbing head, the marquess hoisted himself up from the chaise longue and shuffled over to the window. He pulled aside the curtain to squint at the bright

London morning and then gave a long sigh. 'I wasn't thinking anything in particular. I was intoxicated. Befuddled… Lost my head for an instant.'

'I should jolly well say you did. A Key of Solomon, branded on the thigh of a common whore? These things aren't to be taken lightly.'

'She's not a whore. She's one of Astarte's dancers… Tallulah, I think. With those damned haircuts, they all tend to get mixed up in the old noggin. But listen, it's not what you think; I was experimenting, d'you see?' The aristocrat clasped his hands together as he turned to appeal to his friend. 'I think I'm finally beginning to understand some of the spiritual techniques of the Order. I've been spending a lot of time recently trying to achieve that state of gnosis which you spoke of. That moment of abandonment. In fact, that's what the girl and I were doing when she had her little… accident.'

'What!' roared Dubois, grasping the arms of the chair. 'Do you mean to tell me you were sharing the secrets of the Order of the Thelemic Knights with a showgirl?'

'Now, steady on, Simeon. All I meant was—'

'My God! You behave just like a child at times. You're going to have to learn a little discipline if you want to gain your promotion to Adeptus Minor, you know.'

'Discipline?' spluttered Fitz Corbet. 'Whatever happened to "Do what thou wilt"?'

'As I've explained a thousand times before, the Thelemic law is not a licence for your silly schoolboy lusts. It describes the acceptance of the will, the commitment to seek out your true path in life. I must say, it can be incredibly tiresome at times, this inability of yours to grasp even the most basic of concepts. It was exactly the same at school, nursing you through each and every subject. I do sometimes wonder why I bother.'

'You wonder why you bother, do you?' Fitz Corbet flicked a tress of lank hair from his face, his complexion now approaching puce. 'Well, I can tell you it's no wonder to me. No wonder at all. Money! That's why. After all, where would you be without the Fitz Corbet coffers? There would be no more playing at running a supper club; no travelling the globe on – what is it you call them – your little "gastronomic odysseys"? No more girlish-boys, or boyish-girls, or whatever else you've proclaimed *en vogue* this month. And there'd certainly be no more OTK. I must have given you at least two hundred for the Order over the last few months, on the pretence that you might have things ready for this holy visitation. And I'm beginning to think it a little strange that you're the only one of us who's had any personal contact with this Preceptor of yours. I do hope this isn't all just some elaborate hoax.'

Dubois sat for a while in silence, stroking his saturnine beard. Then, striking his cane on the floor, he rose and puffed out his chest.

'Well, if that's how you really feel, I shall bid you adieu. It is indeed a blow to watch you so effortlessly squander a friendship as long and as dear as ours, but I trust you have your reasons. Of course – contrary to your assumptions – there is, in fact, a long line of associates who would simply jump at the chance of sponsoring the Order. So, you can rest assured the preparations for the Preceptor will proceed undeterred – it's just a pity you won't be there to reap the benefits. Ah, well, c'est la vie.'

Dubois made to leave, but paused with a hand on the doorknob, keeping his back to the room to conceal his sly smile. 'I shall arrange to have Tallulah's body dropped off sometime today. I assure you, my men will be quite discreet.'

'Body? But I thought you said things had turned out alright?'

'Oh no, I'm afraid our delightful little chorine is quite the corpse, Hugo. I kept it from you to protect your delicate nerves. But now you no longer require my services, well…

I'm sure you'll find someone else to deal with her. One of the gamekeepers on the estate, perhaps? Send word to the club where you want her sent. Good day!'

As Dubois had expected, before he had even made it to the lobby he felt a chubby hand clamp down on his shoulder.

'Where are you going, you silly old thing?' Fitz Corbet was a little breathless after the rush across the room. 'You don't for a moment think I meant it, do you? You're my rock, Simmy, my guiding light. Come and sit down, you obstinate fellow.' The marquess grabbed Dubois's hand and dragged him back into the room. 'We'll have some lunch. Somewhere fun. I expect that's what all the excitement was earlier – you know how crabby I get when I forsake the old eggs and b in the morning.'

With Dubois once more safely ensconced in his chair, Fitz Corbet shambled over to the drinks trolley.

'We've time for a little pick-me-up first,' he said, as he began clumsily splashing Fernet-Branca and crème de menthe into a cocktail shaker. 'A Prairie Pullet. Withers always makes this look so blasted easy. Dashed inconvenient when he's not here… Supposed to have an egg in it, but Lord knows where those blighters are kept. Interest you in one?'

'Good Lord, no,' said Dubois, looking disdainfully at the bright-green concoction. 'It will ruin your palate for lunch.'

Disregarding this advice, the marquess chugged away noisily at the shaker for a few seconds; when he reappeared it was with the addition of a luminous moustache.

'So, the Preceptor. When might we expect him, d'you think?'

'Oh, quite soon, Hugo, quite soon. We must be patient, of course, but between you and me… well, let's just say that the planets are almost in perfect alignment for his triumphant return from the wilderness.'

9

HARLEY SAT AT his desk, dog-tired, trying to suck some stimulus from a Gold Flake cigarette. He'd had a ruinous night's sleep, and there could be little doubt as to the cause – Osbert Morkens. For almost six months he'd been on a relatively even keel; half a year of blissfully peaceful nights without having to drink himself into a stupor or resort to the stupefying charms of the opium pipe. But all that had changed when he'd spied those sinister features leering at him from the back of a cab in Piccadilly Circus. Now the bouts of insomnia had returned; and when he did manage to sleep… well, it was just another opportunity for the nightmare to slither back into his mind.

Just as it had the previous night. As usual, a portion of the dream was faithful to what he'd actually experienced – little Eddie Muller standing terrified in his sailor suit, the heavy Luger gripped tight in his chubby hands, the bloody footprints on the carpet. But for some reason, in this nightmare version of events, Harley wore his old battledress – the cloying mud from his trench boots leaving an ugly trail on the runner behind him – and the elegant design of the wallpaper had been replaced by the gaudy stripe of a child's peppermint stick.

But regardless of these strange embellishments, it always ended just as it had that awful night in Cynthia's apartment, almost four years ago now: teasing open her bedroom door… turning back the bedclothes…

Harley was yanked from his gloomy introspection by a sharp rap on the office door.

'It's open!' he called out, getting up from his desk.

'What's all this then, Mr Aitch? Gone up in the world, ain't we? I mean – your own suite of offices?'

The unexpected visitor was a remarkable-looking individual: small and gangly, and in a constantly fidgeting state, which gave the impression he was in possession of more than his fair share of elbows and knees. Alfie Budge, known to his close associates as Squib, on account of his diminutive stature and explosive energy. As usual, Budge was kitted out in standard mini costermonger's garb: shabby jacket, waistcoat and muffler. This was topped off with a shock of unruly red hair, the luminous effect of which had been tempered a little by the application of a razor at the back and the sides, and of a large pancake cap on top. To the casual onlooker, Budge's age would have been difficult to ascertain; though juvenile in physique, he had the mannerisms of an old lag, and his pale face – smeared in equal parts with freckles and grime – wore a jaded, world-weary expression. He could have been any-thing from eighteen to forty-five. However, on enquiring, our casual onlooker would have learnt from Master Budge – with, no doubt, some surprise – that he was, in fact, a mere fifteen and three quarters years old.

'Squib! I haven't seen you in weeks. Thought you were dead.'

'But I couldn't be dead, could I?' said Budge, philo-sophically, pausing to wipe his snub nose on the back of his hand. 'I mean, you wouldn't be inviting a corpse in for a cup of tea and a smoke, would you? Not a sharp bloke like you. That'd be morbid, that would.'

'A cup of tea and a smoke, is it?' said Harley with a chuckle. 'Alright, in you come. You can't stay long, mind. I've got something on. I'm just waiting for my secretary to arrive.'

'Secretary?' Budge made a little excited rearrangement of his shoulder blades.

'Assistant, actually,' said Harley, correcting himself. 'And I don't want you distracting her. We've got a case on.'

'Budge never outstays his welcome,' said the youngster, retrieving a voluminous satchel from the floor and swaggering past Harley into the office. 'You just nod me the wink when you want me to sling me 'ook.'

These impromptu visits from the young lad served two useful purposes for Harley. The first was to present him with a choice of any new jazz recordings which the apprentice wide-boy might be offering – jazz being one of Harley's passions in life, and Budge having a profitable agreement with a number of sailors working the American merchant ships. The second purpose was to act as one of his several sources of intelligence from the city's underbelly. Budge was well placed for such a role – working part-time as a runner for the infamous fence Sonny Gables, he got to rub shoulders with many of the names and faces of the capital's criminal fraternity.

'So, what's the word on the street?' asked Harley, after furnishing the youth with a mug of sweet tea and a cigarette.

'Let me see, now...' The lad took a loud slurp of his tea. 'Well, for starters, Chimp Mason's had his collar felt again. Lumbered for a string of jobs around Mayfair.'

'Was it him?'

'Makes no odds, does it? Not with the bogeys. You know that. His mouthpiece ain't much bottle, so I expect he'll go away for a bit again. You should see this brief of his,

George. Talk about called to the bar. He's sozzled most of the time – it's a wonder the bloke can put his syrup on the right way round.' Budge shook his head in a chuckle as he pulled on the cigarette, cupped tightly in the palm of his hand.

'Doing a bit of stir is an occupational hazard for the likes of Chimp,' said Harley. 'There's a lesson for you there, son. What else is happening?'

'Well, there are some new faces in the manor. San toys. Only a small crew, four or five of them at the most. But by all accounts, they're proper hard nuts. The big man's a jock, Glaswegian; right ugly bugger, an' all – got a face like Lon Chaney.'

'Glaswegian? What's their angle?'

'I don't know yet. Might have something to do with this business with the Italians and the Elephant and Castle mob.'

'What business?'

Budge leant in and adopted a conspiratorial whisper. 'The rumour is they're joining forces, trying to muscle in on Mori the Hat's turf again.'

'That's all we need,' said Harley, with a sigh. 'How reliable is this particular bit of intelligence? I mean, it's not the first time that's been put about.'

'Just a rumour at the moment. But if it is kosher, you can bet your life Mori's on top of it.'

'That's stone ginger. Bound to end a bit messy, that… Alright. So, what have you got in the bag for me?'

Budge showed Harley the briefest of little boy smiles before bending down to delve into his satchel. He came back up with three shellac disks, all bearing the Brunswick label.

'I got two Dutch Elleringtons.'

'It's Duke,' corrected Harley. 'Duke Ellington.'

'Yeah, that's the fella… and this other one's the latest from The Midnight Moochers.'

Harley examined the records. 'Alright. I'll take the two Ellingtons.'

'Not the Moochers?'

'Already got it.'

'*Garn!* You can't 'ave. The bloke told me it's only just out in America. Says he got it in New York as a new release. How could you have one already?'

'Because I happen to be mates with the leader of Munro's Midnight Moochers, that's how.'

'You know Jumpin' Johnson Munro?'

'Indeed I do.'

'Get out of it. No you don't.'

'Alright then, I don't.'

'Do you?'

'Yes. And the last time he was over, he gave me a fresh pressing of "The Cat's Pyjamas".' Harley sparked up a Gold Flake and pushed a plume of smoke out of the side of his mouth. 'And a real keen toon it is too,' he said, in a hammy American accent.

'Please, Mr Aitch. Don't embarrass yourself.'

Harley laughed and fished out some coins from his pocket.

'There you go. Now, you'd better get on, I've got things to do.'

Budge pocketed the money and gathered up his misshapen satchel. He was just taking his leave as Bunty arrived. Before Harley could intervene, the young entrepreneur was halfway across the room, doffing his pancake cap with a generous application of elbow.

'And a very good morning to you, madam.'

'Gosh!' said Bunty, a little taken aback.

'The name's Budge, Alfie Budge.' With a quick flick of his bony wrist, Budge produced a calling card from a hidden pocket within his hat. 'New in town, by any chance?'

'Well, as a matter of fact, I am,' she said, squinting at the inscription on the card.

'That's me: Budge by name, but not by nature – if you know what I mean,' said the youth, with the addition of one of his knowing nose-taps.

'I'm not sure I do.'

'And if you are new in town,' continued Budge, who regarded it highly unprofessional to allow a punter to answer any of his rhetorical questions, 'you won't find a better friend than Squib.'

'Squib?'

'That's what they call me.'

'But I thought you were Budge?'

'Oh yes,' continued the youngster, beginning to build a decent head of steam. 'Squib's a real good friend, alright. Theatre tickets, nylons, American lipsticks, Parisian scent. Then there's all the local knowledge on tap. Little nuggets of wisdom, the result of years of experience.'

'Years?' said Bunty, silently calculating the age of the little animated huckster.

'Could save you a lot of grief, asking Squib first, you know. Which landlord's been watering the gin; which cabbies you can trust; the restaurants that have back alleys strangely devoid of cats; the livelier of the bottle parties.' Another nose-tap here, followed by a quick wink. 'Think of me as a walking *Pears' Cyclopaedia*. And that's not all. Not by a long chalk. You see—'

'That'll do, son!' interjected Harley. 'Leave the lady alone now.'

'Not a problem, not a problem. Only, if you do change your mind, Miss… erm?'

'Bunty.'

'Bunty…? Most unusual. Alright then, *Bunty*, if you do change your mind, you can always leave a message with the tobacconist's just up the street there; you probably passed it on the way here. Just tell them it's for Alfie Budge. Got it?'

'Yes, I think I'm unlikely to forget that now. After all, I do have your card.'

'Alright, then. Mr Aitch, you be lucky now!'

✳ ✳ ✳

'Well, I don't think I've ever met anyone quite like Alfred before,' said Bunty, after the ragamuffin had left.

'They broke the mould when they made that one.'

Harley put the records away in his desk drawer then got up to fill the kettle at the sink in the back office.

'So, how are you finding the new digs?' he called out.

'Oh, Violet has made me feel very welcome. And the room is perfect, of course; and at a very reasonable rate… By the way, you were up awfully early this morning. I came around for you after breakfast, but you'd already left.'

'Yeah, I had a few things to sort out,' he said, heaping spoonfuls of tea into the pot and placing the kettle on the small camping stove. 'By the way, I want you to hold the fort here this morning. I've got an appointment, with a copper friend of mine.'

'Really? Anything to do with the Louise Parker case?'

'No, just tying up a few loose ends from a previous job. You'll be alright here, on your own?'

'Of course. There's simply tons to do. All those boxes to unpack and a heap of filing.'

'That's what I like to hear.' Harley glanced at his watch. 'Right. I've just got time for a cup of rosie before I go. I'll be mother.'

10

HARLEY TOOK A sip of his ale and cast a ruminative eye around the Soho pub. Only in the last few weeks had he felt able to return to the Shabaroon, so intrinsically linked was it to his memories of Cynthia, and in particular to that blissful period they'd spent together immediately following Morkens' arrest. It had been in the Shab's saloon bar that the locals had thrown a party to celebrate his capture of the Nursery Butcher – that particular night had turned into a joyous bacchanal, earning itself a place in West End folklore and culminating in him accepting Cynthia's proposal of marriage. Over there, by the fire, was the cosy nook in which he and Cynthia had spent many a Sunday afternoon in the weeks following, planning the rest of their lives together; a state of domestic bliss which was, of course, doomed never to come to fruition.

He took another pull on his pint and sparked up a smoke.

Since then life had changed so much. *He* had changed so much – he understood that all too well. But though the grief he felt for Cynthia was still as raw, he found it far more difficult to lament the passing of the old George Harley, sitting up there on his high horse, so full of pride and hubris.

But some things did remain unchanged. There, for example, was the indefatigable Juney, working the beer machine with her calm self-assurance – queen of the pub, so comfortable in her own skin, surrounded by all the polished brass and lacquered mahogany. And the landlord, Hal Dixon, leant there on the bar, studying the *Racing Times*, his ginger toupee adorning his scalp like a hibernating woodland animal. And in the corner booth, sipping demurely at a whisky and peppermint, the ribbons of smoke escaping lazily from the Black Cat cigarette in her onyx holder, was Dora, Empress of the West End courtesans. And scattered about the bar, enjoying as much solace and quiet contentment as any library visitor or Sunday morning worshipper, were the other denizens of Bohemia: the theatrical agent immersed in his crossword; the chorine of modish beauty, touching up her tangerine lipstick, while the young man sharing her table – by far the prettier of the two – picked dejectedly at a sodden beer mat; sat on a high stool at the bar was a dark, menacing creature in a billycock hat, one thumb in his waistcoat pocket, gimlet eye fixed on the pub's entrance – a villain, if ever there was one; and at the table next to Harley's sat a struggling artist with paint-flecked tresses, nursing a half-empty glass (and no doubt an empty belly) and a battered copy of *Les Fleurs Du Mal*. Here it endured, in all its welcoming familiarity: the Shab.

He closed his eyes and breathed in the warm, tobacco-spiced, yeasty fug of it all.

'It seems a pity to disturb you, George… but you said it was urgent?'

Harley opened his eyes to the wholesome figure of Detective Sergeant Alec Franklin. Fresh-faced and with the hearty demeanour of a sportsman, Franklin looked indisputably out of place among the Shab's shadowland punters (two of whom had made a swift exit at the sudden appearance of one of His Majesty's Metropolitan Police Force). Like his late father before him, DS Franklin was one of a rare breed: a straight bogey serving in the West End. Franklin senior had worked alongside Harley on the Nursery Butcher case and had been all set to enjoy a well-earned retirement when, on the very same night Cynthia was killed, he was found dead in his bed. Although the subsequent coroner's inquest returned an open verdict, Harley was convinced Osbert Morkens had somehow been responsible for the detective chief inspector's demise (even though the child-killer was already incarcerated in Broadmoor by then).

'Sorry, I was miles away.' Harley smiled ruefully, as he recognised a hint of his old comrade's earnest good nature in his son's eyes. 'Good to see you, Alec. Why don't we go through to the snug? It'll be a little more private back there.'

* * *

'Congratulations on the promotion, by the way,' said Harley, once they were ensconced in the small partitioned-off area at the back of the pub. 'Nice to see the Met recognising the emerging talent in their ranks for once.'

'Thanks… Although, I'm not so sure it was judged on merit.'

'What do you mean?'

'Well, if I'm honest with you, I think the top brass felt guilty about how they allowed DS Quigg to sideline Dad in the Morkens case. And as they couldn't do any more for him, I think I might have got a little leg-up as a consequence.'

'What a load of old madam! That's not how these things work. They made you up to detective sergeant because you're a natural. The apple never falls far from the tree – it's in your bones.'

'Thanks. That's appreciated. If I turn out to be half the copper Dad was… well, I'll not complain. You know, George, if it hadn't been for your tenacity in hunting that monster down, my father would have ended his long and distinguished career as a broken and humiliated man. I'll be forever in your debt for that, you know.'

Harley shrugged. 'Much good it did him in the end.'

'Oh, but you're wrong! He went out on a high. Dad was so proud he'd made that arrest, that he'd been a part of it all. And at the end, well, I'd like to think he went quickly, in his sleep, knowing absolutely nothing about it. I know you think otherwise, but I don't see how Morkens could have had any-thing to do with it, locked up as he was in Broadmoor. I don't *want* to think he had anything to do with it, d'you see?'

'I can understand that,' said Harley with a reassuring smile. 'What about that shicer Quigg? I hear he's long gone.'

'Yes, but he's still in the job. Somewhere in the Midlands, I've been told. I wouldn't be surprised if we don't see him crop up here again in the future, once the dust has settled a little. Quigg was a prominent local Lodge member; they like to protect their own, that lot.'

'Don't I know it. Glad to hear you've steered clear of all that malarkey, though.'

'Something else I inherited from Dad… Anyway, what was it you wanted to talk about? Something to do with a new case of yours?'

Harley shook his head. 'Not a new one, no. It's about Morkens, actually. I need someone to reassure me that the shicer is still safely banged up.'

'Why would you think otherwise?'

Harley took a pull on his cigarette and regarded the policeman for a moment before answering.

'Because I think I might have seen him.'

'What?! When?'

'Last week. Piccadilly Circus. And later on, my assistant saw someone matching his description mooching around outside the agency.'

'But it couldn't have **been** him, could it?'

'You tell me.'

'Well, I haven't **heard** anything about him for ages,' said Franklin. 'And there's your answer, isn't it? Surely, if a criminal lunatic of Professor Morkens' calibre had escaped from Broadmoor we'd all know about it?'

'Not necessarily. He'll still have some loyal friends in high places. His type always does.'

'Oh, come on! You're not seriously suggesting that someone in the corridors of power would be willing to help a psychotic child-killer escape?'

'Let's just say I'm a little more cynical than you, Alec… Listen, you said you owed me one for your old man? Well then, I'd like you, in your professional capacity, to contact Broadmoor and have them assure us that that cowson is still securely within their control and hasn't left the confines of the asylum since he was declared unfit for trial. Will you do that for me?'

'Of course. I'll get on it straight away.'

'Great,' said Harley, sighing as he ground the remnants of his cigarette into the pub ashtray. 'Because otherwise I'm never going to get any poxy sleep.'

'I'd be glad to help, George. Consider it done.'

'That's appreciated. There is one other thing.' Harley handed Franklin one of the copies of the photographs he'd had made.

'A case I'm working on. Missing persons. Louise Parker. She's a dancer, I've put all the details on the back. If she turns up in a cell – or, God forbid, on a slab in the morgue – I'd appreciate you letting me know.'

'Of course… That's quite a hairdo; not easily missed. If we cross paths, I'll let you know.'

'Thanks, Alec. I owe you one.'

Being on duty, and with another appointment to keep, DS Franklin declined Harley's offer of a drink and left. A few minutes later, as Harley was about to re-enter the saloon, he noticed Juney gesticulating to him behind the bar.

'I suggest you pop back out of sight, love,' she said, nodding towards Hal Dixon, who was dealing with a dishevelled-looking woman in a mangy fur coat. 'Avoid the drama.'

'Who is she?'

'Haven't the foggiest. But she mentioned your name. Don't look all there, if you ask me.'

He was just about to take Juney's advice and slip back into the snug when the woman fixed her bleary gaze on him.

'Harley? Is that you?'

After a brief tussle, the woman managed to break free of Dixon's grasp and made a beeline for the private detective.

'Thank God, I found you!'

Harley scrutinised the haggard face, trying to place her – the waxy, pallid complexion; the watery eyes with constricted pupils.

'It's me, George. *Pamela Chisholm.*'

He gripped the edge of the bar.

The Honourable Pamela Chisholm. Once the darling of the society columns. Now addict and social pariah. It had been Pamela who had brought Cynthia to the attention of that predatory German warlock, Fedor von Görlitz, by luring her to his occult society gathering. In Harley's eyes, this wreck of a woman standing before him bore at least some responsibility for his fiancée's horrific murder.

'Don't you remember me?'

'We've never met.' Harley tried to keep his voice measured, his anger already stoking his heart. 'As well you know.'

'But you know who I am?' She grabbed at his arm. 'I was Cynthia's friend.'

'Friend? You've got to be kidding me!' He prised her fingers from his arm and pushed her hand away. 'If it was up to me, you'd be banged up in Holloway for what you did to her.'

'For what I did…' Pamela's eyes lost focus for a moment. She swayed a little, placing a hand on a bar stool to steady herself. 'I don't follow.'

'No? It's simple enough. You touted your so-called friend like fresh meat. Lured her to that lunatic cabal, so they could have their way with her. And for what? Filthy lucre? Another grubby fix from that quack Jeakes?'

'Oh, but you simply don't understand!' She grabbed the lapels of his jacket as she pleaded with him, her breath foul with plaque and stale liquor. 'What else could I have done? I'm as much a victim as she was!'

'You? You're no better than a soddin' ponce!'

No longer able to contain his rage, Harley wrenched Pamela's hands from his jacket and gave her a violent shove. She stumbled back into a bar stool, toppling to the floor.

'Oi! That's enough!' shouted Juney, rushing from behind the bar to attend to the distraught woman, who was now sobbing on her hands and knees, her matted hair fallen across her face in a greasy veil.

'There was absolutely no need for that, George,' scolded the barmaid, giving Harley a stern look. 'That's not like you.'

'You don't know the full story. She was the—'

'I don't care! D'you hear? Now, go and sit down while I deal with her.'

But as Harley backed away, Pamela grabbed at his trouser leg.

'Wait!'

With Juney's help she managed to struggle to her feet.

'I have something to tell you. Something we can't discuss here.' She pushed a crumpled piece of paper into his hand. 'My address. Come… come and see me… *tonight*.'

'I don't think so,' he said, handing back the scrap of paper.

'Oh, but you must, George. Believe me! I have something important for you… something about *them* – about Fedor and the others.'

He glanced at Juney's reprimanding look. With a huff, he took the address and stuffed it into his inside pocket.

If he hadn't had been in such a foul mood as he left the pub, Harley might have noticed the figure loitering in the darkened doorway opposite: a woman with the collar of her green wrap coat turned up, her face obscured by the floppy brim of a soft felt trilby. But though her gaze was fixed doggedly on the private detective as he made his way up Meard Street, this mysterious figure remained resolutely in position – until, that is, Pamela Chisholm exited some five minutes later. Then she slipped silently from her hiding place, shadowing at a safe distance, as the former socialite took a meandering route back towards Piccadilly Circus.

* * *

Ten minutes' walk away in Fitzrovia, Frankie Roscoe had just stopped outside the Joseph Grimaldi pub. He needed time to compose himself before entering. The flutter in his gut may have been down to another missed breakfast, but it was more likely nerves. After all, waiting inside was possibly the last genuine opportunity he had to clear his debts with the ruthless Mori Adler. And, who knew, maybe also earn a little extra dough on the side? And by Christ, the timing couldn't be better – only the previous evening, Adler's enforcers, 'Big' Terry Lampton and Pony Moore, had made a personal visit to explain to Roscoe his imminent obligations pertaining to the loan; the main gist of which was he had just four days to stump up the repayment arrears or they'd return with their colleague Benny Whelks, who'd extract it, in kind, with his rip-throat razor.

Roscoe knew the job in hand would have to be carried out with a certain finesse. Simeon Dubois was no run-of-the-mill mug. Working the black on him over the death of the showgirl, Tallulah, would take charm and nerve. But Frankie Boy could sing that particular song, alright. Charm and nerve? They ran through him like the letters in a stick of Brighton rock.

The wide-boy took a deep breath, adjusted the brim of his lucky fedora, fitted a fresh match in the side of his mouth and pushed on through the studded wooden doors.

The saloon bar of the Joseph Grimaldi was unusually spacious and inviting for a West End watering hole. Displayed on the walls were various framed posters featuring the eponymous King of the Clowns, his uncanny face grimacing in gaudy make-up. The furniture was a mix of oak tables and chairs and slightly shabby leather settees, punctuated here and there with large ceramic pots containing robust aspidistras. This being the back end of the lunchtime trade, the clientele was reduced to a few late stragglers.

'Half a Burton's please, love,' said Roscoe, having finally caught the landlady's attention. He laid the coins down on the counter. 'I'm actually here to meet someone. Mr Dubois about, is he?'

It was then, as he made another brief scan of the room, that the wide-boy noticed the small group in the corner, partially veiled in a blue fug of cigarette smoke. These three individuals now paused in their game of dominoes to turn and scrutinise the newcomer.

Each had a face advertising danger. These were hard men, in tailored suits, playing pub games at lunchtime. *San toys –* mobsters – no doubt about it.

Roscoe quickly averted his gaze and turned back to the bar to accept his drink.

This don't look good, Frankie Boy, he thought. *This don't look good at all!*

He'd only had a quick glance, but they didn't look like any of Adler's crew.

'Well?' asked the landlady, laying down the change.

'Sorry?'

'Is he expecting you?'

'Oh, yeah. I telephoned through to the club last night. He said to meet him here, this lunchtime.'

'Alright then. You'll find him in the private room, just around there, to your left.'

'Much obliged.'

Roscoe was relieved to find Dubois alone, sitting with a half-bottle of a decent Montrachet and a small, leather-bound tome.

'My word, Frank! Did someone actually sell you that tie?' Dubois gave a little tut and went back to his reading. 'Ah well, *le style c'est l'homme même.*'

'You don't mind if I join you, Simeon?'

Roscoe slipped into the seat opposite the dandy. The surprise at having just discovered the presence of a crew of hardened villains in the pub had unnerved him a little, but he was determined not to let it put him off his stroke.

'Nice drop of vino?' he said, forcing a note of cheer into his voice.

Dubois held his glass up to the light.

'It's admirably restrained. One mustn't be too over-stimulated at lunch.'

'S'pose not… So, this is where you have your club, is it?'

Dubois pointed distractedly to the floor.

'Oh, right, 'course. Down in the basement. Not been there myself yet.'

'And I'd say that's unlikely to change in the near future.' Dubois licked his finger to turn the page of his book. He graced the wide-boy with the briefest of insincere smiles. 'We run a very tight door policy.'

Undeterred, Roscoe took a swig of beer and soldiered on. 'What you reading there, then? Something racy, is it?' He squinted at the gold leaf on the spine. '*Oera Linda*. Who's she, when she's at home? I expect you've got sophisticated tastes, when it comes to the ladies, eh? You and that pal of yours, Hugo. I mean, take that little brama, Tallulah. She was something out of the ordinary, weren't she? Real bit of class, that one.'

Dubois closed his book with a sigh and removed his half-moon reading spectacles. 'I can see there'll be no peace until we've played out your little charade. So, tell me – what is this all about, Frank? Have you finally decided to branch out into full-time pimping? Well, if the merchandise is of high enough quality, one might be able to put a little business your way. What are you proposing?'

'Now hold on a minute! I'm a little offended at what you're insinuating there. I'll have you know I'm no Joe Ronce. I mean, a fella's got a reputation to keep, ain't he?'

'Really? You? Reputation? I had no idea… So, then – why is it you needed to see me so urgently?'

'What it is,' said Roscoe, glancing behind him and shuffling his chair a little closer to the table. 'What it is, is that I've come into possession of a little information. Information regarding your mate Hugo and that Tallulah we were just talking about.'

He studied the dandy's face, but there was still no hint of the desired reaction on his rakish features.

'Do go on. You have my full and undivided attention.'

Roscoe leant over the table. 'I know what happened,' he whispered dramatically.

Dubois cocked his head quizzically.

'I know what Hugo did, Simeon. To that poor girl.'

'What did he do?'

'He bloody killed her! That's what! And you did away with her body somehow. And I know about the dope. And about the way he branded her like some piece of livestock.'

Satisfied he was finally getting somewhere, Roscoe sat back in his chair and took up his glass of beer. ''Course, as well as not being a ponce, I'm also no copper's nark. So, never fear – I won't be scurrying off to the bogeys with all this.'

'Heaven forfend!'

'But information of that calibre? Well, it's got to be worth something, ain't it? I mean, I've heard that mate of yours is some kind of aristo.'

'Indeed. Hugo is the fifth Marquess of Clenham.'

'Well, there you are, then. The Honourable Hugo wouldn't want it known up in the House of Lords that he's creased some little doll in a knocking shop in Seven Dials, would he? Accident or no accident. Nor that he's partial to a bit of the old Doctor White, or whatever that muck was they were injecting. And let's face it, sullying his reputation will be the least of his worries. I mean, if she is dead, it'd be the drop for him if word got out, wouldn't it? He could plead manslaughter, I s'pose, but then—'

Roscoe was startled into silence by the low chuckle emerging from Dubois. A chuckle which soon evolved into a full-blown roar of laughter.

'Oh, how wonderfully entertaining!' Dubois slammed his hand down on the table, making Roscoe jump back in his seat. 'Why, Frank, I do believe you're attempting to blackmail me.'

'Well, I wouldn't call it blackmail, not as such.'

'Wouldn't you? Well, I would, dear boy... How utterly idiotic of you. I'm afraid you've made a grave error. You see, you can't blackmail me.'

'Oh yes? That's what you think, is it?' said Roscoe, trying his best to pretend he still had a little control of the situation. 'And why's that, then?'

'Where does one start? There are so many reasons, Frank, many more than I'd care to name. But there are three which spring to mind immediately. Shall I point them out to you, hmm?'

The wide-boy quickly popped a fresh matchstick into his mouth to hide the nervous twitch which had developed in his upper lip. 'Go on then. I'm all ears.'

Dubois rose elegantly and indicated that Roscoe should follow him to the door.

'Impressive, aren't they?' he said, pointing to the clique of hard men playing dominoes. 'The army taught them their trade, of course; an apprenticeship with the gun and the bayonet. And then subsequent bouts of incarceration at His Majesty's pleasure added the requisite bitterness and rage. They're my pack of hounds, Frank. Extremely loyal. And quite deadly.'

Noticing the attention from Dubois, one of the group now got up and sauntered over to join them.

'Everything alright, Mr Dubois?' he asked in a thick Gorbals accent.

'Oh, quite alright, Irvine. Thank you for asking. By the way, this is Frank Roscoe. Commit his face to memory, would you? You might have some dealings with Mr Roscoe in the near future.'

Irvine turned his bulldog countenance to the wide-boy and gave him the once-over.

'Aye, got it,' he said, reaching into his jacket pocket, causing Roscoe to take an involuntary step back.

A smile flickered across Irvine's thick lips as he brought a monkey nut to his mouth. He cracked it open with his teeth and spat the empty shell at Roscoe's feet.

'That'll be all. I'll call if you're needed,' said Dubois, before leading the now ashen-faced wide-boy back to his seat.

'So, there we have it, Frank. I do hope by now you're beginning to realise the potential consequences of your ridiculous actions. And, of course, regardless of any repercussions from my associates there, if I do hear any further mention of these scurrilous accusations, regarding

Lord Clenham and that little chorine, I will bring the full might of the law down upon your head. Is that clear?'

'Crystal,' said Roscoe, swallowing hard.

'One would imagine you've got yourself into some kind of desperate situation, to hatch such a ridiculous plot. Money problems, is it?'

'You could say that.'

'How desperate is it?'

'I haven't got a ha'penny to scratch myself with, and I've got four days to make the sizeable interest on a loan I took out with… well, with someone who has his own pack of wild dogs.'

The dandy leant back in his chair and gave a thoughtful stroke to his pitch-black goatee. 'Well now. It would seem you're in a bit of a pickle, dear boy. Maybe I could offer some assistance?'

'You, Mr Dubois?'

'Yes. You see, I have an associate. A very powerful man, you understand.'

'Go on.'

'This individual has certain tastes, Frank. Exotic tastes. Ones that can't be catered for in the usual establishments.'

'Righto,' said Roscoe, beginning to chew enthusiastically on his matchstick again. 'I think I can see where this is going. And you want me to…?'

'I'd like you to procure a girl for my associate. One who conforms to his particular needs. If you manage this task, you will be handsomely recompensed. Does that sound of interest to you?'

'I should cocoa!'

'Ah, but as you've pointed out, you do have your reputation to think of. Most would regard this assignment as somewhat in the procurement line. I wouldn't want to offend.'

'Oh no! I was only playing with you, Simeon. Don't take any notice of all that old nonsense. Now, you said *handsomely recompensed* – just how handsomely are we talking?'

'Well, what would it take to pay off that little loan of yours?'

'Pay it off? Well, it was a tenner originally. I had a tip on a nag at Newmarket, see. Couldn't lose according to my mate. "Put everything you have on it, Frankie" – you know the script. Net and bice, it was – that's twelve-to-one to you – tasty little earner if it'd come in. Works for one of the trainers, this fella, so I thought he knew his onions. Cor! I'd have done better listening to old Prince Monolulu. Talk about a donkey! It was a wonder it finished at all.'

'How much, Frank?' said Dubois, getting impatient.

'Ah yes, sorry.' The wide-boy scratched at his head. 'Well, let's see now… it's ten per cent vig a week. This is the third week I've missed now, so… to make it go away, it'd be thirteen quid. Unlucky for some – namely yours truly.'

'Thirteen? Well then. Let's say twenty pounds, shall we?

'A score?' said Roscoe, with a little whistle. 'Really? Alright – I'm in! What's this bride got to look like, then? You said your mate had a specific taste in the ladies. Like 'em big, does he? Or dressed up in a uniform? That kind of thing? Now, I know a bloke, who knows a bloke, who—'

'Young,' said Dubois, cutting the wide-boy off mid-ramble. 'Unsullied. Virginal.'

'Blimey! That's an ask, around these parts. How young, exactly?'

'It is of utmost importance that the individual is uncorrupted; the utmost importance.'

'Well, there are ways of telling. You're a man of the world, Simeon, you know what I'm talking about.' Roscoe added a wink by way of explanation.

'Nevertheless,' continued Dubois, pouring himself another glass of wine. 'To avoid any doubt, I think we should stipulate that the female in question is no older than… oh, let's say nine years old. Younger would be better, of course.'

'What?!' Roscoe let the match drop from his mouth,

immediately feeling a little queasy. 'Nine?' He pushed himself up from the table. 'No, no, no! I want no part in any of that old nonsense. No, sir. You can count me right out.'

'Indeed?' The dandy gave an amused smile. 'And what if we upped the fee to, oh… let's say, *fifty* pounds?'

'Fuck me!' Roscoe sat back down again. Hard. 'Fifty quid?!… Still… Nope. No can do.' But though he was vigorously shaking his head, a part of Roscoe's brain was whirring through the calculations. 'I mean, I couldn't get messed up with all that malarkey, could I? It's, it's…'

'Well, let's not rush into any hasty decisions, Frank. This could be the answer to all your prayers. But just think what you could do with fifty pounds. Why, it wouldn't only pay off your debts, you could establish a foundation for the future. A little business somewhere, perhaps? And, of course, you'd know just where to get her from, wouldn't you? The girl.'

'What do you mean?'

'Oh, you must remember bragging to me that night, about that little nurse you were taking advantage of, at the children's home? You see, I always make a point of paying attention to such little points of detail. You never know when they're going to come in handy.'

With a devious smile on his satyr-like face, Dubois took a sip of his Montrachet.

'Now, you say you've been given four days' grace by your creditors. Well then, I will give you forty-eight hours to decide. Come to me here, within two days, with your answer. I couldn't say fairer than that, now, Frank, could I?'

11

T HE EVENING HAD brought a damp chill to the air. Harley paused in the narrow side street, rubbing his hands against the cold. He studied the drunken row of decrepit houses with bowed brick walls, shored up here and there with makeshift timber buttresses. This dismal enclave of Bethnal Green had obviously been overlooked in the clearance project which had razed the Old Nichol slums – the birthplace of his Uncle Blake. Actually, this wasn't too far from where he himself had grown up.

He looked at the shabby street and considered the relative opulence of the Fitzrovia townhouse he'd inherited from Uncle Blake. The thought of it was suddenly disorientating. For a moment, he felt untethered somehow, as though observing himself as a character in a film.

He closed his eyes and pinched the bridge of his nose.

There was no getting away from it – all the booze and dope he'd inflicted on his constitution in the last few years had taken its toll. He was feeling decidedly off his game. Still, here he was, back in the saddle. He'd just have to get stuck in and start grafting again… and hope it wasn't too long before those once well-honed skills came back to him.

Harley took stock of his surroundings once more. On further consideration, this place was far worse than the street he'd grown up on. It was like something out of a Dickens novel. Certainly not the kind of area you'd expect a viscount's daughter to be living in. He'd begun to suspect the whole thing might be a setup – a conjecture only strengthened by the brief glimpse he'd had earlier of someone he thought was shadowing him as he made his way along Shoreditch High Street. But Pamela Chisholm had mentioned Fedor von Görlitz, and if there was even the slightest chance of getting any intelligence on the whereabouts of that shicer, then it would be worth the risk.

After having reassured himself he wasn't being followed, Harley slipped into a tight snicket between two buildings, which he hoped would lead to the small square he was searching for. The cut-through was so narrow as to expel almost all the meagre light offered by the streetlamps, and he had to stop for a moment to allow his eyes to adjust to the gloom. The ammonia reek of urine in the alleyway was almost overpowering, and he was about to spark up a cigarette to mask the smell, when—

What was that?!

He quickly flattened himself against the brickwork and peered into the gloom.

Somewhere up ahead – the crunch of broken glass underfoot.

There! The silhouette of someone, outlined briefly against the pale strip of light at the far end of the alleyway.

His hand moved instinctively to the brass knuckles in his jacket pocket.

He listened carefully. Above the faint trickle of water

running in the gutter at his feet, he could just make out the domestic sounds from the buildings around him: a banging door; the monotonous bark of a dog; the clatter of pans from an upstairs room.

He started as someone thrust open a sash window a few feet ahead of him.

With a pounding heart, Harley watched as a scrawny hand now appeared and…

… emptied a chamber pot into the passageway.

Jesus! What was happening to him? Ex-trench-raider, secret service man, and here he was quaking in his boots like some milky schoolboy.

He hurriedly struck a match on the brickwork and lit his smoke.

Of course, he mused, pulling hungrily on the cigarette, it wasn't only the effects of his time spent malingering in that no-man's-land of grief which had put the mockers on his nerves; it was also the glimpse of that cadaverous face, leering at him from the back of a cab in Piccadilly Circus. His nemesis. Osbert Fucking Morkens – or someone doing a good impersonation of the cowson, anyway.

Having composed himself a little – and carefully avoiding the foul puddle produced from the contents of the chamber pot – Harley stealthily set off again down the passageway. When he reached the end, he found the little quadrangle he'd been searching for, the meeting place of four alleyways. The air here was a little fresher; the predominant smell was of a coal fire, with the hint of fried food. Someone nearby had a gramophone playing and the tinny strains of Eddie Cantor singing 'If You Knew Susie' drifted over the square.

He sought out the communal stairwell to Pamela's apartment block and made his way up to the first floor – where he found the door to flat six slightly ajar.

Trying to peer in through the living room window proved

no help at all – it was almost impossible to make anything out beyond the grubby net curtain.

Harley slipped his fingers into his knuckleduster and teased open the door.

'Pamela?'

No light burning. Silence.

'Pamela? It's George!'

He could feel it in his gut – there was something off here.

He knew he should have abandoned the visit then and there, had it away on his toes while he still could, but something made him step inside.

He stood in the hallway with his hand on the door, listening for a moment, and then quietly secured the latch.

There was sufficient light from the streetlamps to see the place was in a state, cluttered with the confused mess of a life lived on the edge. No domestic staff here to pick up after the Honourable Miss Chisholm.

Harley checked his watch, giving himself five minutes to make a quick reconnaissance.

It took him less than half that time to find her. She was in the bedroom, tangled up in a clammy sheet.

He struck a match: a wide-eyed, uncanny mannequin stare; pallor mortis complexion; bluish tinge to the lips.

Already knowing it was a futile gesture, he placed a finger to Pamela's carotid artery. Her neck was cold, waxy – like the skin on a joint of pork. Unsurprisingly, there was no trace of a pulse.

So, here he was, alone with the corpse of a viscount's daughter, who, only a few hours earlier, a dozen or so witnesses had seen him verbally and physically attack.

Time to take a run-out powder.

He took out his handkerchief and quickly rubbed away any prints from the bedstead, the doorknob, anywhere else he thought he may have touched. He checked his watch again, noting he was still just under the five-minute mark. In his mind he quickly revisited the journey from Soho to Bethnal Green, the interactions he'd made, who might have seen him, the when and where; all the fragments of witness statements which might possibly be stitched together to form a troubling narrative for his defence. All in all, on reflection, he concluded he'd left a minimal footprint.

That was good, and he was pleased to find his old training had finally kicked in: there was no panic now; his hand was steady; he was working efficiently, quiet and calm.

However, upon returning to the living room, Harley spotted, through the grubby net curtain, the unmistakable outline of a Metropolitan Police constable's helmet.

A copper! Striding purposefully towards Pamela's front door.

The knocker sounded infeasibly loud in the still of the room.

He ducked down behind the sofa and held his breath as the bobby's voice rang out purposefully.

'Miss Chisholm? It's the police! Are you quite alright, miss? Only, we've had a report, you see. About a disturbance. Miss Chisholm?! If you don't answer I'm afraid I'll have to force the door!'

12

W ELL, IT HAD to come sooner or later. Until now he'd somehow managed to navigate a liminal space between the city's demi-monde and respectable society, breaking bread with both the villains and the law-keepers. But it seemed Harley's luck might finally have run out. He only had himself to blame. After all, he'd crossed the line that cold, foggy night at the sewage works in Beckton; a line drawn by his own hand. No use mewling like a kid about it now.

It was fight or flight. And Pamela's rooms had only the one exit – the same door the burly police constable was now hammering on with his leather-gloved fist.

Fight it was, then.

He hefted the weight of his brass knuckles.

From what he'd seen through the net curtains, the bobby was well-built; a few years younger than himself and a foot or so taller. The lad could obviously handle himself or he wouldn't be walking the beat in Bethnal Green. But, surely, he hadn't the same experience – all those skills Harley had picked up as a trench-raider and a field agent? He felt confident he could, at least, get a few digs in. Enough to have it away on his toes. The question was whether he'd be identified later. Even if he did manage to amscray, there was bound to be a manhunt. And if the bobby managed to summon assistance by getting in a blast on his police whistle, there was a fair chance he'd be recognised. Bethnal Green wasn't far from his old manor – there'd be plenty around who might recognise George Harley's ugly mug. Since the Nursery Butcher case he'd become something of a local celebrity.

On the other hand, he was innocent – of Pamela's murder, anyway. And who was to say it was even murder? From what he'd seen, there were no obvious signs of foul play. It was far more likely she'd just overdosed on the dope. Maybe he should stay and face the music?

Sod that!

Harley made a quick scan around for anything that might be used as an impromptu weapon, his eyes settling on the companion set in the fireplace. The poker would do nicely. Two foot of wrought iron plus his trusty brass knuckles, versus a standard-issue Metropolitan Police truncheon? Sounded like good odds.

He was just beginning to shuffle over to the fireplace on his hands and knees when something made him stop in his tracks. A woman's voice: Received Pronunciation; plummy; cultured elocution – vaguely familiar – hailing the copper out on the landing.

Having scrambled back behind the sofa, Harley now attempted to slow his breathing, straining to hear what was being said.

'I say! Constable? I wonder if we might continue this inside. The neighbours, you understand.'

'Of course, miss. I was just trying to—'

'You mentioned forcing the door? I have a key, so that

won't be necessary. I think we've had quite enough drama around this rotten business as it is, don't you? Come along, then. I must warn you, though, Pamela's housekeeping leaves a little to be desired.'

Harley's fist tightened around the knuckleduster as the latch turned. As the mystery woman ushered in the bobby, he hunkered down on one knee, ready to pounce at the first sign of his discovery.

'You are a friend of Miss Chisholm's?' continued the bobby.

'Second cousin, actually.'

'I see. Might I have your name, miss?'

'Mowbray. Lady Angela Mowbray.'

'*Lady* Mowbray?' The copper's voice lost a little of its previous authority.

'Miss Mowbray will suffice, Constable. I don't think there's any need to stand on ceremony, given the present circumstances.'

'Thank you, miss.'

'Hopefully we can get all this sorted and be on our way soon. You see, I was just dropping in to pick up a few of Pamela's things before driving out to see her at the sanatorium.'

'Sanatorium? Miss Chisholm's not here, then?'

'No. Thankfully the family doctor convinced her to accept the fact she needs medical intervention for this vile habit of hers. The nurse and one of the viscount's men picked her up an hour or so ago. She's being driven out to Norfolk as we speak. Marvellously bucolic place. Simply stunning views.'

'I see. Only, we've had reports of a disturbance. Some kind of altercation. Screaming.'

Harley heard the woman give a resigned sigh. 'I expect that was Pamela getting cold feet at the last moment. But I can assure you, Constable, she eventually agreed to go quietly. We received a telephone call from the doctor, confirming they were on their way. That's why I've popped down here to pick up some things for her. The family are awfully relieved, of course. My father has had to field some rather awkward questions about the whole affair. He was accosted by some awful reporter outside the Lords, last week. He's a stickler for convention, you understand. It's all been excruciatingly embarrassing for him.'

'The Lords, miss?'

'Daddy's Lord Granville. Actually, I think he goes shooting with your commissioner. So, you see, we'd be awfully grateful if you could keep any further embarrassing reports of altercations and suchlike to a bare minimum.'

'Of course, miss. Quite understandable. Well, it seems like you have everything in hand here. Is there anything I can do to be of any assistance?'

'That's very kind of you, Constable, but I think I can manage. It's just a few of her personal things. I'll be sure to explain to the family how accommodating you've been.'

'All part of the service. Well, if there's nothing else you need, I'll be saying good day.'

'Good day! And thanks awfully!'

The woman waited until she'd seen the bobby take the stairs back to the ground floor before she closed the front door.

'I'd say it was safe for you to come out now, George.'

Puzzled, Harley tentatively raised his head above the back of the sofa.

'Surprise!'

She looked just as she appeared in his nightmares: the strawberry-blonde hair, the exquisite bone structure, the haunting beauty of those azure eyes – Morken's she-devil, in all her flawless glory.

'Cat got your tongue, George?'

Harley rose up from his hiding place, the poker still clenched in one hand, the other balled into a fist around the brass knuckles.

'Well? Aren't you pleased to see me? How did you like my little turn as Lady Mowbray?'

Harley began to ease his way from behind the sofa.

'Oona.'

'Oh! You've discovered my real name. How clever of you.' She snapped open the clasp on her handbag, conjuring a small silver revolver. 'That's quite close enough, I think. And we can lose those thuggish items. This isn't some public house brawl. Drop them there on the floor, where I can see them.'

Harley stood glaring at her, trying to calm his breathing.

'Come on.'

The weapons thudded onto the rug at her feet.

'Good boy.'

'I'm sure I could yell loud enough for that copper to still hear me.'

She snorted. 'You were the one hiding behind the sofa. Look, this is ridiculous.' She pointed with the gun at the shabby sofa. 'Sit down, won't you? I feel we've got off on the wrong foot here.'

'Are you kidding me?! Got off on the wrong foot?'

'Listen. Any involvement you assume I may have had in either those child killings or—'

'You framed that poor bastard Collins for it!'

'No, I didn't. I simply supplied you with those photographs – which were quite genuine, by the way. If you remember, I told you at the time I didn't really suspect him. You, George, were the one who jumped to the wrong conclusion.'

'But it was your con. You, posing as Madame Leanda, just like that little charade just now for that copper. You were part of it all. I saw you there with them! Morkens and the Bulgarian, laughing and joking in that kitchen, above that soddin' chamber of horrors. You must have known what was down there in that cellar.'

'Really? You were there, watching me?' Her scowl relaxed

to a feline grin. 'How fascinating. But there you are, you see. Your conclusion that I was involved in what happened to those children and your unfortunate fiancée—'

'She was fucking butchered!'

Oona took a deep breath before continuing with exaggerated patience, as though talking to a small child. '— is merely a result of flawed inductive reasoning: the professor and Whispers are murderers. The professor and Whispers are in the kitchen. Oona is in the kitchen with them. Ergo: Oona is a murderer. Personally, I blame that credulous buffoon, Conan Doyle. In fact, you know absolutely nothing about me.'

'Illuminate me, then.'

'I don't think so. Not here.'

She took a quick look at her watch.

'Now, much as I'd dearly love to continue this scintillating conversation, I don't think it's awfully sensible for either of us to be hanging around, do you? Not with a corpse in the next room.'

'How did she die?'

She touched a finger to the glistening vermilion lipstick at the corner of her mouth but remained silent.

'You killed her?'

'I'll pretend I didn't hear that. What you should be asking yourself is why I'd risk my neck coming here to dig you out of such a tight spot.'

'Is that what's happening here? Really? Because Pamela told me she had some information on your German pal, Fedor von Görlitz. Maybe you came here to silence her before she could talk to me.'

Her grin was less convincing this time. She pointed to a tatty bureau in the corner of the room. 'Go and take a look in the top drawer. And no funny business.' She waggled the gun. 'Remember – I'm a cold-hearted killer.'

The drawer stuck a little at first, but when he'd finally forced it open, Harley discovered three large photographic prints inside.

'Up to your old tricks again?'

'I suggest you take a closer look,' said Oona. 'They were taken at Beckton Sewage Works. Ring any bells?'

Harley's fingers clenched around the edge of the drawer.

That sense of looming danger he'd felt that night – had his instinct been correct all along? Had there actually been someone hiding in the shadows, watching him exact his savage revenge on the Bulgarian?

He surreptitiously spread the prints in the drawer to get a better look, a measured frown set on his face. 'Means nothing to me.'

The images were grainy, underexposed; thankfully ill-defined. A dark, fog-smeared scene. But he knew the hunched figure close to the ground was Whispers, kneeling in his shirt-sleeves, his shackled hands held before him in supplication... and he knew who the figure standing over him was.

The blood began to sing in his ears.

'Pamela lured you here to blackmail you, George.'

'So you said. Over what? What are these supposed to be?'

'Don't play games with me. Pamela knew what you did... That's why she had to be dealt with.'

He found himself caught for a moment in the icy glare of those alluring eyes.

'So, you did kill her.'

'No. I just furnished her with the means to do it herself.'

'Why?'

She took a step towards him. When she spoke, her voice was softer, almost a whisper; as though she'd given up playing her role.

'Isn't it obvious? We're tethered together now, you and I.'

'Don't kid yourself. There's nothing between us.'

'Oh, but there is! I could never have dreamt it were possible, but since you had him incarcerated—'

'That shicer Morkens?'

She nodded, seemingly still a little amazed at the thought. 'Since then, I've been… *changed*. Liberated! A planet set adrift from its star.'

She put a hand to the exquisite line of her neck and smiled. A seemingly honest smile this time, but nonetheless as beguiling as before. Standing there, with the faint glow of the gas lamp on her porcelain skin, with those azure eyes wide and entreating, she was doll-like, otherworldly.

'We are indeed tethered by this, you and I… And so, I vouch to help you, George.'

'Help me? With what?'

'Why, to seek your retribution, silly. You see, they also took something from me. Something I loved, so dearly. Just like your Cynthia.'

'Morkens and von Görlitz?'

'And others. There have always been powerful people in the Order. But the professor was unique. Unrivalled.'

'Evil.'

'I'm not sure I know what that means… But powerful, certainly. Frighteningly so. Always there to oversee us.'

'Always?'

'You must understand I've known nothing different… until now. It was my school, my church. I'd imagine you're the kind of man who operates on an instinctive level, yes? You pride yourself on being able to read people, discern their motives? Well, you'd struggle to read me, George. They made me so.'

'The Ancient Order of the Unicursal?'

'I was one of their little experiments, you see.'

Her brow wrinkled as she seemed to search for something in his eyes.

'You know, Fedor once took me to see a film, in Berlin: *Metropolis*.'

'Fritz Lang.'

'Yes... And when the *Maschinenmensch* was revealed, Fedor said: "That's you, Oona. Our beautiful little robot." He started to call me Maria for a while. The irony was, I found it chilling. So, you see, I must have some emotion, mustn't I?'

'Well, you can certainly lie convincingly. You worked the gammon on that bobby like a pro.'

'Oh, that's simply acting. I've been told I have little sense of jeopardy.'

'Or guilt. Working with those shicers, those child-killers.'

Oona's frown deepened. She glanced down at the silver revolver in her hand, then she stepped back and levelled the gun at him, the spell suddenly broken, her voice once more confident, businesslike.

'Guilt? A pathetic emotion. What good has guilt ever done anyone?'

'A moral compass, then.'

She chuckled, menacingly. 'A dubious gizmo. Peddled by charlatans. Oh no, I've never felt the need for one of those, George. That's my secret weapon, you see. That's why, unlike you, I seek only retribution... And not *redemption*.'

She smiled archly, studying his face for a reaction.

'Now, I've enjoyed our little chat immensely, but I think that's quite enough for the time being. I'll be off now. But don't worry, I'll be in touch soon.'

'What if I don't want that?'

Oona nodded towards the open drawer. 'Let's just say it would be awfully foolhardy of you to spurn my offer of assistance. Remember to take those photographs with you. Leave a suitable gap before you exit... and don't dream of following me. I know where you live, remember?'

13

DESPITE ITS EARLIER reticence, the rain was now hurling down on the London streets with some confidence. Roscoe reluctantly hauled himself up from the bench with a groan. He'd been out for hours now, trudging the streets under a private cloud of despondency, contemplating his dismal prospects, always coming back to the same conclusion: Frankie Roscoe was finally out of the race.

He started off again down the Mall, passing the ranks of tramps dossing for the night on the patch of green behind Admiralty Arch. Was that his future now? A round of the cheap kip shops, then the casual wards, swiftly followed by a fully-fledged tumble into the purgatory of the down-and-out. He'd experienced a period of tramping two years earlier – just after he'd finished a stretch in Wormwood Scrubs – so he knew all too well the level of degradation which lay ahead of him. On the road meant days of gruelling hardship and nights of interrupted sleep; an incessant cold and damp that settled into the very marrow; the misery of foot-rot, the pariah treatment from Joe Public and victimisation from Old Bill. And the hunger. Christ! That hunger, which started as a mild hollowing in the gut but grew more insistent, hour by hour, working itself into a poisonous lethargy, almost impossible to break free from. But a night in the spike was hardly better: petty regulations and wheedling tramp majors; the rotten shell-shock cocoa and the chalky bread smeared with margarine that tasted of petrol. And of course, Roscoe knew the worst of it would be the humiliation of having to admit to himself that he'd once again been tested and found wanting. Stamped as a loser. Just another mug.

His mood now worsened by the drenching rain, Roscoe decided to make his way up into Soho, to seek shelter in one of the all-night cafés, where he could nurse a three-ha'pence cup of coffee for an hour or so, safe in the knowledge that he'd fit right in with all the other bedraggled creatures of the night that frequented such establishments. The wet cobbles of Piccadilly Circus reflected the dancing neon, extolling the virtues of Schweppes Ginger Ale, Telemac raincoats and the 'non-stop' fun to be had at the London Pavilion. But even this free light show – which would normally have lifted Roscoe's spirits a little – failed to impress itself on his dreary frame of mind. With his head down and his hands thrust deep into his pockets, he strode off into Coventry Street.

The downpour had all but emptied the streets, but here and there, a number of Piccadilly daisies – an order of low-class prostitute which had proliferated in the area during the Great Slump – could be seen lurking in doorways. As he made his way through the rain, he batted off a few unenthusiastic solicitations from these women, most of whom displayed the exhausted pallor and broken spirit of having to skivvy away at some menial day job, as well as coping with working the streets of a night-time.

Before long he found himself outside Alberto's café bar in

Lisle Street. He hurried inside and was immediately embraced by the café's distinctive warm fug – a mixture of cigarette smoke, sweat, fried food and the cheap floral scent liberally applied by the street girls. At a table by the window sat a couple of dilly boys – teenage rent boys who plied their trade around the main thoroughfare. One of these youths sat doodling patterns in the condensation on the inside of the window.

'Ooh, things might be looking up.'

'I wouldn't waste your time with that one, dear,' said his associate, after a brief glance in Roscoe's direction. 'Nanti dinarly – vada the clobber.'

Roscoe scowled at the lad, before nodding to a familiar face – one of the small-time ponces who treated Alberto's as an unofficial HQ for running their janes. The pimp gave Roscoe a half-hearted acknowledgement before going back to berating the sullen-looking girl sitting at his table. The girl sat silently through the lecture, playing listlessly with a small heap of spilt sugar.

There were a few other customers dotted about the café, the usual Alberto's mix of night folk and ne'er-do-wells – luckily, though, nobody who Roscoe owed money to. Just along from the dilly boys an old street hawker sat carefully arranging and rearranging his meagre stock of bootlaces and matchboxes in a battered, rain-sodden cardboard suitcase. He shared a table with a market porter, who was sleeping off a skinful, his head slumped on the table, dribbling onto the shabby Formica top. Further in was a gent in full evening dress, treating a giggling young woman to a plate of egg and chips – an investment which he hoped would pay a healthy dividend before the night was through – and opposite them a couple of young men in cheap suits and gaudy American-style ties sat whispering conspiratorially over their mugs of tea, one of them sporting a freshly split lip.

Roscoe looked to the back of the café, where he spotted

two veterans of the street – Vera and Gracie. No part-time Piccadilly daisies these two, but fine examples of the old-school nymphs of the pave.

'Frank! What you doing standing there like the spare mug at an idiots convention?' hollered the inimitable Vera. 'Come and park your arse over here, ducks.'

Roscoe gave a sigh, shook some of the rainwater from his jacket and trudged over to join them.

'Blimey!' exclaimed the thinner, sardonic Gracie. 'You're looking pleased with yourself.'

'Don't be sarky, Grace. Look at the poor thing.' Vera took Roscoe's cold hand in hers. 'You look as cheerful as a kiss from a cold kipper on a windy night. What's the matter, love? You're usually the chirpy one. Girl problems, is it? Got some little brama in trouble?'

'Chance would be a fine thing,' said Roscoe, his stomach beginning to groan at the aroma of fried bacon wafting from the kitchen. 'It's the usual, ain't it? *Money* – or the lack of it.'

'Well, you sit yourself down and we'll treat you to a cuppa. We ain't had a bad night so far, have we, Grace?'

Gracie gave a non-committal sniff.

'Mind you, not as good as Jack Mundy's over there.' Chuckling, Vera nodded to where the porter was out cold on the table. 'Should have seen him earlier – drunker than a fiddler's bitch.'

'He's got to be up for market at four, an' all,' added Gracie.

'There you are,' said Vera, leaning over to pinch Roscoe's cheek, bringing with her a unique perfume of face powder and strong spirits. 'You don't have to look too far in this town before you find someone worse off than yourself. Things can't be that bad, can they, love?'

'They can, actually. Well, that's what it looks like from this end of the telescope,' replied the wide-boy, indulging himself for a moment in the motherly attention.

'You know what I always say when I'm down on the knucklebone of my arse?'

'Something will turn up,' answered Gracie.

'Thank you, dear. That's right – something will turn up. And it always does. Now, I'll tell you what you need: something hot in your derby kell. I'm guessing you missed your supper?'

'Yeah,' said Roscoe, with a rub of the stomach for additional effect. 'And breakfast and lunch.'

'Alright, Ronald Colman. Don't lay it on too thick, or I might just change my mind. What'll it be? A sav and a slice?'

'Just the ticket – much obliged.'

Vera shouted out the order to the overweight Pietro, who sat at the counter, engrossed in a paperback with a lurid cover. With a short grunt to demonstrate the inconvenience of this new turn of events, he dog-eared the page and struggled off his stool to attend to the tea-urn, the sudden movement dislodging half an inch of cigarette ash, adding to the tally of stains on his apron.

'So, how much are you in for then?' asked Vera.

'Enough,' answered Roscoe, dejectedly. 'And I seemed to have made a few new enemies, an' all.'

Just then Pietro brought over Roscoe's cup of tea, splashing a good quarter of the liquid into the saucer.

'That silver service training is quite something, ain't it?' joshed Vera.

'*Prego*,' mumbled the Italian, moving the sheen of grease around a little on the tabletop with his tea-towel, before presenting a small plate bearing a bright red saveloy, served on a slice of bread and margarine.

'There you are, Frankie. Get that down you.' Vera produced a hip flask from her voluminous handbag and splashed a generous measure of gin into Roscoe's tea. 'And there's a little eye-water to pep you up.'

'Ta very much,' said Roscoe, rubbing his hands. But before he'd had chance to take a bite, the café door crashed open, revealing a thin, bedraggled individual in a flat cap.

This newcomer glared at the dilly boys, flicking the rainwater off his sleeve in their direction. 'What you staring at? Soddin' lavenders!' He yanked off his cap and pulled out a comb, dragging it through his oily hair while eyeing up the clientele with a threatening glare.

This individual's nervous body language was all too recognisable to Roscoe, as was the pasty countenance and the caged-animal glint in his eye – here was a fellow not long out of prison, and by the look of it, with some old scores to settle.

'Oh, God help us, that's all we need,' said Vera, taking a swig from her flask.

'Who's that, then?' asked Roscoe.

'Stingo Spinks – nasty piece of work. He's just out of stir for almost killing his girl; beat her to a pulp one night when he came back late from the pub to find his dinner served cold.'

'What a gent,' said Roscoe, attacking his saveloy with gusto.

'Ain't he? Now he's on some kind of death wish by the sounds of it.'

'How d'you mean?'

'Well, before he went away, he used to do a bit of work for Mori Adler; nothing too serious, by all accounts, I get the impression he wasn't much more than an errand boy. Anyway, when he got lumbered for doing his missus, he was under the impression his boss would make it all go away. Now, you know Mori.'

'Unfortunately, yes,' mumbled Roscoe, through a mouthful of cheap sausage.

'Well then, you know how he likes to give it the big 'un that he's some kind of family man, right? He's hardly going to step in to save someone who knocks his bird about, is he?

'So, what's this about a death wish?'

'Well, since Spinks got out, he's been doing the rounds, bad-mouthing Mori left, right and centre.'

'Get out of it!'

'It's true. He's saying that Mori's days are numbered, that there'll soon be a new order in town. The cackle is that Stingo has – or more likely just thinks he has – formed some kind of allegiance with the Italians.'

On hearing this, Roscoe immediately stopped chewing, craning his neck to get a better look at Spinks, who had now settled himself down beside the ponce and his girl at the front of the café.

'Does Mori know about this?'

'Mori knows about everything,' said Gracie.

Roscoe half-stood for a moment, catching sight of something at the front of the café. He then quickly ducked back down into his seat.

'What's the matter, Frank?' asked Vera. 'You look like you've seen a ghost.'

'Worse than that – it's Benny Whelks!'

Roscoe gulped down his gin-laced tea and grabbed his sodden hat from the table.

'I swear he just pressed his face to the glass.' Roscoe pointed to the silhouettes of two figures who could be seen through the fogged-up window, loitering outside. 'I can't be found in here by Mori's mob, not with that nutcase Spinks in here; they might think we came in together.'

'What are you getting all milky about?' said Vera. 'You've had nothing to do with him, love – we'll vouch for you.'

'But you don't understand, Vera. It's Mori I owe the dough to.'

'I see… In that case, it's probably best you go out the back way. Slip out now while you still can. Good luck, ducks.'

'Yeah, good luck,' added Gracie, helping herself to the remains of his saveloy.

But, true to form, Roscoe's escape attempt was over before it had begun. For, as he rushed through the beaded curtain that covered the kitchen doorway, he immediately collided with the formidable frame of 'Big' Lampton. The mobster clamped a hand on Roscoe's damp shoulder and leant down to purr in his ear:

'Going somewhere, Frankie?'

A few moments later, as a clutch of Adler's heavies frog-marched Roscoe and Spinks out through the front door of the café, Gracie arranged her knife and fork on the empty plate and wiped her mouth on her sleeve.

'Seems like you were right, after all,' she said to Vera, offering her a cigarette.

'How's that, dear?'

'Well, looks like something turned up for Frankie, alright.'

14

T HE MAÎTRE D' of the Café Royal gave a barely perceptible sigh.

'It's quite impossible, I'm afraid, madam,' he announced, giving the extraordinary woman standing before him another quick appraisal. 'We're fully booked this evening. And, as I've explained, without a reservation…'

Ilse Blau let her monocle drop as she raised one painted eyebrow, the violet shimmer on her angular cheekbones darkening a little. 'You ridiculous man,' she said in a rasping Berlin accent.

She took a pull on her cigarillo and blew a plume of smoke in his direction. 'As I explained, I have arranged to meet some acquaintances. Perhaps they are here already?'

'Really?' said the maître d', with a doubtful little tilt of his head. 'Perhaps madam would care to furnish me with their names?'

'Names? Who knows? Rupert, I think. You have him on your little list, hmm? Rupert? It seems everyone in this damned city is called Rupert, or Johnny... or Frrreddy,' she added, with a guttural trill.

'Ah, you see, without a surname, I really can't—'

'I can describe him for you, if you like. He is a banker – as rich as Croesus... and he has a belly, this banker – like an old sow, you know?'

She puffed out her cheeks and performed an exaggerated mime of obesity. 'A gross belly... but a little tiny pee-pee, like a schoolboy... Ah! But his wife? Such a body. Perfect breasts, and the arse of a goddess.'

'Please, madam!' The maître d' removed a handkerchief from his sleeve and dabbed at the tiny beads of sweat which had begun to prick his bald pate. 'There's really no need for impropriety.'

'Ach! You English. You're a nation of eunuchs!' This last comment echoed around the ornate foyer, causing a number of guests in the dining room to snap out of their state of snooty boredom and arch their necks, trying to get a view of the cause of the commotion.

'I appeal to you not to make a scene, madam.'

'You think this is a scene, my friend?'

Blau stepped closer and pulled open her sable fur coat, revealing herself to be quite naked beneath – apart from an impressive string of pearls. The flustered man's gaze was drawn uncontrollably to the thatch of pubic hair, dyed the same copper red as her severe bob.

'I... I...' he stammered, tugging desperately at his starched collar as he watched her sensuous fingers make their way through the scarlet curls, inching slowly downward.

'That's quite enough!'

Finally locating his stiff upper lip, the attendant began to stride towards the front doors to summon the burly doorman. But he was stopped in his tracks by a commanding voice.

'Astarte! There you are – we thought you weren't coming.'

Sir Rupert Heathley – financier to the nobility. A man of power and influence, and one of the blessed whose wealth appeared to have remained unscathed by the devastating effects of the Great Slump. 'Matthew, what is the meaning of this? Why the devil are you making our guest wait out here in the lobby?'

'Sir Rupert, I do apologise,' said the maître d', trying his best not to conjure images of the corpulent banker's diminutive member. 'Some mix-up with the name… You see, we weren't quite sure which—'

'Alright, alright. Take the young lady's coat and we'll have her through to our private room.'

'Take her coat, sir?'

Sir Rupert had always regarded the maître d' of the Café Royal as one of life's little constants – like the quality of the Beef Wellington at his gentlemen's club, or the dulcet chime from the quarter-minute repeater he kept in his waistcoat pocket. But now the confounded fellow seemed to be suffering from some form of brain fever, blushing like a schoolgirl and stammering to find his words.

'But, Sir Rupert, I… I…'

'What the deuce are you waiting for, man? Take her coat, I said.'

With a blast of raucous laughter, Blau buttoned her white sable, repositioned her monocle and elegantly strutted over to the banker, going up on tiptoes to whisper in his ear.

'Well, I'll be damned!' he exclaimed. 'Well, in that case, my dear, best you come through just as you are, what? Ha ha!'

He proffered his arm and led the cabaret dancer into the main dining room, parading her past the ranks of the distinguished and the grey-haired like some exotic pet.

* * *

Two and a half hours later, after a selection of cocktails, four courses of service à la russe, three bottles of hock, one of champagne – and for Blau, a number of surreptitious dips into an antique silver pendant in which she kept her cocaine – Sir Rupert Heathley released the last straining button on his waistcoat and announced to his wife that it was time to go.

'Oh, but Rupee,' complained Lady Antonia (who was, indeed, quite exquisite to look at – if a little dim when engaged in conversation), 'you really are a beast! There's a super party in Hanover Square that Asty says I simply must attend. All the right people will be there. That's right, isn't it, Asty?'

'Oh, *ja, meine Liebe*,' said Blau, sounding decidedly bored as she poured herself another drink. 'All the *right* people.'

'I know you've got this tiresome board meeting in the morning, but can't I go?'

'No, you jolly well can't,' scoffed Sir Rupert, smoothing down his Kitchener moustache.

'Whyever not, honeybun?' said Lady Antonia, a pout spoiling the perfect rosebud of her mouth.

'Because, my dear girl, I'm not at all sure I could trust our Fräulein here with such a treasured possession.'

With a flutter of her lashes, the banker's wife shuffled over to her husband to nestle her face against his formidable neck; the effect wasn't dissimilar to that of a young fawn embracing a walrus.

'But what on earth could we get up to that you haven't already witnessed… and positively encouraged, you naughty man.' She gave a little giggle and tweaked his bulbous red nose. 'I really can't see what the difference is.'

'The difference, Antonia, is that I wouldn't be there to gain any pleasure from the experience. A little sapphic titillation to spice up the marital bed is one thing; having the two of you gallivanting around Mayfair like something out of the *Ladies' Almanack* is quite another. You've had your answer, now let that be an end to it. Gather your things, we're leaving.'

Sir Rupert tossed his napkin onto the table and struggled

to his feet. 'Order yourself another cognac, my dear,' he said to Blau. 'And another dessert, if you care to – for that sweet tooth of yours. You can put it all on my account.'

'Oh, but you're too generous, Rrrrupeeee.'

'Yes, quite,' said Heathley, who wasn't quite calibrated for the cabaret artiste's unremitting sarcasm. 'I trust we'll see you at the Grimaldi Vaults on Friday, hmm? Dubois tells me you have a new performance to unveil.'

'*Ja! Heliogabal*… You know of this Roman emperor?'

'No, no, I'm not sure that I—'

'He was "quite a character", as you English say.' Blau lounged flirtatiously across the banquette, lighting up another of her acrid cigarillos. 'Infamous and decadent. Sexually dysphoric. He had a secret chamber built within his palace, you know, where he'd paint his face as a young girl…' She encouraged her fur coat to fall open, revealing the pale white flesh beneath. '…and force his supplicants to use him as a temple prostitute. On Friday we will re-enact these ancient rites of sin before your very eyes.' She threw him an alluring glance and let a thin stream of smoke curl out from her painted lips. 'It will be most exquisite.'

The corpulent financier placed a steadying hand against the wall, his complexion running to a dangerous shade of puce. 'Will your girls be as… ahem… as scantily clad as usual?'

'*Oh ja, wie immer,* practically naked. Can you imagine such a thing, Sir Rupert? This choreographed vision of ecstatic defilement?'

'Ecstatic defilement, eh?' managed Heathley, following up with a little apoplectic squeak.

'I say, are you quite alright, Rupert?' asked his wife, sharing a conspiratorial smirk with Blau. 'Only, you do seem to have turned an awfully strange colour.'

'Quite alright, thank you. Just a little reaction to the lobster, I think. You know how seafood sometimes gives me the gyp.'

With his blood pressure raised to a dangerous level by these erotic musings, Sir Rupert now released the button on his starched collar. 'It all sounds jolly intriguing. However, Antonia and I must be off now – things to do. Come on, my dear, stop dawdling there. Say *auf Wiedersehen* to Astarte.'

And with a last resigned kiss blown to the dancer by a now rather sulky Lady Heathley, the couple departed.

However, Blau wasn't left to her own devices for very long, for within a minute or two of the Heathleys' exit there came a tentative knock on the door. With a sigh, she sat up, pulled her coat around her, emptied Sir Rupert's unfinished cognac into her own glass, and called out: 'Come!'

There entered a balding waiter, in round, metal-rimmed glasses, pushing an empty trolley.

'Mendel!' exclaimed Blau, with an astonished grin on her face. '*Bist du es wirklich?*'

'*Nicht so laut*, Ilse!' urged the waiter, hurrying to close the door behind him. '*Übrigens, man kennt mich hier als* Josef – Josef Maier.'

'Josef Maier?!' She guffawed. 'Sounds like some fat grocer from Nuremberg.'

'That is exactly why I chose it,' he said, beginning to clear the table.

'Ach! But it's so good to see you; and to be speaking German again. English is so sloppy – like some cobbled together peasant's stew. Leave that! Come, sit.' She patted the banquette. 'I was so thrilled to get your message. There is much for us to catch up on… Why won't you sit with me?'

'I can't. What would it look like if the head waiter comes in and finds me with my feet up, engrossed in conversation with one of the guests?'

'The Mendel Einhorn I knew ran… how many clubs? And your café, and—'

'Yes, well,' he interrupted, continuing to gather the dirty

plates. 'Those days are long gone; this you must understand, my dear. Besides, I'm Josef – remember? And Josef is just a waiter… for the time being, anyway.'

'Come here, I say.'

Einhorn finally relented, laying down the stack of plates he was holding to perch on the edge of the seat. Blau reached up to place an affectionate hand to his cheek.

'You've aged, *Liebling*. You look, I don't know… beaten, somehow.'

'Haven't you heard?' he said, pushing her hand. 'We've all been beaten.' He splashed some wine into a glass and gulped it down.

'Oh, forget about that. We'll talk of the old days. Here…' She popped the lid of the silver pendant. 'There's plenty to share.'

'My poor girl,' said Einhorn, with a sad shake of his head. 'Can't you see? The party's finally over. After all, one can never dance forever.'

'You sound just like all the rest of them. You know I can't abide dull people.' She dug into the pendant with a long, painted fingernail and snuffled up a small heap of cocaine. 'So, if that's all you have to say, don't let me keep you from your pots and pans.'

'One moment.'

He slipped across the room to open the door, making sure no one else was in earshot, before closing it again and wheeling the trolley across it to prevent any sudden interruptions.

'There is something urgent I have to discuss with you. Something of grave importance.'

'What?'

'Hedwig.'

'Hedwig is here?! Where?'

'No, no, it's not that. You see, she is…'

'Yes?'

He placed a hand on her arm.

'What?' she said, batting it away.

'Hedwig is dead,' he whispered. 'Murdered.'

'Ridiculous!' She grabbed at her cognac with a shaking hand. 'It's quite impossible. Who would want to murder Hedwig?'

'You know the answer to that.' Einhorn sighed. 'They caught up with her in Vienna. She'd been there a few months; changed her name, kept her head down, even began to wean herself off the dope.'

'She has always had a soft spot for Vienna,' said Blau wistfully.

'She found a job, singing in a bar; a dingy little place, just off the Ringstrasse. Quite a comedown for our wonderful shining star. Anyway, one night, a customer buys her a drink. A handsome young man, a fellow Berliner, he says. They get talking, one thing leads to another, and before long, he invites her to move in with him.'

'Oh yes? And how do you know all this, huh? Are you reading fortunes in your spare time now?'

'It is quite simple: she wrote to me. We kept up a regular correspondence. You have to remember, my dear, Hedwig and I were good friends well before the two of you met.'

'Please spare me all this sentimental rubbish. Why are you telling such stories? You think I still care?' Despite the harsh tone, a slight waver could now be detected in Blau's voice.

'He sold her out, of course, this boyfriend,' continued Einhorn, undeterred. 'No doubt sent to entrap her in the first place; encourage her to let her guard down, share her secrets… *our* secrets.' He watched her face closely for a reaction. 'You know, of course, of what I'm speaking – what they were after. Do you still have it, Ilse, the roll of film?'

Blau shot him a petulant look; then gave a brief nod.

'Yes, of course you do. Where did you get it? I don't ever remember anyone taking photographs at the rituals.'

She laughed. 'It's a wonder we remember anything from those nights, eh? The state we were all in.'

'Is it genuine?'

'Yes.'

'So, where did you get it?'

'We stole it. From some madman. An Englishman, named Turpin. An artist, visiting Berlin. He'd tracked us down, wanted to see the show. He was quite the little disciple.'

'And how did he come by it?'

'Fedor gave it to him, would you believe?'

'Von Görlitz?'

'Yes. You see, Turpin was part of the London chapter of the AOU. For these neophytes, our original Berlin gatherings had taken on a kind of mythical status. Anyway, he'd been commissioned by Fedor to make artistic prints from the negatives. The Englishman had brought some to show us. Actually, they weren't bad. He had some talent, this lunatic. He wanted us to tell him all about the rituals in the pictures. He'd become obsessed with the images.'

'When were they from, these photographs?'

'My guess is from those last few weeks of the Berlin gatherings, when things had started to turn a little crazy.'

'Those rituals… with the girl?!'

'You remember?'

'How could I forget?' Einhorn's eyes blinked nervously behind his glasses. 'The things we did. I must have relived them a thousand times or more, when I close my eyes to sleep. Haven't you?'

'No, I haven't. You Jews, with your guilt. That God of yours should go a little easier on you every now and then. But anyway, the point is, this lunatic Turpin hadn't recognised our little watercolourist in the photographs. I mean – how could you miss him, with that stupid little Chaplin moustache of his? But, of course, Hedwig and I immediately saw the potential. It was easy enough to persuade Turpin to invite us back to his hotel room. While I rode him in the bedroom, Hedwig stole the roll of film.'

'When was this?'

'In the winter. Near Christmas time – '28, I think.'

'Why didn't you use it then, Ilse? He was already leader of the National Socialists. You could have gone to the press; in '28 they still had some teeth. I mean, photographic evidence of the Führer taking an active part in an occult ritual…?' Even though they were still speaking in German, Einhorn lowered his voice at this point. 'One that culminated in the sacrifice of an innocent young girl? They would have published in the blink of an eye. It might have put a stop to all this madness there and then.'

'Why didn't I go to the press? Because *we* too were at that ritual, you idiot! Besides, I thought all this Nazi nonsense was just that: a brief madness – just another outbreak of the lunacy we've all had to endure since the Black Hand decided to put a bullet through dear old Franz Ferdinand's thick skull. I mean, little Adolf? Who, in their wildest dreams, would have thought he'd ever amount to anything?' She laughed loudly, a deep, resounding guffaw. 'Do you remember him at the ceremonies? Too terrified to speak? You can see it in those photographs. His eager little piggy eyes—'

'Enough!' hissed Einhorn, casting a nervous glance towards the door. 'It is no laughing matter, believe me. That joke has turned into a nightmare. Evidently Hedwig had been boasting about your little find. She always did have loose lips. Somehow, the Party got wind of it. Naturally, they now see it as a matter of national security.'

Einhorn sighed and pulled a battered cigarette from the top pocket of his uniform jacket.

'This Berliner who befriended her in Vienna,' he said, taking a light from the candle on the table. 'He turned her in. They took our dear shining star of the Nachtlokals and dragged her from this man's apartment to a disused factory – so many to choose from these days, of course. There they...' He paused to bolster himself with a pull on the cigarette, pushing his spectacles back up his nose. '...they tied her to a chair. And shot her; in both legs. You remember Hedwig's legs, Ilse? Like a gazelle... After shooting her they kept her alive for a week, to extract the information they required. At such work, these devils are experts. So, of course, it is beyond any doubt: Hedwig knew what you have in your possession, so now they also know.'

'And did she write you all of this as well? On a postcard? Scrawled in blood with her tortured little fingers?' she sneered. 'How on earth could you know that's what happened? I see your little game, Mendel – you're trying to trick me into telling you where it is. Well, it won't work. That little secret is my insurance policy, a pension for my old age.'

Einhorn smiled and shook his head slowly. 'My dear, if they do know what you have, then I'm afraid there won't be any old age. You'll be lucky if there's a next month.'

'You're just trying to scare me. There's no way you could know such a thing happened to Hedwig.'

'You think I could invent such a thing? How I wish it wasn't so.' He stubbed out his cigarette and stood up. 'It happened, Ilse. I've seen a copy of their report.'

'How could you have?'

'Oh, there are still a few who are loyal, on the inside. Some who stay in contact. We've formed our own little network of trusted emigrees. In some ways it's easier to get information over here, you know. The English do adore their little spy games; and all of Europe is bristling with nerves at the moment, of course.'

'But how did they track her to Vienna in the first place?'

'The Frenchman.'

'Noiret, her agent?'

'Pimp, more like,' said Einhorn, with disdain. 'They arrested the little rat in a round-up – one of Röhm's little surprise parties. Apparently Noiret had some dealings with the communists.'

'Röhm?' scoffed Blau. 'I remember that fat queen when he was picking up doll boys at the Zauberflöte.'

'Shush!' hissed Einhorn, with a concerned glance towards the door. 'No one speaks like this anymore. It's too dangerous… even here.'

'*Mein Gott*! The world has turned on its head! To think that anyone would take such boorish morons seriously.'

'Please, Ilse!'

'Stop pleading like a little girl. Go on – tell me about Noiret.'

'Well, apparently, he was released the day after he was picked up – highly unusual nowadays. A fortnight or so after this I received the report about poor Hedwig. Noiret must have sold her out to save his own skin. You know he had her hooked on that stuff… no doubt she blabbed all sorts of things to him.'

'Listen to you! So righteous. There was a time when you were as bad as any of us.'

'Yes, well, as I told you – the party is over. It's time for us all to sober up.'

As if this were a challenge, Blau fixed him with a withering stare, before dipping once more into her silver pendant.

'I must go,' said Einhorn, glancing at his watch. 'I've spent too long in here already. But tell me one thing – did Hedwig know you intended to come to London?'

'No,' answered Blau, dabbing at her nostril. 'I was heading for Paris the last time I saw her.'

'Good. Then we may have a little time yet. And do you have any reason to suspect that anyone here knows your true identity? I mean, it's not as if you're keeping a low profile, is it? Continuing to perform. And all of this…' He waved his hand at her extravagant appearance.

'I didn't come here to hide from those Bavarian bully boys.'

'No? Well, maybe you should have done. Why change your name, then?'

'Oh, I don't know,' she said, dismissively. 'A new start, perhaps.' She stubbed out the remains of her cigarillo on a side plate. 'But tell me – this report you saw, of Hedwig's interrogation, did it actually mention what we have?'

'What *you* have, you mean. No, not specifically. But it mentioned certain information which was "of great importance to national security".'

'Are they after Fedor as well?'

'Of course not. Haven't you heard? He's sold his soul to them – that is, he would have done, if he possessed such a thing.'

'What do you mean?'

'I mean he's now SS-Standartenführer von Görlitz.'

'Fedor joined the Schutzstaffel?!'

'With special occult duties, apparently. He's always been obsessed with all that pagan runic nonsense. They call him "Himmler's Rasputin" now. As you say, the world has turned on its head, *Liebling*.'

Shaking his head resignedly, Einhorn stood up and handed her a piece of paper.

'Here. If you need to contact me. Please remember to ask for Josef. As for what you're holding? My advice is to find someone here you can trust and get it to the British authorities. You never know, it might still do some good.'

There was a knock at the door. Einhorn jumped out of his seat to push the trolley out of the way. He opened the door and exchanged a few words with one of the waiting staff.

'I'm needed elsewhere, madam,' he said in English, giving Blau a curt nod. 'It was extremely interesting to talk to a fellow countryman. Good evening.'

'Wait!' She beckoned him to the table. 'I need to ask you something.'

'Be quick,' he whispered. 'They're already suspicious.'

'Come now, my good man,' she said loudly, for the benefit of anyone listening in. 'I'm a guest of Sir Rupert, I demand you entertain me further with your charming conversation.'

He made his way back over to her, keeping one eye on the door. 'Well, what is it?' he asked with a sigh.

'Do you remember?' she continued in German, almost whispering now. 'In those last few weeks of the Berlin ceremonies. Just before… before the unfortunate accident.'

'Accident? My God! What happened to that young girl was no accident.'

'Alright! How were we to know Fedor was so out of control?' She tossed her head dismissively. 'We cannot be blamed.'

'We all knew what Fedor von Görlitz was capable of. We were all just too cowardly to stop him.'

She mimed a sympathetic face and chucked him under the chin. 'Poor little Mendel. It must be so tough trapped inside that bourgeois conscience of yours. For me? What is done, is done. I simply refuse to waste another second thinking of it. So, let me please get to my point… Before the incident with the young girl, do you recall that other Engländer? You know, with the bald head, and those eyes?'

'That devil? Of course! He was the one goading Von Görlitz on… Such depravity.'

'Depravity? Have you really forgotten all the excitement? Those moments of ecstasy?' She gave a wistful sigh and shook her head. 'For me, there's simply nothing else to match the thrill.'

With a pained look on his face, Einhorn leant across the table, placing a hand on her shoulder.

'Please tell me you're not still dabbling in it all, Ilse. After all that happened?'

'Ah, it's nothing serious,' she said, inspecting her nails.

'The impresario at the club, a pompous little peacock called Dubois, he has his own little order. Nothing like our Berlin chapter, of course – after all, the English lack the required sense of abandonment.'

'How could you?'

Blau shrugged. 'I needed to get out of Paris in a hurry. Some of the old gang suggested I should contact this Dubois; said he had a perfect venue for the act here in London. It turned out he was delighted with the idea – even offered to pay for our passage over. How could I refuse? When I got here, I discovered he was more interested in my connection with the Order than in my theatrical reputation. Just like that madman Turpin, he's forever questioning me about the old days. About Fedor, the rituals.'

'And so you begin the descent to Hell once more.'

'Why should I worry? According to you, we'll all be assassinated in our beds by National Socialists before the end of the week.'

Einhorn pulled away, walking stiffly back to his trolley. 'I can see you won't listen to reason – you never did. I wish you luck, my dear. *Auf Wiedersehen.*'

'Wait, Mendel! That Englishman, with the bald head. Can you think of his name?'

Einhorn thought for a moment. 'I'm not sure I ever knew it… Sometimes Von Görlitz called him "Professor", remember? He was simply *der Engländer* to the rest of us. Why do you want to know? Have you seen him again?' He suddenly looked concerned. 'Ilse, please don't tell me the fellow is somehow mixed up in this little amateur cult of yours.'

'I don't know. I can't be sure. There's someone who I've only seen from afar. Talking to Dubois. The Preceptor, they call him. He is different to how I remember him. But there is something about the way he holds himself, something about his eyes… Ah! But what does it matter?'

'If it is the same man, it matters a great deal. You must avoid him, at all costs. He is extremely dangerous.'

'Don't you worry, little Josef,' she said, clicking open her silver pendant once more. 'I can look after myself.'

15

S AT AT HIS desk, in his office overlooking Regent Street, Mori Adler plucked the smouldering double corona from his mouth and peered into the cardboard box in front of him. A frown set upon his face as he ran his fingers through his thick waves of pomaded hair – traced here and there with a few distinguishing streaks of grey. He plunged his hand into the box and squinted at the quivering creature as he placed it gently on the green leather of the desktop.

'What is this, Fayvel? It's a dog I wanted.'

'And it's a dog you got,' answered the bespectacled Fayvel Greenspan, Adler's long-suffering accountant. 'A pug.'

'Are you sure?' The mobster peered closely at the pug's bulbous, watery eyes. 'Looks like a frog in a balaclava – I wouldn't put it past that shyster Gables to pass something off like that, he's as wide as they come.'

'It's a pug, Mori. Pedigree, no less, according to Gables – and therefore, thinking about it, we should probably be highly sceptical of the creature's lineage.'

'Hmm… And for this I paid a guinea?'

'Well,' said Greenspan, with a diplomatic clearing of the throat. 'That was Sonny's asking price; but as per your instructions, no money has actually changed hands yet.'

'Let's keep it that way,' said Adler, taking his cigar from the ashtray and billowing a few plumes of blue-grey smoke towards the ceiling. He took another look at the dog, whose purple tongue was now flicking back and forth across its squashed little muzzle. 'D'you think Esther could grow to love such a thing?'

The accountant sighed. 'As I've told you before, my particular expertise lies in double-entry bookkeeping. Profit and loss, that's my schtick. And I'd like to think I have a certain knack for it. As for the inner workings of the female mind?' Greenspan held out his hands. 'What do I know of such mysteries? You may as well ask me about the surface of the moon… So, what's the occasion for such an act of generosity? Birthday, is it? Anniversary?'

'Peace offering,' said Adler, tentatively plucking at the layered skin of the pug's neck. 'She caught me with that little shicksa, Valerie.'

'Again, Mori?'

Adler gave a shrug.

'And you think this'll do it?'

The mobster peered at the dog's crumpled face. 'I'll be honest with you: I was expecting something a little more along the lines of a fashion accessory.'

'Fashion accessory?'

'Yeah. See, Esther's always poring over those Hollywood magazines – *Picture Show, Movie Classics*, you know the kind of thing. Last week she was reading an article about Bette Davis. There's Ms Davis in the photograph, sipping a cocktail in some luxury penthouse, with her little black Scottie dog plonked on the baby grand. "Ooh, Mori," says Esther. "Would you look at that – such elegance. See? The little dog matches her Chanel outfit." Then she fires me one of her looks.'

'I see. And this you interpreted as her wanting a dog?'

'Of course. I can read her like a book,' said Adler, with a self-assured stroke of his chin.

'You don't think, maybe, she wanted the Chanel outfit instead?'

Adler turned to the twinkling lights of Regent Street as he considered this suggestion; then looked back at the pug.

'Alright, you clever momzer,' he said, pointing his cigar at the accountant. 'Let's get back to the books, shall we? I'm paying you by the hour here, remember.' He slumped down at the desk, grabbing the frightened animal by the scruff of its neck. 'And when we're done you can take this monstrosity and throw it in the river.'

Suspended in mid-air, the dog began to kick its back legs, mewling its concern. Adler pulled it close in to his face. 'What are you complaining about, ugly?'

With a final resigned yelp, the pug stopped struggling and experimented with two gentle licks to the end of the mobster's nose.

'Oh, I see,' said Adler, his bad mood immediately evaporating. 'A dirty fighter, eh? Well, I admire a fella who can think on his feet. Shows initiative.' He lowered the dog into his lap and began to massage its neck. 'On second thoughts, I'll keep the mutt… Now, what were you saying before, about the slots?'

'Well, it's not good news, I'm afraid.' Greenspan opened one of the large black ledgers piled on his lap. 'It would appear that last month's dip in our slot machine takings was no aberration; this month we're also down – almost twenty per cent versus last year's figures. The downturn seems to be concentrated in the Soho area alone; the returns on the machines we have elsewhere, around the suburban transport cafés and such, don't appear to have been affected. We're also down on some of our bespoke "insurance" lines; public houses mainly – again, in the Soho area.'

He looked up at Adler, who was tickling the pug behind its ear. 'I must say, Mori, you're taking all this a lot better than I'd expected. Which leads me to suggest that maybe you already have a good idea of the cause?'

Adler nodded. 'The word on the street is that our Italian friends have made a tentative alliance with the Elephant Boys.'

'I thought they were sworn enemies.'

'It seems the rumour's kosher – I've had it from more than one reliable source.'

'And this new coalition – they're making inroads into our business ventures?'

Adler nodded. 'Hence the downturn.'

'I see.' Greenspan closed the ledger. 'Left unchecked, I fear this will escalate.'

'Don't worry. Uncle Moriel has a plan.'

'I'm sure he does,' said the accountant, removing his spectacles to polish them with his handkerchief. 'But if it's all the same to you, I'd rather not know the details.'

'No need to be so squeamish. Just a little well-engineered statesmanship, that's all that's needed here.'

There was a knock at the door.

'Wait!' shouted Adler. 'Stick around, Fayvel. If I'm not mistaken, you're about to have the opportunity of witnessing the first step in my grand scheme. You'll get to see what pays your wages.'

'Thank you, but no thank you,' said Greenspan, rapidly gathering his books together and struggling to his feet. 'Unfortunately, I have problems of my own to attend to. Shona's sister is coming for dinner tomorrow. This, in our house, is a state visit, no less. The cleaning from top to bottom, the schlepping back and forth to the deli, haircuts for the kids… So, Moriel, I'll bid you goodnight, and I wish you luck.'

'Luck? Feh! A man makes his own luck in the world. You poodle off home to the loving arms of your family and leave the downturn to me. My love to Shona.'

With the accountant safely out of the way, Adler called Benny Whelks into the office.

'Well then, Benjamin. Who are the first pupils you've got lined up for our little lesson?'

'We've got three of them back there, boss: Stingo Sp-Sp-Sp-Spinks, F-F-Fingers Flynn and Frank R-R-Roscoe.'

'Roscoe? He weren't on the list. What gives?'

'We found him in Alberto's with Sp-Sp-Spinks. I figured – as he's only got a couple of days to come up with the vig on his loan – it might not be a c-c-c-coincidence that he's hanging around with that r-r-rat.'

'Good boy. Smart thinking.'

Whelks allowed himself the briefest of smiles.

'Alright, let's be having 'em.'

But the chiv-man remained fidgeting in front of the desk, chewing nervously at a hangnail.

'Benjamin, I've known you long enough to see you've got something on your mind. So – spit it out, son.'

'It's Sp-Sp-Sp-Sp-Spinks, boss.'

'What about him?'

'If there's any settling to do, I want to do it.'

'He been winding you up, son? About your affliction?'

Whelks looked at the floor and nodded.

'Alright, he's all yours,' said Adler, letting a thick ribbon of cigar smoke escape lazily from his tiger's smile. 'But you go easy, now. I know you've got a thirst for the work, but remember – they're here to fetch a message back to the Italians; corpses don't make for good errand boys. Got it?'

'G-g-g-got it.'

A few minutes later, Roscoe, Spinks and Paddy 'Fingers'

Flynn were ushered into Adler's office, to stand in front of his desk like three mischievous schoolboys sent to receive the cane. Now on the downward slope of his all-day bender, Spinks had lost a little of his earlier belligerence and stood mumbling to himself, with his cap clenched tightly in his hands. Paddy Flynn, on the other hand, appeared a little more resigned to his fate.

Flynn was a seasoned pickpocket, who sometimes diversified during the week by working the 'wash up' – stealing from jackets hung up in public baths – but whose main source of income was to be found among the weekend crowds of Oxford Street, Piccadilly Circus and Trafalgar Square. Now, everyone knew that to ply such a lucrative trade in the West End (and for an expert 'whizzer' such as Fingers Flynn it certainly was a most profitable pursuit) you needed to pay a levy to Mori the Hat – something that Paddy had failed to do for the last month or so, having been assured by one of the Elephant and Castle mob that they were soon to take over as tax collectors for the area. But even though he'd now been accosted for his transgression, Flynn was quietly confident he'd escape the confrontation with Adler's crew relatively unscathed. After all, hadn't he kissed the Blarney Stone when he was a kiddie? And if it turned out that he couldn't wheedle his way out of it, he had a pocketful of notes that would do the talking for him.

Out of the three summoned to Adler's office, it was Frank Roscoe who looked the most concerned. Convinced now he was caught in the irrepressible slide of the worst run of luck of his life, and knowing he had the princely sum of 2/6 in his pocket with which to repay the mobster's loan, he could see no other outcome to this little gathering than one which involved a lot of pain and fear.

Maybe I should plead my case? he thought. *Get in quickly before this Stingo character has a chance to rub Mori up the wrong way.*

'Mr Adler...' he began, his tongue suddenly dry and sticking to his palate.

But the loquacious Flynn was too quick for him. Taking advantage of Roscoe's brief hesitation, the Irishman elbowed him out of the way, cleared his throat and began to embark on his own story. And quite a story it was, too:

'Now then, Mori. Let me just start by saying I've been a complete and utter eejit. There's no denying it, and that's a fact. But here's the thing, you see – there's a woman to blame. "Isn't there always?" I hear you say. And why wouldn't you? After all, aren't you a man of the world yourself? I bet you've a great eye for the ladies, and no mistake. But this doll, now?' Flynn sketched out an hourglass figure with his hands and gave a whistle. 'Jesus, Mary and Joseph, now there's a ride. Let me recount it for you and you'll understand. Now, it all starts, you see, on the Tuesday morning... or was it the Wednesday? No, no, it was definitely the Tuesday, because there were kippers for breakfast – and Mrs Donaghy only produces such a treasure on Tuesday mornings, on account of her youngest, Brian, making a habit of staying over on a Monday night. For which auspicious event she presents us with a shepherd's pie, by the way. Shepherd's pie on a Monday night, kippers on a Tuesday morning, that's how it's always been at the Donaghy's place, as far as I can tell. And who am I to complain? For doesn't she do a lovely plate of shepherd's pie? And, let's face it, who doesn't like a little consistency in their life, eh? Even if the portions are on the woeful side. So, there I was, Tuesday morning – as I've already mentioned, I believe – minding my own business, sauntering down the road when...'

Flynn continued in this vein for several minutes, negotiating his way through a meandering picaresque adventure, presumably designed to eventually arrive at an explanation as to why he was late with his payments, but on the way taking in the penguin enclosure at London Zoo, a fortune-teller's booth on the pier at Southend, and the Royal Pavilion in Brighton.

'And would you believe it, Mori,' he continued. 'I wake up, dripping wet on the beach, with the donkey still tethered to me ankle. Well, now, I knew I had to get the first train back to London, so I—'

'Schtum!' barked Adler, finally growing weary of the Irishman's prevarication. 'I know how this one ends.'

'Oh yes?'

'Yeah – you escape by talking the hind leg off that donkey you're tethered to.'

This quip garnered the appropriate sycophantic chuckles from the pack of heavies at the back of the room.

'You've certainly got some spiel, Flynn, that's for sure,' continued Adler. 'It's a wonder you don't knock that whizz lark on the head and take up as a confidence man. But what I want to know is what you've paid out to the other mob so far.'

'The other mob?' said Flynn, looking shocked at the very suggestion. 'A fella would have to be as mad as a hare to do such a thing. I've not paid them a penny.'

'The truth now. Tell it as if you were sitting in that little confessional box. You know what'll happen to you otherwise.'

'I swear it. Not a penny.'

'Hmm… I'll admit you've always been a good earner. But I can't be tolerating dissent in the ranks, can I?'

'And you'll not be getting any from this quarter, Mori. I swear to God. If only you'd let me finish the story, I could explain exactly what happened. You see, I—'

'Enough already!' shouted Adler. 'Keep schtum for a minute. Let me think.'

Adler looked the pickpocket up and down for a while, sucking pensively on his cigar. 'Any gelt on you?'

Flynn nodded, patting his jacket pocket.

'How much?'

'Enough.'

'Lucky for you,' said Adler, holding out his hand.

With a wonky, resigned smile the Irishman handed over a plump fold of bank notes.

Adler licked his thumb and counted out two-thirds for himself, handing the remainder back with another glint of his gold tooth. 'Then, of course, there's the message.'

'The message?'

'Well, I've got to send a message back out there, haven't I? Otherwise every little gonif working the manor will start forgetting about the grease for poor old Moriel. Now, what's the name of those little punishments the priest hands out to you boys when you've been naughty?'

'Is it the Hail Marys you'd be thinking of, Mori?'

'*Hail Marys*, that's it.' Adler gestured to the two heavies standing sentinel at the back of the room. 'Big, Pony? Take Mr Flynn downstairs and give him ten Hail Marys. Don't go too boisterous, but do make sure you leave a mark on that pretty face of his. But avoid the fingers... You see, Paddy? I'm a reasonable fella – I wouldn't want to take away the tools of your trade.'

'Thanks,' mumbled Flynn, uncharacteristically terse as he was shoved towards the door by Big Lampton.

'Now, Frankie boy.' Adler looked to Roscoe as he chucked the pug under the chin. 'What have you got to say for yourself, son?'

Having witnessed the pickpocket's fate, the wide-boy was even more dubious of a pain-free outcome for himself. He swallowed repeatedly to try to get some moisture to his dry mouth and then stepped forward to make his case.

'I've had a run of bad luck, Mr Adler – you know how it is.' He looked at the cut of Adler's Savile Row suit, the expensive jewellery on his hands, the box of Romeo y Julieta on the desk. 'Well, maybe you don't... But believe me, I'm working on a tidy little scheme right now which should bring in a flock of dough; and when it does, you'll have your money back, plus all the interest of course, straight away – no worries.'

'Well, that's all fine and dandy. Just make sure it's in two days' time. 'Cause that's all you've got left, son. As well you know.'

''Course I do,' said Roscoe, with a nervous little giggle. 'Only, I think there's been some dreadful mistake here, Mr Adler.'

'You do?'

'Yeah. I mean, I've got nothing but the utmost respect for you and your boys. Always have – you ask anyone. There's absolutely no way I'd be mixed up in this thing with the other mob.'

'What thing's that, then?' asked Adler, suddenly losing his smile.

'You know the, erm…' Roscoe pulled a pained face and indicated over his shoulder with his thumb. 'This business, between the Eyties and the Elephant Boys.'

'And what exactly do *you* know about that?'

A twinge of the wide-boy's street sense indicated to him that it was time to change tack. 'Nothing, Mr Adler. Nothing at all. I swear it. On my mother's grave. That's what I'm trying to tell you. I just happened to be in that café, enjoying a tightener, when in walks this fella…' He nodded at Spinks. 'Never even seen him before. What's his name? Stinko something, ain't it?'

Spinks growled something incomprehensible through a curled lip.

'Yes, well,' said Roscoe, stepping a little closer to Adler's desk and lowering his voice. 'The meat in the pie, as they say, is that I don't know him from Adam, see? And I've had nothing whatsoever to do with all this old gammoning he's been doing, neither.'

'Is that right?' said Adler, blowing on the glowing end of his cigar. 'So how come you were taking stoppo when Lampton got hold of you? I mean, if you were just in that café for a bit of nosh, why feel the need to slip out the back door when Benny and the boys roll up?'

'Because,' said the wide-boy with a sigh. 'Because I thought they were after me for the dough, didn't I? And with what I've got in my pocket, well, that was going to be a difficult conversation. Oh, but don't you worry, you'll get that money, Mr Adler, you'll get her alright.'

'Oh, I know that, Frankie.' Adler placed his hands behind his head and contemplated Roscoe for a moment. 'Alright. Go and stand back over there… Stingo? Come here.'

But Spinks wasn't so compliant as the two previous interviewees. He remained firmly rooted to the spot, muttering incomprehensibly, mangling his cap as though he were wringing someone's neck.

'He ain't going to listen to sense, b-b-boss,' said Whelks, slipping a hand into his jacket pocket.

Spinks stopped mumbling and shot Whelks a black look.

'All in good time, Benny,' said Adler. 'Leave him there for the moment – he can still hear what I've got to say to him. Now, Stingo. The boys inform me you had a lot to say for yourself in the back of the motor on the way over here. Care to repeat any of it for my benefit?'

Spinks fixed his stare somewhere above Adler's head and remained silent, clenching and unclenching his fists.

'What's the matter? Cat got your tongue?'

Visibly shaking now, his upper lip curling away a little from his yellowing teeth, Spinks dropped his head and clenched his eyes shut. The drinking binge, which had begun at ten o'clock that morning, had worked as a catalyst on the grumbling sense of injustice he'd developed during his months in prison, building up the pressure throughout the day into a furious rage that now, even given the perilous situation he found himself in, threatened to explode in one almighty outburst.

'Come on, Spinks,' continued Adler, leaning forward

across the desk. 'If you don't give it up voluntarily, I'll have Benny here work it out of you.'

You could have almost heard the *tink* in Spinks' brain. With a defiant laugh he threw his cap to the floor and took a step towards Whelks, his eyes wide and burning with a maniacal light. 'Oh no!' he pleaded sarcastically, dropping to his knees and clenching his hands together. 'Anything but th-th-th-th-th-th-th-th—'

But Spinks' stuttering parody was cut short as the chivman's lethal hand whipped out from his pocket, augmented by five inches of vicious steel razor.

The first pass was a loose, upward-arching swing, taking off a good slice of the nose. The second blow was delivered with more speed and accuracy, finding its target just to the side of Spinks' left eye, biting through to the bone and cleaving down through the soft flesh of his cheek.

Spinks collapsed with a guttural howl, clutching his hands to his butchered face, the blood pouring through his fingers to puddle on the ornate Persian rug.

'Benny!' shouted Adler, dislodging the terrified dog as he jumped to his feet. 'What the bloody hell...?! Are you meshuggener?' He rushed around the desk, hitched his trousers and got down on one knee. 'Look at this mess! Do you know how much I paid for this rug?'

He pulled out a handkerchief and begun to mop at the blood. 'This'll never come out...'

Sickened by the violent assault he'd just witnessed, Frank Roscoe doubled over and began to gag into his hand.

'No you don't, you little shicer!' said Adler, grabbing him by the scruff of his neck and pushing him towards the group of heavies. 'I don't want you adding your filth to my cleaning bills. Get him out of here. On second thoughts, all of you get out of here. Go on – amscray!' He gave a kick to the bloodied, sobbing form of Spinks, who was now curled into a foetal position on the rug. 'Take this schmundie over to Doc Shandy and get him sewn up. And understand this, Benjamin – you are not in my good books.'

'Sorry, b-b-b-b-boss,' said Whelks, wiping his blade clean on Spinks' shirt.

'So you should be… Now, where's that mutt gone?'

Adler went down on his haunches to search out the pug, who was busy nuzzling away at something under the desk.

'Oh, you dirty little chazzer!' he exclaimed, as he tried to prise away the half inch of bloody cartilage from the dog's jaws.

16

'**W**ELL, THAT'S JUST about exhausted all my contacts in the West End clubs,' said Harley, returning with Bunty to the Frith Street building after a visit to the Blue Lantern club in nearby Ham Yard. 'We've worn out some shoe leather, that's for sure, but still not a sniff of our Parker girl.'

'Rather seedy looking, that last club, I thought,' said Bunty, closing the street door behind her. 'Actually, they're all rather seedy, wouldn't you say?'

'That's because you're visiting them during the daytime… and you're sober.'

'Ooh! Look, George.' Bunty picked up a letter which had been partially concealed by the coir doormat. 'I wonder how long this has been here… Hand-delivered.' She removed her gloves. 'It could be another of those mysterious messages.'

'Let's see.' Harley took it from her. 'The envelope's a cheaper make. And the last one was typed, this is addressed by hand… a female hand, I'd say. See the way the letters are rounded? And they're almost all the same size, regardless of whether they're capitals or not. It's not infallible, but that normally indicates a female writer.'

'Intriguing.'

'I'm guessing it's not connected to our earlier messages.'

'Well, there's one sure way to find out,' said Bunty, plucking the envelope from his hands.

'Whoa! It needs to be done carefully, with a letter-opener. We don't want to destroy valuable evidence. Let's do it upstairs.'

Up in the agency, Harley hung up his hat and coat and made his way into the front office. 'How about a cuppa? But let it brew a little this time, eh? I don't want—' He stopped in his tracks, looking at his desk. 'Bunty! Come in here a moment, will you?'

'Whatever is it?' she said, wandering in with the kettle in her hand.

'That blue file. Did you move it at all, just before we left this morning?'

'No, I don't think so. Why, what's in it?'

'It's not what's in it, it's how it's sitting on the desk. I purposefully left it at a slight angle to the rest of the pile when we left the office. It's a "trig", just like the bit of horsehair I gummed across this upper drawer… one end of which is now flapping loose.'

'A trig?'

'A way of telling if someone's been in here while we were away. I've been taking a few extra security measures lately, on account of this Morkens business.'

'Goodness! You might have let me in on it, George.'

'What d'you mean? You've not been in here rummaging around, have you?'

'Of course I haven't. Is there anything missing?'

'They wouldn't be after nicking stuff – it'd be about information. Anything that could be used against me, is my guess. Personal details, maybe addresses of those close to me.'

'Colleagues?' said Bunty, looking concerned.

'Possibly.'

'Gosh!'

Bunty put the kettle down and walked over to the window.

'But couldn't this be to do with the Parker case, George? What makes you so sure it's linked to Professor Morkens? Didn't your policeman friend confirm that he's still safely locked away in that asylum?'

'He did. But that doesn't rule out any collusion with the staff there. I've been trying to persuade DS Franklin to arrange a visit, so I can confirm it with my own eyes, but he's going to take a little more convincing.'

'Well, it sounds like a jolly good idea to me.' Bunty put a hand to her throat, as she began to scrutinise the passers-by in the street below. 'The thought that that monster might be out there somewhere, hiding in the shadows, spying on our movements...' She gave a little theatrical shudder. 'It makes the skin crawl.'

Harley sat down at his desk and sparked up a Gold Flake. Talk of Morkens had brought his thoughts drifting back once more to the dungeon in that infernal charnel house. The sordid butcher's block... body parts rendered down for the professor's insane experiments... the cherubic heads floating in jars. He looked over to Bunty as she gazed out of the window, in her sensible skirt and her cashmere twin set, with that flawless, country girl complexion, so at odds with the painted, modish masks of the Soho girls. Whatever had he been thinking of – exposing another innocent to the risk from such abject evil?'

'We have a visitor,' said Bunty, snapping Harley out of his gloomy reflection.

He rushed to join her at the window, half-expecting to see Osbert Morkens creeping up to the front door. But rather than an imposing character in an astrakhan coat and top hat, what he saw was a brief flurry of elbows beneath an oversized pancake cap.

'Squib,' he said, with some relief.

A few minutes later, Alfie Budge sat ensconced in the back room with a mug of sweet tea and a digestive biscuit.

'Come on then, son,' said Harley, stirring the sugar into his own mug. 'What's this hot bit of information you have for us?'

''Fraid I'm going to have to charge you for this one, Mr Aitch.' The little cocksparrow adopted his most earnest expression to deliver this bad news. 'Had a tight week, see.'

Harley gave a sigh and rummaged in his trouser pocket. 'How hot is it, exactly?' he said, looking at the coins in his hand.

'That florin looks about the right temperature.'

'Bit strong, that. One-and-six?'

Budge pondered this for a while as he dunked his biscuit. 'Throw in a couple of smokes?'

Harley shook his head. 'You've been knocking about with Sonny Gables too much, son… There you go. It'd better be worth it.'

'Don't think you'll be disappointed,' said Budge, pocketing the coins and secreting the two cigarettes within the tumble of ginger curls beneath his flat cap. 'See, it's about that Fritz you've been looking for.'

'Ilse Blau?' asked Bunty, eagerly.

'No…' said Budge, with a puzzled frown, concerned his nugget of information might not be quite as valuable as he first thought. 'I thought it was this Star T character you were after.'

'Astarte,' said Harley. 'Don't worry, it's the same woman.'

'Thank Gawd for that! For a moment there I thought we were talking refunds.'

'Can we get on with it?'

'Sorry, Mr Aitch. So, this… *A Star T*? Cackle on the street is she's tight with Limehouse Lil.'

'Really?'

'That's the rumour. Best of pals, apparently. I've heard she even bunks at Lil's place off and on.'

'Lil still got the restaurant?'

'The Lotus Blossom? Yeah, 'course she has. But you should know that – you're almost family, ain't yer?'

As sharp as he was, Budge couldn't help but notice the pained look flash across the private detective's face.

'Lumme! Sorry, Mr Aitch!' he said, with a little nervous flurry of his elbows. 'I didn't mean to… you know… remind you of…'

'Let it be, son. It's fine.'

'This *Limehouse Lil*,' said Bunty, trying desperately to pick the facts from this confusing exchange. 'I gather you have some personal connection to her, George? Shouldn't we get around there straight away and see if Blau's staying with her?'

'The thing is, I haven't seen Lil for a good while. I can't really just turn up out of the blue.'

This struck Bunty as very uncharacteristic. 'Whyever not?'

'It's complicated.'

'I see. Well, couldn't we send Alfie around there with a note?'

She slammed her cup and saucer down on the desk, causing Budge to jump and spill his tea.

'The note, George! From under the mat.'

'Blimey! I completely forgot.'

Having retrieved the envelope from the front office, Harley teased it open with a letter opener and extracted the folded sheet of paper.

'Right! You need to drink up, Squib. Bunty and I are off out.'

'Really? What is it?' asked Bunty.

'It's from one of the girls at the Rendezvous next door. Looks like we might finally have a lead on Louise Parker.'

'Don't s'pose there's any chance of another biscuit before you go?' asked Budge.

* * *

Having been let into the club by Jimmy the caretaker, Harley and Bunty were met on the stairs to the basement auditorium by a pair of showgirls in a flurry of garish, yellow feathers.

'You're keen, ain't you, ducks?' said the lead girl, making a half-hearted attempt to cover her breasts. 'We ain't open yet… Oh, it's you, Georgie! How are you, love?'

Harley was lost for a moment in faux plumage as the young woman leant in to give him a peck on the cheek.

'Don't laugh – it's canaries this week.'

'Budge over, Jacq!' said the smaller girl, behind her. 'Your tail feathers are going right up my 'ooter.'

'You here about my note?' asked Jacqui, trailing an arm over Harley's shoulder. 'We're just up to the roof for a smoke. Why don't you keep us company, eh? We can discuss it up there.'

'I should throw something on, if I were you,' said Bunty, with a disapproving look. 'It's not as warm as it looks.'

'Who's this then, your maiden aunt?' The showgirl placed her hands on her hips, giving a little involuntary spin to the tasselled pasties covering her nipples. 'Any other pearls of wisdom, sis?'

'Alright, Jacqui, play nicely,' said Harley. 'You said in your note you might have something for me?'

She flashed Bunty a glare before turning her attention back to the private detective. 'Jerry said you were looking for some hoofer with zhooshy riah, that severe Louise Brooks cut?'

Harley produced a photograph of the missing girl. 'There you go: Louise Parker. Though she could be working under a moody name, of course. Recognise her?'

'I think I might, yeah. And definitely that hairstyle. I was

158

at a bottle party a week or so ago, and there was a bunch of them there, all with the same hairdo.'

'She's working with a German act,' pitched in Bunty. 'Ilse Blau. A little risqué, by all accounts.'

'Well, we ain't exactly the Salvation Army here ourselves, love.'

'In Berlin, Blau was known as the Queen of Depravity.'

Unimpressed, Jacqui curled her lip and inspected a chip in her nail polish. 'And she's over here, is she, this Queen of Depravity? Well, for God's sake, don't tell Jerry – we'll all be out on our arses with her top of the bill before you know it. Listen, George, I've not heard a peep about this Elsie Blue character, but—'

'Ilse Blau,' corrected Bunty.

'As I was saying,' continued the showgirl, flashing Bunty another black look, 'I doubt whether this Fritz is working the regular venues; we'd have heard something on the grapevine by now. You only have to fart in the bath round here for it to be the main topic of conversation at the Gargoyle Club. But, you know, I worked with an act from the Berlin clubs, at a private do, a couple of years ago.'

The showgirl's compatriot sighed and planted her backside on the stairs. 'Our Jacqui's famous for her private dos.'

'If you don't mind, I'm trying to tell a story here…! Anyway, this German was a drag act, see. Bit near the knuckle. But the punters seemed to like it. He was telling me about what they get up to over there, in the Berlin clubs. It's a bugger's daydream, by all accounts. Fellas trussed up like chickens, beaten with riding crops. Anything goes, apparently.' Jacqui broke off to chuckle at the look on Bunty's face. 'All I'm saying is, if this Blau character is known in that scene as the Queen of Depravity, then her schtick is going to be far too rich for the type of punter we get around here.'

'Not to mention the Lord Chamberlain,' added the other showgirl.

'Exactly. Which means, if she is working her act in this town, then she's doing it on the underground scene.'

'She is,' said Harley. 'At the Grimaldi Vaults.'

'That new place in Fitzrovia? 'Course, I've done a bit of that, you know – those underground joints. And nice work it is too, if you can get it. Better than standing on that draughty stage down there, freezing your thrupennies off for two quid a week. You get to meet a better class of gent in that kind of establishment, I can tell you.'

'Yes, it's a wonder you didn't bag yourself a duke, dear,' quipped her colleague, pulling herself up by the handrail. 'When you've married your viscount, you can spend all day reminiscing about the good old days, but as it stands at the moment, we've got twenty minutes before we're due back downstairs with our tits and our teeth. I'm off for that smoke.' And with that she sashayed up the stairs, shedding little puffs of yellowy down as she went.

'She's right,' said Jacqui. 'I need to skedaddle.'

'Hold on,' said Harley, taking out his notepad. 'You didn't say where this bottle party was.'

'Seven Dials, Shorts Gardens. Above the Crown pub. Is your girl British?'

'From the Midlands, originally.'

'Well then, I reckon I might have been chatting to her that night. See, the rest of that troupe with the haircuts were all foreigners – Frenchies, I think, most of 'em. Apart from this one girl, Tallulah.'

'Tallulah,' repeated Bunty, making her own notes now. 'Go on.'

The showgirl rolled her eyes at her, before continuing. 'Anyway, she said she was in digs just around the corner to the party – at the Sunny Side. It's a boarding house a lot of the girls use. The landlord's a bit of an old souse, but he's an easy touch, by all accounts.'

'Where exactly is this gaff?' asked Harley.

'Erm, Little Earl Street, I think it's called.'

'Righto. That's been helpful. Thanks a million, Jacq.'

'Don't mention it. Just remember to put in a good word about me to Jerry.'

* * *

'It's a bit dowdy, isn't it?' said Bunty half an hour later, as she gazed up at the Sunny Side's dishevelled façade.

'That's Seven Dials for you,' said Harley. 'The whole area's like a graveyard for rented accommodation; it's where all the shabby little boarding houses come to die. We're on the outskirts here of what used to be the old St Giles Rookery, see. The miserable inspiration for many a great artist: Dickens, Hogarth, Doré, Fielding… they've all wandered down these streets to take a tentative sniff through a cologne-scented handkerchief – so they might better conjure an authentic rendition of the decrepit heart of this fair city of ours.'

'I say, that's rather poetic. You know, you're quite the surprise at times, George.'

'Oh yeah?'

'Yes. Take all those curios at your place. And your obvious love of literature. I would never have guessed that someone from your background would have—'

Harley tipped his hat back an inch and gave her an old-fashioned look.

'Sorry. I didn't mean that to sound condescending,' continued Bunty, a little flustered. 'It's just that… well, what I mean to say is—'

'Alright, loosen your corset. No offence taken.' Harley killed his cigarette beneath his heel. 'Come on – we've got ourselves a missing dancer to find.'

Harley's vigorous bang on the doorknocker dislodged a little flurry of papery paint flakes. Receiving no reply, he redoubled his efforts. Soon a sash window squealed open on the first floor and a pair of smudged, belladonna eyes stared down at them from above.

'Give it a bleedin' rest, won'tcha?' The voice was throaty, rough as a docker's. 'I've only just hit the sack!'

'Sorry, love,' said Harley, moving back to the pavement so as to get a better view of the young woman. 'We're after the landlord. Is he in?'

'You from the Council?'

'Oh no, it's nothing like that,' said Bunty. 'We're looking for a young lady.'

The woman raised one slender bow of plucked eyebrow, made a quick scan of the street, and leant further out so that she might continue the conversation in a husky whisper. 'Well, it's a bit early for most of the girls, but I expect Flo would be up for it. She's always game, that one. Second floor, at the back. You both wanting a go, are you?'

'No,' said Harley, chuckling at Bunty, whose neck had coloured in embarrassment. 'We're looking for a missing girl – Louise Parker. You might know her as Tallulah?'

'You ain't a bogey, are you, mister?'

Harley shook his head. 'Don't worry, there are no coppers involved. Not as yet, anyway. I'm a private detective, working for the family.'

The young woman gave a sniff and rubbed at one of her kohl-rimmed eyes. 'Tallulah, you say?'

'That's right. D'you know her?'

'Depends.'

'On what?' asked Bunty.

'On the usual,' said the woman, rubbing her thumb and forefinger together.

'Well, why don't you let us in? I'm sure we can come to some arrangement,' said Harley.

'Alright… Give us a mo', I'll just throw something on.'

Five minutes later the three of them were standing in the Sunny Side's grubby hallway.

'Is there somewhere a little more private we can talk?' asked Harley.

''Fraid not – I've got company upstairs, and he ain't come around yet. I was working late, you see.'

Bunty tried her best not to look too judgemental.

'I'm in show business,' said the young woman, flashing her a cold stare.

'Well,' said Bunty, producing the portrait of Louise Parker. 'Our missing girl is a dancer. Do you dance at all?'

'Among other things.'

'You might know her, then?' She held out the photograph.

'Let's see the wherewithal first.'

Harley passed her some money.

She gave him a seductive pout, tumbling the coins in her hand. 'Any chance of a smoke, handsome? I'm gasping here.'

Having transferred some of her carmine lipstick to the end of one of Harley's Gold Flakes, the girl settled herself on the stairs and adjusted the man's overcoat she was wearing so as to reveal just enough bare leg to hold his attention.

'Let the dog see the rabbit, then.' She held out her hand for the photograph. 'Yeah, that's her alright, Tallulah. Had the big room on the top floor; the best in the house. No surprise there. Right little madam, she was. Proper pound-noteish. She's moved on, though. Always banging on about how this place was beneath her. And about all the high-flyers she was meeting at that bleedin' club she was at.'

'Which club?' asked Harley.

'Some place on the underground scene, where the waiters dress up as clowns.'

'The Grimaldi Vaults?'

'Is that what it's called? I don't know. Sounds daft, if you ask me.'

'Did she ever talk about the German she worked for?' asked Bunty. 'The leader of the dance troupe? Ilse Blau, or Astarte? Do either of those names mean anything to you at all?'

'Nah,' said the girl, handing back the photograph. 'She kept her cards pretty close to her chest where work was concerned. Mind you, I don't blame her – you don't want to broadcast it when you're onto a good thing. Not nowadays. Not with this bleedin' Slump. I mean, there's only so much to go around now, ain't there?' She gave Harley an appraising look. 'And there's always someone younger and prettier, ready to jump into your shoes as soon as you look the other way.'

'When did you last see Tallulah?' asked Harley.

'I don't know. A month ago? Three weeks? Hard to say, really. It's not as if we were pals.'

'And you've got no idea as to where she might have moved on to?'

'I couldn't care less, could I? Good riddance, is what I say; stuck up little cat.' The woman took a long drag on her cigarette and then stood up, ready to return to her beauty sleep. 'I tell you who you should ask, though.'

'Who?'

'That good-for-nothing waste of space, Frankie Boy. He was sniffing around her skirts for a good couple of weeks, trying his luck.'

Just then the door leading to the basement stairs was jerked open by Walter Smethwick.

'Who's there?' murmured the befuddled landlord, still a little worse for wear from the previous night's drinking, and yet to have his hand steadied by a hair of the dog. 'What's going on out here?'

The young woman quickly pulled the coat around her and started off up the stairs. Harley grabbed at the coat.

'Oi! Leave off!' she hissed. 'I can't let the old bugger catch me with money, he'll have it off me for rent.'

'This Frankie Boy,' whispered Harley. 'He got another name?'

'Roscoe, Frank Roscoe. On the third floor.'

She wriggled free of his grasp and turned to address the landlord, who now stood bracing himself against the grubby wall.

'This gentleman's a detective, Mr Smethwick,' she said, emphasising the words as though he were simple-minded. 'He wants to ask you a few questions – about Tallulah.'

On hearing this shocking revelation, Walter Smethwick collapsed to the floor in a gibbering mess, suddenly overcome with a fit of delirium tremens.

* * *

While Harley and his assistant were attending to the needs of the incapacitated landlord in his basement apartment, Roscoe let himself in through the Sunny Side's front door and began a slow trudge up the stairs. He was in a royal blue funk. Witnessing the violent attack on Stingo Spinks had been a turning point for him, a final confirmation that he was in a miserably tight spot; the worst in his life, in fact. On the one side, he had his outstanding debt to the Adler gang; and on the other, Simeon Dubois and his pack of wild dogs were trying to pressurise him into kidnapping a child. A rock and hard place didn't come close. And so he'd arrived at the difficult decision to flee the capital for a while and take to the open road. He could see no other way out.

His plan now was to gather his meagre possessions and have one more night's sleep in a decent bed – for, even with its greasy pillows and resident bed bugs, he knew getting his head down at the Sunny Side was leagues ahead of what lay in store for him tramping on the road. Then, first thing in the morning, he'd make his way out of town to some decent-sized transport café and hitch a ride with a wagon heading north.

As he stood outside the door to his room, rummaging for his key, Roscoe became aware of something crunching underfoot. He lifted his shoe.

Nutshells.

The cast-iron features of Dubois's lead hound, Irvine, flashed into his mind.

'Bugger!' he whispered, making a quick scan of the stairwell.

Finding no one there, the wide-boy returned to his door and gave it a tentative push.

It swung open, unlocked.

He thought for a moment about running straight back down the stairs and out the door. But you needed a decent coat on the road, a good pair of boots; he wouldn't last long in what he was wearing. And he certainly didn't have the funds to replace the perfectly good examples he had sitting in his wardrobe.

He took a cautious step into the room.

With one eye on the open door, he checked behind the curtains. In the wardrobe. Under the bed.

All clear. Dubois's dogs had gone.

But they had left something behind – a small suitcase, sitting on the green candlewick bedspread.

Roscoe locked the door and picked up the envelope tucked into the handle. The note inside was typewritten and succinct:

IN CASE THE PREVIOUSLY SUGGESTED REMUNERATION
IS NOT AN ADEQUATE ENOUGH INCENTIVE, PLEASE
ACCEPT THIS GIFT AS A LITTLE ADDITIONAL
MOTIVATION TO CARRY OUT MY PROPOSAL.

Roscoe immediately seized on this tiny glimmer of hope. His mind began to race, sketching out the broad strokes of a new, more optimistic plan. After all, though he still had no intention of going through with Dubois's request to procure a child for his perverted cronies, what was to stop him taking this gift and disappearing as planned? Pawning whatever was inside – and knowing that stuck-up berk, it was probably something classy – was bound to give him enough for a decent stake. If he played his cards right, studied the form, made only low-risk bets... well, he could easily win enough to get a decent little room somewhere; in the Midlands, say, or maybe Liverpool, where he had some distant cousins. Start again. Lay low for a while. No need, after all, to return to tramping, with all the drudgery, the blisters, the impetigo.

After pushing a fresh matchstick between the beginnings of a smile, the wide-boy took the small key from the envelope and popped both locks on the case. He stood for a moment, rubbing his hands together in anticipation, then flipped the lid.

Roscoe sprang back against the chest of drawers with an involuntary yelp.

Inside the case, on a bedding of bloodstained newspaper, her once-stunning violet eyes transformed to the milky-eyed stare of a dead fish, was the decapitated head of the show girl, Tallulah. And tucked in neatly beside it, like a pair of nightmarish slippers, were her dismembered feet.

Roscoe slammed the lid shut.

He staggered over to the hand-basin – his head reeling, in serious danger of bringing up his meagre lunch – and gulped greedily at the icy water from the tap. After giving his face a liberal splashing, he slapped at his cheeks.

'Come on, Frankie – think, *think*!'

He began to perform a nervous little dance around the bed, continuing this mantra, '...think, think, think...' all the time regarding the suitcase as though it were a hissing cobra, ready to strike. Every neuron in his brain was firing at full capacity, sprinting through a thousand dodgy escape plans... all of which seemed to culminate in Frank Roscoe swinging at the end of a rope.

After a while, the rush of adrenaline began to fade, leaving his head thumping with a dull ache.

Exhausted, he slid down the wall to a sitting position on the stained lino – not daring to share the bed with the hideous package. He took out a grubby handkerchief and mopped at his face.

There was nothing else for it. He had to get rid of the suitcase. Immediately.

After all, while he was still useful to Dubois, it was unlikely that the dandy would set any kind of trap with the police. But as soon as it became clear he wasn't going to kidnap the little girl for those perverts… well, then he was bound to get a knock from the bogeys. And with that in his room it'd be the drop, for sure.

Roscoe struggled shakily to his feet. With a little involuntary shudder, he forced himself to secure the clasps and then gave the case a vigorous wiping down with a flannel, to remove any fingerprints.

Now all that was needed was to walk smartly down the stairs and into the street. Don't stop, don't talk to anyone. Just a bloke walking along the road with a suitcase – the most natural thing in the world. Make his way to the river, some-where not too busy – maybe one of the little back alleys round the Pool of London. Drop the suitcase in the drink and away on his toes. It'd be out in the Channel before anyone was any the wiser.

That's it, Frankie. That's using your crust!

Now the wide-boy's survival instinct had begun to kick in. He quickly searched out a pair of gloves from his sock drawer, donned his thick overcoat with its collar turned up, and pulled his hat down low on his head. After a quick appraisal in the mirror, he decided on the addition of a woollen scarf wrapped around the lower part of his face. Having made all the necessary preparations, Roscoe carefully picked up the suitcase from the bed, squirming as he felt the body parts settle inside.

It was then that someone hammered on the door.

'Frank Roscoe? You in there?'

Roscoe almost screamed out in panic. He stood there, stock-still, his heart thumping in his chest, praying to a god he didn't believe in.

More knocks on the door, louder this time.

The wide-boy opened his eyes and crept over to the window, half-expecting to find the street below swarming with coppers and Black Marias. What he actually saw was almost as frightening: leaning against a lamppost on the opposite side of the road was the Glaswegian, Irvine.

The hard man tipped his hat in recognition as he shucked another monkey nut.

The door handle rattled violently, making Roscoe jump and give a little yelp.

'I know you're in there! Listen, I just want to ask you a few questions, that's all. About Tallulah.'

Roscoe looked down at the anonymous-looking suitcase in his hand and began to mouth a litany of obscenities.

17

'**I**'M SURE I can hear someone moving around inside,' whispered Bunty, with her ear to the door. 'The fellow must have something to hide.'

'Shush!' said Harley, gesturing for her to follow him back down the stairs a little, so they wouldn't be overheard. 'He might well have something to hide, but it might not have anything to do with our missing girl. From Smethwick's description, this Frankie sounds like a typical wide-boy; there are a hundred and one reasons why he might not want to open that door.'

'Wide-boy?'

'Wide awake – living by his wits. Into a bit of petty crime, of one form or another.' Harley pulled out his notebook. 'Let's slip a note under his door. You never know, if he's not involved in Tallulah's disappearance he might get in contact.'

As Harley was scribbling his message, he became aware of approaching footsteps from below. Soon a pair of broad shoulders and the top of an expensive-looking fedora appeared in the stairwell.

The newcomer stopped on the landing and gave them the once-over, his thickset jaw grinding away mechanically. He cracked another nut between his teeth and took a step forward.

'Mr Roscoe?' asked Bunty. 'Frank Roscoe? Mr Smethwick said you might—'

Bunty was shocked to discover the Scot's forefinger thrust hard against her lips.

'Wheesht, Blondie! I'm nae your man. And even if I was, I would nae talk to you.' He began to trace a line down Bunty's neck. 'But there are other things I might consider.'

'Alright, pal, let's ease off there a bit, shall we?' said Harley, pulling his assistant out of harm's way. 'Wait for me downstairs,' he said quietly.

'I'm perfectly alright here, thank you,' said Bunty, obviously a little flustered by the encounter, but continuing to hold Irvine's lecherous gaze, nonetheless. 'After all, we have the landlord's consent to be here.'

Irvine smiled and spat a mouthful of soggy nutshell to the floor.

'Come on, George. Put the note under the door and we'll come back some other time.'

'George, is it?'

Harley noticed the subtle change in Irvine's demeanour, the way his right hand had dropped to the bulge in his jacket pocket.

He's pouching, thought Harley. Though the bulge looked too big for just a razor. *A shooter, then?*

From just the way the man held himself it was obvious to the private detective that the character now squaring up to him was professional trouble. No doubt this was the Glaswegian san toy Budge had been talking about. A face like Lon Chaney, the lad had said; well, that certainly checked out.

Harley gave a gentle pat at his own jacket pocket, feeling the reassuring weight of the brass knuckles.

'Who wants to know?'

'Oh, I don't think we need any formal introductions,' said Irvine. 'Not just yet, anyhow. But I've a little advice for you, George.'

'Go on then – I'm always open to a little friendly advice.'

'I didnae say it was friendly.' Irvine paused to pick out a plug of chewed nut from a back molar. 'That wee lassie, Tallulah? I'd forget about her, if I were you.'

'Would you now?'

'Aye, I would.'

'Well, thanks for the advice.'

'You're welcome.'

'Come on,' said Harley, keeping one eye on Irvine as he eased Bunty towards the stairs. 'I think we're done here.'

'You take care now, Blondie,' said Irvine, with a broad smile.

* * *

'You'll need to pull yourself together, son,' said Irvine, offering the nervous-looking Roscoe a cigarette. 'You've an important job to do for the boss tomorrow night. Come and sit on the bed, eh?'

Roscoe shot a look at the suitcase and gave a vigorous shake of his head. 'I'm not sitting next to that.'

'Don't be a jessie. After all,' Irvine grabbed the offending case and slid it under the bed, 'when all's said and done, we're all just bags of meat. The sooner you learn that lesson, the better.'

Roscoe risked engaging the Scotsman's pallid blue eyes for a moment, before quickly turning his attention back to the street. 'What if they come back? Bring the bogeys with 'em?'

'They'll nae come back. Not today, anyhow.'

'Can't you take it away with you now? I've got the message. It's giving me the collywobbles something rotten. I've told you, I'll grab the little…' Roscoe took a consolatory pull on his cigarette to try to calm his nerves. 'You know… I'll do that job. So, do we really have to keep that thing here?'

'Let's just call it a wee bit of insurance.' Irvine patted the bedspread. 'Come on now, Frankie. Why don't you take me through your little plan, hmm?'

Reluctantly Roscoe slumped down on the bed. He sat despondent, smoking silently as he contemplated the nightmare predicament he was in.

'Listen, Mr Irvine,' he said after a while. 'What do you think about this lark? Personally, like? What Simeon's asking me to do. You've been around the block a bit, right? I mean, don't get me wrong – I like a bit of skirt as much as the next fella, but… well, it's a no-no, ain't it? Messing about with a kiddie.' He turned to appeal to Irvine's savage, grey features. 'Just plain wrong?'

The Scotsman laughed as he unfolded the large cut-throat razor, a third of its blade bound with sticking plaster.

'I think you're asking the wrang fella, Frankie Boy. Anyone can be a commodity as far as I'm concerned. Now…' He pointed the cold blade at the wide-boy's quivering eyelid. 'Why don't you take me through that wee plan of yours, eh? There's a good laddie.'

18

'THIS FRANK ROSCOE you're talking about,' said Solly Rosen, laying down a plate of cheese sandwiches on the table in the Bag O'Nails' saloon bar. 'I know him.'

'There you are,' Harley said to Bunty. 'What did I tell you? Deadbeats and lowlifes – they're his speciality.'

'Oi! D'you want this or not?'

'Don't listen to him, Solomon,' said Bunty. 'We'd be delighted to hear anything you can tell us about this Roscoe character.'

'Alright then. Well, the lad was a regular at the Twelve Ten for a while. That's a little supper club, run by Mr Adler.'

'A *little supper club*?' Harley shook his head. 'It's a rough-house drinking and gambling den, Bunty. What we call a *spieler*.'

'From the German, presumably?' said Bunty, sipping cautiously at one of Marni's gin specials.

'From the Yiddish, actually,' said Rosen. 'But it's the same difference, ain't it? Anyway, as I say, this Frankie Roscoe was a regular there for a while – until he ran up too many gambling debts and got himself barred. I've seen him out and about, at the gee-gees and the dogs. He's just some tuppenny-ha'penny wide-boy; there are thousands like him. But here's the thing: it just so happens that right now Roscoe is on his last warning for a loan he took out with Mori. That means that Frankie Boy has got just a few days to either stump up the cash or jump ship; assuming he doesn't want to take the third option.'

'Which is?' asked Bunty.

'A long swim down to Southend,' said Harley. 'In a hessian sack.'

'Crikey! Oh, George, that reminds me. Tell Solly about that rough character we met at the boarding house.'

'The jock? He's already told me,' said Rosen. 'You got a handle on him yet?'

'Not as yet. But I had a quick word with John Franklin's lad, on the QT, to keep his ear to the ground in case Vine Street get a sniff of him.'

'Didn't recognise him yourself, then?'

Harley took a pull on his pint and shook his head. 'And believe me, you'd definitely remember that ugly boat. It's a face only a mother could love. I'd say he's working strongarm for someone with a bit of dough – had on a nice bit of schmutter, Savile Row by the look of it. I've also been trying to get hold of Squib, he mentioned something about a new crew in town.'

'I reckon I might have a lead on that one for you, as well.'

'Well, come on then, you big lump! Don't leave us in suspense.'

'I can't be too long.' Rosen looked over his shoulder towards the bar. 'Marn'll have me guts for garters. They're three deep at the bar up there.'

'Solly! Who's this jock?'

'Well, I don't know whether you've heard, but there's this new club on the underground circuit – the Grimaldi Vaults.'

'There it is again,' said Bunty.

'You been?'

'No,' said Harley. 'But Jerry Paladino mentioned it to us the other day. Rathbone Place way, ain't it?'

'That's it. The geezer running it has been stirring things up a bit lately, treading on people's toes. I can't remember this bloke's name. Something foreign sounding.'

'Dubois,' said Harley.

'That's the fella. Bit pound-noteish by all accounts. Anyways, the word is that this Dubois has brought in some out-of-towners to act as muscle. Not just on the door, but for his own protection as well, like a bodyguard. So, he's got to be into something a bit heavier than just running the club, right? I've heard that one of his crew is a face from the Glasgow gangs. Sounds like it could be your man at the Sunny Side.'

'There you are, George – it all comes back to the Grimaldi Vaults,' said Bunty, looking pleased with herself as she took another tentative sip at her drink. 'I told you we should prioritise the Ilse Blau lead. We ought to get that invitation to the club sorted out as soon as possible.'

'Hark at this,' said Harley. 'Five minutes in the job and she's writing it like Agatha Christie. Don't you worry, Miss Chatterton, it's all in hand. In fact, I heard today that Lil's back in town. I'm off to Limehouse tomorrow to sort out the invite.'

'You're going to see Lil?' Rosen looked surprised at this news. 'Blimey! How long's it been, now?'

'I don't know. A long time.'

'Since the funeral?'

'Probably.' Harley buried his face in his glass of beer.

Rosen sat back in his chair and crossed his arms over his formidable chest. He knitted his brow, deep in thought. 'Well, you know what? I think it's good you've finally plucked up the courage to go round there, George.'

'Plucked up the courage? That's what I've done here, is it?' Harley looked warily at Bunty, who was desperately trying to follow the gist of the conversation.

'I reckon it's progress. Part of the healing process.'

'Well, Dr Freud, I thank you for those insightful observations,' said Harley, looking over at the bar where something had attracted his attention. 'But I'd say, judging by the old-fashioned look your Marni's giving you, the Yiddish Thunderbolt might be needing a little healing of his own pretty soon.'

At that precise moment, as if to emphasise Harley's point, Marni Rosen's caustic shriek cut through the clamour of the busy pub:

'Solomon! Must be thirsty work, sitting there gassing like an old yenta, while the mother of your children works her backside off, earning you a living! You got everything you need, love? You want I should bring you a glass of beer over, maybe?'

'Ouch!' said Harley, grinning at his friend as he raised his glass in a toast. 'Stopped in the first.'

Rosen let out a sigh of resignation as he hauled his large frame out of the chair. 'Right. Duty calls. Abyssinia! Say hello to Lil for me.'

With a hefty pat on the back for Harley and a wink for Bunty, he was off through the crowds… and then immediately back again.

'I forgot this. Here you go.' He handed Harley a small white envelope. 'Marni said someone left it on the bar for you. Not sure why they didn't just come over and give it to you themselves.'

Harley showed Bunty his typewritten name on the front of the envelope.

'The same as our Greek message,' she said.

'Yeah… Did she say who left it?'

'Nah,' said Rosen. 'She finished serving a punter, turned around and there it was.'

'We must have been followed,' said Harley, scanning the crowded bar to see if he could catch a glimpse of any likely culprits.

'Probably just one of your many admirers, George… Right, I'd better be off. You be careful out there, you two.'

'Let's hope there's more to go on than last time,' said Bunty, watching Harley tear open the envelope.

He slid out a postcard, depicting the ornate, colonnaded façade of a neoclassical building.

'British Museum,' he mumbled, turning it over.

But before Bunty had a chance to read the message written on the reverse, Harley had already squirrelled the postcard away in his jacket pocket.

'George!'

'It's nothing. Something private.' He stood up, grabbing his coat from the empty chair next to him. ''Fraid I've got to go meet someone.'

'Now?! Who?'

'Tell you later.'

Harley looked over to the bar, where Rosen was now engaged in an animated conversation with a dubious-looking character in a wide-check suit.

'Listen,' he said, pulling the brim of his hat down low. 'When you get a chance, tell Solly I've gone for a meet at the museum.'

'The British Museum? Because of the postcard? But won't it be closed now?'

'Please, Bunty, this is important.'

She was concerned. It was the first time she could remember seeing him rattled.

Harley glanced at his watch. 'Tell Sol, if I haven't phoned here to give the all-clear by nine-thirty, then he's to come to the museum and check I'm still in one piece. But no police! You got that? Strictly no police.'

'But if you really believe that awful creature Morkens is somehow behind these messages and you go along there now, without any kind of preparation… Well, it's madness, don't you see? You'll be walking straight into a trap.'

But Harley was already off, weaving his way through the crowded pub towards the exit.

'George! Wait! I'm coming with you!'

Harley spun on his heels.

'No fucking way!' he growled at her, immediately silencing the lively hubbub of the saloon bar.

All eyes now turned to follow the passionate exchange.

'Do you hear me? If you follow me out that door, you'll be back at the Labour Exchange come Monday morning!'

* * *

Just as Harley turned the corner onto Great Russell Street, the nickel-coloured moon emerged from a ragged pennant of cloud, casting a cool metallic sheen onto the façade of the British Museum. He regarded the sombre stares of the allegorical figures high up on the neoclassical pediment and – with an uncharacteristic flutter of nerves – wondered whether they might not hold for him some ominous warning.

'Milky,' he mumbled, then spat into the gutter.

The stately Bloomsbury avenue was deserted, and the contrast to the clamour he'd left behind in the Soho pub gave him pause to reflect on his current course of action. He felt bad about the way he'd snapped at Bunty, but the chilling thought that he might have unwittingly exposed her to the risk of violence – at the hands of the same ruthless criminals responsible for Cynthia's brutal murder – was almost beyond contemplation. He sparked up a Gold Flake, silently cursing himself for employing such an ingénue in the first place. He pulled hard on the smoke, savouring the welcome burn of the Honey Dew tobacco, and then reread the typewritten message on the postcard:

IT WOULD APPEAR YOU MAY HAVE 'LOST YOUR HEAD' WITH BROTHER WHISPERS AT BECKTON. BUT IF YOU REALLY DESIRE THE RETURN OF THAT EXQUISITE TROPHY YOU SEEK, YOU MAY FIND A HELPFUL CLUE TO ITS WHEREABOUTS TONIGHT IN THE HALL OF GREEK & ROMAN ANTIQUITIES, AT THE EXHIBIT MARKED FOR YOUR ATTENTION.

Exquisite trophy? He liked to think he had a strong stomach, but the abject evil at the heart of this teasing little message brought the bile to his throat.

His head now swimming, Harley imagined, for one terrifying instant, Cynthia's hazel-green eyes, gazing out pleadingly from one of the professor's hellish specimen jars, her raven-black tresses playing lazily about her ashen face in the preserving fluid.

'Bastards!'

He looked to the museum again. Who had lured him here? The old goat, Morkens himself? Von Görlitz? Or was it that she-devil, Oona, up to her mind tricks again? Whoever it was behind this new message, Harley knew his knee-jerk reaction went against all his training. But even if it were a trap, with the message hinting at what he'd done to the Bulgarian, Whispers, at Beckton Sewage Works, there was simply no way he could involve the police. He'd have to deal with this alone, swiftly and emphatically.

Time to go over the top, Corporal.

He pocketed the postcard, killed his cigarette under his heel, and set off around the perimeter of the museum. After all, he might be walking headlong into a trap, but there was no need to make it easy for them by appearing through the front door.

A few seconds after Harley has made his move, someone emerged from the shadows of the darkened doorway of the Atlantis Bookshop, just a stone's throw away in Museum Street. Passing beneath the streetlamp, this figure was revealed to be dressed in a forest-green sway coat and wide-brimmed trilby, pulled low to obscure the face. The figure carried on into Great Russell Street, following the private detective at a discreet distance, moving through the night with the instinctive slink of a nocturnal feline.

Five minutes later, Harley was lowering himself through an open window he'd found in the museum's rear elevation on Montague Place. Landing as quietly as possible, he took stock of his surroundings: a workbench, shelves crammed with pots of paint – the small store obviously belonged to the maintenance department. He spent a moment quietly searching through a set of drawers, and before long had acquired a wood chisel to accompany his set of brass knuckles. He stowed the new weapon in his jacket, teased open the door and slipped out into the corridor. The dark was almost impenetrable in this back-of-house area, so he worked his way through the maze of corridors with a series of lighted matches. After a few wrong turns, he eventually found a door leading to one of the large public galleries.

Harley was no stranger to the delights of the British Museum – he'd spent many hours touring its exhibition halls, and he sometimes used the reading rooms as part of his case research – so it didn't take him long to get his bearings in the galleries, and he was soon on his way to the Hall of Greek & Roman Antiquities. There was no longer any need for the matches: the angled beams of moonlight projecting through the skylights offered a surprisingly bright – if somewhat eerie – illumination to high-ceilinged spaces. He realised, of course, this meant he would be easier to spot by anyone lying in wait, so he stayed close to the gallery walls and made use of the shadows cast by the larger exhibits.

Before long, he'd arrived at his destination and took a moment to steel himself, crouching down behind one of a pair of caryatids flanking the gallery entrance, listening carefully for any evidence of movement in the room beyond.

Silence.

Keeping low, Harley ventured a quick peek into the large exhibition space. There was no obvious sign of a welcoming party, so he slipped quietly inside.

On his guard for any signs of ambush, he now worked his way along the ranks of display cabinets, looking for an exhibit marked for his personal attention, as the mysterious message had promised.

He stopped at the last cabinet in the row and peeled off the handwritten label which had been pasted to the glass. It had on it one line of what he now knew to be ancient Greek: Πρόσεχε τί ἐπιθυμεῖς – the same phrase he'd had translated from the first mysterious message. But, even without this, Harley would have known he'd found the exhibit that had been singled out for him.

There on the shelf – between a Dionysian drinking cup and a small verdigris-covered figurine of Apollo – sat a large, weathered chunk of sculpted marble, depicting three classical figures. He read the exhibit card:

Marble column drum from the Later Temple of Artemis at Ephesus, showing a draped woman, between a youthful Thanatos (Death) and Hermes Psychopompos (Conveyor of Souls).

As he took a step back to regard this remnant of ancient architecture – sculpted some two thousand years previously – Harley felt the familiar icy dread creeping across his scalp. The reference was an obvious and chilling one.

At some stage over the many centuries of its existence the sculpture had suffered significant damage, with the result that the woman in the diaphanous gown, depicted between the two Greek gods on her way to the underworld, was now missing her once exquisitely rendered head.

'Cynthia...' he whispered, involuntarily, the susurration of her name returning to him in mocking echoes from the cavernous gallery walls.

He forced himself away from the exhibit. With the blood now singing in his ears and the chisel clenched tightly in his fist, he began to move quietly around the gallery, checking behind the larger display cabinets and life-size statues, searching the shadows in the window niches for someone lurking, ready to pounce.

But there was nothing to find. He appeared to be completely alone in the gallery.

Maybe there was a message waiting for him? Secreted about the sculpture somewhere?

He struck another match and moved back to examine the marble.

Which was when he caught sight of the blood.

A staggered line of dark crimson spots on the polished floor, leading away from the exhibit towards the large doorway to the next hall.

His hackles now well and truly raised, Harley followed the crimson trail into the adjacent gallery. He stopped by an imposing frieze of eagle-headed deities, where the spots became smudged into broad smears, indicating to Harley that the injured party had fallen here and had begun to drag themselves (or had been dragged) further into the room.

He struck another match and soon discovered this theory confirmed.

Ahead of him, lying face-down with one outstretched hand still clutching his now-shattered lamp, was the museum's nightwatchman. The man was obviously in a bad way, a dark, viscous puddle of blood forming around him on the gallery floor. Harley was just about to rush to his aid when he was stopped by a voice from the gloom:

'Turn around… slowly.'

19

'YOU'VE COME, THEN. Just as he said you would.'

The voice appeared to be emanating from a giant *lamassu* – a towering, sphinx-like effigy of a winged bull with the regal, bearded visage of an ancient Assyrian. But this voice was humdrum and pedestrian – more Metropolitan line than Mesopotamian. Then Harley caught sight of its real owner, edging out from the shadows between the sculpture's front legs: a mousy-looking, middle-aged woman in a beret and horn-rimmed glasses – with a revolver aimed directly at his head.

'Alright,' he said, dropping the chisel and putting his hands in the air. 'Easy now.'

'You're really him?' asked the woman. 'You're George Harley?'

She seemed a little dazed, as if she were confused to find herself in such strange surroundings, like a sleepwalker awakening from a spell of unconscious wandering. The gun, however, remained determinedly pointed in his direction.

'You see, I couldn't bear to have any more disturbances. If you're not him, I'm afraid I'd have to—'

'Yes! I'm George Harley. Who are you?'

'Me?' said the woman, looking a little surprised at the question. 'Why, I wouldn't have thought that's important.'

'You're the one with the shooter, lady. In my book, that makes you a somebody. So, why don't you tell me your name, eh?'

The woman thought for a moment, placing a hand to her pale cheek. Harley began to suspect she might be under the influence of drugs, or suffering from some mental affliction. Neither of which, in his experience, was conducive to the safe handling of firearms.

'Pendleton,' she ventured after a little hesitation. 'Joyce Pendleton.'

'Well, you look like a reasonable kind of person, Joyce. What say I just go and check on our friend over there? See if I can do anything to help him.'

'I assumed he was dead.'

'Was it the gun? Has he been shot?'

'It was so loud, you know. Quite frightening, actually.'

'I'm sure it was. They're scary things, shooters. Where did you get that one?'

'It was my father's – his service revolver.'

'I see. Do you think you could put it down now, Joyce?'

'No. I don't think I can do that.'

'Pity… But you will let me go and see to him, won't you? Where was he shot?'

'In the leg, I think.'

'Least it's not the gut. But he's lost a lot of blood. Probably not got long, if we want to save him.'

'His name is Feathers. Arnold Feathers. I always thought it such a poetic name.'

'You know him?' asked Harley, beginning to edge his way over to the casualty. 'You know Arnold?'

'Not well. But I see him most nights. He starts his lock-up round in the Reading Rooms – that's where I work, you see.'

She paused to think, pushing a tress of hair back into the beret. 'You know I've been in here, each night, for this past week now. Practising. Tonight was the first time that Feathers discovered me. The funny thing is, when he did find me here, before I shot him, he didn't seem to know my name. I've worked here all those years, and he didn't have a clue who I was.'

'The Reading Rooms? I've spent some time there myself.' Having reached the unconscious nightwatchman, Harley began a quick assessment of his injuries.

'I know. He said you were quite the dilettante…' Miss Pendleton's voice trailed off as she leant back against the statue, looking a little faint.

Harley worked quickly, removing the nightwatchman's tie and using it as a tourniquet on his thigh. All the time he kept one eye on the pistol in Miss Pendleton's hand, which now, thankfully, had begun to sag towards the floor.

'Who said I was a dilettante?'

Appearing to be on the verge of a swoon, Miss Pendleton slumped down to a crouching position and began to mumble something.

'Joyce? I can't hear you.'

'*Pickle herring…*' she mumbled, her eyes closed now, her head swaying as if to imagined music playing in her head. '*Pickle herring.*'

'What?'

'The gathering… it's so hot, so hot! Hands pawing at my body… drums so loud…'

Now in the midst of some kind of trance, the librarian let the gun tumble from her hand and began to tear at the buttons of her blouse, her thin lips stretched into a lascivious grin. 'Love is the law, love under will!' she chanted, her eyes still clenched tight. 'Love is the law, love under will!'

Seeing an opportunity to disarm her, Harley began to pad quietly across the marble floor.

But as he did so, he became aware of a slow glissando of musical notes, a simple, plaintive phrase, from some flute-like instrument. The strange music seemed to immediately revive Miss Pendleton. She snatched at the pistol and scrambled to her feet.

'What are you doing? Stop it! Stop it at once!'

She aimed the gun at Harley's face.

'He said you'd be devious. It's Feathers' fault, bursting in on me like that, making me lose my concentration… Back off there. Back off!'

'Alright,' said Harley, with his hands up again. 'Who said I'd be devious?'

'Why, the Preceptor, of course. Didn't you hear? That was him calling me.'

'That music? D'you mean Professor Morkens, Joyce? Is that what he's calling himself now, the Preceptor?'

'Stop talking! Tell me – did you find her, Harley? Did you find your Cynthia through there, in the gallery?'

Harley struggled to stay calm, forcing himself not to react.

'So prescient,' she continued, now full of maniacal confidence. 'It was sculpted in the fourth century BC, for the temple of Artemis. Artemis, whose birthplace was Mount Cynthus.'

Harley took a deep breath, trying to quell the fury which had begun to rage inside. 'Bravo. So, you happen to have found an exhibit which, with a big stretch of the imagination, could be used to make some sick reference to the brutal murder of an innocent, talented young woman. You must be very proud of yourself. So, come on then, Joyce – what's all this old palaver really about, eh?'

'What's it about?!' she screeched, her face suddenly livid. 'What's it about?!'

She strained for a few seconds, squeezing hard on the trigger, finally succeeding in letting off an explosive round.

The bullet ricocheted off the floor, worryingly close to Harley, peppering him with a spray of marble fragments.

'Now,' continued Miss Pendleton, smoothing down the rucks in her cardigan as the gun's report reverberated around them, the air thick with the acrid smell of cordite. 'It's time for your lesson, Mr Harley. The Preceptor has spoken.'

She took some crumpled notes from her skirt pocket, straightened them out and began to read.

'You have a cat, I believe?'

'What?' said Harley incredulously, keeping his eye on the wavering muzzle of the pistol.

'A pet cat – you have one, yes?'

'What the fuck has that got to do with—'

'Do you, or do you not, have a cat!' yelled Miss Pendleton, aiming the gun between his eyes.

'Yes, I have a cat. Called Moloch, if you must know.'

'And there we have it – *Moloch*. So frivolous; so disrespectful.'

'What?'

'Moloch was once a name to conjure terror, you know. A god besmeared with the blood of human sacrifice and parents' tears.'

'Jesus Christ! What is all this bollocks, Joyce?'

'Shut up!' She fumbled for a moment with her notes, trying to find her place. 'Yes… You see, the Preceptor can no longer regard your behaviour as just simple foolish impudence. And so, Harley, he has decided to punish you for your hubris. It now pleases our glorious teacher to liken himself to Moloch, that terrible god of antiquity. Indeed, as we speak, the Preceptor gathers around him his own clan of Ammonite worshippers, bold adepts who need not resort to the noise of drums and timbrels to drown out the cries of their victims.'

'Victims?'

'Yes, victims,' she said with relish. 'The first of whom you will soon be hearing of. And when you do, George Harley, you will be humbled by the knowledge that they were chosen purely to teach you this lesson: that… that man… knows not—'

With Miss Pendleton concentrating on her notes once more, Harley seized the opportunity and pounced across the floor, ploughing into her with his full body weight. She gave a startled yell and doubled over, the gun slipping from her grip to go clattering off into the shadows behind them.

Clamping his hands around her wrists, Harley dragged the bewildered librarian across the floor and slung her against the large plinth of the lamassu, where she slumped her head in her hands and began to sob.

'Listen!' he said, shaking her by the shoulder violently. 'Pull yourself together. You've got a bucket full of trouble ahead of you, lady. A spell in Holloway, I shouldn't wonder. First, I'm going to get Feathers to hospital. After that you can explain yourself to the local constabulary. Maybe though…'

He gently raised her chin, so she was looking him in the eye.

'Maybe I could put in a good word for you? Tell them you've been coerced, right? But you need to meet me halfway, Joyce. What are you mixed up in here, eh? Is it the AOU? What have those shicers been doing to you?'

But Harley noticed something behind him had caught the librarian's attention. Something which had widened her pupils in terror.

He spun around to see what it was.

This time there could be no suggestion of mistaken identity; this was no fleeting glimpse in the back of a cab in a crowded Piccadilly Circus. There, twenty feet or so above their heads, with his malevolent face pressed up against the gallery skylight, was the Nursery Butcher himself – Osbert Agamemnon Morkens.

Harley quickly scrambled to the area behind the large statue and began a frantic search in the shadows for the discarded gun. Glancing back at the roof, he saw the professor pulling something from inside his Astrakhan overcoat. Harley launched himself across the polished floor to take cover behind the marble plinth. But he soon realised that what the criminal lunatic held in his anaemic, long-nailed fingers was no weapon, but an ivory-coloured penny whistle.

Morkens placed the whistle to his feminine lips and drew from it three sustained, melancholic notes.

Though quieter than the previous performance – which Harley guessed had been delivered from a much closer location – the music still managed to penetrate the glass of the skylight, eliciting an immediate response from Miss Pendleton, who let out a panicked screech and began to fumble for something in her cardigan pocket.

By the time Harley had realised her intentions, the distraught woman was busy stabbing away at her upturned wrist with a pair of needlework scissors.

He rushed over to wrestle the weapon away from her, her forearm already slick with blood.

Above their heads the eldritch melody played on. Its insidious effect seemed to cause the librarian physical torment, making her wail and gnash her teeth as she fought desperately against Harley's restraints. Glancing back up to the roof, he was met by the child-killer's piercing, hypnotic stare, so well-known to him from his nightmares.

'Don't hold his gaze, George!'

This urgent, whispered instruction had come from some-where beyond the lamassu.

Unnerved, Harley hauled Miss Pendleton around so he could peer into the shadows.

'Who's there?' he hissed.

She emerged from the shadows, into a shaft of silvered moonlight: Oona.

'We need to go, George. The police are on their way.'

'Why should I trust you?'

She pulled up the brim of her felt hat and gave him a beseeching look with those deep azure eyes. 'You really have no choice.'

'What about the nightwatchman? He's lost a lot of blood.' He looked down at the librarian, who had sunk to her knees, moaning in his grasp. 'And this one?'

'Leave them.'

'She'll do herself in.'

'They're of no consequence. It was a trap.' She placed a finger in the air. 'Listen!'

Above Miss Pendleton's whimpering, Harley could now make out the discordant clanging of a brace of approaching Metropolitan Police Q cars.

Oona held out a gloved hand to him. 'We must go! I know a safe way out, through the basements.'

Harley looked once more at Miss Pendleton, squirming on her knees in front of him.

He sighed and let go of her wrists.

'Sorry, Joyce.'

'Good boy,' said Oona, placing a hand to his cheek as he joined her behind the lamassu. 'You're learning... One second, though.'

After a cautious glance to the gallery skylight above, Oona sprinted to the bloodied scissors lying on the gallery floor. Harley was thankful at first, thinking she was about to wipe them clean of his prints, but was puzzled to see her then yank Miss Pendleton's head up by the chin and dangle the scissors in front of her. The crazed librarian snatched them greedily from her hand.

Oona smiled and tucked something into the distraught woman's blouse. Then she was back at Harley's side.

'What the fuck was that?'

'An improvised confession. Let's just hope they don't check it against her real handwriting.'

'I don't mean the note – giving her back those scissors! She'll open her veins with them.'

Oona sighed, a puzzled knot marring that exquisite brow.

'Can't you see? She's AOU, George. Think of her as an enemy combatant. I'm sure you did far worse things in your trench raids.'

'It's not the same,' he muttered, pushing her aside.

But any plan of returning to the aid of the suicidal librarian was quickly scotched when he felt the muzzle of Oona's revolver, digging into his lower back.

'We have just seconds to get to those basements,' she hissed into his ear. 'Will you please get it into your thick skull that I am here to rescue you, Corporal Harley!'

From the sudden increase in the volume of the clanging bells, it was obvious that the police – in the form of the Flying Squad, most likely – had now arrived at the gates of the museum and would, at any moment, come crashing through the gallery doors, to find him alone with the bodies of two fatally wounded civilians.

It galled him to admit it, but – psychopathic witch or not – he had little choice but to go with Oona.

Hoping to get a fix on his nemesis before he left, Harley glanced one last time at the skylight, but all he saw there now was the nickel-coloured moon, hung like a flyblown mirror on the murk of the London sky. It was an image which held little optimism.

Then, with a sigh, and against his better instincts, he turned to follow Oona into the shadows.

20

TILLY BIGELOW RETURNED the sock she'd just finished darning to the wicker basket and slumped back in her chair. Among her closest friends, Tilly was known for three things: a nose reminiscent of W. C. Fields; a constant hankering after sweet things; and a voracious sexual appetite. She now sighed and gave that nose a vigorous rub. It had been a full six hours since she'd last pandered to her sweet tooth – with a slice of Victoria sponge at the Lyons Tea Shop – and over a fortnight since she'd indulged herself with that other predilection. Even then, she'd been restricted to a quick knee-trembler with a docker down a gloomy back-alley on the Isle of Dogs. Mind you, he'd thrown in a couple of bars of knocked-off chocolate. She smiled wistfully at the memory; it had to be said, those stevedores had the roughest of hands – and the foulest of mouths.

She looked up at the clock and let out another sigh of boredom; with only two hours gone of her nightshift at the orphanage, there was little hope of scratching either itch in the near future.

As night matron of the infant block, Tilly was solely responsible for the care and well-being of sixty children between the ages of four and seven. Much like the majority of her colleagues at Stockwell Green Orphanage, any modicum of natural affection she may have once held for the orphans had been gradually eroded by the constant regime of bed-wetting, night terrors, croup and nits. Unlike some, though, this shift of opinion had not veered all the way into the realms of petty cruelty, but had stalled somewhere in the area of ambivalence, leading Tilly to regard her young wards much as a herdsman might his stock.

Tilly's eyes were a little tired from the darning, and after trimming the smoking wick of the oil lamp, she leant back in her chair to rest them a while, her thoughts soon drifting to the comparative attributes of Eccles cakes and Chelsea buns. Just as she was drifting off into a fully-fledged nap, a sharp rap at the window jolted her back into consciousness.

She sat up and rubbed her eyes, not quite believing what she saw. Grabbing the lamp from the table, she got up to illuminate the face at the window.

She hadn't been dreaming. There he was, in the flesh – that cheeky Frank Roscoe.

'Frankie!' she squealed, opening the door to the rear courtyard. 'It's been weeks without a single word from you, you naughty thing.'

'I know, I know,' said Roscoe, holding up his hands in submission. 'But I've been busy, see, down in Brighton. Had a little thing going on the giddyaps. But I'm here now, ain't I?'

'Oh, Frank, you don't half talk funny. Come on in. I'll put the kettle on. Afraid there's nothing to go with it, though.'

'Oh, no?'

With a flourish, Roscoe produced a brown paper bag from behind his back.

'Cake?' said Tilly, her eyes widening.

'Well, it ain't kippers, now, is it?' said Roscoe, revealing the large Madeira cake he'd pilfered from the grocer's that afternoon. 'Oh, and I got you these, an' all. You like them, don't you?'

'Mint creams? They're my favourite! I must say, I was planning on being a little stand-offish – what with you vanishing into thin air like that. But I think I just might be persuaded to become proper friendly again.' She pushed in close and grabbed a handful of buttock.

As usual, Roscoe avoided staring at Tilly's extraordinary nose, focusing instead on her generous cleavage.

'Sit yourself down,' she said, placing the cake on a little table which contained a primus stove and other tea-making paraphernalia. 'I'll be mum.'

But Roscoe remained standing at the window.

'Is it just you on tonight, Till?' he asked, pressing his face to the glass.

'Yeah, in the Infant Block, anyway. What are you doing over there?'

'It's just I thought I saw someone when I came in, loitering out there in the yard.'

She joined him at the window. 'Who did you see, Frank?'

'It was a bloke, I think. He had something covering his head, something dark, like.'

'Oh, get away with you!' Tilly gave him a playful slap and returned to her tea-making. 'I know what you're about, Frank Roscoe, pulling my leg.'

'No, straight up. I swear there was someone there.'

She frowned at him and picked up the oil lamp. Surrounded, as she was, by little flesh-and-blood examples of the harsh realities of life, Tilly Bigelow was not one to be easily spooked by ghost stories. The cruel bite of icy water on a chapped hand; the iron grip of lumbago in the morning; the sweet release of sugar on the tongue; that exquisite ache between the loins: these were the things whose concrete existence was unquestionable – she had no time for hobgoblins and bump-in-the-nights. Armed with such resolve, she swung open the door and stepped into the courtyard, holding the lamp high to illuminate the dark corners.

'Hello?' she hollered. 'Who's there? Show yourself! Or we'll have the constable on you!'

But the only reply was the creak and groan of the shunting wagons in the railway sheds on the other side of the high perimeter wall.

'Must have scarpered when they saw me come in,' said Roscoe, laying a hand on her shoulder. 'Come on, gel, let's get that tea on the go. I'm spitting feathers here.'

After two helpings of cake and a decent sampling of the mint creams, Tilly was in a suitable mood to reciprocate. From an early age she'd understood the true nature of such transactions; for though she could amuse herself as much as anyone in the escapist pleasures of a whimsical novel or a romantic movie, she knew, without money or social standing, the realistic matrimonial prospects for a girl with a face like a musical hall act were somewhat limited. The boxes of chocolates, trips to the picture house, the evening sprees fuelled by port and lemon – well, they all came at a price. And Tilly was alright with that.

'Right now, little Frankie,' she said, pushing the wide-boy back in the old, battered armchair and dabbing the last couple of cake crumbs from her chin. 'What's matron going to do about you being such a naughty boy, eh? I mean, you were away for such a long time. I'm not even sure I can remember how to play our special little game.' She started to walk her fingers up his trouser leg. 'Remind me – was this how it started?'

'Yes, miss,' said Roscoe, hastily gulping down the last mouthful of tea. 'I think it went something like that.'

'Ah yes,' she purred, popping the buttons on his fly. 'It's all coming back to me now.'

Just then, with a creak of its hinges, the door leading to the children's dormitory swung slowly open. Roscoe fumbled at the buttons of his fly, toppling his cup and saucer off the arm of the chair in the process. Tilly scrambled up off her knees and span around to confront their unexpected guest, doing her best to shield her visitor from view. But when she saw the little forlorn figure standing in the doorway, she broke into a fit of relieved chuckling.

'It's alright,' she said, turning to Roscoe, who was still hurriedly rearranging himself. 'It's only little Poppy.'

'What d'you mean, it's alright?' he hissed. 'Little Poppy there almost got an eyeful of old Mr Peaslin, didn't she? And what about when she starts yapping to her mates about the little game matron was playing with the gentleman in the parlour, eh? You'll be in right shtuck.'

'No, I won't,' replied Tilly. 'The poor little mite is stone deaf. Can't hear a thing. And a little feeble-minded with it, if truth be told. She won't be yapping to anyone; and she won't have a clue what's going on here, neither, bless her.'

'Stone deaf and feeble-minded, you say?' said Roscoe, contemplating the child. 'She's a pretty little thing though, ain't she?'

And in that moment, little Poppy's fate was sealed.

'How old is she, then?' he asked, following Tilly as she escorted the child back down the whitewashed corridor, redolent of carbolic soap.

'Six... maybe seven; I'd have to check. Why you so interested, all of a sudden? Getting broody in your old age?'

'Get out of it! Nah, it's just this deaf thing – makes you think, don't it?' Roscoe started clicking his fingers behind the little girl's head. 'Can she really not hear anything at all?'

'Will you stop it, Frank! She's not a plaything. Why don't you go back to the office and get yourself ready? After all, we were only just getting started, weren't we?'

Roscoe nodded to a set of double doors at the end of the corridor. 'So, is that where they all sleep, then? One big room, is it? Like in the spike?'

'That's right, the dorm. But I'm going to put Poppy to bed in the sanatorium; she likes it in there. Sometimes she's up for hours, see, making her little moaning noises. I don't want her waking the other kiddies. I won't be long. Why don't you go and get comfy? Throw some more coal on the fire, if you like.'

'Right you are,' said Roscoe, with a wink. But he hung around just long enough to make sure he knew exactly which door led to the sanatorium.

When Tilly finally returned to the office, she was surprised to find Roscoe at the main window again, brandishing the bread knife she'd used to cut the Madeira cake.

'What on earth are you up to?'

'He's back, Till – that bloke I saw. He came right past the window.'

'No!'

Seeing how agitated the wide-boy was, Tilly didn't dare venture outside this time.

'He looks like a wrong 'un to me,' said Roscoe, 'and no mistake. He's got this thing over his head, like the old executioner's hood. With eyeholes cut out of it.'

'Oh, stop it, Frankie! You're scaring me.'

'It's true, I tell you… Right!' He grabbed hold of the door handle. 'I'm going out there.'

'Don't, Frank. Stay here with me, please.'

'I'd love to, Till, really, I would. But what about them kiddies, eh? What if he's here for one of them?'

'Why would he be?'

'Well, there's all sorts of perverts about, nowadays. Unnatural types. They can't stop themselves, you know, once they've got the craving.'

'My God! Don't!' She slumped down into the armchair with her hand held to her breast.

'Right. Make sure you lock the door behind me.'

Tilly sat with her gaze fixed steadfastly on the courtyard, waiting eagerly for Roscoe's return. In response to each creak of settling timber, or pop from the burning coal in the grate, she gave a quick nervous rub to her ever-reddening nose. After five minutes with neither sight nor sound of the wide-boy, she decided to try to calm her nerves a little by resorting to the box of peppermint creams. It was as she got up to retrieve the sweets from the table that she was presented with a most terrifying sight.

There, staring back at her from through the narrow sash window on the opposite side of the room, was a nightmarish scarecrow figure in an old, dishevelled greatcoat. In place of a head, this creature had a blackened, shapeless sack with large eyeholes ripped out of it.

Tilly looked away for an instant, searching for something to defend herself with. When she looked back again, the terrifying figure had disappeared.

Suddenly there was shouting. The sound of someone sprinting across the gravel. Then, silence.

'Frankie?' she murmured, tentatively approaching the window.

A frantic pounding at the courtyard door had her running to cower behind the armchair.

'Tilly! Open up! It's me!'

She scurried to open the door and let Roscoe in. He stumbled into the room, his collar hanging loose around his neck. There was grime on his face and what looked like blood on his hands.

'Are you hurt, love?'

'Not me,' said Roscoe, trying to catch his breath. 'Not me... I got one of them, with the knife.'

'There was more than one?'

'Two of the bastards. Done up in weird hoods.'

'I saw one! He was there – at that window.'

'They didn't get in, did they, Till?'

'No. He was there for just a second.'

'I reckon they was after screwing the place. One of them came at me with a crowbar. I stuck him, though, stuck him good. In the arm.' Roscoe held up his bloodied hand as evidence. 'I chucked the knife over the wall – can't afford to get lumbered for it.'

'Have they gone, d'you think?' asked Tilly, rushing over to lock the door again.

Roscoe nodded.

'You sure?'

'Saw them scarper away out the yard.'

Tilly tried to compose herself. 'Right, then. We're going over to the main block to get help. They've got a telephone over there; we can call in the law.'

'Hold your horses,' said Roscoe, placing a restraining hand on her arm. 'You can't call in the bogeys, not while I'm still here. I'll get lumbered for wounding with intent. And you'll lose your job for having me in here in the first place.'

Tilly pondered the problem for a moment, then gave a quick rub of the Bigelow nose.

'Well, how's this, then?' she said. 'You make yourself scarce and I'll go over to the main block on me own.'

'That's more like it, Till. But you've got to give me time to get away, mind. If I'm caught skulking about the grounds, they'll have me as one of the burglars. Give me ten minutes, then you go over and sound the alarm.'

'Don't you want to clean up a bit first?'

'Nah, I'll be alright… Blimey, what a palaver, eh? And we didn't even get to play our little game, did we?'

'Don't you worry about that, my brave little man,' she said, giving him a peck on the cheek. 'I'll make it up to you next time, I promise. Off you go, then. You take care now, Frankie Boy.'

'Alright, Till. Don't you let on I was here though, will you? And remember – give me ten minutes to get away.'

* * *

Having pawned his watch two months previously, Roscoe had no idea how many of those ten minutes were left as he crept his way over to the coal shed by the orphanage gate. It had certainly taken longer than he'd hoped to open the heavy steel lid of the large refuse bin and hide the greatcoat, the hood and the little bag of pig's blood he'd used to bloody his hands with. The success of his dangerous and despicable little adventure now lay in the ease with which he could escape with the prize.

He placed a hand on the rusted handle, and, with a little jitter of nerves, yanked open the coal shed door, half expecting to discover a couple of burly constables ready to handcuff him and lead him away to chokey.

He held his breath and struck a match… and exhaled with relief.

There she was. Little Poppy. Still curled up in the red blanket. The bottle of butyl chloride had obviously worked its magic.

Then a worrying thought occurred – *what if he'd used too much of the stuff*? Three drops on a handkerchief, Irvine had said; but maybe that was for an adult? How much for a six-year-old? And such a tiny, frail six-year-old, at that. Wouldn't three drops be too much?

Panicking now, Roscoe placed his face up close to the child's. No, it was alright, she was still breathing. Just in a deep sleep.

He put a hand to her cold little cheek. She looked so fragile, like a doll.

My God, Frankie Boy! Whatever have you done?

He thought about leaving her there. Scarpering. Going back to his original plan of tramping around the country for a while.

Then a set of images flashed into his panicked brain: Spinks' face opened up by Benny Whelks' razor; the milky sheen of Tallulah's dead eyes; and the ugly promise of violence in Irvine's gimlet stare.

You've no choice, son. This is about survival now. Anyway, the little mite won't have a clue what's going on – feeble-minded, that's what Tilly said.

Spurring himself on with these reassurances, Roscoe retrieved the folded coal sack from behind the door, shook it out the best he could, and then, with much fumbling, manhandled the child inside.

Besides, she'll be far better off where she's going. Growing up in an orphanage? That's no kind of a start in life – just like doing bird. These toffs know how to live. She'll have nice clobber, loads of nosh, little treats.

So, like some dybbuk in a folk tale, with the sack containing the kidnapped child slung over his shoulder, Frank Roscoe slipped out of the orphanage gates and stole away into the night.

21

Roscoe scanned the street one more time for any sign of movement. Where were Irvine and his mob? Did they really expect him to just sit in his room, waiting patiently for them to saunter over, while, for all he knew, half of Scotland Yard might be out looking for him?

He pulled the blanket up over the sleeping child. It was getting chilly with the window open, but the sickly smell that emanated from the suitcase under the bed soon became overpowering with it closed. He'd tried to mask the stink by emptying a can of Vim over the body parts; this had helped at first, but now it just seemed to add to the overall nauseating effect. Whatever happened, he'd have to get rid of that case soon, before the other tenants started to complain about the reek.

But it shouldn't be long now. After all, he'd gone through with his side of the bargain. Once he handed over the little girl, all his problems would disappear: Irvine would take care of poor old Tallulah, and with the fee for the kidnapping he could pay off Mori the Hat and have plenty to spare for a new start somewhere.

So, where were Irvine and his crew? For the last twenty-four hours there'd been at least one of those bastard san toys loitering around outside, ensuring he didn't have it away on his toes. Now – nothing.

Who was he kidding? Roscoe knew exactly where they were. Now the deed was done, they were keeping their distance, waiting to see whether the net would close in on the little mug they'd fooled into doing their dirty work for them. Well, if they wanted the kid, they'd just have to come and get her, and that bundle of horror in the suitcase.

He sat on the edge of the bed and gently placed a hand on Poppy's cheek; she squirmed a little under the blanket, but still seemed to be sedated by the knock-out drops. He'd only be a little while. Back in no time at all. A quick trip down to the ground floor to telephone Dubois and back up again – a couple of minutes at the most. After one last check of the street below, Roscoe slipped out of the room, locking the door behind him.

He'd just reached the telephone in the hallway when the street door burst open.

'Blimey, Frankie! What you looking so guilty about? You up to no good as usual?' It was the girl with the kohl-rimmed eyes from the first floor, looking a little worse for wear.

'Get out of it!' said Roscoe, shrugging a shoulder and immediately adopting his wide-boy grin. 'You just surprised me, that's all. About to use the phone, weren't I?'

'Got one of your surefire tips, have you? Here, hold on a mo'…' She leant on him as she slipped off her shoes. 'Cor! That's better… You're out of luck with the blower though, love. Old moany-guts ain't paid the rental in weeks, they cut it off yesterday. You'll have to use the one at Cambridge Circus.'

'Bugger!' exclaimed Roscoe, shooting back up the stairs.

'Here! You keep out that bathroom, now!' she shouted up after him. 'I've already called dibs on it. It's my tub night tonight, that's why I'm back early!' She padded heavily up the stairs in her bare feet, mumbling to herself. 'Got to do me smalls an' all. No peace for the wicked.'

Back in the third-floor room, Roscoe was over by the window; but there was still no sign of Irvine and his boys. Cambridge Circus was only ten minutes' walk away, but he knew the phone box was a popular one; there was bound to be a queue.

A door slammed on one of the lower floors, prompting Poppy to turn over in her sleep and let out a little whimper.

Roscoe took the butyl chloride from his jacket pocket. He'd probably be away for a good twenty minutes at least. If she woke up in strange surroundings – and God forbid, if she found that suitcase under the bed – well, she was bound to scream the place down, wasn't she? Could little deaf girls scream? Well, if not, they could certainly thump the door and stamp their little feet, make a right old rumpus.

He fingered the little blue glass bottle nervously. Dare he risk giving her another dose? He already had the remains of one corpse in his room. Maybe he should gag her instead? Tie her up, so she couldn't make a noise? He approached the bed and yanked back the blanket.

What are you thinking, you swine! Look at her – she's just a little kid. You can't tie her up like some pig for slaughter.

Roscoe swore under his breath and turned to his dresser mirror, looking to his reflection for inspiration. But all he saw there was a pasty chancer in a cheap suit, chewing nervously on a lousy matchstick.

Then he had an inspiration – Walter Smethwick's little shrine to his dead daughter!

He quickly retrieved his emergency quarter bottle of gin from the sock drawer and slipped out of the room again, the beginnings of a plan forming in his brain.

It took a couple of minutes of knocking to get Smethwick to answer. When he did finally open the door, it was obvious the landlord was in a bad way.

'There he is!' said Roscoe, jostling the befuddled landlord towards the kitchen table as he invited himself into the flat. 'The man himself. Been having ourselves a little party, have we? You're looking a little under the weather, Walter. But don't you worry – I've got the very thing for that.' With a flourish he produced the small bottle of spirits from his jacket pocket. 'There we go, nice little drop of mother's ruin, courtesy of Frankie Boy. Just what the doctor ordered, eh?'

Roscoe grabbed the chipped glass from the table and poured out a healthy measure. 'You get that inside you, chum,' he said, pushing Smethwick down into the chair and thrusting the drink into his hand. 'Hair of the dog. Do you the world of good, that will.'

It took a little longer than expected for Roscoe to get enough gin into the landlord to render him insensible enough for what he had planned, but Smethwick eventually succumbed, laying his head on the table with one last incoherent mumble. The wide-boy seized his moment, dashing over to the Welsh dresser, where he helped himself to a colourful Rupert Bear annual and Piecrust, the doll in the polka-dot frock, who took pride of place in the dead girl's shrine.

Back up on the third floor, Roscoe leant over the handrail for a while, listening out for anyone who might be coming up to use the bathroom. Once satisfied that the coast was clear, he went back to his room and gathered the necessary items for the next part of the plan – moving the slumbering Poppy to a temporary hidey-hole, just in case she came to while he was away at the phone box. Covering her with the orphanage blanket, he gently lifted the child onto his shoulder and, with the dolly tucked under his arm, quietly stepped out onto the landing.

It was the grumbling belly of the Sunny Side's ancient boiler which roused Walter Smethwick from his drunken stupor, soon followed by the familiar insistent knocking of the pipes and the creak of expanding timber – all telltale signs that someone was running a bath on the top floor of the house.

Having doused the guilt with a suitable amount of hard liquor, Smethwick found himself temporarily liberated from his usual self-disgust, and as he listened to the little domestic symphony play out around him, he found it conjured a swell of sordid memories – the furtive archive of a life before all the tragedy and degradation had strangled his libido. Recollections of balmy summer nights flooded back to him, holed up in his secret cloister, gorging himself on the delectable visions of his naked tenants; all those slippery, lithe bodies, unknowingly parading themselves before him, while he rubbed himself to a sweet release, his eye pressed tight against the knothole in the boards.

Smethwick emptied the glass of the remaining quarter inch of gin and tried to focus on the calendar on the wall. Tuesday night, Tuesday night… Yes, it would be that little minx on the first floor. She always bathed on a Tuesday. A mouth like a docker, but, my God, that body!

And suddenly, in the midst of these carnal meanderings, Walter Smethwick suffered a blinding moment of revelation. A ray of logic so bright and true that it instantly penetrated the alcoholic haze to deliver a surprising shock to his crapulent brain. The cause of this sobering moment of clarity? It was the simple realisation that the death of his darling little Lorna had been just a tragic accident. Nothing more. Not an act of divine punishment. Just misadventure. For how could it have been holy vengeance? What god would be so wicked as to take the life of an innocent, just to cure him of his little unsavoury habit? To believe in such a concept was laughable; and indeed, Smethwick – now consumed with an intoxicating sense of relief – threw back his head and let out a rambling, drunken guffaw, staggering around the kitchen as he hooted in contempt.

'How can it be a sin?'

After all, who – if not God – was responsible for such lustful thoughts in the first place? Wasn't this passion for the naked female form simply a result of his true nature as a man? What could be less perverted than that?

This train of thought soon led Smethwick to a most exciting conclusion – for if it were no longer to be regarded as a sin, then what was to stop him simply taking up where he'd left off? After all, wasn't the Sunny Side still crammed with ravishing examples of the female form? And given the ribald nature of their occupation, who was to say these girls would even object to being spied upon in the first place? Why not steal up to the attic at that very moment? Pull up the step ladder behind him, position himself above that secret spyhole – it was all he could do to stop himself breaking into a run.

Patience now, Walter, you mustn't alert any of the tenants. That's it, quietly up to the third floor. Hover a moment outside the bathroom door. Yes – taps turned off, the little splash and lapping of the water as she gets in, lowering that enchanting body into the hot water, a scarlet blush already caressing the pale skin. Come on now, you really mustn't miss a second of this!

There's the little ladder in the store cupboard, just where it always was. Wait for the topping up with cold water – there's the tap running again, masking the little knock as you rest the ladder against the frame... Pull it up quietly behind you, that's it... Close the hatch with your thumb on the catch to muffle the spring... Ah yes, there it is, that old familiar smell, like the almond mustiness of an old book... Take a moment for the eyes to adjust to the gloom... The slow creep across the boards, easy does it… There's the chink of light from the knothole… Unbutton the fly now; the reassuring swell of arousal already straining against the cloth… Ease yourself down, any moment she'll be in sight. Any moment now…

But that was as much time as the unfortunate Walter Smethwick had to enjoy his brief respite from torment and self-loathing. For it was just then – as he knelt on the dusty attic floorboards, his now flaccid member still grasped in his trembling fist – that the drunken landlord was presented with a most terrifying vision. An apparition so ominous it seemed ridiculous to have ever questioned the vengeful nature of his cruel and wicked god. For there, stumbling towards him in the dark attic, still stiff from her resurrection and with her precious little Piecrust clutched tightly in her emaciated hand, was the spectre of his dead daughter, Lorna. And what reason would she have had to make that harrowing journey back from the grave, other than to admonish him for his bestial perversion? The same wicked aberration which had engrossed him that night; the night when Maureen was away at her sister's in Bournemouth; when he was once again up there in the dark playing with himself like a wicked little schoolboy, spying on that petite blonde from No.3, as his little princess gasped for her last breath in the basement, suffocating from a violent attack of asthma.

'N-No, Lorna,' he stammered, fumbling with his trouser buttons. 'Go back to your rest, now. There's a good girl.'

But the little figure shuffled on relentlessly, one hand outstretched, her dolly dragging in the dust beside her. And all the time she mewled in torment – so Smethwick supposed – through a mouth still stopped up with cemetery loam.

'Go back! Leave me alone, can't you? No… No! Back, I say!'

He stumbled to his feet and scrambled over to grope at the clasp on the hatch. But the alcohol and the panic had rendered his fingers all but useless, and so all that was left to him was to stagger towards the rear wall, backing away, unable to tear his eyes from the ghost of his dead little girl.

And then, as he felt the rough brickwork against his back, Smethwick finally understood that the outstretched hand was in fact pointing, showing him a way out, a release from all the degradation, all the filth of life.

'Oh, thank you, my dear. Yes!' he said, biting on his thumb, trying to staunch the sobbing which had begun to rack his thin frame. 'Thank you! And you must know, my little princess, you must know that Daddy loves you. Yes, he does. And he's so, so very sorry!'

With that final confession, Walter Smethwick finally experienced a moment of serenity. Now all that was left to do was to tuck in his shirt tails, climb the two wooden steps to the attic window, force open the catch… and launch himself into the night.

* * *

On his way back from Cambridge Circus, a now buoyant Frankie Roscoe allowed himself the luxury of a little smile. The phone call with Simeon Dubois had gone better than expected. Roscoe was to deliver the girl immediately to the back door of the Joseph Grimaldi pub, then, assuming all was to the dandy's satisfaction, he would be paid his fifty pounds (fifty pounds!) in cash and one of Irvine's men would return with him to collect the suitcase containing Tallulah's remains.

'Fifty nicker!' he mouthed, adding a little whistle.

Could it really be that, against all the odds, he might actually make up the lost ground in the final furlong and win this race by a nose? That certainly would be a turn-up for the books. And then what? Once he'd paid off Mori Adler, there'd be a cool thirty-seven left. Thirty-seven quid – that was a flock of dough in anyone's books. A bloke could make a decent go of something with that kind of money.

Giving a little joyous shrug of the shoulders, the wide-boy hurried off up the street. He was still engrossed in his scheming when he arrived back at the Sunny Side, and if it hadn't been for a shout from the side alley that divided the boarding house from the pawnbrokers, he might have missed the small crowd which had begun to gather there.

'Oi! Frank! Over here!'

It was Begsy: a weasel-faced petty thief, often found hanging around the Sunny Side, attracted by its clutch of female residents.

'Can't stop, I'm afraid, pal,' replied Roscoe. 'Got something on.'

But Begsy wasn't to be fobbed off so easily. After giving a quick tap on the side of his nose, followed by a melodramatic check of the street in both directions, he sauntered over to Roscoe with the air of a man in possession of valuable information.

'Well, let's hope this thing you've got on is nothing moody, Frank,' he said with a knowing smirk.

Roscoe tried his best to adopt a nonchalant expression. 'Oh yes? Why's that then?'

'Because in a couple of minutes this gaff's going to be teaming with bogeys, that's why.'

'You don't say?' said Roscoe, struggling to ignore the little worm of anxiety which had begun to squirm in his gut. 'And why would the bogeys be so interested in this old place, chum?'

'Oh, let's see now – maybe because the landlord of said establishment has just launched himself out the window, and is, at this moment, doing a passable impression of raspberry jam on the pavement over there.'

'What?!'

'Come and have a look yourself, if you don't believe me.'

Still not sure if he was being set up for some elaborate prank, Roscoe followed Begsy into the alleyway. But after only a few paces, a sudden gap in the crowd revealed the unmistakable figure of Walter Smethwick, sprawled out on the cobblestones in an impossible ragdoll pose, a dark mess oozing from his oddly misshapen head.

Whispering a string of expletives, Roscoe span on his heels and ran back as fast as he could, oblivious to the stares of the growing crowd and to Begsy's sarcastic jeers. After fumbling with his keys for a moment, he went through the front door and sprinted up the stairs. The clamour on the landing awakened the belladonna-eyed girl from the first floor, who had been snoozing in her tepid bathwater, blissfully ignorant of the tragedy unfolding about her.

''Ere, what's all the commotion?' she hollered.

But Frankie Boy didn't bother to reply – this situation went far beyond the realms of a little sweet-talking. If he didn't grab little Poppy and disappear before the bogeys arrived, he was looking at a long stretch in chokey.

Come on! Just grab that ladder, and get up in that attic and—

It wasn't there! The ladder had disappeared.

Frantic now, Roscoe hurled aside the mops and brooms from the small cupboard in which, less than half an hour previously, he knew he'd replaced the attic ladder. But it was no use. It simply was not there. Not there! Which meant… what, exactly? That someone had discovered little Poppy in her hiding place?

He stood back and gawped up at the hatch for a while, overwhelmed for the moment by this turn of events, the adrenaline pushing his heart to a nauseating rate.

Then the moment of hesitation was over. Once again, his innate sense of survival kicked in, spurring him on into his own room and back out again with the chair. Taking up one of the discarded brooms, he leapt up and stabbed at the catch; once… twice… finally opening the hatch on the third attempt.

And there she was! He could hardly believe his own eyes: little Poppy. Framed in the opening. One small fist rubbing at her cheek as she clutched the dolly to her chest.

Roscoe held out his arms to her and… Oh, you clever little thing!… she obligingly sat herself down on the edge and dropped into his embrace.

He held her tight for a moment. Planted a kiss of relief on her dear little head. Couldn't help it. Anyone would think he was rescuing her from a blazing inferno.

Then he was off. Pounding down the stairs with his illicit prize gripped tightly to his chest.

And just in time – wasn't that the clang of a Q car he could hear? Heralding the imminent arrival of Scotland Yard's finest? But what did that matter now? He was there, standing in the Sunny Side's hallway, the front door teased open ready to slip away into the night, off to collect his prize money; off to a new start.

It was at that exact moment that Roscoe remembered the suitcase filled with body parts, festering away under his bed.

Another trill from the squad car bells. Closer now. A couple of blocks away at the most.

Before he knew what he was doing, his feet had taken him back up the stairs and onto the third-floor landing. The mad rush of blood thrummed in his temples as he pushed open the door to his room, his chest heaving with exertion, his shirt plastered to his back with cold sweat.

Once inside, Poppy was tossed onto the bed as he scrambled underneath it for that hideous package. She stood up immediately with a muted little giggle, holding out her arms for a repeat, thinking it all just a silly game.

He stood, she jumped, and they were off down the stairs again in a mad dash.

Roscoe paused in the entrance lobby, his heart pounding in his chest. He held his breath and listened: the screech of brakes... the slamming of car doors... the pounding of service-issue footwear.

He looked down at the case in his hand – a personal ticket to damnation. There was no way he could risk walking out into a street teeming with police in possession of such an article. A kidnapped child was one thing – there were stories already forming in his head to wheedle his way out of that little number if the need arose. But a case full of decomposing body parts? Not even Paddy Flynn could talk his way out of that one.

And so Roscoe made his way back along the hallway. But this time he headed down, down the short flight of steps, down to the landlord's basement flat.

'Sorry, Walter,' he mumbled, as he swept aside the empty spirit bottles to make room for the suitcase in the centre of the kitchen table. Then, after a quick wipe of the handle with his handkerchief, he was away, out of the side door leading to the rear courtyard, with his stolen prize clinging tightly to his neck.

22

THE SOUND OF an engine idling close by in the street below drew Bunty to the office window. She peered down expectantly, watching closely as the passenger got out of the stationary taxi. But it was soon apparent it wasn't Harley.

She glanced at her watch: eleven o'clock. He was never this late for work.

The last time Bunty had seen her employer was when he'd left her standing in the saloon bar of the Bag O'Nails, bristling with embarrassment from his dressing down, watching him rush off to what was obviously some kind of perilous rendezvous at the British Museum. Following Harley's instructions, when she still hadn't heard from him by nine thirty, she'd persuaded Solly Rosen to accompany her to the museum, to see whether they could track him down. But on arrival they'd found a phalanx of black Wolseley police cars lining the street outside and a huddle of CID detectives and uniformed bobbies surrounding the porticoed entrance to the building. No police, Harley had said, so they'd slunk back off to the pub, more than a little concerned.

And now this.

She picked up the copy of the Daily Oracle and reread the headline:

LIBRARIAN SHOOTS NIGHT-WATCHMAN AT BRITISH MUSEUM!

The article went on to explain how the body of one of the museum's librarians, a Miss Joyce Pendleton, had been found in the Hall of Greek & Roman Antiquities alongside a note confessing to the shooting of Arnold Feathers, the museum's elderly nightwatchman. Feathers had survived the shooting but was now in a critical state at University College Hospital.

Thankfully, there was no mention of Harley. But it seemed ridiculous to assume he wasn't somehow tied up in this troubling incident. On first seeing the headline that morning, Bunty had immediately telephoned the Bag O'Nails and suggested to Rosen that they go to see Harley's contact at Vine Street, DS Franklin. A suggestion which provoked quite a strong response from the ex-boxer.

'Are you meshuggener?!' he said. 'No police! George was clear about that. You could be landing him in all kinds of schtuk if you put the squeak in to the bogeys that he was there.'

Which she'd deciphered as meaning it wouldn't be at all in her boss's favour for her to contact DS Franklin. But it had been more than twenty-four hours now and still no word from Harley. Rosen had tried to reassure her it was quite normal to go to ground for a bit after a big 'shemozzle' and that Harley was bound to turn up again after a couple of days, but she was finding it extremely hard to adopt such a laissez-faire attitude. She'd contemplated confiding in her new landlady. After all, from the stories she told about her late husband, Vi Coleridge was bound to have some sage advice on dealing with this kind of shady affair. But would it really be prudent to involve a third party in agency business? She wasn't sure Harley would approve of such a breach of confidence. The whole thing was frightfully frustrating, especially as they seemed to be finally getting some progress in the Louise Parker case.

These musings were interrupted by a neat tapping on the frosted glass of the office door.

She folded away the newspaper and went to open it.

'Wotcha, Bunty!' chirped Alfie Budge, as though they'd known each other for years.

'Alfred. Do come in.'

'Much obliged,' he said, doffing his pancake cap with the usual little flourish of elbows. 'So, I got the message you left with the tobacconist. Sounded urgent.' Budge gave the office a once-over. 'No Mr Aitch?'

'No, he's not here at the moment. Actually, you wouldn't happen to have seen him around, yesterday or this morning, would you?'

'No, I ain't. Nothing amiss, I hope?'

'Oh, it's probably nothing. I've been left a little in the dark, you see – Mr Harley is pursuing a line of enquiry he insists is far too dangerous for a poor, defenceless girl such as myself.'

The street urchin gave a little sniff and a shrug. 'George usually knows what's o'clock. If he reckons it's a bit hairy, then it probably is.'

'That's all very well. But if he thinks I'm going to just sit here, dusting the aspidistras until he deigns to return, he's got another thing coming. We've got a missing girl out there somewhere, whose family are no doubt sick with worry. I, for one, am going to do everything in my power to try to find her for them.'

'Well, that's very spirited of you, I must say,' said Budge, a little taken aback. 'But it's going to be tough working this sherlock lay on your own, what with you being new in town.'

'That's where you come in, Alfred,' she said, pulling on her coat and checking her hat in the mirror. 'I'm taking you up on your offer to act as my cicerone.'

'Come again, miss?'

'My personal guide. Don't you remember? All that local knowledge you offered to impart? We're off to a public house.'

'Oh, yes? Any one in particular?'

Bunty consulted her notebook. 'The Joseph Grimaldi. Off Rathbone Place. Do you know of it?'

'Can't say as I've ever been inside, but I know where it is.'

'Capital! Oh, hang on. Are you allowed inside public houses?'

Budge deflected this insult to his street credentials with a convulsive parry of his elbows and knees. ''Course I am! What d'you take me for? Some kind of milksop?'

'Jolly good. Off we go then!'

A few moments later, as Bunty was locking the street door, Budge's keen eye was drawn to a sleeping vagrant, huddled in a doorway on the opposite side of the street.

'Look at that milestone-monger.'

'Sorry?'

'That tramp over there. See, I know most of 'em round these parts, but I don't recognise this fella.'

'Another poor soul down on his luck,' said Bunty. 'A sign of the times, I'm afraid. There's an army of young men just like him, in the prime of their life, forced to sleep rough. No work and no obvious prospects of it, either. It's a crying shame our government seems so ineffectual in coming up with a solution.'

'This one's a bit odd though, ain't he? I mean, look – he's clean-shaven, for one thing.'

'Well, we don't know his story, do we? He may have only just lost his job, poor fellow. Anyway, come on, it's rude to stare. We've got a job to do. Rathbone Place – lead on.'

'Yes, madam. How d'you want me? Fast trot, or a canter?'

'That's quite enough of your sarcasm, thank you, Alfred,' said Bunty, heading smartly up the road behind him.

The vagrant in the doorway opposite now stirred from his grubby nest of blankets. Once he was satisfied a sufficient gap had been established, he set off, stealthily shadowing the pair of trainee detectives from the opposite side of the street.

* * *

'So,' said Budge, looking around at the collection of lunchtime drinkers filling the saloon bar of the Joseph Grimaldi pub. 'What's this judy's name again?'

'Ilse Blau. But remember, she's using the pseudonym *Astarte*.'

'She drinks in this boozer, does she, this Fritz?'

'I'm not sure about that. But I believe she performs at a private club located in the basement.'

'And she's the missing showgirl we're after?'

'No. That's Louise Parker. Though we think she's using the stage name Tallulah.'

'Clear as mud.' Budge removed his cap to scratch at his head. 'Why ain't we just looking for this Tallulah, then?'

'Well, my theory is that, as the star of the show, Astarte should be far easier to track down. She's quite an extraordinary character, by all accounts – not easily missed. So, if we can locate her, hopefully she'll lead us to Louise. D'you see?'

'Think I've got it.' Budge nodded towards the bar. 'As you're in charge of this secret mission, am I right in thinking you'll be standing the drinks?'

Bunty removed her gloves and began to rummage through her handbag. 'I suppose I could manage a couple of ginger beers. Would you mind, awfully?' She held out a few coins for him.

'Ginger beer?'

'You're far too young to be drinking alcohol, Alfred. I know George seems to think it acceptable, but in my opinion,

220

one shouldn't really drink on the job anyway.'

'Strewth!' Budge gave a sigh. 'Alright. I'll get the ginger beers in, and you start asking around after that German hoofer.'

As he stood waiting to be served, gazing longingly at the foaming pints being passed over the counter, Budge felt a light tap on the shoulder.

'Boots! Well, I never! How are you, pal?'

Boots Naylor – who was of a similar age to Budge and cut from a similar cloth – gave a quick rub of his shabby footwear on the back of each calf – a nervous tic which had earned him his little epithet.

'Mustn't grumble, Squib, mustn't grumble. Yourself? Still working for that shark, Sonny Gables?'

'Oh, Sonny ain't so bad, not when you get to know him.'

'Get out of it! He'd steal the pennies off a dead man's eyes, that one.' Naylor grinned, revealing two rabbity front teeth. 'But enough of old Sonny. How are you off for stock?'

Naylor hoisted a tattered suitcase onto the bar and sprang the two catches with a well-practised flick of the thumbs. He opened the case to reveal a row of colourful neckties, hanging from the inside of the lid.

'Need any stranglers? Hot off the boat, this lot. Apparently, they're all wearing these out in Hollywood this season.'

'Bit loud, ain't they? My customers have a bit more of a refined taste, Boots.'

'Refined? Alright, take the kettle off the hob for a moment. Here you go, have a butcher's at these… Silk cami-knickers, all the way from gay Paree. Luxury item, that.'

'Gay Paree? More like the Caledonian Road. And that ain't silk, neither.'

'Alfie Budge. You're a hard man to please, and no mistake. But, seeing as you're an old pal…' Naylor gestured for Budge to move in a little closer and then lifted a false bottom in the suitcase, revealing a collection of pornographic magazines.

'How's about a little light reading? And trust me, these *are* French.'

'Lummie!' exclaimed Budge, with a little spontaneous flick of the elbow.

Naylor began to demonstrate his wares by flicking slowly through one of the illicit publications. It was just as he'd reached an image of an attractive blonde, who had somehow got herself into a rather compromising position with a Catholic priest, that Budge remembered he hadn't arrived at the pub alone. He looked over to where he'd left Bunty.

'Strong, ain't they?' said Naylor. 'You can knock these out for five bob a go, you know. I'll let you have a dozen for— Squib? Hey! Where you off to, son?!'

But having just caught sight of a distressed Bunty Chatterton being manhandled through a side door by a couple of dangerous-looking toughs, Budge had forgotten all about the tempting merchandise in Boots Naylor's suitcase.

* * *

'You brute!' exclaimed Bunty, as Irvine clamped her arm tight behind her back in the side alley by the pub. 'I know who you are, you know.'

'Is that right?' The thick Glaswegian brogue purred uncomfortably close to her ear. 'It's a pity your boyfriend's nae here to look after you today, Blondie. Does he know you're snooping around here, asking your nosy questions? Did you never hear curiosity killed the cat?'

He gestured to his sidekick, a lanky individual with a gaunt face plagued by a rash of acne.

'Go and start the car, Woody. I think we'll have a wee bit of fun with this one.'

Woody flashed a row of grey, tombstone teeth and then lumbered off towards a black Humber saloon, which stood waiting at the end of the passageway.

'You won't get away with this,' said Bunty, continuing to struggle. 'I didn't come here on my own, you know.'

'Aye, we saw. Your wee brother, is it? Does his mammy know he's out?'

Irvine whipped out a cut-throat razor, pressing the cold blade against Bunty's cheek.

'I dinnae think that squirt's gonna help you out of this spot of bother, do you?'

'I wouldn't count on it!'

Irvine turned to discover little Alfie Budge standing in the alleyway, brandishing a broken beer bottle and trying desperately to calm the nervous twitching of his elbows.

'You'll end up getting hurt, sonny, playing with sharp things like that.'

Budge took a tentative step forward. 'Why don't you let the lady go, pal? After all, the punters back there in the boozer, they all saw you leaving with her. If...' He swallowed awkwardly, trying to moisten his dry mouth. 'If something happens to her, there'll be witnesses.'

'Oh, I don't think so, wee man. See, this pub's my turf. All those folk in there know just what a nasty old bastard I am. They wouldnae dare cross me.'

'Let her go,' continued Budge, queasy with fear now. 'You might not believe it, but... but I happen to be acquainted with Mori Adler. He won't be best pleased when he finds out you've been throwing your weight around on his manor.'

'The Jew-boy? I'm nae scared of him. You can tell him what you like. Now, I've enjoyed our wee chat, son, but me and my pal there have got a spree planned with your sister. So, you best run off home, eh? Woody, get her into the car.'

'Halt!'

This latest challenge hadn't come from the plucky cockney sparrow, but from a figure who had suddenly appeared from behind the parked Humber; someone who Budge immediately recognised as the derelict he'd seen sleeping in the doorway back in Frith Street.

'Christ on a bike!' exclaimed Irvine. 'What we got here?'

'Do as I say,' continued the tramp.

Budge's keen ear caught the hint of a foreign accent in the newcomer's voice. *A Yiddisher boy, maybe?*

'Let her go and we will all walk away from this safely.'

No… more like German. What was a bleedin' Fritz tramp doing riding to their rescue, like Gary Cooper?

'This jakey's wrang in the head, Woody,' said Irvine. 'Get Blondie in the car and I'll deal with the both of 'em.'

But before the sidekick could carry out this instruction, the mysterious tramp had produced a pistol from his shabby jacket.

'Easy, pal,' said Irvine, suddenly more willing to take the stranger seriously. 'That's a gallus move, there, right enough. You sure you're prepared to use that thing?'

'Be quiet now… You! Let the lady go.'

'Boss?' Woody appealed to Irvine, his lugubrious face in a state of acned confusion.

'Let her go. Now!' barked the stranger, then calmly pumped a round into the tyre of the Humber's back wheel.

The explosive discharge in the small alleyway made Budge yelp and drop his bottle, and even had Irvine ducking instinctively for cover.

The vagrant held out a hand to Bunty. She hesitated for a moment, then pulled herself free from Woody's grasp to join him.

'Young man?' he said, gesturing to Budge to follow suit.

'Careful now,' said Budge, thrusting his hands in the air like he'd seen in the movies. 'I'm one of the good guys.'

As he crept past Irvine to join Bunty and their mystery rescuer, Budge happened to glance back at the pub, and what he caught sight of there sparked an additional shock to his already overwrought nervous system. Looking out from a top-floor window, transfixed by the scene unravelling below, was a small child with closely cropped hair and tears glistening on its grubby cheeks. Looming behind this child was a sinister figure, bearing a startling resemblance to Joseph Grimaldi, as depicted on the eponymous pub sign suspended a few feet below the window; though in that image, the pantomime clown was portrayed with a friendly, if mischievous, demeanour – whereas the uncanny greasepaint mask of the clown in the window was of a far more grotesque and terrifying nature.

Not quite believing his own eyes, Budge turned to Bunty, shaking her arm to grab her attention. But when he looked back to the window, the child and the clown had vanished.

There was no time, however, to ponder further on this disturbing little scene, as the mysterious tramp now began to slowly advance on the two mobsters, his pistol held out steadily before him.

'Gentlemen, please discard any weapons you may have and then turn to face the wall behind you.'

'I dinnae think you know what you're getting yourself into here, pal,' said Irvine, brandishing his cut-throat razor.

'Do it now, please. Or I shall be forced to shoot you.'

This last instruction was delivered with such an air of professional confidence that Irvine's sidekick withdrew his own razor from his pocket and tossed it to the ground.

'Better do what he says, boss.'

But the Scotsman wasn't ready to yield. With a malevolent grin he took a step towards his adversary.

'Let's see what you're made of.'

The tense face-off was suddenly curtailed by the distinctive sound of a Metropolitan Police car's bell, approaching from a nearby street – a sound which produced a Pavlovian response in the two gangsters, who promptly dashed back into the side door of the pub. A similar reaction was triggered in the streetwise Budge.

He grabbed at Bunty's hand.

'That's the bogeys, miss! We need to scarper. I can't afford to have me collar felt.'

Bunty looked to their rescuer.

'Yes,' he said, pocketing his gun. 'We should all go.'

He gave her a curt nod and then was away himself, sprinting to the end of the alleyway, where he disappeared through a wooden door leading to a dishevelled-looking back yard.

For the next few minutes, Bunty did her best to keep up with the fleeing Budge, as he scampered away through the back streets of Fitzrovia. Before long she found herself tumbling out of a narrow side street into the throng of shoppers on Oxford Street.

'Stop running now, miss,' said Budge, thrusting his cap into his pocket and removing his jacket. 'Don't make yourself look too obvious. Take your hat and coat off, in case someone clocked us. We'll go down into the tube. If someone's reported there's shooters involved, the heavy mob will be onto it – the Sweeney. Believe me, you don't want to mix it with those fellas.'

Five minutes later they were travelling down the escalators in Tottenham Court Road Underground Station, with Budge keeping a wary eye out behind them for anyone following.

'Blimey!' he said, wiping the sweat from his forehead. 'Talk about a guardian angel. You realise that was the same bloke we saw kipping in that doorway in Frith Street? I told you there was something weird about him, didn't I? You ever seen him before?'

'Never.'

'Hold on!' exclaimed Budge, suddenly grabbing at her arm.

'What is it? Are we being followed?!'

'No – sorry, it's not that. I've just remembered – the clown. Did you see him?'

'Clown?'

'At the window. With the little kid?'

'I'm afraid I have no idea what you're talking about, Alfred.'

'Up in one of the rooms above the pub. All made up with greasepaint, he was, like some villain in a pantomime. Creepy as hell. And the kid looked dead scared to me. Urghh…' Budge gave a little involuntary shudder. 'Gives me the collywobbles just thinking about it. I've always had a thing about clowns.'

'Well,' said Bunty, reaching into her handbag for her compact, 'I'm not exactly sure what's going on at that place, but there's little doubt in my mind they have something to hide. Something that warrants further investigation.'

'That may be true… but do me a favour, will you, miss? Get Mr Aitch back on board as your partner. I'm done with this sherlocking lark – it ain't good for the heart. Tramps with shooters? Lunatic jocks? Nightmare clowns? No thank you very much! I'd rather deal with the likes of Sonny Gables and Mori the Hat, any day.'

And as if to validate this sentiment, Alfie Budge delivered a little nervous flurry of the elbows.

23

FRANK ROSCOE WIPED the beery foam from his top lip and contemplated his recent change of luck. Things certainly did look rosier on a full stomach, that was for sure. To think, just a few days ago he'd been seriously contemplating packing it all in for a stint of tramping on the George Robey! He gave a little chuckle to himself. Not now, though. Now Frankie Boy was properly in clover – for the first time in his life.

He patted his breast pocket, just to reassure himself it wasn't all just a crazy dream. No, there it was: an indisputably thick wad packing out his wallet. Fifty nicker! Minus the price of a plateful of Irish stew and a couple of pints of wallop, of course. Now all that was needed was to bowl over to the Twelve Ten club, square his debt with Mori Adler, find himself some new digs, and then put his feet up for a few days while he worked out what to do with the rest of the dough. Which would be, what? Oh, about thirty-five quid, after he'd set himself up with a new suit, and had a couple of decent nights on the spree.

Thirty-five quid!

He gave a little whistle and took another celebratory slurp of his pint.

It was as he was checking the pub clock that Roscoe caught sight of a familiar face at the bar. Trevor Heggerty was a well-respected stable lad who'd worked for a succession of the more prosperous racehorse trainers in the South-East. The lad was a likeable character in his own right; but it was his access to first-rate inside knowledge on the horses which held the attraction for Roscoe. And so, over the last couple of years, the wide-boy had put the effort in to nurture this acquaintance.

The odd thing was, he couldn't ever remember seeing Heggerty in the capital before. In fact, he was sure the country boy had stated categorically, on more than one occasion, that he had an aversion to the bright lights of the city, preferring instead the pastoral delights of the Sussex downs. A Saturday night in Brighton was about the limit of his excitement. So, what had brought him up to London? Obviously something important, because Heggerty was looking decidedly nervous, sipping half-heartedly at his pint as he eyed his fellow drinkers with the usual fear and suspicion of a hayseed in the Smoke.

Roscoe was just about to call Heggerty over when he noticed another familiar face entering the pub, someone whose appearance offered a likely explanation for the stable lad's sojourn to London. He watched with growing interest as 'Honest' Joe Cox – one of the South-East's more successful turf accountants – approached the bar, perched on the stool adjacent to Heggerty, ordered a drink, and then walked out again without drinking it. Behaviour that may have appeared odd to the casual onlooker, but not to Roscoe, who was in no doubt at all about the contents of the bookie's folded copy of the *Sporting Life*, which Heggerty was now self-consciously stuffing into the inside pocket of his raincoat.

So, our boy Heggerty was on the take, was he? Well, well, well! Quite a result. After all, if a bookmaker of Cox's stature was greasing the palm of a stable lad, it could only mean one thing – a sure-fire bet. Not just a juicy tip, but evidence that a race was about to be rigged. A dead cert. Stone ginger. And having witnessed the clandestine transaction, Roscoe knew there was a good chance he'd be able to worm his way into the action. And not just for hush money. With a stake of thirty-five quid, spread across a number of bookies, with the right kind of odds… well, that would be a serious flock of dough: a life-changing amount. And why stop at thirty-five nicker? Why not chuck the whole lot on it? After all, it was well known that this type of bribe was only made just before the race in question, so that had to mean it was at one of tomorrow's meets. All he need do was tap Heggerty up for the name of the winner, get down to the racecourse in time to spread the bet judiciously, and then sit back and watch his ship come in – not forgetting to avoid any of Mori the Hat's heavies in the meantime, of course. But how difficult could that be? Half a day of lying low? Why, he might even go so far as to add a little interest when he finally repaid the debt, as a gesture of goodwill. And who knew? With the kind of money he'd have lining his pocket by then, the opportunity might arise to do a little business with Adler himself. A little investment in one of the mob's entertainment establishments, say, or involvement with their import and export lark. Yes, Mori was bound to turn a blind eye to him being a couple of days late if it meant he was going earn out of it; after all, wasn't he first and foremost a businessman?

'Trevor,' said Roscoe, placing a hand on Heggerty's shoulder at the bar. 'Sorry, pal. Didn't mean to startle you.'

'That's alright, Frankie. No harm done.' Heggerty pulled out a handkerchief to mop at the spilt beer on his shirt. 'What a coincidence, seeing you here.'

'You're looking a touch milky there, Trev. Not up to no good, I hope?'

'What d'you mean, up to no good?'

'You just look a bit pale, is all. Maybe you're coming down with something, eh? So, what brings you to this fair city of ours, then? I thought you preferred it out in the sticks.'

'I, erm…' Heggerty glanced nervously at his watch. 'Listen, Frank, I'd love to chat. But I'm here to visit a sick relative, see. I only stopped off for a quick one. I'd better be going. Visiting hours, and all that.'

'Sick relative?'

'That's right. My aunt. Might have to operate, apparently.'

'Oh, yes. Your aunt, is it? I see.' Roscoe gave a nonchalant sniff and inspected his fingernails. 'And what about Joe Cox, then? Is he coming along to the hospital with you? Just nipped out to get a bunch of grapes, has he?'

'What?' Heggerty now looked decidedly queasy. 'Oh Christ! You won't say anything, will you? I mean, I'll lose my job if they find out. Or worse. It's the first time I've ever done anything like this, I swear it is.'

'Say anything? What d'you take me for?' Roscoe looked suitably affronted. 'I'm no nark.'

'Oh God, no! I didn't mean that—'

'No, I should think not. The very idea. Now, let's all calm down a bit and have a drink, shall we? What's your poison?'

'Thanks all the same, Frank, but I really should be going.'

'Get out of it. What's the rush? We both know there's no sick aunt to be visiting. What there is…' The wide-boy glanced over his shoulder to make sure no one was listening. '…is Honest Joe's bunce wrapped up in that newspaper in your pocket. I must say, I had you down as a civilian, honest-as-the-day's-long type.' Roscoe tugged at the wings of his bow tie. 'Didn't imagine you'd be involved in this kind of chicanery. If I'm honest, I'm a little shocked.'

'You've got to believe me – it's the first and the last time. I swear it!' Heggerty slumped down on the bar stool, looking like he was on the verge of tears. 'I need the money, you see.'

'What is it, son?' said Roscoe, adopting a conciliatory tone. 'Got yourself into a bit of bother with the gambling?'

Heggerty nodded.

'Yes, well, you always were a bit of a mug for the cards, weren't you? What did you do, borrow a lump to try to win it back? Now you're chasing your own tail. Is that it?'

'That's it exactly. It's going up by the week.'

Roscoe tutted and shook his head. 'A common mistake with your amateur. Still, if you do this number for Honest Joe, everything'll be squared, right?'

'I bloody hope so.'

Roscoe now leant in to whisper into the groom's ear. 'So, what we talking here? A bit of gingering up the arse, or a nobble?'

'A nobble,' whispered Heggerty.

'I see. And I take it that once the favourite has stopped halfway around the track to take his forty winks, Coxy has a rank outsider ready to take everyone by surprise, yes?'

'That's about the size of it.'

'Righto,' said Roscoe, rubbing his hands together. 'I'd say this is a chance for us all to have a nice little touch, wouldn't you?'

* * *

At two o'clock the following afternoon, Roscoe was comfortably ensconced in the grandstand at Brighton racecourse. To his great relief, he'd managed to avoid any encounter with Mori Adler's boys, and now, having placed a selection of large bets on Spicer's Life in the two o'clock with various bookmakers around the course, all that was left to do was to sit back and soak up the atmosphere, while he waited for the race to start.

Spicer's Life. That just had to be a good omen, didn't it? His mother's maiden name? On a horse that was about to make him his fortune? Yes, after all the madness, all the gloom and doom, here, finally, was something that made sense. No dismembered corpses in suitcases here. No kidnapped kiddies. Just a day at the gee-gees – his world, something he understood.

Roscoe closed his eyes and savoured the little flutter of anticipation in his gut; it felt like the kiss of the first gulp of booze on an empty stomach. This was living, alright. The fleets of charabancs parked out by the gates. The expectant hubbub from the stand. The tic-tac men with their white gloves and binoculars. The seething mass of spectators, made merry with excitement and alcohol – all the judies in their finery; the sharply dressed men chewing on cigars; the excited factory workers, determined to wring every last drop of entertainment from their works' beano.

Look at those mugs, he chuckled to himself, watching the groups of punters milling around the bookies' pitches, waiting eagerly as the odds were chalked up on the boards, placing their little tuppenny-ha'penny bets. If only they knew. Roscoe fingered the wad of betting slips in his pocket, reassuring himself they were still there.

Over at the starting line he could see the runners had begun to gather, some of the thoroughbreds tossing their heads nervously as they approached the tape. Only a few minutes to go now, a few more moments of anxious anticipation before Frankie Boy was finally on velvet for life.

As the bookies dealt with the last flurry of bets, the crowd turned their attention to the track, with groups of spectators pushing eagerly up against the whitewashed barriers. Soon they were under starter's orders. Roscoe leant forward onto the edge of his seat, slipping a fresh matchstick into the side of his mouth. Just five furlongs to sit through and he'd be collecting the biggest win of his life. He felt like a kid on Christmas Eve.

Hello, what's all this? he thought, seeing a small group of uniformed police pushing their way through the crowd. One of the razor gangs raising Cain again, no doubt.

He glanced anxiously back at the starting line – but was reassured to see the starter was about to get proceedings under way.

There we go! They're off!

Roscoe stretched his neck to see above the animated couple in front of him.

He followed the tightly grouped runners as they made their way towards the grandstand. Alright, mate, take it easy, don't make it look too obvious now… There we go, that's the way… But don't hold her back too much… He frowned as the field thundered past the grandstand, with his horse second from last and the favourite already a good few lengths out in front – surely they were leaving it a bit late? After all, it was only a sprint; there was just a third of the race left to run.

Roscoe now became aware of a scuffle breaking out in the crowd ahead of him. Standing up to get a better view, he discovered the disturbance was coming from one of the bookies' pitches. It appeared the small group of bobbies he'd seen earlier were now doing their best to arrest a bookmaker, but were experiencing a good deal of resistance from his entourage, including two burly individuals who looked like they were no strangers to the inside of a police station.

With a creeping realisation of what might be playing out before him, Roscoe read with horror the sign above the pitch of the unfortunate bookie: 'Honest Joe Cox'.

Roscoe's brain was suddenly awhirl with a series of disastrous scenarios as he felt the flutter of excitement in his gut beginning to sour into something far more unpalatable.

He glanced back at the track, just as the first horse was thundering across the finish line…

It was the favourite.

The horse that was supposed to have been nobbled by Heggerty.

He watched in disbelief as Spicer's Life – the nag on which he'd just bet more money than he'd ever had before in his life – sauntered home in last place.

Just before the full gut-wrenching nausea overcame him, Roscoe experienced a strange moment of calm. After all, if he'd given it any real thought, it would have been obvious this would be the outcome: standing there once again, with just a few coins in his pocket, not knowing where the next meal was coming from, having just squandered the biggest opportunity of his miserable loser's existence. This, after all, was the natural order of things.

Then the wave of despair broke. He collapsed into his seat, his head in his hands, and began a low wail of misery. As he paused for breath in this wallow of self-pity, he felt an iron-like grip on his shoulder.

'R-R-Roscoe?'

The wide-boy opened his eyes to Benny Whelks' unwholesome countenance.

'What's up, Frankie?' said Big Terry Lampton, grinning as he loomed over Whelks' shoulder. 'Had a bit of bad luck?'

'Now listen, fellas,' said Roscoe, his mouth engaging automatically as he scrambled to make sense of this additional shock. 'I was going to come around to see Mr Adler yesterday, honest I was. Only, see, what happened was—'

'Schtum!' barked Whelks, flashing the briefest glint of his razor from inside his jacket. 'You n-n-need to come with us, now. It's time to p-p-pay up.'

'I can't, Benny. I've lost everything.' By way of demonstration, Roscoe pulled out the wad of betting slips and let the wind take them from his hand.

The chiv-man fixed him with his cold shark stare. 'There's more than one way to s-s-settle a debt, F-F-Frankie.'

'Please, Benny! Just a few more days. I'm begging you!'

Whelks shook his head slowly, then stood aside to allow the rangy Lampton through to extricate his victim.

As he was being manhandled down the steps of the grandstand, with the groups of spectators parting eagerly to allow the dangerous-looking mobsters room to pass, Roscoe happened to look over to the track, where the results board was being hauled up via the pulley system.

The first four places were displayed in a vertical stack, and as he gazed at these wooden panels, he was suddenly reminded of a scene from his childhood – the display of hymn numbers on a rare visit to church, while attending the funeral of a distant uncle. And in that instant, on what felt for all the world like a final walk to the scaffold, Frank Roscoe was filled with the same terrifying dread of oblivion he'd felt back then, contemplating for the first time the brief mortality of the runners in life's handicap sweepstake.

This stark realisation of his imminent fate acted upon Roscoe's nervous system like a cattle prod, awakening in him the last vestige of his wide-boy's survival instinct. Without pausing to think twice about what he was doing, he twisted quickly at the waist and swung back an elbow, clipping Whelks in the groin. With a little nervous yelp, he then heaved with all his might against the broad back of Big Lampton, who was walking ahead of him down the grandstand steps. Lampton went over like a felled tree. Seizing the moment, Roscoe launched himself over the prostrate hard man and flung himself headlong into the heaving mass of spectators gathered at the trackside. Then he was off, pelting along as fast as he could, barging his way through the crowd, oblivious to the insults and blows he received on the way. With the adrenaline pushing his heart to a sickening pace, he fought his way out into an open space where he was able to increase the speed, sprinting now around the broad curve of the parade ring and out into the parking area.

As his feet hit the gravel of the main driveway, Roscoe risked a glance behind him.

No one there… No one there!

He could see the entrance gates up ahead of him, and beyond them, freedom.

He bent double, panting heavily, his hands on his hips and tears of relief streaming down his face.

'I've fucking done it! Where are you now, you shicers, eh? Make a mug out of Frankie Boy? Never! I'm here to stay! D'you hear me? Here to stay!'

It was at that moment – as he bellowed his ersatz victory hurrah to the heavens, oblivious of his surroundings – that the seven-and-a-half-ton motorised horsebox ploughed into Frank Roscoe from behind.

The driver hadn't stood a chance – pulling out of the parking bays there was no need to look to his right, it was a one-way exit, and anyway, the wide-boy stood well below his line of sight in the raised cab.

He heard the thump of the collision, though, that was for sure. As he stood on the brakes and jumped out of his seat, the driver began to run through a silent litany in his head, praying he hadn't hit a child. He stopped praying at the first sight of Roscoe's crumpled body, turning instead to lean against the side of the truck and heave up the remains of his fried breakfast.

Inside the horsebox, the thoroughbred, made jittery by the emergency stop, snickered loudly and kicked out against the back door of the truck, dislodging the plate which bore the horse's name; a name which – if he were still alive – Frank Roscoe might well have found a little portentous: Little Orphan Annie.

24

H ARLEY SAT AT his kitchen table, with a steaming mug of sweet tea and a thick slice of buttered toast before him. It had gone two by the time he'd got cleaned up and hit the sack. Then it had been an age before he'd finally dropped off to sleep – hardly surprising following all that excitement at the museum. And, of course, he'd been visited by the usual nightmares.

Still, he had to admit, the gods had certainly been smiling down on him recently; albeit gods with an ironic sense of humour, seeing as they'd sent that she-devil to save his skin again.

As she'd promised, Oona had successfully led him out of the clutches of the Flying Squad to safety, via the labyrinthine basements of the British Museum, then through a bulkhead door leading to the London sewer system. They'd parted company at a junction a few hundred yards into the dank, noisome tunnels. She'd directed him to take the right-hand fork, and then navigate his way to the nearest access ladder and wait an hour for things to cool down before making his exit. As she'd just saved him from getting arrested – and was still in possession of that silver revolver of hers – he'd felt obliged to comply. The last he'd seen of her, she was wading off into the forbidding gloom of the left-hand sewer tunnel.

Of course, it had been no walk in the park to stay down there in the cold and dark, with the excrement of the good people of Bloomsbury swilling around his feet. But it was nothing compared to that night he'd endured in '17, trapped in a crater in no man's land, the howitzers ripping the sky apart above his head, with just his Lee-Enfield rifle and the legless torso of Corporal Jimmy Miller for company. Compared to that horror, it had been a breeze. Even if the smell kept reminding him of that fateful night with Whispers at Beckton Sewage Works.

An hour later he'd emerged through a manhole cover in Brunswick Square. He'd walked the rest of the way home, eager to rid himself of some of the stench from the sewer. Once he'd arrived at Bell Street, he'd hidden himself in a doorway and kept his own front door under surveillance for over half an hour. Of course, it wasn't nearly long enough to be completely certain the coast was clear, but he'd seen no evidence of any uninvited guests – either from the Met or other, more nefarious, quarters – and by then he really did need to get out of those disgusting trousers.

He took a sip of tea and let his eyelids close for a moment.

Immediately it was there again: that malevolent hypnotic stare, leering down at him from the gallery skylight.

Harley jerked himself awake with a yell, ricking his neck and spilling some of his tea.

The bastard!

There could be no doubt about it now – Morkens had definitely managed to escape somehow from the confines of Broadmoor Asylum. He really needed to alert Scotland Yard as soon as possible, get them to initiate a manhunt. Although she'd obviously been under the influence of some kind of hypnotic state, the librarian, Joyce Pendleton, had made it all too clear the Nursery Butcher was planning more of his despicable acts against children. It was paramount he was apprehended as soon as possible.

The trouble was, Harley couldn't be absolutely certain he hadn't been spotted there at the museum. Who was to say he wasn't himself currently at the top of the Yard's most-wanted list? If he just nonchalantly sauntered into Vine Street Police Station, he could well be condemning himself to a long stretch in prison.

Just as he was sparking up a Gold Flake to help ponder this predicament, Harley's heart kicked in his chest at a shockingly loud and confident *rat-a-tat-tat* on the front door knocker.

Immediately charged with adrenaline, he sprang over to the kitchen window to check for bogeys encamped in the back yard – which would be a sure sign he was about to get lumbered.

But all looked clear outside.

He took a moment to compose himself and then made his way into the hallway… where he was a little alarmed to make out – for the second time that week – the distinctive outline of a bobby's helmet, this time through the obscured Muranese glass of his own front door.

Maybe the gods had turned their back on him, after all?

Harley guessed the copper on the doorstep would have already seen the movement in the hallway. There was nothing else for it. He took a deep breath and opened the door.

'George! You're in. I tried earlier, got no reply.'

Harley gave a little sigh of relief. It was the local beat bobby – and as constables went, Percy Burns was about as chummy as they came. Nevertheless, he still made a quick, surreptitious check behind the policeman, just to make certain he wasn't acting as the beard for a CID raid.

'Sorry, I must have been out cold. Had a late one… You well, Perce?'

'Mustn't grumble.'

'What is it, then? I'm not in some kind of schtuk, I hope?'

The PC chuckled amiably. 'No, nothing like that, George. I'm here to give you a message from Vine Street. John's lad – DS Franklin – wondered whether you could pop round there. Says he's got some important news for you; about some case you're working on.'

'Sounds promising. But I'm just finishing my breakfast. You got time for a cuppa?'

'Don't mind if I do,' said Burns, unstrapping his helmet and following Harley into the kitchen.

* * *

DS Alec Franklin decided it would be prudent at this stage to close his office door, to prevent his colleagues overhearing his conversation with Harley, which had taken a rather disconcerting turn.

'But look, George, we've been over this already. It couldn't have been Morkens. I checked, remember? He's still safely under lock and key in Broadmoor.'

'But you didn't go there in person, though, did you? You didn't see the shicer actually in his cell? Because I'm telling you it was definitely him.'

Franklin dragged his hand through his hair and sat back down behind his desk. 'Alright then… Euston Station, you said; busy, was it?'

Harley obviously couldn't admit to Franklin that he'd actually seen Osbert Morkens at the British Museum, but he figured Euston would be close enough.

'Fairly busy.'

'And your view of Morkens was from across the concourse? Was anyone else there with you to witness this?'

'No. And I know what this sounds like, but it was him, I tell you.'

'But how can you be so sure? After all, there must be hundreds, if not thousands of sixtyish, balding gents in London with a white goatee beard. And… Well, the thing is… With the way Cynthia passed…'

The young policeman paused for a moment, doodling nervously on his blotter, trying to choose his words carefully. 'What I mean is, the condition you found her in… Well, who wouldn't be affected by such a thing, George? It's only natural that you might have become a little… What I'm trying to say is, it's perfectly natural if you've found yourself obsessing a little about the professor.'

'Obsessing?!'

Harley stood up and squashed his cigarette in the ashtray. 'Right! Get them on the blower again.'

'Who?'

'The asylum, of course. I've got some specific questions for them.'

'Come on, now! You don't really expect me to just drop everything and—'

But the policeman's protestations were interrupted by the trill of the telephone.

'DS Franklin… Yes, that's right… Really? And the address?' He scribbled down some details. 'Righto. Thank you.'

Franklin tore off the page from his notepad. 'Listen, forget about Morkens for a moment.'

'How can I? I'm obsessed, remember?'

'Please, George! This is important. That missing person you're working on – the lead in Seven Dials? You were asking about that Glaswegian tough?'

'You got something on him?'

'Not him, the place.'

'The Sunny Side?'

'Yes. It seems they had a bit of excitement at the boarding house last night. A suicide, by all accounts.'

'Alright. You've got my attention. Who?'

'The landlord.' Pearson consulted his notes. 'One Walter Smethwick.'

'Well, that's a bit of a coincidence.'

'There's more. You see, while CID were searching the premises, it seems they made a rather gruesome discovery. Human remains. Female. Probably in her twenties. Dark hair, cut in a severe bob. It looks like we might have found your missing dancer for you... Or what's left of her, anyway.'

'What are we standing around here for, then?' Harley grabbed his hat from the desk. 'Let's get over there, pronterino.'

'Hold on. I'm not so sure that's a good idea.'

'What? You said it yourself – the haircut, the boarding house: it's got to be Louise Parker.'

'I know, but... You see, they found the girl inside a suitcase.'

'Poor kid... And?'

'They didn't find all of the girl inside the case.' Franklin hesitated, avoiding eye contact by rearranging some of the papers on his desk. 'I thought it might, you know, bring back some bad memories.'

Having donned his hat, Harley now pushed it back an inch or so – an indication to those who knew him well that he was somewhat vexed.

'Get your coat, Alec. And stop treating me like some sodding milksop.'

* * *

'Thank you, Constable. If you'd give us a moment.'

Franklin held a handkerchief to his nose as he peered into the open suitcase. He turned to Harley, who was studying the photograph of Louise Parker.

'What do you think?'

'It's our girl, alright. Poor old Bunty will be upset.'

Oh Christ, Bunty! thought Harley, realising he hadn't seen her since he'd stormed out of the Bag O'Nails on the way to the museum.

'Bunty?'

'My assistant. Actually, I'll give her a bell in a minute and get the details of the girl's family for you.'

'Thanks, that'll be helpful.'

Harley moved in to get a clearer view of the young woman's decaying head and feet, neatly packed into the gingham-lined case. 'It's weird, ain't it? When you get over the initial shock, there's a kind of gruesome fascination about it. Like some uncanny doll.'

'Well, I, for one, wouldn't want to look at it for a second more than I have to,' said Franklin, giving the private detective a puzzled look. He was aware of the severe depression Harley had suffered following his fiancée's brutal murder and decapitation, and couldn't imagine what disturbing memories the situation might be provoking. 'Come away now, George.'

They squeezed past the police photographer dismantling his apparatus in Smethwick's basement apartment and made their way out through the French windows into the Sunny Side's dismal little back yard, where a trio of bobbies in their shirtsleeves were busy upending the heavy flagstones.

'You know, I don't think you'll find the rest of her out here,' said Harley.

'Why do you say that?'

'Well, you put stuff in a suitcase to move it, right? And you don't have to be Bernard Spilsbury to work out that those particular cuts of meat aren't the freshest. So, if she was butchered here, at the Sunny Side, how come the suitcase is still around?'

'Maybe Smethwick hadn't had a chance to get rid of it yet?'

Harley shook his head. 'Unlikely. Walking down the

road with a suitcase, in an area chock-a-block with boarding houses? Not exactly suspicious behaviour, is it? Anyway, who's to say Smethwick's our killer?'

'It seems the likeliest conclusion. The case was found in his flat, and there's his suicide to take into account.'

'What do you mean?'

'Well, you've seen all those empty bottles in the kitchen. It's evident the fellow had taken to drink. My guess is it was guilt that drove him to it. In his cups, maudlin, overcome with remorse at what he'd done to that poor girl, he staggers up to the top floor and throws himself out of the window.'

'And the head and feet? Why cut them off?'

'So the body couldn't be identified?'

'What, by her feet? And why then just leave them lying around the gaff? No. It doesn't make any sense.'

The policeman stood and pondered this for a moment. 'Well, I have to admit, I don't have an answer for that one at the moment.'

'Nor do I… Let's have a look at the attic, shall we? That's where he went out of the window, right?'

'There's no need for that. They've already given it a comprehensive search. If there was anything worthwhile up there, we would have—'

But Harley was already back in the house.

Franklin hurried in after him. 'Wait up, George! This is Met business now!'

'If you are coming up there with me,' shouted Harley from the hallway, 'make sure you grab a couple of them Wootton lamps from the bobbies.'

* * *

Harley pointed to the constellation of motes wafting around in the patrol lamp's beam. 'I like dust – dust tells stories.'

He directed the light to the floor of the attic by their feet.

'Here, for example, is where a herd of service issue size nines came traipsing in to stomp all over any evidence that might have been there. Luckily, it seems all your inspired CID colleagues did was climb up the ladder, walk over to the window, scratch their crusts for a bit, and then clamber back down again. What they didn't do was venture any further in.'

He swung the torch beam along the rough floorboards, highlighting a distinct trail of footprints leading off into the gloom.

'Over there, for example.'

'But it looks like somebody else certainly did,' said Franklin.

'Smooth sole. No heel. Could be Smethwick's,' said Harley. 'He was in his slippers when he jumped, wasn't he? See how they lead all the way across to the window?'

The policeman nodded, following Harley's beam of light as it picked out the direction of the trail.

'What about this, here?' asked Franklin. 'I'd say that's a child's foot, wouldn't you?'

'Yeah. And barefoot at that... and there's another cluster of them, over there, in the corner.'

'A frightful place for a kid, up here in the dark.'

'Look, there!' Harley switched off the Wootton lamp and pointed to an area that had been cleared of the boxes and old tea chests which littered the rest of the attic.

Franklin peered into the gloom. 'I don't follow.'

'Wait a bit. Let your eyes adjust... There – see that bright spot of light, like a golden penny? I'd say that's a hole through the ceiling. And Smethwick's tracks lead right up to it.'

'What's below it, d'you think?'

Harley made his way carefully across to the point of light and got down on his knees to put his eye to the hole.

'The communal bathroom. Spyhole. Looks like our land-lord might have been a bit of a peeping Tom.'

'Do you think maybe someone caught him at it? There was some kind of a struggle and Smethwick ended up being pitched out of the window?'

'Unlikely. And the tracks certainly wouldn't suggest it.' Harley turned the torch back on and made a sweep of the area. 'Hold on...'

He plucked at something sticking up from between the joists at the edge of the narrow walkway.

'Look at this.' He held up a small woollen blanket. 'Property of Stockwell Green Orphanage,' he read, shining the lamp at the label sewn into the edge. 'Clean. No dust on it. Can't have been here very long.'

'Orphanage? That's odd. Not an obvious fit with the Sunny Side's clientele.'

'Does Smethwick have kids?' asked Harley. 'I saw some stuff downstairs in his basement flat.'

'Did have: a daughter. Deceased, sadly. Unfortunate case. She died in the throes of an asthmatic seizure. There were some rumours of neglect, apparently. Nothing ever proven. Broke up the marriage, though, by all accounts.'

'Well then, I'd say you need to contact this Stockwell Green Orphanage as soon as you can, Alec. See if any of their kids have gone missing.'

'Missing? What makes you say that?'

'Morkens.'

Franklin shook his head and turned to climb back down through the hatch.

Harley clasped a hand on the policeman's shoulder. 'Hear me out on this one.'

'But he's been under lock and key,' said Franklin, 'in the secure wing of an asylum for the last four years. How could he possibly be involved in the murder of your missing dancer?'

'Well, that's just it. I'm now not so sure any of this has actually been about Louise Parker.'

'What? We've just discovered the butchered remains of an innocent young woman down there. If it's not about that poor soul, then what is it about?'

'This!' Harley held up the blanket. 'Orphanage kids. Dismembered bodies. This has got Osbert soddin' Morkens written all over it. You mark my words – that shicer's planning something.'

'Based on what evidence, exactly?'

But, of course, Harley couldn't tell Franklin about the message he'd been given by the spellbound librarian at the British Museum; of how Morkens might now be modelling himself on the ancient Ammonite god, Moloch, a deity once synonymous with ritual sacrifice of children. Or about the child-killer's plan to capture fresh, innocent victims, as part of some perverted punishment for Harley's hubris.

'There's no evidence, is there? Listen, you've been a great help here today, George, but I'm afraid this is a CID case now. You're going to have to let us take over from here.'

'The other day you told me you'd be forever in my debt for what I did for your old man on the Nursery Butcher case.'

'And I meant it.'

'Well then, I'm calling in that debt. I'm telling you Osbert Morkens has escaped. And, what's more, he's about to lay fucking siege to the innocents of this city again. So, DS Franklin, you and I are going to take a trip to Broadmoor Lunatic Asylum. If we get there and find that shicer safely under lock and key, I swear you won't hear another peep out of me. But if he has gone over the wall, then you're going to do all you can to convince your oppos at Scotland Yard to get that monster back into custody, before he kills again.'

25

'AND WHAT, EXACTLY, is this?' exclaimed Bunty, holding up the front page of the *Daily Oracle*, featuring the shooting at the British Museum.

She had ambushed Harley as soon as he'd stepped into the office, and the emotional quiver in her voice, matched with a slightly manic glint in her eye, suggested he'd have to handle things tactfully.

'I know how it must look, Bunty, but believe me, I had nothing to do with that shooting.'

'I should jolly well hope not! But why on earth didn't you let me know you were alright? I've been beside myself with worry.'

'I'm sorry. I got caught up in something afterwards; something at the Sunny Side.'

'My immediate thought was that you'd been injured in some way,' continued Bunty, interrupting him, her cheeks flaring. 'Or worse! But then, when I read the story, and there was no mention of you... well, I began to think you might have been arrested, and they'd held back the information from the press. I wanted to get hold of that policeman chum of yours, at Vine Street.'

'Franklin? Please tell me you didn't do that. I told you – no police, remember?'

'Remember? How could I forget? You practically screamed it in my face in front of the whole pub. And no, I didn't go to the police, Solly persuaded me not to.'

Good boy, Sol! thought Harley.

'Yeah, I'm sorry about that. I was out of line. But I was worried about you. Thought I might be putting you in danger.'

'I don't think I was the one in danger. What on earth happened there, at the museum?'

'It was a trap,' he said, a little sheepishly. 'Like you said it would be… Morkens was there.'

'It was really him?'

'I'm certain of it. I was lucky to get out of there in one piece.'

Having built up a decent head of steam, Bunty now puffed up her cheeks and gave a long, exasperated huff.

'Oh, George… You told the police, of course?'

'Kind of. I told Franklin I'd seen Morkens at Euston Station. I couldn't admit to being at the museum, in case I got lumbered for the shooting of that nightwatchman.'

'I see… And did he believe you?'

'No. But I got him to agree to make a visit with me to Broadmoor, to prove it one way or another. We're going tomorrow.'

'Is that wise, do you think? After… well, after what happened to Cynthia. Are you ready to confront that foul creature again?'

Harley was perplexed to discover he couldn't immediately answer this. He managed a half-hearted shrug.

'I really was concerned about you, you know, George. Charging off to confront that lunatic on your own like that. You might have let me know sooner you were safe.'

'I didn't know you cared,' he said, a smile breaking on his face. 'Listen, I won't let it happen again. I promise.'

'Thank you.'

A blush rose on her pale neck as she stood there, smoothing out the creases in her skirt.

'But remember,' said Harley, breaking the awkward silence, 'you mustn't ever tell anyone I was at the museum that night, got it?'

Bunty held up a three-fingered salute.

'Guide's honour!'

'Alright. I'll take that. So, Miss Chatterton, can I now take off my coat?'

'Of course. I'll put the kettle on in a moment, but listen, I had a nice chap telephone me from Vine Street Police Station, wanting the contact details for the Parkers. You mentioned something about the boarding house. Have they found her?'

'Ah...'

Harley pictured the grim contents of that shabby suitcase, lying among the clutter on the kitchen table in Walter Smethwick's apartment.

'I'm not sure you'll want to hear all the grisly details.'

'Really, George! You've left me completely in the dark here, gallivanting off on your own. I've been beside myself with worry. The least you can do is furnish me with all the details of the case, grisly or otherwise. I am supposed to be your assistant, after all.'

'Alright! Alright! Get that tea on the go and I'll fill you in. But I warn you – it's not nice and cosy like one of those Agatha Christies. You might need a nip of brandy in your cuppa. There's a bottle in the bottom drawer of the filing cabinet.'

Ten minutes later, having described in explicit detail the recent events at the Sunny Side Boarding House, Harley watched his assistant sit back in the office chair with a slightly queasy look on her face.

'I think I'll have a little more of that brandy, George,' she said, pushing her teacup across the desk. 'Only a smidgen, though. And might I have one of your cigarettes?'

'Blimey, that bad, eh? I didn't know you smoked,' said Harley, tossing her the yellow Gold Flake packet.

'Only on special occasions.'

'Go easy on that, it's not one of your fancy cork-tipped jobs.'

'Thank you,' she said, coughing a little as she emerged from behind a small cloud of smoke. 'That poor girl. Her parents will be devastated, of course. To think of one's child meeting such a fate. Her poor mother. How have they taken it?'

'Well, that's the weird thing. According to Franklin, they were a bit surprised by the news, by all accounts.'

'I should jolly well imagine they were.' Bunty took another tentative pull on the Gold Flake, then held it out at arm's length, so as not to get the smoke in her eyes.

'No. What I mean is, the Parkers were surprised to hear about their daughter's death because she had already died from diphtheria, at the age of five. Ten years ago. It turns out the Louise Parker we were searching for didn't exist. That character posing as her father sent us out on a wild goose chase. The likeness he showed us wasn't Louise Parker at all.'

'But he paid us good money, didn't he? Why on earth would someone go to such lengths, just for some kind of practical joke.'

'Oh, this is no joke,' said Harley, splashing more brandy into his own cup. 'I've been mulling it over. See, I reckon our Mr Parker, whoever he is, wanted us to find a missing person alright. But the person he really wants us to track down is Ilse Blau. Remember how he steered us down that path from the very start?'

'But why not just engage our services to find her in the first place? Why all the subterfuge with the Parker girl, or Tallulah, or whoever she really is?'

'Was.'

'Gosh! Yes – was.'

'I'm not sure. But my guess is that this Ilse Blau, or Astarte, character is mixed up in something far heavier than just a missing persons case. I think whoever is after her has been using us as a shield, utilising my inside knowledge of the seedier parts of this fair city to get in close to her, undetected.'

'According to Alfred, your friend Lil knows Blau. Have you had a chance to visit her yet?'

'Not yet. It got a bit forgotten in all the excitement.'

'Well, I think we should jolly well get over there as soon as possible, don't you? I mean, if what you say is true about Blau being the main focus of things now.'

'Have you forgotten that animal Morkens is out there somewhere? Running around, scot-free. I think you'll find that's the main focus now.'

'Surely you need to leave him to the authorities, George.'

'That's what I did last time and look how that turned out. If they'd hanged that monster in the first place, rather than deeming him unfit for trial, then he wouldn't have… Well, things would have worked out differently.'

Harley swigged down the brandy and got up to walk over to the window. He stood for a moment, silently contemplating the passers-by in the street below, massaging the back of his neck.

'You look awfully tired,' said Bunty. 'Would you like me to go to Limehouse for you? You can't have had much sleep over the past few days, what with everything that's been going on.'

'No, I'll be alright. But listen – Morkens and Blau? Maybe we can investigate both things at the same time.'

'How do you mean?'

'Well, I think there's a strong possibility the professor is messed up in this business at Sunny Side somehow. I told you about that blanket we found in the attic, right? Franklin had it checked out, and after a little reticence at first, the orphanage finally admitted they had lost one of their wards. A little deaf girl, six years old.' Harley consulted his notebook. 'Poppy Chandler. Went missing a few days ago. By all accounts they wanted to complete their own internal investigation before handing it over to the authorities. The matron on duty at the time reported seeing a suspicious character on the premises and believes the little girl was kidnapped out of her bed.'

'And they didn't call the police?'

'Probably weren't too bothered, were they? Could be seen as one less mouth to feed.'

'Don't be so cruel, George!'

'I'm not being cruel, I'm being realistic. It doesn't help to get too emotionally attached in this game.'

'Hold on!' exclaimed Bunty. She thought for a moment, nibbling the end of her thumb. 'When Alfred and I were at the Joseph Grimaldi pub, he swore he saw a small child in one of the upstairs windows. He said the child looked like they were there under duress. He couldn't be sure whether it was a boy or girl, because the hair had been shorn so close, you see.'

'Whoah!' said Harley, with his hand up. 'What do you mean, *when you and Alfred were at the Joseph Grimaldi*?'

'Ah, yes… of course, you don't know about our little run-in with that Scottish brute and his friend, do you?'

'Run-in? With that san toy? Please don't tell me you went snooping around there on your own.'

'I wasn't on my own,' she said, a little peevishly. 'I had Alfred with me.'

Harley came back to the desk, spun his chair around and sat on it back to front.

'Right, Miss Chatterton. You're going to sit there and tell me every single thing that happened from start to finish. Everything, mind!'

26

'I MUST SAY, THIS is most irregular,' said the principal attendant, as he led them down the dismal corridor of the secure wing. 'We usually have a few days' notice for such an interview.'

'We obviously appreciate you accommodating us at such short notice, Mr Johnson,' said Franklin. 'As I mentioned on the telephone – we're investigating a murder enquiry which has a possible link to a child abduction. Given the professor's history... Well, we have a few questions for him.'

'Has he been displaying any unusual behaviour recently?' asked Harley. 'Anything out of character?'

Johnson stopped walking and pulled out his snuffbox. 'Funny you should say that,' he said, after helping himself to a generous pinch. 'We did have an incident with one of the night staff a few weeks back.'

'Incident?'

'Unfortunate business. Chap called Smythe. Poor fellow was prone to bouts of melancholia, you understand. Ended up taking his own life.'

'Here, at work?' asked Franklin.

'Oh, no. He was off duty at the time.'

'So, what's that got to do with Morkens?' asked Harley.

'Well, just a rumour really. There was some talk among the staff that Smythe had developed a rather inappropriate relationship with the professor. Nothing was ever substantiated, of course.'

'Inappropriate? You mean sexual?'

'Good Lord, no!' exclaimed Johnson, punctuating this with an energetic sneeze into a tobacco-stained handkerchief. 'No, the suggestion was the professor had managed to attain some kind of influence over the fellow. But as I say, nothing was ever proven. Other than that, I'd say he is a model patient. Always obedient and courteous in my experience. Not surprising really, given the man's pedigree.'

'Oh yeah, he's a real gent, is Osbert Morkens.'

'Recently he's even managed to win over Mr Bullen,' continued the attendant, oblivious to Harley's sarcasm. 'No mean feat, I can assure you – Bullen is one of our more disciplinarian members of staff. A little overzealous at times, if truth be told. Hard chap to please. However, it would seem he has nothing but good words for our professor… You know, in a strange way, I wish all of our patients were more like Osbert Morkens.'

Johnson proceeded to trumpet loudly into his handkerchief, masking Harley's foul-mouthed response to this observation.

'Right then. Shall we proceed, gentlemen?'

The attendant turned to the steel-enforced door, flipped open the observation plate and bent down to peer into the cell.

He gave a little amused chuckle.

'Well, I suppose that's the way with these academic types. Looks like the old fellow has fallen asleep at his desk again, poring over his studies.'

'You allow him his books in here? Like he's on some kind of jolly?'

'Broadmoor is an institution of cure and rehabilitation, Mr Harley,' said Johnson, wagging an admonishing finger. 'Not a place of punishment. We leave that to other establishments.'

'Of course,' said Harley, faking a charming smile. 'I'm sorry, sir, would you mind if I just…?'

The attendant moved aside to allow Harley access to the observation window.

'Jesus!' he exclaimed loudly, jumping back from the door. 'Open it up!'

'I'm sorry?' said Johnson, trying to push the private detective aside to take another look. 'I really must insist that I—'

'Open the bloody door, man! Do it! *Now!*'

The startled attendant began fumbling with the large key ring attached to his belt.

'Got your shooter, Alec?'

'No. Why?'

Harley pointed to the door. 'Whoever's in there at that desk, it ain't Morkens.'

'Ridiculous! I… I,' stammered the befuddled Johnson.

'It ain't Morkens, I tell you! And he ain't sleeping, either.'

Having finally identified the correct key, the ashen-faced attendant unlocked the cell door with a trembling hand.

'Careful,' said Harley, grabbing him by the shoulder. 'I think there's someone else in there with him.'

* * *

'Christ, what a mess,' said Franklin, regarding the foul sludge of vomit and blood splattered across the open books on the small deal table.

'Have a smell of that,' said Harley, offering up a small hip flask he'd found on the floor. 'Go easy though, don't put it right up to your nose.'

'Pretty pungent. Some kind of acid?'

'Spirits of Salt is my guess. It would have eaten through his insides in seconds.'

'Good grief! That's horrible.' Franklin looked at the figure slumped forward on the table. 'Who is this, then?'

'I don't know. But it's obvious who he's meant to be: the shaved head, bleached goatee beard. He's roughly the same height and weight… though a bit younger, I'd say. It's pretty obvious this poor sod was employed to imitate Morkens.'

'Do you think this is who you saw, at Euston Station?'

'No. I think that was the old goat himself. I reckon this bloke was being smuggled in here whenever Morkens fancied a trip outside.'

'In collusion with the staff?'

'Yeah. Specifically our friend over there.'

Harley nodded to where a male nurse was attending to the warder, Bullen, who sat huddled in the corner of the cell, cradling his knees and rocking back and forth.

'Can we have a moment with him now, pal?'

'Alright,' said the nurse. 'But I'm not sure how much sense you'll get out of him. Could you help me get him up on the bed?'

Though he had quietened a little, Bullen's eyes were still wide and maniacal. Every so often he jerked his head around, as though he'd caught sight of something malevolent in the shadows.

As he approached the bed, Franklin noticed the large dark stain at the crotch of the warder's trousers. Johnson had intimated the man was something of a hard-nosed disciplinarian; what on earth could have reduced him to this state?

'I'm from the Metropolitan Police, Mr Bullen. Detective Sergeant Franklin.' He crouched down by the side of the bed. 'It's quite alright. You're perfectly safe now.'

Bullen's wild eyes snapped into focus. He fixed his stare on the policeman with a low, sinister chuckle.

'Safe?! How can I ever be safe? While he's in there.' He stabbed a finger against his temple. 'In there!'

'Alright, pal, calm down,' said Harley, adopting a harsher tone than his colleague. 'What happened here, Bullen? Who is this poor sod with his guts all burnt out?'

'It's not important. He's a nobody.'

'I'd like to think we're all important to somebody. Do the right thing. Give us a name, so his family can be contacted.'

Bullen moaned and rubbed the heel of his hand in his eye. 'Eric Stoker. He drinks in my local.'

'And I'm guessing you chose poor old Eric here because he bore a bit of a resemblance to that shicer Morkens, right? Smuggled him in here at night and allowed that maniac to go roaming free out there, among the public. What did you do it all for, eh? A few shekels?'

'You couldn't understand… I had no choice.'

'What do you mean?' asked Franklin.

'The professor. He gets into your head.' Bullen risked a quick, frightened glance at the corpse slumped across the table. 'Makes you do things.'

'You mean he made this fellow drink the acid himself?'

Bullen nodded, his eyes wide and terrified again. *'Finish your medicine,'* he murmured, in a low growl. *'There's a good boy. Drink it all up. Every… last… drop.'*

'Where is he now?' asked Harley.

There was no answer from Bullen, who had placed an arm across his face and had started to mumble incoherently.

Harley pushed Franklin aside, grabbing hold of the warder's jacket by the lapels. 'Where is he!?'

But all this elicited was a bout of jabbering, maniacal giggling.

'Alright. I think that's enough now, gentlemen,' said the nurse, approaching the bed with a charged syringe. 'Quiet now, there's a good fellow. Let's have another little dose, eh? Help you get some sleep.'

But before the additional sedative could be administered, Bullen leapt to his feet, thrusting the medic to one side. He gave a painful bellow. Lowered his head. And charged at the wall.

The collision with the thick stone produced a sickening thud. The bloodied man reeled back, dazed, but – to his obvious dismay – still conscious. With another anguished howl, he charged again.

By the time they had managed to restrain him, the white of Bullen's skull could be clearly seen, shining through the pulped flesh of his forehead.

'My God! What are we dealing with here, George?' asked Franklin, watching the crazed warder – now securely trussed up in a straitjacket – being extracted from the cell by a cohort of burly psychiatric nurses.

Harley tapped out a cigarette and sat on the edge of the low, metal-sprung bed frame. 'Osbert Agamemnon Morkens, that's what.' He sparked up and drew greedily on the smoke. 'I've been trying to tell you – he's a soddin' monster.'

'The thing I don't understand,' said Franklin, 'is why he'd suddenly blow his cover like this. He's had a perfectly good system running here, by the looks of it. The mimic taking his place here in the cell, leaving him free to slip out whenever he wants. Why ruin all that with such a brutal act; one that was guaranteed to be discovered within a few hours?'

'Because he doesn't need his little stand-in anymore, does he? My guess is he has absolutely no intention of returning to captivity. Ever. And he wants us to know it. This is a message… Probably intended for me.'

'Really? So what, exactly, is he saying?'

'What's he saying?' Harley exhaled a long plume of smoke. 'You'd better lock up your kiddies, 'cause Professor Morkens is coming out to play.'

27

'**H**ONESTLY, SIMEON, IS this really necessary?' asked Hugo Fitz Corbet, as Dubois led him blindfolded up the front steps of the suburban townhouse. 'Correct me if I'm wrong, but haven't I supplied the funds to set up this little bolthole for the Preceptor? It seems dashed unreasonable to keep the location secret from me.'

'As I've explained to you before, it's merely a precaution.' The dandy removed the silk scarf from Fitz Corbet's rubicund face. 'You must understand, the Preceptor is a powerful and gifted man. There are certain individuals out there who would be jealous of his potency and cautious of the effect his teachings might have on the masses.'

'Who, exactly?'

'Those who have a vested interest in maintaining the status quo.' Dubois paused to fit a Turkish cigarette into an elegant amber holder. 'As for your recent generous donations to the Order, as I have explained before, there are many others willing to step into your shoes should you wish to withdraw your funding. Remember – the day will soon come when the Order of the Thelemic Knights of the Unicursal is a dominant force in our society. Our Preceptor is the prophet of a new age. Most people of insight would consider themselves lucky to have the opportunity to invest in such a cause.'

Fitz Corbet blinked his piggy eyes, studying his old friend's inscrutable features.

'Very well,' he said with a sigh. 'But remember, you promised me this would be an extraordinary experience. I'm expecting thrills. I'm also expecting my promotion to Adeptus Minor in the not-too-distant future. I must say, this First Degree level stuff has been most disappointing – it would be more stimulating if I'd joined the Boy Scouts.'

'Please don't embarrass me by speaking like this in front of the Preceptor, Hugo. You're sounding like a spoilt child again. Now, come along. Our other guest will be waiting.'

'Other guest?' said Fitz Corbet, hurrying to follow Dubois down the elegant hallway. 'I thought it was to be a private audience.'

'And so it is – for both you and another of our important Zelators; a First Degree level, like yourself.'

Dubois opened the door to a sumptuously decorated room: vermilion flock walls, adorned with erotic prints, rococo sconce lamps and ormolu mirrors. On one side of an ornate fireplace stood a black lacquered harpsichord, the underside of its opened lid inlaid with delicate chinoiserie. On the opposite side of the room was a dining table, set for four, and beyond that a handsome bookcase displaying shelves of books bound in green and mustard Moroccan calf skin. On the settee, enjoying his third glass of hock, sat the corpulent banker, Sir Rupert Heathley.

'Sir Rupert, may I present Hugo Fitz Corbet, the fifth Marquess of Clenham. Hugo, I believe you may have met Sir Rupert before.'

'Indeed he has,' said the banker, crushing Fitz Corbet's chubby little paw in a vigorous handshake. 'When he was still in knickerbockers. Knew your father well.'

'Yes, of course.'

'Quite a character, old Fitzy. Droll sense of humour. Decent shot as well, don't you know.' Seemingly satisfied with this potted history of Fitz Corbet's father, Heathley turned his attention back to his wine.

'Pour yourself a drink, Hugo,' said Dubois. 'I'll let the Preceptor know we're all here.'

'Are there no staff?' asked Fitz Corbet, looking a little bemused, as he sauntered over to the drinks cabinet. 'I thought we were dining.'

'We've kept it to a bare minimum, for confidentiality reasons,' explained Dubois, shooting his friend a cautionary look from the doorway. 'I'm sure you'll manage, just this once.'

Ten minutes later – during which time Sir Rupert had regaled his fellow guest with a rambling, and rather bawdy, account of a recent visit to the brothels of Budapest – Dubois returned to the room and busied himself with dimming the gas lamps.

'Please remain seated when he enters, gentlemen,' he said, lighting the candles on an elaborate Art Nouveau candelabrum which stood in pride of place in the middle of the dining table. 'And, of course, there's to be no physical contact, unless the Preceptor instigates it himself.'

Just then, three plaintive flute notes could be heard from the hallway outside. At this signal, Dubois took his position by the fireplace. The two guests turned their heads expectantly towards the door, which now opened, the gentle waft of air causing the candles to jitter momentarily, casting dancing shadows across the ceiling.

Osbert Morkens had altered somewhat since his escape from Broadmoor. The once silver-grey goatish tufts of eyebrow and saturnine beard were now dyed raven black. With a bold line of kohl to elongate the eyelids, and a lavish silk turban to cover his famous domed cranium, the ageing Oxford professor now resembled a Middle Eastern mystic; an effect which might have appeared a little vaudevillian, if it hadn't had been for the malevolent glint in the child-killer's pitch-dark eyes.

He paused in the doorway.

An expectant hush descended on the room.

'*Ave fratres*,' he said, sonorously.

Morkens gave the merest hint of a bow and then walked over to take his place at the head of the table.

'Won't you join me, gentlemen?' He smoothed the creases from the tablecloth on either side of his place setting. 'I'm sure we're all eager to partake of our repast.'

'Actually, Preceptor,' said Fitz Corbet, 'I should like the chance to pose a few questions first.' He frowned earnestly as he made his way over to the table. 'You see, I've been preparing for my advancement to the next degree for several months now. Of course, Simeon has been extremely helpful, but there are a few parts of the text I'd like clarifying. Take, for example, the—'

The aristocrat was shocked into silence by the professor as he growled and thumped the table with his fist.

'Sit!' he barked, the reflections of the candle flame dancing in the dark mirrors of his eyes.

Overcome by a nervous agitation he'd not experienced since his schooldays, Fitz Corbet hurriedly took take his seat.

'There we are,' purred Morkens, resuming his cunning smile. 'Now, listen to me carefully. The content of the Libri of the OTK – the wording of the rituals, the expounding of the laws, et cetera – is merely a conduit for the Will. Do you see? Your advancement through the ranks of the Order cannot simply rely on you learning your lines verbatim. You are not cramming for a viva here. It is elegant wisdom, not its brutish sibling knowledge, which is required. And wisdom comes with experience, not swotting. Do you understand?'

'Yes… I think so.'

'Very good,' said Morkens. He now turned his attention to the boorish Heathley, who'd been taking great delight in Fitz Corbet's dressing down.

'Sir Rupert, I trust you appreciate the difference?'

'Hmm? Oh yes, of course. Man of action. Always have been. No need to teach me about experience, sir. Experience is everything. It's the opportunity of encountering unique experiences that drew me to the Order in the first place.' The banker smoothed down his Kitchener moustache and inclined his head towards Morkens, lowering his voice to a conspiratorial whisper. 'Talking of which – Dubois here tells me we might be in for a little treat in the near future. *Une petite ingénue*, eh?'

Morkens exchanged a dark look with Dubois before producing a long-stemmed pipe from his robes. 'Sir Rupert, I wonder if you'd furnish me with a light?'

'Why, of course, old man,' said the banker, offering up his silver lighter.

Having ignited the plug of strangely coloured tobacco in the bowl of his pipe, the professor now blew a small cloud of its aromatic smoke into Heathley's face. This had an instant, stupefying effect, leaving Sir Rupert slumped in his chair, with a dazed, apoplectic look in his eyes.

At the sight of this assault, Fitz Corbet choked a little on his wine and began to appeal to Dubois; but his friend gave him a reassuring smile and gestured for him to hold his tongue.

Morkens adopted a languorous smile, seemingly satisfied with Heathley's reaction to the intoxicant. Then, with an exaggerated, theatrical flair, he conjured a small instrument from his sleeve – the same penny whistle, carved from bone, which he'd employed in the British Museum. He held the instrument to his lips and played a few bars of a doleful, enchanting melody.

'Mark it well, Heathley,' he murmured into the ear of his dazed victim. 'This is your motif.'

A loud snap of his fingers drew the banker to an upright position.

'Where are you now, would you say, Sir Rupert? Look around you. Tell us where you find yourself.'

'I'm...' But Heathley stopped himself abruptly, a look of intense panic on his face. His eyes began to scrutinise the walls and cciling, as if he were trying to make sense of some complex puzzle. 'But I don't understand... How could I...?'

'Do tell us,' murmured Morkens.

'Why, it's...'

'Yes?'

'Well, I'd swear it's the old wadi, at El Mughar... Hot, of course.' Heathley tugged at his tight collar and looked behind him, becoming increasingly unnerved. 'Damned hot!'

Still smiling, Morkens took up the salt cellar from the cruet set and began to pour a stream of salt into his upturned palm, close to Heathley's ear. 'And now, Heathley? Where are you now?'

The banker jolted in his seat; his look of puzzlement transformed to one of fear. He held a hand up to his face, warding off some invisible attack.

'Lost in the dunes, somewhere. Alone... Can't move... Bally sun! Burning! My face, eyelids, burning... Up to my chest... Buried... in the sand. Damned sand; never-ending. As far as the eye can see!'

Morkens leant across and let the salt spill from his hand.

'Yes. Never-ending. Each grain a life wasted, a soul squandered. The inestimable sum of man's folly. Millions after millions. A desert of mediocrity.'

He blew the last few grains from his palm.

'And now?'

At first Heathley was silent in his seat. But then there came a low sob from his corpulent frame. His protruding gut, clamped tight within its expensive waistcoat, juddered in small, rhythmic bursts.

'I... I...'

'Hmm? Do speak up, there's a good chap.' Morkens grinned spitefully as he cocked his head in anticipation of Heathley's answer.

'I am... nowhere. I am *gone!*'

A fat tear rolled down the banker's ruddy cheek, disappearing into the thicket of his walrus moustache.

'Yes,' nodded the professor. 'Gone. Another brief existence frittered away on capricious schoolboy fancies. Just one more grain now, among all the other billions, the trillions... Ah, well. When men know how to live, they will die no longer.'

Morkens sat back and clapped his hands. 'Enough! Awake!'

Heathley spluttered back to his senses, performing the embarrassed double-take of a man caught rubbernecking on a commuter train. 'Hmm? What?'

'You know, Dubois,' said the professor, pouring himself a glass of wine. 'I do believe I've worked up an appetite. Perhaps you might serve our dinner now?'

* * *

'So, Preceptor,' said Fitz Corbet, shovelling another spoonful of roast potatoes onto his plate. 'Might one ask...'

He paused. Though now emboldened a little by the wine, he was still wary of incurring the wrath of the strange mystic. Charismatic as the man might be, he obviously had a dangerous, and sadistic, side to him.

'Come now, Lord Clenham.' Morkens offered a reassuring smile. 'There's really no need to be so cautious. We'll have no more demonstrations… not this evening, anyway. Besides, it would be churlish of me to be so ungenerous to my host. Dubois tells me you are responsible for supplying us with this charming pied-à-terre. And that you've been a faithful sponsor of the Order over the last few months.'

'Well,' said Fitz Corbet, wiping a little gravy from his chubby chin. 'One does what one can. My question is about our little gathering here.'

'Ah, yes?'

'Well, as delightful as the food – and the company, of course – may be, I was expecting rather more of a…'

Fitz Corbet hesitated. Glancing up from his plate, he found the professor watching him with a chilling intensity, somewhat reminiscent of the stare of the Komodo dragons he'd once experienced on a visit to the Reptile House at London Zoo.

'…of a unique experience.'

'Unique?' repeated Morkens, raising one of his prominent eyebrows. 'And have you not found our sumptuous repast a unique experience?'

Much to Fitz Corbet's puzzlement, this comment was met with a flurry of titters from around the table.

'Well, I…' Deciding to bolster himself with another gulp of wine, he shot a quick look across the table at Dubois; it seemed there was to be no support from that quarter. 'Of course, your demonstration earlier was most intriguing.'

'But the food itself, Lord Clenham,' interrupted Morkens. 'This delicious cut of meat – do you not find this intriguing?'

'Well, I for one certainly do, Preceptor,' chipped in Heathley, still a little chastened from his earlier dalliance with Morkens' devilry. 'Just as you promised, Dubois – puts one in mind of a top-notch veal.'

'The meat?' asked the baffled Fitz Corbet. 'But I don't…'

It was then that he glanced around at the others' plates and noticed his fellow diners had, for the most part, eschewed the vegetable dishes and were applying themselves, with unusual concentration, to the pale, succulent meat.

'Perhaps another slice?' asked Morkens. 'Before you make up your mind?'

As the professor turned the serving plate towards him, Fitz Corbet caught sight of the familiar symbol, stamped into the skin of the roasted joint.

The Key of Solomon!

It was a sickening revelation.

'But… but that's the…'

'Indeed!' exclaimed Morkens, a thunderous look in his eye. 'A sacred unicursal. One you saw fit to brand upon the thigh of this common slut of yours.'

Fitz Corbet looked down at his plate with horror. 'You don't mean to say that this is… that we've been…'

'Eating Tallulah? Yes!' Morkens grinned and flicked his tongue across his sensuous lips. 'And wasn't she quite delicious?'

Fitz Corbet grabbed at his napkin and retched.

'Pull yourself together, man!' barked Dubois, pouring a glass of water for his friend.

'You knew, Simeon?'

'Of course I knew.'

The fifth Marquess of Clenham looked incredulously at his fellow diners, their lips slick with grease, then promptly gagged once more.

'Stop acting so childishly,' hissed Dubois. 'What's the matter with you? When you thought it was veal you were shovelling it down your throat like there was no tomorrow.'

'It's hardly the same, is it?' said Fitz Corbet, gulping at his water. Horrified, he glanced at the morsels of meat left on his plate, then hurriedly pushed the offending article away.

'Calm yourself,' instructed Morkens, adopting a more magisterial tone as he sat up and spread his willowy fingers on the tablecloth. 'Take a moment to think on it, to relish the thought… How many others alive today could lay claim to such an experience, hmm?'

'But it's horrific!' screeched Fitz Corbet, his face uncharacteristically pale and waxy. 'It's… it's against nature!'

'Against nature?' Morkens grabbed another slice of meat and pushed it into his mouth, sucking the fatty juices from his fingers. 'You disappoint me, Lord Clenham.'

In an instant the professor was up on his feet, a fierce intensity now burning in his eyes. 'Look at me, you snivelling fool! Look here!'

But Fitz Corbet continued to stare in horrified astonishment at the polished white head of the femur, protruding from the abhorrent joint of meat on the serving plate.

Having worked himself into a feverish rage, Morkens now leant across the table, pushing his cadaverous features close in to the aristocrat's face. *Against nature?!*' he screamed. 'And just what is the nature of Man, in your opinion? Do you know what he has become, in this civilised age of ours?'

Fitz Corbet began to gag again as he fumbled with his collar stud.

'No?' continued Morkens, flecking Fitz Corbet's now ghastly complexion with the froth of his spittle. 'I'll tell you, shall I? He's been shackled by his intellect; dragged, kicking and screaming, away from his sublime, bestial origins. In these so-called enlightened times, Man has been condemned to a miserable, embittered existence, in which he is eternally denied the fulfilment of his most basic desires; denied by an iron cage, wrought of petty laws and social mores. *That* is against nature, *my Lord!*'

With a swish of his silken robes, Morkens sat down again. The urbane dinner guest had returned, his tempestuous fury dissolving as quickly as it had appeared.

After a period of awkward silence, Heathley laid down his

knife and fork and, keeping his eyes fixed on the table, said, 'May I speak, Preceptor?'

'You have a question?'

'Indeed.' The banker risked a little eye contact. 'Are we, then, to believe that without such restrictions, without our laws of society, we might liberate our true nature?'

Morkens smiled serenely and poured himself some wine, then stood and went over to sit at the harpsichord.

'What is it that keeps a man from murdering his business rival, would you say? Or from bedding his neighbour's daughter...? Lord Clenham?'

Fitz Corbet looked pleadingly to his friend Dubois for assistance. But the dandy was avoiding eye contact.

'His conscience?' he offered.

Morkens shook his head. 'His *fear*; fear of punishment, of social castigation. His conscience is merely a construct of such fear.'

'But surely,' said Heathley, joining his hands across his prodigious belly, 'if one were to remove the rule of law... well, there'd be mayhem. Rioting in the streets. Anarchy.'

'Undoubtedly. But I'm not talking about freeing the whole of society of those laws; just the minds of a select few. Do you see? Therein lies the secret to our pathway.'

Morkens began to pick out a simple melody on the keyboard.

'Look at our so-called civilised Man. How has his intellect served him, would you say? What friend to Man is his reason...? No friend at all. His reason has become his gaoler and also the feeble light which illuminates his cell, bringing greater clarity to his suffering. And if the majority of that suffering stems from the frustration of his unattainable desires, and if those desires are rendered unattainable by his elevation and intellect, then...'

Morkens placed his left hand on the keyboard now, offering a subtle counterpoint to the melody.

'…shouldn't he become more like the beast? For, who among us, apart from the ascetic fool, would disagree that the sane goal of any existence is to avoid suffering? Look to the wolf – does he suffer? Well, perhaps, sometimes…' He turned his threatening stare once more on Fitz Corbet. 'But only when he lacks the prey to satisfy his needs.'

Feeling a little woozy from his recent shock, and with numerous glasses of wine beginning to take their effect, the aristocrat found the mournful song of the harpsichord and the cadence of Morkens' soliloquy combining to produce a mesmerising effect. He lowered his head onto his arms, closed his eyes… and found himself immediately plunged into a nightmare vision of a spiralling gaping maw, with vicious carnivorous fangs, drooling strings of bloodstained mucus.

With a boyish, soprano scream, Fitz Corbet jerked himself awake, gripping tightly at the arms of the chair while staring about him in confusion.

'What the…?!' He coughed and wiped the line of dribble from his chin.

'My, we are receptive, aren't we?' said Morkens, closing the lid on the harpsichord. 'Ready for a little more showgirl, Lord Clenham?'

The aristocrat pushed back his chair, the florid blush returning to his cheeks as he threw his napkin on the table.

'Keep away from me! What devilry have you got me into here, Simeon?'

'Careful, Hugo,' said Dubois, keeping one eye on Morkens. 'We don't want to upset our guest now, do we?'

'Upset him? Good Lord! That's rich. Please remember I'm the one bankrolling your little cannibal club, here.' He grappled with the silver cigarette box on the table, his chubby, childish hands shaking uncontrollably now. 'I'm sure it wouldn't take much for the authorities to trace this place back to me in some way. I'd be implicated in the whole sordid affair if it ever came out. I do have the family reputation to think of, you know. You hoodwinked me into this, with your outrageous promises.'

'Preceptor, I do apologise,' said Dubois, concerned to see Morkens getting up from the harpsichord. 'I think Lord Clenham has taken a little too much wine.'

'It's quite alright, Simeon,' said Morkens, removing the long-stemmed pipe from his robe as he approached the table. 'Our friend here is just a little overexcited. A common reaction, easily dealt with.'

'Overexcited?!' blustered Fitz Corbet. 'No! You keep away from me! Simeon! Do something!'

As the panicking Fitz Corbet turned to confront Morkens, he found himself engulfed in a pungent cloud from the mystic's pipe.

'Pass me a teaspoon, would you?' said the professor, easing back the head of the now unconscious Lord Clenham.

'Might I ask what you intend to do with him?' asked Dubois.

'There's no need to be overly concerned.' Morkens unscrewed the lid of the small jar he held, containing a bright green paste. 'There'll be no permanent damage. But I don't think our friend here is quite ready for the next stage yet, do you?'

Using the spoon, he smeared a little of the paste onto each of Fitz Corbet's temples.

'A tiresome individual… Still, this should keep him quiet for the evening. And in the morning, he won't be sure whether it wasn't all just an elaborate dream… There we are.'

He resumed his place at the head of the table.

'Now then, gentlemen. As enthralling as the delectable Tallulah may have been, consuming the roasted flesh of a common whore is, at best, merely an Epicurean experience. It's fine on the palate and the stomach. Indeed, it might even offer an admirable solution to the problem of birth control in the lower classes.'

This elicited a nervous chuckle from the banker.

'But it adds nothing to one's potency and nourishes the soul not one jot. For such mystical delicacies we must look to the occult masters for guidance. And there we find, in the teaching of such luminaries as Hermes Trismegistus and Eliphas Levi, the instructions for the consumption of innocents.'

Morkens paused to take in a deep breath, his eyes having suddenly acquired an avaricious lustre.

'An act which, if carried out following strict guidelines, can confer all manner of powerful qualities. Of course, this was once a well-known custom. It is no coincidence that our ancient folk tales are populated with hordes of powerful ogres and cunning witches, simply ravenous for the sweet flesh of children.'

Morkens sat forward with his elbows on the table, his long fingers arched before his face.

'Take the Catholic doctrine of transubstantiation. The faithful brethren believe, when they fall to their knees and poke out their tongues to receive that little wafer, that they are about to consume, not just a symbol, but the very flesh of that pale Nazarene; who, if he were to be believed, was the most innocent of innocents. And that through this act of cannibalism they might assume a little of his power.'

Heathley began a guarded response, but Morkens cut him off.

'*Whoever feeds on my flesh and drinks my blood has eternal life*, that was his claim, was it not? And who are we to scoff at such powerful magic, practised for centuries by a third of the world's population, hmm?'

Morkens got to his feet and walked over to an etching on the wall, depicting a priapic rake about to ravish his maid. He smiled lasciviously as he traced a long nail across the glass.

'And, of course, it's not just the Christians who believe in the power of consuming the flesh of innocents. In the Middle

Ages, Chinese eunuchs would kidnap and kill virgin boys to feast upon their brains, in order that they might imbibe the potency with which to grow back their shrivelled apparatus. And in English medieval apothecaries, one could purchase the grease rendered from a child's corpse, as a panacea against numerous diseases… Of course, such a powerful ingredient has many other, interesting applications.'

With a malevolent chuckle the professor waggled the pot of green ointment, before pocketing it again in his robes. He pointed to the unconscious Fitz Corbet.

'You see, the reason our little friend here was so disgusted by our repast is because he has allowed his intellect to guide his true nature. The ancient Gauls, the Aztecs, the Iroquois Indians, certain negro tribes of the Congo, the *Secte Rouge* in Haiti – for eons man has consumed the flesh of his fellow man, in order that he might take on another's power. And then, of course, there are those who refined the practice to a form of artistry: Vlad Tepes, Elizabeth Báthory, our exquisite baron, Gilles de Rais… true visionaries,' purred Morkens.

He returned to the table to spear one more slice of the pale flesh on his fork.

'But enough idle chatter. I shall now introduce you to our next offering, Heathley. Our own innocent, procured for the forthcoming ceremony. It'll give you something to look forward to until we meet again. Whet the appetite, so to speak… Simeon, if you would?'

Dubois smiled and left the room, returning after a short while with the little orphan, Poppy, clinging tightly to his hand.

'Come now, dear. Don't be shy in front of the nice gentlemen,' said Dubois, ushering her over to stand in front of the fireplace.

Poppy glanced nervously around the table. When she caught sight of the turbaned Morkens, she quickly dropped her gaze, clenching her nightgown tightly in her fists.

'Well now,' said the professor, walking over to place his hand on top of her head. 'Here she is. I trust your men have had strict instructions, Simeon? The maintenance of her purity is fundamental to the success of the ritual, you understand.'

'Of course, Preceptor,' said Dubois, with a nod of assurance.

'Yes,' continued Morkens, bending down to pinch Poppy's cheek. 'She's fattening up quite nicely, I'd say. After all, we need to make sure there's enough to go around, don't we?'

As she felt the deep reverberations of the laughter, the little deaf girl looked up – and was much alarmed to see the row of gaping, red, glistening mouths.

* * *

Later that evening, as Morkens sat at his dressing table, cleaning the kohl liner from his eyes with a cotton pad daubed in cold cream, there came a knock at his door.

'Come…! Ah! Dubois. Do sit down, I've something to discuss with you. Now then, your little cabaret star, Ilse Blau – what is it she's calling herself nowadays?'

'Astarte.'

'Of course; how fitting. You're aware that Fräulein Blau was an early member of our Berlin chapter?'

'Indeed, Preceptor. One of the reasons I sought her out in Paris was because of her history with the Order. She was one of the original members, I believe?'

The professor gave a little patronising smile. 'Oh, Ilse was of no real significance from an occult point of view; she's a hedonist at heart. Of course, she added to the aesthetic of the gatherings, helped draw in new, influential members. One of Fedor's little ornaments, you might say. But I've recently received a communication from Berlin about her, which is a little troubling, to say the least.'

'Really? In what way, exactly?'

'Fedor has informed me he has it on good authority that

the new German government has sent a cadre of secret agents to London to apprehend Ilse Blau.'

'Good Lord!' Dubois began to fiddle nervously with the signet ring on his little finger. 'I know Herr von Görlitz has close access to Himmler, but… well, do you think he might be mistaken? It all sounds rather incredible.'

'Well, apparently, there's some friction between the head of the intelligence service, Konrad Patzig, and Himmler, so, unfortunately, Fedor isn't privy to all the details at the moment; but fundamentally, he believes the intelligence to be reliable.'

Dubois thought for a moment, screwing one of his Turkish cigarettes into his amber holder.

'I've heard the National Socialists are keen to crack down on what they consider to be "decadent" artists, but I'm surprised they feel so strongly about it they'd send agents abroad to search them out.'

'Ah,' said Morkens, holding up a willowy finger, 'there's a little more to it than that, I'm afraid.'

The professor then recounted the story of the incendiary negatives of Hitler, which von Görlitz had entrusted to the Maltese pornographer, Victor Manduca, but which had disappeared in a police raid in Soho, some four years earlier.

'Fascinating!' said the dandy, tickled at being on the periphery of such international intrigue. 'Well, even though Astarte is one of the main attractions at the club, I realise these things can't last forever. If the Nazis really believe she's in possession of these negatives, I'd be happy to turn her over to them – if you think it would help the cause.'

Morkens sat for a moment, pulling contemplatively on his goatee beard.

'No… I think not. It's not beyond the bounds of possibility that Fedor informed them of the existence of the negatives in the first place. In my opinion, he's a little too enamoured of his new friends. Hitler may well become an important part of our grand scheme, but it might be prudent to keep our cards close to our chest for the time being. I want you to find out if Blau really does possess those negatives. We may want to use them ourselves in the future.'

'Of course, Preceptor. Consider it done.'

Dubois sat up in his chair, a serious expression on his face.

'Before I leave you, might I just discuss one more thing? About the upcoming ceremony?'

'I sincerely hope you're not about to spoil my evening, Dubois,' said Morkens, with a darkening look. 'I intend this ceremony to be a milestone in the history of the occult sciences in this country. I'm relying on you to make sure everything runs smoothly.'

The dandy gave a reassuringly obsequious smile.

'No, it's nothing like that. I can assure you all the preparations are in hand. It's just...' He paused a moment, smoothing down his pomaded beard as he decided on the most diplomatic way to phrase his concerns. After all, he had witnessed, at first hand, the cruel effects of the Preceptor's occult power.

'I just wonder whether it might be prudent to limit the size of the congregation. Perhaps just include the upper degrees? You see, the ritual you are honouring us with at this event is of such... well, such magnitude, that I fear it might be, erm... misconstrued by some of the newer members.'

'Too shocking for them, you mean?'

Dubois cleared his throat.

'Perhaps, Preceptor.'

The professor gave a long sigh and eased back into his chair.

'You must understand that, as well as the profound occult importance of the ritual, the ceremony will hold another valuable lesson for the congregation. You see, to be able to achieve the fundamental reorganisation of society which stands at the very heart our doctrine, we require the masses to become culturally desensitised to actions and behaviours they might currently regard as abhorrent. Through repetitive exposure to organised ritual based on such actions – actions which they were once taught were wicked and sinful – such things will become normalised. Banal. Only then can we expect the uncritical obedience needed for our revolution.'

Morkens smiled archly and leant in closer to the dandy, the globes of the gas lamps reflected in his dark pupils.

'Do you see, Dubois, how our cause might prosper from such banality of evil?'

28

'IS THERE A bus to Limehouse from here, George?' asked Bunty, as they emerged from Goodge Street Tube Station.

'No, I'll probably take the Norton. It could do with an outing, keep things ticking over.'

'Your motor car?'

'Motorcycle: a Norton CS1.'

'Really? I've always been intrigued with the idea of riding on a motorcycle. Do you take passengers, on the back?'

'It's a combination. There's a sidecar.'

'Well then,' said Bunty, looking down at her skirt. 'I shan't even have to change.'

'Listen. I was just about to say – you're not coming with me. Sorry.'

'What?'

Harley shrugged and set off up the road.

'Whyever not?' she said, rushing to catch up with him. 'If Lily Lee *is* friends with Ilse Blau, why, she might even be there this very minute.'

'Don't worry, I'll make sure I fill you in on everything when I get back. I need to do this alone, Bunty. I've some private business with Lil.'

He stopped walking and looked at her earnestly, placing a hand on her arm. 'Look, I'm sure, by now, Vi has told you about what happened to my fiancée?'

'Cynthia? Not everything. But yes, I think I know the basics. It sounds so… so ghastly.'

'Yeah. Well, Lily Lee? She's Cynthia's sister, see? And I haven't been to see her for ages. Not since the funeral.'

'Whyever not?'

'That's not something I want to discuss here.'

Harley began to walk away again, but she grabbed at his sleeve.

'Vi's right, you know.'

He sighed. 'About what?'

'This guilt you feel, for what happened to Cynthia. It's ridiculous, George.'

'Listen, you don't know the first thing about—'

'No, you listen for once! From what I've been told you did absolutely nothing wrong. After all, you helped bring that foul creature Morkens to justice. Just think of all those lives you saved. No one on earth could have predicted what would happen afterwards.'

'It'd be lovely to believe that, but it's not true. If I hadn't had—'

She put her finger to his lips.

'Shush! You're a good man, George Harley. I can see how you may have forgotten that in all the madness with Morkens…' She touched her fingers to his cheek now. '…but I'm sure Lily won't have forgotten.'

Good man? He conjured the image of Mr Whispers, handcuffed and pleading to him from the hold of the sludge vessel, those mollusc-like eyes blinking in terror, magnified through the lenses of the pebble-lensed spectacles.

Bunty smiled at him and straightened his tie.

'Now, if you're feeling awkward about meeting Lily after all this time, well, why don't I come along with you?'

'I don't think that's a good idea.'

'Why not?'

'I was engaged to her little sister, remember? I don't think Lil would take too kindly to me turning up out of the blue with an attractive young woman in tow, do you?'

'Attractive?' said Bunty, a little colour rising on her cheek.

'Alright, Miss Chatterton. Don't let it go to your head… Now, don't worry. If Ilse Blau is at Lil's, I'll get everything I can out of her, I promise. And if she isn't there, then I'll make sure that Lil gets us into the Grimaldi club somehow.'

He checked his watch. 'I think I'll shoot straight around to the lock-up and get the bike now. I shouldn't be longer than a couple of hours. Why don't you go back to the office and type up those notes for the case file? I'll be back before you know it.'

'No.'

'Sorry?'

'Quite frankly, George, after having to deal with your little disappearing act at the British Museum, I'm simply not prepared to go back to spend another few hours alone in that office, worried sick, not knowing if you're going to return in one piece or feature as a headline in tomorrow's newspapers. On top of that, after your comments the other day, with that killer Morkens now at large, I don't think I'd feel safe all alone in Frith Street. He obviously knows the address. No, I'm going with you to Limehouse. I shall wait outside in the sidecar if you don't think it appropriate for me to come in with you.'

Harley shook his head. 'I'm not having you hanging around the streets of Limehouse on your tod. It ain't exactly the safest of places.'

'Safer, I'll warrant, than being left alone in an office

registered to George Harley with that criminal lunatic Morkens on the warpath. That's what they call a sitting duck, I believe.'

Harley looked to the heavens and gave a little groan.

'Sod it! Come on then!'

'Where are we going now?' she said, setting off after him.

'To bloody Limehouse, of course.'

'That's the ticket! You won't regret it, you know.'

'I already am.'

* * *

Half an hour later they were motoring down the East India Dock Road, Harley astride the growling Norton CS1 and Bunty beside him, clasping tight to the sides of the sidecar and grimacing against the onslaught of the wind, her peaches-and-cream complexion masked by the ungainly leather cycle helmet and goggles.

As they drew up at a set of traffic lights, Harley glanced over his shoulder, to check if the green Daimler was still trailing him. The car had first drawn his attention as it drew up alongside them at Tower Hill – the way both occupants had so assiduously avoided his gaze had seemed a little odd. A quick minor detour, with the car following the Norton's every turn, had proved his suspicions beyond a doubt.

But who were they? Certainly not bogeys – CID wages didn't run to such expensive suits. And this was a Daimler Fifteen Coupé, a sports model, a calibre of vehicle not usually found in the Scotland Yard carpool. Maybe a couple of wide-boy heavies, associated with Dubois and the Glaswegian nut-cruncher? Whoever they were, by the time the lights had changed, Harley had decided he needed to shake them off before they got to Lil's.

* * *

Bunty looked up at the slightly neglected-looking shopfront they'd pulled up outside of.

'*Aida's Café?* I thought you said Lil lived above a Chinese restaurant.'

'So she does,' he said, helping her out of the sidecar. 'This is a little bit of evasive action. Don't look, but we've had some unwanted company for a while now. Two blokes in a green Daimler who look like they can handle themselves. Don't look, I said! Right. Listen. We'll stow our gear in the sidecar and then we're going to walk into the café, go straight behind the counter, through the kitchen and out into the back yard. Just follow my lead. Aida's an old mate; I'll tip her the wink, so we won't have any bother.'

'Gosh!' said Bunty, removing her goggles. 'Who on earth do you think they are?'

'I don't know, but they look like trouble,' said Harley, beginning to unstrap his leather helmet.

A few minutes later, having successfully executed the little evasive detour through the back of the café, Harley and Bunty were making their way through a neglected-looking alleyway, populated with small clusters of Malays and Chinese, huddled together, loitering against the brick walls and smoking in doorways. Bunty noticed that these men – some in pigtails and silk tunics, others in the everyday working garb of the Lascar – eyed them warily as they passed; one fellow even hawked a gobbet of pink betel nut juice into the gutter after them.

'Are you sure we're quite safe here, George?'

'No, I'm not. And I told you so, but you insisted on coming, remember?'

He noticed her face was ashen with worry.

'Look, don't fret too much,' he said, putting an arm around her shoulder and hurrying her on a little. 'We'll be alright, as long as we keep ourselves to ourselves. Lil's isn't too far now.'

Keeping a keen eye out for trouble, Harley continued to lead Bunty through the back streets of Limehouse. Interspersed with the more mundane shopfronts they passed – the ship's chandlers, newsagents and dingy bottle shops – were retailers of a more exotic nature: outlets for Chinese medicine, with serried rows of jars full of gnarled roots, dried fungi and multicoloured flower heads; grocers touting strange sweet cakes and ceramic pots of fiery stem ginger; and humble eating houses, their windows strung with the exotic bunting of mummified fish and golden-skinned ducks. The air here was redolent with the spiced promise of oriental delicacies, and every now and then, from a basement grate, could be detected the sweet, pungent aroma of the opium pipe – a perfume to which Harley himself was no stranger.

'Gosh! It's like we've been transported to another country,' said Bunty, stopping to study the Chinese Hanzi characters on some newssheets pasted onto the brick wall. 'Quite exhilarating once you get over the initial shock.'

'Alright, Dr Livingstone; stop dawdling there. We need to crack on.'

They continued to weave their way through the strange labyrinth of back alleys for a while, until, on emerging from a damp, narrow tunnel, Harley said, 'Here we are – this is Lil's place.'

There, before them, in all its scarlet-and-gilt finery, shining jewel-like among the dismal, smoke-blackened terraces, was the Lotus Blossom.

They approached the restaurant's entrance and Harley rapped sharply on the door. This drew the attention of a Chinese youth with a thatch of raven-black hair, who was busy laying tables inside.

'We close, mister! No eat yet – close!'

Harley gestured for him to approach the door.

'We close, mister! Go Tai Ling, round corner. Tai Ling,

good breakfast… You want to play puck-apu? Wong Chin, maybe he open.'

'No. I'm here to see Lil.'

'You want girl? Too early for girl, mister. You come back later. Girls sleepy now.'

'Listen, son. I don't want to eat. I don't want to play puck-apu. And I don't want a bleedin' girl. Alright? I'm here to see Lily Lee – you understand?'

'No, no,' said the waiter, beginning to walk away. 'She busy-busy. Too busy see you.'

'Are you sure we have the right place, George?'

Harley began thumping on the window.

'Oi!' he shouted. 'Open the sodding door, won'tcha?!'

Bunty pushed her face to the glass and peered into the dark interior of the restaurant. She could just make out another figure, looming in the background – a hulking individual, dressed in dirty chef's whites, who was now gesturing towards the window with the large meat cleaver he held tightly in his fist.

'Oh dear!' she said, taking a step back. 'I think we might be in for a spot of bother, George!'

29

Harley swore under his breath as he watched the enormous Chinese chef lumber over to the door. He really didn't have time for all this palaver; after all, if the two characters in the green Daimler were professionals, it wouldn't take them long to realise they'd been hoodwinked. And then there was Bunty – what on earth had possessed him to bring her along? The idea that she might be safer accompanying him to Lily Lee's, in the rough back streets of Limehouse, than sitting all warm and snug in his West End office… Christ! He must be losing his marbles!

Cursing again, he watched as the corpulent, sweaty face, sporting a thin mandarin moustache, pushed up against the glass.

He sighed… told Bunty to move to the corner of the street… stepped back a few paces… fitted his brass knuckles… and adopted a defensive stance.

The door burst open, the cleaver glinting in the morning sunlight.

'Fuck me!' exclaimed the chef, in a broad Cockney accent. 'George 'arley!'

'Quong?'

'Alright, I know I've put on a few pounds, but who were you expecting, Anna May Wong?' He turned to the young waiter and waved the large blade. 'I told you, silly bollocks – it's George!'

'Who George?' said the lad, keeping his eyes warily on the chopper dancing a few inches from his nose.

'You know, Cynthia's—' Quong stopped himself, sneaking a nervous look at Harley. And then, in order to deflect attention from his little faux pas, he delivered a sharp clip around the ear of his young colleague. 'What did I tell you? I told you to open the door, didn't I?' He curled his lip and repeated the assault. 'Come on, now. Chop-chop. Out of the man's way. He's tight with the boss… Come on in, George. And who's this?'

'Bunty, my assistant.'

'Come in, Bunty. Sorry about this one. I wouldn't mind, but he's been here three years now. Every day it's like he's just stepped off the bleedin' boat.'

'Thanks, Quong. Lil in, is she?'

'Yeah. Go on up. You know the way. I'll tell her you're here. She'll be chuffed to see you, after all this time.'

'Could Bunty stay down here with you? Maybe give her a taste of your delicious grub?'

'Of course! I'd love to.'

* * *

Harley sat waiting for Lil in her office above the restaurant. The opulence of the room jarred somewhat with the stark landscape framed by the window: a slate-coloured sky, punctuated by tottering smokestacks and the skeletal cranes of the Limehouse docks. He closed his eyes for a moment, the familiar surroundings having stirred memories which were never far from his mind's eye.

'Hello, George.'

'Lil! Sorry, I was miles away.'

He clasped her hand, with its exquisitely painted nails. 'Blimey! Look at you – all togged up, and it ain't even lunchtime yet.'

Lil gave a slow, theatrical twirl, showing off the figure-hugging emerald dress of finest Huzhou silk. Her lustrous dark hair was piled into an elaborate bun and set off with a beautiful jade headpiece. From her costume, she might have stepped straight out of one of the decorative oriental scrolls which lined the walls. But her face was pure English rose – as beautiful as Cynthia's in its way. Only Lil's eyes were harder than her late sister's, and of the most striking viridescent hue. A little like the eyes of a predator.

'Oh, you know how it is,' she said. Her voice was measured and cultivated, delivered as though she were on stage. 'One must keep up appearances. Besides, I've found it helps in negotiations: you men are so easily distracted.'

'Well, I can see how it'd be effective – I must say, you're looking lovelier than ever, Mrs Lee.'

'You always were a smooth talker,' she said, placing her hand on his cheek again. 'Now, I'd like to say the same about you, but quite frankly, darling, I'd say you've not been looking after yourself awfully well. Those rugged good looks have begun to fade a little.'

'Well, there's been a lot of water under the bridge since we last met, ain't there? Things take their toll.'

'Hmm. Perhaps… But it really is wonderful to see you. Let's have some tea and you can tell me what you've been up to.'

'I'd love to, Lil, only I'm in a bit of a hurry, see. On a case. Something big.'

Lil arched an exquisitely pencilled eyebrow. She had a way of challenging with a glance – her lips pouted, unequivocal – that reduced most men to the role of naughty schoolboy.

'A bit of a hurry?' She snorted and walked over to an ornate box, inlaid with mother-of-pearl. 'I'd offer you one of these,' she said, fitting a thin cigarillo into a jade holder. 'But I'm guessing you still prefer those awful Gold Flakes.'

She accepted Harley's light.

'So, we don't see anything of you for years, and when you do finally turn up you won't even stay long enough for a cup of tea? You used to have a little more class, you know.'

'You're getting me mixed up with someone else,' said Harley, sparking up his own smoke.

'Seriously, why on earth haven't you been to see us? How long has it been?'

'You know exactly how long it's been – almost four years.'

'Yes. And in those four years… well, for a start, Cynthia's nieces have grown into beautiful young women.'

'Dolly and Jasmine.' Harley tried to keep the emotion out of his voice.

'You know how attached to you they'd grown. You used to visit at least a couple of times a week. But it would appear that after Cynthia's—'

'Please, Lil! I really don't want to talk about it.'

'My God!' she said with another little derisive snort. 'Really? Does everyone walk around on eggshells when you're about, scared of mentioning her name?'

He looked at her, incredulous.

'Why would you let those bastards do that to you, George? Allow it to eat you up inside like that? Isn't it enough that they murdered that beautiful girl? Butchered her?'

'I know what they soddin' did,' he said, quietly. 'I'm the one who found her, remember?'

'Exactly! You know what they did. Stripped her naked.

Hacked off her head. Took it away with them as some kind of sick trophy. Left my beautiful, talented sister defiled, like some animal carcass.'

'Stop!'

'And you still think all that was simply revenge for what you did, George? For capturing Morkens?'

'What was it, then?'

'I'll tell you what it was: pure, evil insanity! A perversion of nature for which you, George Harley, cannot hold yourself accountable. Do you understand?' She sent a long plume of smoke towards the ceiling. 'Solly told me about the state you've been in these past few years.'

'He did, did he?'

'Yes, he did. He's a friend; he cares about you. We all do. For a supposedly intelligent man you really can be quite moronic at times, you know. You do realise the only person holding you responsible for what happened to Cynthia is *you*? Stop being so bloody self-indulgent. Get on with your life. That's what Cynthia would have wanted.'

'Self-indulgent?'

'Yes! Those black moods of yours, locking yourself away for months on end, losing yourself to the drink and the chandu. Don't you think we all miss her? Mourn for her? Don't you think we all wish that bastard had hanged for what he did to her? Dear Lord! That darling, sweet, talented girl. She was my little sister, remember? Do you think I've not lain awake at night, wondering what that son of a whore did with her head?'

'Lil. Don't…' Harley pushed himself up from the chair, walking to the window, where he stood smoking silently.

'Well, I do miss her,' said Lil. She moved across to the drinks cabinet, where she splashed a generous slug of gin into a tumbler. 'I miss her every day. And I miss my Sammy. But do I mope about? Do I shut myself off from the world? No. And you know why?'

'Look, I can't do this right now.'

'I'll tell you why, shall I?' she continued, undaunted, stabbing the air with her cigarillo. 'Because I know that, for some, this world can become just one big festering maw; lying in wait, ready to gobble them up. The decent people, the hard-working… the likes of Sammy and Cynthia. Ready to chew them up and spit out their bones. But I refuse to play that game. The world's going to lose a few teeth before it ever gets any nourishment from Lily Lee. And my girls? They'll be the same. I'll make sure of it.'

'How?'

'The best tutors, deportment lessons, language coaches… anything money can buy. I know what you think about the upper classes, George, but you mark my words, I'll see my Dolly and Jasmine marrying the crème de la crème, if it kills me. You should see it – they've already got a little fan club of moon-faced suitors, drooling along after them whenever they're out on the town. The poor, well-connected chumps don't stand a chance. Those girls make me so proud.'

She laughed, pushing a plume of smoke through her painted lips. Then she narrowed her eyes.

'All the money I've made since those bastards did for Sammy, every single penny from the restaurants, the chandu, the gambling, the girls.'

'That's what it's all about now, is it?'

'That's what it's always been about. Those girls won't be chewed up and spat out. Not if I can help it.'

'I don't doubt it. But you might just risk turning them into the ones who do the chewing and the spitting out.'

Lil's tigress eyes fixed Harley with a calculating regard, and, for just a second, he found he could believe all the infamous stories reported by the popular press about Limehouse Lil – the cruel and callous widow, head of a nefarious oriental crime gang who'd amassed a fortune from drugs, gambling and prostitution.

Lily broke the spell with a blast of her throaty, mannish laugh. She downed her gin and sashayed over to him.

'Oh, I've missed you, George Harley,' she said, delivering a loud kiss on his cheek. 'But you really do need to let all that nonsense go… You know it's what she would have wanted.'

'I'll try.'

'You do that… So, if you're not here for a social visit, why are you here?'

'I've got some bad news… and I need a favour.'

'Anything else?'

'No, I think that's it.'

'The bad news first, then.'

'That shicer, Morkens; he's escaped.'

There it was – a fleeting shimmer of shock across those exquisite features.

'How?'

'A bit of murder, mesmerism, collusion… after all, our professor's nothing if not resourceful.'

'And why haven't I heard anything about this? There's been nothing in the papers, no word from my contacts.'

'I'm not sure. It's early days yet, but my guess is they're sitting on it while it's being discussed at a higher level. After all, it looks bad, don't it? Misplacing a criminal lunatic. It's all this government needs at the moment, with public opinion as it is.'

'Who told you?'

'That's just it,' said Harley. 'He did.'

'Whatever do you mean?'

'He's been targeting me. Winding me up. I think he's planning something; something big. This escape is just the start of it. He's already tried to lure me into a couple of traps.'

Lil thought for a moment, tapping a manicured nail against her empty glass. 'Morkens at large? Well, maybe that's not such a bad thing.'

'How so?' asked Harley, stubbing out his Gold Flake.

'It's open season now. Tell me something, George – would you kill him, given the chance?'

Harley laughed. 'Hold on, you've just been telling me that I should forget about all that nonsense, get on with my life.'

'Yes, but that was when I thought that cockroach was safely under lock and key, rotting away in some miserable asylum.'

'Well, I'm not sure. Taking the law into your own hands, like that?' He allowed himself a little rueful smile. 'It's not always guaranteed to end well.'

He noticed the crystalline glare had returned to Lil's eyes.

'What about you? Would you kill him?'

'In the blink of an eye. If I thought I could get away with it. Unlike you, George, I'm not hobbled by some ridiculous moral compass… You said he was targeting you. Do you need a gun? We received a shipment a couple of weeks ago.'

Lil walked over to her desk and began to flick through a large black ledger.

'We have a few cases left.'

'No. I don't need a gun. And I don't want to hear about you dealing in them, either.'

'Of course, I forgot – you have that little phobia thing.'

'It's not a phobia, Lil. Shooters kill people. Their sole purpose is to rip big, irreparable bloody holes in human flesh. And since the war, there's a lot of them out there. Most of these kids coming up think it's like in the movies – a puff of smoke and a bad guy bends over and holds his belly. They ain't seen the consequences like I have. The gore. The agonising death.'

'No gun, then.'

'No gun.'

She closed the heavy ledger. 'Alright. So, I'll ruminate on your bad news later; decide whether I need to get involved or not… What's this favour you need?'

'Does the name Ilse Blau mean anything to you?'

Lil thought for a moment, then shook her head. 'Nothing, I'm afraid. Should it?'

'How about a cabaret act, called Astarte?'

'Oh, my word, yes! Astarte…' Lil let the name bubble into one of her husky laughs. 'Good Lord, what a handful. I mean, I thought I'd seen it all, but that one? She's turned obscenity into an art form.'

'They call her the "Queen of Depravity" back in Berlin, you know.'

'I can quite imagine. Have you seen her act? No? Well, it needs to be seen to be believed, I can tell you. But, you know, she does have this… well, animal magnetism, I suppose you'd call it. A certain carnality. Simply oozing with it… I must admit to having succumbed a little myself,' she added, with a wry smile. 'Oh dear, I'm not embarrassing you, darling, am I?'

'Get out of it! Listen – I heard that you were close. That you put her up here, from time to time?'

'She has stayed here, but… Well, to tell you the truth, as hugely entertaining as Astarte was to have around, I wasn't really happy with the influence she was having on the girls. I know it's not exactly a convent here, but some of her stories! You know, she told me that back in Berlin she'd made a sexual mistress out of the society wife of a high-ranking army officer. Apparently, she used to beat this poor woman in public with a riding crop if ever her behaviour became in any way bourgeois.' Lil chuckled. 'To make matters worse, she then had the woman bring along her fourteen-year-old son to watch them make love, in order that it might cure him of becoming a pompous boor like his father. There were plenty of other stories – of her stopping her act to urinate on the table of a heckler, making outrageous scenes in restaurants, stealing jewellery from her rich acquaintances, blackmail… Simply incorrigible. Though, a lot of what she says may well be fantasy – she does like to indulge somewhat, and not just alcohol.'

'What's her poison?' asked Harley.

'Anything she can lay her hands on, in my experience. Cocaine, chandu, ether.'

'Ether?'

'Yes.' Lil laughed. 'She soaks her cigarettes in it. But you know, for all her indulgences, for all of her infantile obsession with filth and obscenity, there's something about those dances – inspired by the most macabre of subject matter, by the way: death, suicide, syphilis, addiction, black magic – well, there's something in her performance that's simply transfixing.'

'And this is her act at the Grimaldi Vaults, is it? When is she next—'

But Harley's question remained unfinished as he was interrupted by the roar of a car's engine, reverberating loudly in the quiet back street outside. When he glanced out of the window, his suspicions were confirmed.

It was the Daimler Fifteen.

'I think we might have a problem,' he said, fishing his brass knuckles from his inside pocket. 'Got any useful muscle nearby?'

'Just Quong in the kitchen. It's too early for any of the boys to be around. Is it Morkens?'

'No… I was tailed on the way here. I thought I'd given them the slip.'

'But you hadn't,' said Lily, not bothering to hide her annoyance. 'And exactly what kind of mess are you treading into my carpet, George? What are we dealing with here? Bogeys? The Elephant Boys? The Italians?'

'Not bogeys. That's as much as I know. Tell me, are the girls at home?'

But Harley's question was answered by a shrill scream emanating from somewhere close by.

'In their bedroom, the next floor up!' shouted Lily, already on her way to the door.

'Wait,' said Harley, grabbing at her arm. 'We don't know what we're walking into, here. Let me go.'

'Don't be ridiculous!'

'Please. Leave it to me, Lil,' insisted Harley. 'You go and get Quong and get him to bring his cleaver. We've got more chance of getting these bastards that way.'

'Alright. But I swear, George, if anyone harms those girls…'

There was no need for Lil to complete her threat. She pushed away Harley's hand and dashed off to summon help.

Even though he'd assured Lil that Morkens wasn't involved, in the few seconds it took Harley to scale the stairs to the next floor, he'd already begun to speculate whether he might have led the escaped child-killer directly to Cynthia's two teenage nieces. Now, as he crouched with his ear to their bedroom door, he perhaps hesitated a little longer than was necessary, recalling in all-too-vivid detail the horrific discovery on opening the door to his fiancée's bedroom, some four years previously.

30

Harley burst his way through the girls' bedroom door.

The scene that greeted him was somewhat of a surprise. Since their fifth birthdays, the Lee twins had attended a weekly jiu-jitsu lesson. These two willowy beauties – still clad in their silk pyjamas – were now employing this training to great effect. Though their attacker had an obvious advantage in both strength and height, through a combination of agility and a two-pronged counterattack, they'd so far managed to resist the clutches of the intruder – who Harley recognised immediately as the driver of the green Daimler.

'Uncle George!' squealed Dolly, clinging tightly to the back of the man with her arm around his throat.

'Any weapon?' Harley asked Jasmine, who had just leapt on top of the chest of drawers from where she was now jabbing at the man's stomach with the butt of a lacrosse stick.

'Over there!' she shouted, pointing to a blackjack lying discarded on the floor. 'We've put him down twice, but the blighter keeps getting back up again.'

'Alright, girls, back off now. Let the dog see the rabbit.'

For a second the intruder looked relieved at escaping Dolly's stranglehold. This moment of respite was soon shattered, however, as the private detective's brass knuckles thundered into his jaw.

Harley leapt on his semiconscious victim, and was just beginning to search through his pockets for some form of identification when an individual dressed in the tattered costume of a tramp appeared at the open window. If Harley's assistant had been with him at that moment, she'd have been able to identify him as her mysterious rescuer from the altercation with Irvine outside the Grimaldi Vaults.

'Place your hands in the air and get up slowly, please,' said the newcomer, pointing his gun at Harley's head. 'No surprises now.'

'Get behind me, girls,' said Harley, dropping his knuckle-duster and rising slowly to his feet. 'Don't do anything to provoke him: no sudden moves.'

'This is good advice,' said the man, climbing in from the fire escape. 'Please listen to your friend, ladies. Believe me, we don't wish to hurt you.'

Like Alfie Budge before him, Harley's guess was that the slight cadence in the stranger's accent was of German origin. A quick look at the model of firearm confirmed his suspicion.

'Walther PPK. Issued for undercover work, right? So, that would make you, what…? *Abwehr*? *Schutzstaffel*?'

The tramp answered with a thin-lipped smile. 'Please be quiet, there's a good chap. Now, if you wouldn't mind, two steps back… there we are.'

Keeping the gun trained on Harley, the man crouched down and slapped his semiconscious compatriot around the cheek. 'Come on, wake up! That's it. Quick now.'

Though still obviously a little groggy, the driver of the Daimler managed to struggle to his feet.

'*Sie ist nicht hier,*' he mumbled.

'English!' hissed the tramp, hauling the man towards the open window and then pushing him out onto the fire escape. He turned back to address Harley.

'I apologise for any distress we may have caused the young ladies. However, please don't think of following us. I have an armed colleague downstairs; I couldn't be held responsible for the consequences. So…' He offered a curt bow to Jasmine and Dolly. '…good day!'

And then he was away, out of the window and clattering down the iron stairway.

Harley turned to the twins. 'You alright, girls? Blimey! Look at you two. Last time I saw you, you were skipping rope; now you're knocking seven bells out of fully grown men.'

'Oh, Uncle George,' said Dolly with a huge grin. 'It's so lovely to see you!'

As Harley was engulfed in a hug from the twins, their concerned-looking mother appeared in the doorway, closely followed by the red-faced, breathless Quong.

'George?'

'All clear, Lil. They're fine.'

Having given her daughters the once-over, Lil turned her attention to Harley.

'Well?'

'Two of them up here. Another down below. Armed. German.'

Lil strode purposefully over to the open window, with Quong following close behind.

'Careful, Lil,' said Harley. 'These ain't some snotty-nosed wide-boys.'

'I don't care who they are. Nobody breaks into my place and terrorises my daughters.'

'Well, I don't know about being terrorised. I'd say they were giving as good as they got.' He turned to the twins and gave them a wink. 'Chip off the old block. You ought to be proud of them.'

'Quiet!' snapped Lily, now out on the fire escape, scouring the streets below for a sign of the intruders. Harley was just climbing through the window to join her when he heard the sound of a car's engine drawing near.

Suddenly the green Daimler roared around the corner.

'Is that them?'

'Yeah. But I wouldn't—'

Harley was cut short by the explosive discharge from the small pistol which had suddenly appeared in Lil's hand.

He grabbed at her wrist, wrenching the weapon from her. 'What the bloody hell are you trying to do? You'll kill someone!'

'That's the idea, you idiot. Now give me that back, this instant.'

'Look… They're long gone. And you were never going to hit them from here, not with this thing.' Harley studied the compact firearm. 'These little Colts are for close-up work. To hide in your boot, or in your case, in your, you know…' He nodded towards her cleavage.

The twins gave a little giggle from the back of the room.

'No accuracy, not from any distance. You're more likely to hit some poor kiddie playing hopscotch in the street. Not to mention drawing the attention of every bogey within earshot.'

He noticed an inscription on the side of the pistol.

'For a killer doll.'

'It was a gift,' said Lily, snatching back the gun. 'From an admirer, in Chicago.'

'Chicago? Don't tell me you've started doing business with—'

Lily's smart kick to his shin prevented him from finishing his sentence.

'Not in front of the girls!'

After plucking the gun from his hand, she climbed back into the room.

'Girls,' she said, placing her hands on her daughters' cheeks. 'Be honest now. This man…'

The twins – not quite identical, but so obviously a pair – both quickly dropped their smiles, the admiration for their mother displayed in attentive concentration. Harley marvelled at how quickly Cynthia's little nieces had matured into such beautiful young women. Without their cheeky grins, their unblemished faces were an alluring mix of ethnicity, set off with the inherited jewels of Lil's emerald eyes.

'Yes, Mother?' asked Dolly, earnestly.

'Did he touch you, at all?'

'Only on the foot,' said Jasmine.

'The foot?'

'Yes. I must have caught him at least three times with a groin kick,' she said, unable to hold back her giggles.

'No you didn't, you fibber!' said Dolly. 'Most of the time you were hiding on top of that chest of drawers. I was the one doing all the work. You saw it, didn't you, Uncle George? I had him in a stranglehold and—'

'That's quite enough,' said Lil. 'Young ladies shouldn't squabble. Now, both of you, go and put something decent on. I've got things to discuss with Uncle George.'

'I'd better go and check on Bunty first,' said Harley.

'No need,' said Quong. 'She's down in the kitchen, making short work of a bowl of wontons.'

'You sure she's alright?'

'Yeah. Good as gold, George.'

'Bunty?' said Lil, arching an eyebrow at Harley.

'My new assistant.'

'Can't wait to meet her… Alright, Quong; would you give us a moment?'

'Right you are, boss. I'll be downstairs if you need me.'

'So,' said Lil, once they were alone again. 'Our unwanted guests – who are they, exactly?'

'I can't be sure,' said Harley, retrieving his knuckleduster from the rug. 'But my guess is they're *Abwehr*, German military intelligence. And I think they came here for exactly the same reason as I did – Fräulein Ilse Blau, or Astarte, as you know her.'

'What do they want with her?'

'That I don't know yet.' Harley sparked up a smoke. 'Tell me – when will she next be performing at the Grimaldi Vaults, d'you think?'

'She's there every Friday. I don't expect it'll be any different this week. I can't see Simeon Dubois letting her slip through his fingers; not without a fight. He's built the club's reputation on her performances.'

'What's he like, this Dubois?'

'Tricky. But he seems to have taken a shine to me.' She helped herself to one of Harley's Gold Flakes, plucking the cigarette from his mouth to light her own, then placing it back between his lips with a little condescending tap on the cheek. 'We do a little business, now and again.'

'Yeah, I can imagine… You know, I can't help thinking that shicer Morkens is somehow mixed up in all this. Only a gut feeling, but…'

'But you trust your gut feelings?'

'Exactly. So, I can think of two ways of approaching this. One way involves the bogeys, I'm afraid. I reckon, from what's just happened here, I've got enough on the Grimaldi Vaults to get CID involved. If I can convince them to turn the place over, I'll tip you the nod as to when it might happen – so you can make sure none of your boys are hanging around, alright?'

'Understood. And if Scotland Yard don't comply?'

'Well, the alternative approach is a bit more low-key… Would you be able to get me into the club, do you think?'

'Of course, I'm a member.'

'And a few of my close associates?'

Lil frowned. 'It sounds like either of your plans is going to cost me in lost revenue. I'll have you know that club is proving to be a lucrative little number for me.'

'Come on, Lil. Those shicers broke in here and scared the girls. Imagine if Astarte had still been here. They had shooters, remember – anything could have happened.'

Lil pondered this for a moment.

'Alright. I'll get you into the Grimaldi Vaults, but on one condition.'

'Which is?'

'If you do corner those Germans, you let me have a piece of them.'

'Literally?'

'I have a reputation to uphold, George. As you say, bursting in here, scaring my girls. A lesson needs to be taught… We'll take them down to our basement. Quong's a wonder with sweetbreads… lightly fried, in oyster sauce.'

31

ILSE BLAU SAT silently, contemplating her reflection in the dressing room mirror. Her face was like a waxen effigy glowing in the candlelit room, with dark violet rings accentuating the pale blue of her eyes. She regarded the velvet-covered tabletop, strewn with her personal fetish objects and the paraphernalia of her daily battle with ennui: bottles of absinthe and cognac; portraits of saints and baroque crucifixes; a rabbit's foot; a jar of dead roses; a chipped glass holding a handful of ether-laced cigarettes; an array of expensive perfume bottles caught in a tangle of pearl necklaces. '*Wie langweilig…*' she uttered, in her husky, masculine voice.

She lit one of her Turkish cigarettes, triggering a violent bout of coughing, from which her lace handkerchief came away dotted with little crimson rosettes.

Pulmonary tuberculosis – another of her little secrets. She'd first been diagnosed in Paris, and still found it faintly amusing that after all the hedonistic abuse she'd subjected her body to, it might be this unexceptional, ubiquitous disease that would eventually see her off. That's if the National Socialists didn't get to her first.

'*Wie langweilig,*' she repeated, grinding the cigarette into a dirty wine glass.

There was a knock at the door.

'Miss Astarte?'

'Come!' she said, stuffing the bloodstained handkerchief into a drawer.

'Ah! *Mein Kleiner.*'

It was William, the club's timid, seventeen-year-old runner.

'You seem to have a certain vigour about you tonight, Willy. A potency. Have you finally got around to fucking that little barmaid you were telling me about, hmm? You naughty boy.'

'No,' spluttered the flustered youth. 'No, I… erm.'

'*Ja?* Come on! Out with it.'

'There's a telephone call for you, miss. You can take it in the office.'

'I'm not sure I can be bothered, Willy. I am so bored tonight… Why don't you come over here and cheer me up?'

Blau gave a throaty laugh as the lad scurried back out the room. Then, after fortifying herself with a dip into the silver pendant of cocaine, she hauled herself up to make her way to the office.

'*Ja?*' she said languidly, retrieving the receiver from the desk and slumping into the chair.

'Ilse?'

'No, this is Astarte,' she replied, suddenly alert, sitting forward. 'Who is speaking, please?'

'*Ilse, hier ist Mendel.*'

'*Moment mal!*'

She quickly checked that no one was outside in the corridor and then hurried back to the telephone.

'I thought you were calling yourself Josef?'

'It makes no difference now. They've discovered where I live.'

'Are you sure?'

'I'm certain of it. I returned home last night to find my room had been broken into. Every drawer searched, clothes and papers thrown everywhere.'

'Maybe you were just burgled?'

'Burglars don't rip open the lining of your jackets, Ilse. They don't prise up floorboards. I've got gold cufflinks, a box of decent cigars, a jar full of money – none of these things were taken. No, I'm afraid there can be no doubt as to what they were after.'

'I see.' Blau found herself miraculously cured of her ennui. 'What will you do now?'

'I'm leaving. Tonight… I'm afraid I can't tell you where I'm going.'

'Of course. I understand. You need money?'

'No, thank you. Besides, I think it would be best for us both if we didn't meet up, don't you?'

'Yes… So, why call?'

'To warn you, my dear. After all, I've been keeping a low profile, yet still they tracked me down. For you, Ilse, I'm afraid it can only be a matter of time.'

Blau was racked with another violent bout of coughing.

'Are you ill?'

'No, I'm fine. A head cold is all.' She wiped the bloody palm on her skirt. 'Listen, Mendel. That thing we were talking about. Do you really think I should take it to the authorities here?'

'Hush, Ilse! Who knows who might be listening in…? I must be going now. Take care of yourself, my friend. *Alles Gute für Dich.*'

* * *

Blau slipped into her room on the second floor of the pub and hastily locked the door behind her. As she drew the curtains, she glanced down at the street below.

There it was. The green car. Still parked on the opposite side of the road.

But where was the driver? Arriving a few hours earlier, she'd noticed the man ogling her as she'd entered the pub. Being no stranger to unwanted attention, she'd thought nothing of it at the time; but in light of Mendel's phone call, maybe there was more to it? And then there was the incident in the club. She'd been drinking at the bar, casually observing a group of the venue's 'Joey' clowns as they enjoyed a beer and a game of cards before the start of their shift. When a fourth drinker had arrived at the table, Blau had noticed one of the men knock a few times on the table by way of a greeting – a German custom, one she'd seen many times in the bierkellers of Berlin but never witnessed before in London. To her knowledge there were no Germans on the Grimaldi Vaults' staff. Was it possible, then, that there were agents at the club, working undercover? Abwehr, or worse still, the hated Schutzstaffel? But, if so, why hadn't they already made their move? Were they biding their time? Reluctant to act too overtly on foreign territory?

Blau slumped down on the bed, her mind a morass of gloomy scenarios. One thing was certain – she couldn't disappear with empty pockets, she'd have to complete the night's performance in order to get paid. And even then, she might not have enough. There was always her jewellery; some of the gifts from her more exclusive admirers should fetch a decent price. Or a loan from Dubois, maybe? And once she had the money, the next question would be where to escape to? After all, she was running out of places to hide. Her particular brand of entertainment required a certain refined predilection, only found in the audiences of the more sophisticated cities of the world… New York? Yes, perhaps it was time to unleash herself on the Americans. But that would mean being trapped on board a ship for… how long?

Whatever she might decide, she knew one thing had to

be taken care of immediately – moving the roll of film she had stashed away; the thing for which, according to Mendel Einhorn, those Nazi bastards had tortured and killed her adorable Hedwig. Burglars don't prise up floorboards, he'd said – meaning that these *Schweine* obviously did. The current hiding place simply wouldn't do anymore.

Kicking the rug aside, Blau grabbed a spoon from the bedside table and began to lever up the loose floorboard. She panicked for a few seconds as her hand scrabbled around blindly, trying to locate the small package... There it was! Nestling between the joists.

She tore open the paper wrapping. Just a small, innocuous-looking canister; remarkable, perhaps, when compared with the large older photographic plates, but nowadays something that wouldn't normally garner much attention. Not until you knew the importance of the images contained within. That little bastard Hitler, naked as the day he was born, his lily-white skin drenched in the blood of a sacrificial virgin.

Turning up the gas, she teased out the first few inches of film and held it up to the lamp. Though in negative, it was still easy to make out the thin, naked bodies – the skin tone dark grey, the clumps of pubic hair showing as stark white geometrical patterns. She smiled as she wound the film back into its casing, knowing what power such images could wield in this new, dark era.

It was then that she heard the commotion outside in the hallway.

But this was nothing to concern her; just the mewling of that unfortunate little creature Dubois was holding in the top-floor room. An exotic gift, no doubt, for some affluent client. Why should she get involved? It was no different back home. Since the end of the war, the pandering to such deviant tastes had become something of a growth industry. Though, of course, in Weimar Berlin these things had been done with a certain panache – before that little beer-hall Chaplin had got his hands on things. Where else were there twelve-year-old telephone girls, delivered by automobile, dressed to resemble the female starlets of the day? A prepubescent Dietrich, say, or a Lya da Putti.

Ja, mused Blau, with a certain perverted pride, *we Berliners have always shown a level of artistic flair with our depravity.*

But as she listened to the continued scuffle on the landing outside, a plan began to form in Blau's head. She tossed the film canister in her hands a couple of times. Perhaps she would get involved, after all.

'What are you doing there!' she barked, wrenching the door open and surprising the individual in the Joey clown outfit, who was at that moment attempting to drag the terrified Poppy towards the communal bathroom at the end of the corridor.

'Miss Astarte! You gave me quite a shock,' he said, stooping to pick up the orphan's dolly, which had fallen to the floor.

'I have asked you a question, clown. What are you doing with that little girl?'

'It's an errand. For Mr Dubois.' Even with his mask of thick pantomime make-up, it was obvious that the young man felt uncomfortable with his task. 'I'm to bathe the child, miss. Unfortunately, she's wet herself, again.'

'Are you surprised? Look at her – she's terrified of you. And no wonder, dressed in that horrific costume. Come, give her to me, I shall do it.'

'But Mr Dubois expressly stated that—'

Blau wrenched the child from him and gathered her up in her arms.

'*Und die Puppe?*'

'Hmm?'

'The toy!' demanded Blau, holding out her hand. 'Give me her toy, you idiot!'

'Of course. Here you are… Right,' said the bewildered

clown, as Blau disappeared into the bathroom with the little girl. 'I'll just wait out here then, shall I?'

* * *

Having tested the temperature of the bath water, Blau turned to the little girl, now perched on the toilet seat. As she did so – no doubt precipitated by the cocktail of intoxicants in her bloodstream – the vision of this small child, sitting patiently in her white petticoat, with clouds of steam billowing around her, brought back the memory of another child, on another night. A dark memory, of excess and debauchery; of profane rituals and Hungarian countesses; of Fedor von Görlitz and *der Engländer*... of death... and night... and blood.

Much to her surprise, Blau found these memories provoking the smallest twinge of guilt.

How odd, she thought.

Allowing a smile to form on her lips – a genuine smile, a warm smile – she placed a hand on the child's soft cheek.

'*Liebling*,' she whispered.

But this was simply ridiculous. There was no time for remorse; after all, this was now about self-preservation. She must return to the business in hand.

She pulled the slip off over the little girl's head.

'So, in we go, my dear... There we are. Good and hot, *ja*?'

Poppy chuckled and splashed at the water with both hands, delighted with the warm bath, and with the attention from this fascinating adult.

Blau stood up and placed her ear to the door. 'Remember – no peeking through the keyhole, you dirty little pig!' she shouted, then picked up the doll and poked its face over the side of the bath.

'So, here is your little friend. Do you see?'

Piecrust's merry little dance drew another chuckle from Poppy.

'Oh, what a pity,' said Blau, lowering the doll out of sight and surreptitiously forcing the seam on its back. 'I see she has a little tear in her.'

The little girl frowned, not able to follow the conversation, but aware of a change of mood and eager to know when Piecrust would reappear.

'But that's alright, *Liebling*.' Blau kept the dolly out of sight as she pushed the film canister through the small opening in the cloth, making sure the feel of it would be masked by the thick stuffing. 'I happen to be a superb seamstress.' She smiled as she pulled the needle and thread from her lapel. 'We dancers have to be, you see. Just a few quick stitches… there we are – as good as new, *ja*?'

Poppy gave one of her excited mewling sounds and clapped her hands as Piecrust's chubby little face appeared once more over the side of the bath.

32

H ARLEY DOWNED THE last mouthful of whisky and killed his cigarette in the black onyx ashtray – which Cynthia had given him as an engagement present. He plucked Uncle Blake's 'dreamstick' from its stand and traced a finger over the intricate silver adornments, following the sleek lines of sinuous, snaking dragons and curlicued clouds.

He'd been doing so well up until now – he hadn't been on a proper jag for over six months. But the visit to Limehouse, seeing Lil and the girls… well, it had brought it all back with a vengeance, and he could hear once again the doleful padding of that Black Dog's paws.

With a small sigh of resignation, he steadied his hand to light the small spirit lamp, then extracted a pea-sized ball of the dark opium paste from its silver canister. He watched with anticipation as the drug began to bubble and swell on the end of the needle, soon turning a rich golden colour. He worked the warm goo between his fingers before heating it some more and then pushing it into the bowl of the pipe.

Holding it to the flame, he took a deep pull and closed his eyes.

One more pull and he was plunged with delicious relief into an ocean of black… velvet… calm…

He floated adrift: for hours; years; aeons…

* * *

After – how long? – there came to him a vision:

He lay on his back in the sand, washed up on some desolate island, lapped gently by the waves of a warm sea. His mind was free of worry. He neither knew nor cared how long he'd been there; it was simply enough to lie, basking in the sun, lulled by the hypnotic birdsong filling the air.

But this reverie was interrupted by a sudden, troubling sense of urgency, as though he had forgotten an incredibly important engagement. Sodden with sea water, he dragged himself to his feet to follow a line of perfect footprints left in the wet sand, prints which led to a door, incongruously erected on the beach. A door he had the nagging feeling he'd seen somewhere before.

He placed his ear to the varnished wood. There in the distance – the sound of a piano: plaintive high notes, like the ring of crystal glass.

A voice whispered in his ear: 'Songs of the night.'

He nodded, solemnly, then turned the handle.

Cynthia's hallway.

He was puzzled to discover her chic, geometric wallpaper had been replaced by a childish red-and-white stripe – then remembered the peppermint stick, protruding from the pocket of little Eddie Muller's sailor suit.

He looked down to find he was wearing battledress – the familiar khaki woollen tunic and trousers, and his old service boots, caked with the cloying mud of the trenches.

'Corporal Harley!'

Reacting automatically to the command, Harley marched

towards the bedroom door, leaving a muddy trail on the carpet behind him. He watched as his hand reached out to grab the doorknob, turning it slowly…

* * *

'Corporal Harley!'

He came to – or dreamt he'd done so.

Back in Bell Street. Supine on his unmade double bed. The candles on the Girandole mirror now guttering stubs, their flickering light casting dancing images on the ceiling, like the bioscopes he'd seen as a kid at the Egyptian Hall in Piccadilly.

'Corporal Harley!'

Was he still in the thrall of the opium?

He tried to sit up a little, the room kaleidoscoping around him, bringing on a wave of nausea.

'There you are. Thank goodness! I thought you'd done yourself some permanent damage.'

Someone at the foot of his bed. That voice…

He tried to focus, but found the room suddenly swathed in swirling ribbons of colour. He dropped his head back on the pillow and closed his eyes, relieved to hear the birdsong returning.

'You know, we must do this together sometime. It might be fun.'

Then he knew who it was. At the foot of his bed. Holding the dreamstick.

'Oona,' he heard himself whisper.

'Here I am, my little tin soldier.'

He kept his eyes closed as he felt the thrill of her manicured hands, those exquisitely painted nails, teasing his bare chest. Her melodic cultured voice was close to his ear, each word firing small volleys of coloured globes across his mind's eye.

'Let me tell you a story, George. One Christmas, when I was just a little girl, somebody gave me the most magical of presents: a tin soldier. He was so dashing in his gold-braided hussar's uniform. There weren't many presents in my childhood. I was an awkward, precocious little thing and so this gift was something remarkable to me. You see, little Oona had no friends. No siblings. No pets. Boo-hoo! But here, now, was someone; someone brave and handsome to look out for me...'

A tingling ripple of electricity played across his brain as those cool fingers moved slowly down to his abdomen.

'I'm not sure I'm really qualified to say, but, you know, I think I might have truly *loved* that little tin soldier. He was so brave, handsome and utterly loyal. I could make him do anything I wished. And who was Oona in this little childhood fantasy? A sweetheart waiting patiently at home? A twee virgin fiancée? No! The icy empress, of course! Stern and beautiful. Again and again, I would order my little hussar into the most dangerous, life-threatening adventures. And every time he would willingly comply.'

Her vermilion lips were closer now, her breath the scorched Sirocco wind upon his neck.

'I've come to realise, George, that you might be my little tin soldier, come back to me after all these years... How intriguing it is! We shall see how this develops.'

And as her manicured fingers continued on their journey, Harley once more lost his grip on Bell Street... The electric globes, dancing in his mind, were suddenly engulfed by the star-speckled expanse of an ebony universe; infinite and timeless.

As he watched, a shape began to form in the myriad stellar clusters, galaxies coagulating, lumping together into a vague mass. Hurtling towards him now, becoming more distinct the closer it got, until there before him, floating in space like some ancient celestial being, was...

Cynthia's face.

Beautiful. Serene. The eyes closed in restful repose.

He reached out to her, but in a shocking instant the vision transformed into the cadaverous head of Osbert Morkens, a cruel sneer on the feminine lips, the domed cranium glowing like an alien moon.

Now Harley was struck with a terrifying realisation, a realisation that the professor's devil-goat eyes would soon open; that they were about to open now; and that, for the sake of his sanity, he must look away. Look away!

But he had lost all volition. Caught like a rabbit in the cobra's stare, he was frozen before the godhead, ready to receive his fate. He watched, terrified, as the deathly pale lids began to slowly rise…

33

H ARLEY HAD AWOKEN the following morning to the mother of all hangovers. So bad were the after-effects of his jag that he'd decided to make an early stop-off at Doc Shandy's in Bridle Lane – the Adler gang's tame medic. The quack had injected Harley with one of his infamous 'pick-me-up' shots – something the boys called a Lazarus. God knew what was in it – it was probably best to stay ignorant of the fact – but, as ever, it had proved a miraculous cure and Harley now felt clear-headed and buzzing with energy. Just as well – if all went to plan, he would have a long and eventful day ahead of him.

He could only recall a few tattered remnants of his pen yen session, the most alarming of which was the image of Morkens' planet-like visage; that one continued to give him the jitters whenever it bobbed back up to the surface. But the most bizarre outcome of the hedonistic spree was the discovery of the note, found on his bedside table.

He plucked it now from his jacket pocket, just to make sure it was real:

So, she hadn't been just some opium dream. To think – he'd been lying there in bed, off his head like some stinking Limehouse hophead, defenceless as a babe in arms, with that harpy standing over him. He should count himself lucky he hadn't had his throat slit.

Harpy? Who was he kidding? The woman was the one of the most jaw-droppingly attractive creatures he'd ever set eyes on. He gave an involuntary shudder as he remembered the tease of her fingernails on his abdomen.

Cheese it, you mug! She was there, with Morkens, in that charnel house. You saw it with your own eyes.

What was she up to, the devious witch? Twice now it had appeared she'd rescued him from a perilous situation.

Harley recalled a suspicion he'd held for a while about Oona during the Nursery Butcher case: the possibility that she might be an undercover agent, working for the Secret Service. But at Pamela Chisholm's digs she'd spoken about being in the AOU for a long time. Some kind of sleeper agent, perhaps? Then again, how could he trust anything the woman said? And this *pickled herring* thing – that's what the delirious librarian, Miss Pendleton, had been mumbling to herself at the museum. What the hell was all that about?

He put the thought to the back of his mind for the moment as he emerged from the narrow alleyway off Piccadilly. He pulled a last drag from his Gold Flake, shot his cuffs, and strode purposefully into Vine Street Police Station, giving a curt nod to the bobby standing duty on the door.

'So, come on then, what exactly is being done about Morkens' escape? Why isn't it all over the papers by now? Haven't the great British public got a right to know there's a criminal lunatic roaming free out there?'

'I'm afraid I'm just a lowly detective sergeant,' said Franklin, with a pained look on his face. 'It's being handled by the top brass now.'

'But why would they want to keep it low key? Wouldn't it be better to have Joe Public keeping a lookout for that maniac?'

'Perhaps. But imagine the headlines, the amount of panic they might cause. That damned rag the Daily Oracle, for example, would have a field day.'

'Very diplomatic. What you mean is the powers-that-be don't want it broadcast to the nation that they dropped a bollock by allowing an insane child-killer to slip out of the so-called secure wing at Broadmoor. They should have strung the shicer up when they had the chance.'

'I can completely understand how you must be feeling about this, George, really, I can. Apparently they've instigated a serious review at Broadmoor, to determine exactly how this was allowed to happen.'

'Review?!' Harley pushed his hat back an inch or so. 'A lot of good that'll do. They need to dig those pencils out their arses, get out on the streets and capture the bastard; other-wise they're going to have more kiddies' blood on their hands. They can have all the reviews in the world once that monster gets his hemp necktie.'

Franklin looked to his office door. 'Please, George, try to keep it down a little. I can assure you, everything possible will be being done to apprehend Professor Morkens. Have you thought any more about the offer of temporary relocation?'

'Nothing doing. I've got a living to make. Besides, I'm not

scared of that puffed-up shicer.' Harley tried to dismiss the image of Morkens' giant leering face floating in space which had just popped into his head. 'It's that little orphan, Poppy, you should be concerned about, not me.'

'You still think her disappearance is linked to Morkens?'

'I'm convinced of it… which leads me to the Grimaldi Vaults. Did you get the warrant? Clearance for sufficient manpower?'

'Ah, well… I did tell you it wouldn't be straightforward.'

'This smells like bad news.' Harley heaved a sigh and slumped back into the seat. 'Go on.'

'We didn't get the warrant for the raid on the club.'

'There's a suitcase of body parts, a kidnapped child, an escaped criminal lunatic and a possible nest of foreign agents. And – in my professional opinion – they're all somehow linked to Ilse Blau and that club. Now, would you kindly explain to me, in words of one syllable, why you couldn't convince a magistrate to authorise a warrant to raid the gaff.'

'It wasn't the magistrate. The super filled me in on it this morning. There's been an intervention from above.'

'On what grounds?'

Franklin looked to his notepad. 'Operational conflict.'

'With which department?'

'Nobody's saying. All I know is, there's an injunction from the Yard on us going anywhere near the Grimaldi Vaults, or any of its staff, because of the risk of compromising an ongoing intelligence operation.'

'For how long?'

'Until further notice.'

'This is bollocks! I bet they're just after some minor dealer who Dubois has allowed to set up shop in the club. Ongoing intelligence operation? It'll be some eager PC, fresh out of Peel House, squeezed into some loud suit they've got from C Division's dressing-up box, posing as a snowbird and sticking out like a sore thumb to all the regulars. So, you're not going to look at it, then?'

'I've just told you – we can't go anywhere near the place. I know it's frustrating, but there you have it. We're just not privy to the full story.'

'Privy's about right. The whole thing stinks like an outhouse, if you ask me.' Harley consulted his wristwatch. 'Well, thanks for the meeting, Detective Sergeant, it's been most enlightening. But I'd better be off – I'm out on the town tonight.'

'Oh, really?' said Franklin, getting up from his desk to show Harley out. 'Anywhere nice?'

'Yeah, a little place in Fitzrovia. The Grimaldi Vaults.'

'Now, hold on a minute! I've just told you, we're under strict orders not to approach the place.'

'No, Alec, you're under strict orders. I'm on civvy street, remember? The only person I have to answer to is my new assistant, Bunty.' He gave Franklin a wink and grabbed his hat from the desk. 'Abyssinia! I'll let you know how we get on.'

'Heaven preserve us,' said Franklin, reaching for the telephone.

34

T HE MUSCULAR WOMAN with the slicked-back hair, immaculate in a tailored dress suit, screwed her monocle into her eye as the small group approached the club's entrance.

'Lilian!' she drawled in a thick Berlin accent. She took a pull on her large, torpedo-shaped cigar and gave Lil's Junoesque figure a slow once-over. 'How fabulous you look tonight, darlink.'

Simeon Dubois had discovered Trude at the Mikado Bar on Puttkamerstrasse, during a scouting trip to Berlin the previous year. She had proved an excellent choice for the Grimaldi Vaults' sentinel, endowed with both an innate theatrical sarcasm and the ability to spot an undercover policeman at twenty paces.

'Do behave, Trude,' said Lil, waving away the compliment. 'We both know I'm not your type.'

Lil glanced back at the innocent-looking Bunty, standing in line with Harley and Solly Rosen. 'Miss Chatterton, on the other hand…'

Grinning around her cigar, the Berliner pulled back the velvet drape, revealing the cavernous entrance to the club.

'Hey, sister!' she said, fixing Bunty with a predatory glare. 'Maybe I see you later, eh?'

With Trude's fruity peal of dirty laughter still ringing in their ears, Lil ushered her guests into the small antechamber and pointed to the cloakroom hatch. 'You can check your coats in there,' she said, then pulled Harley aside.

'Listen, George. Once we're in there, I'll be leaving you to it, I'm afraid. I can't afford to get mixed up with whatever little scheme you might have up your sleeve.'

She pointed at Rosen, who was horsing around with Bunty. 'With the two of you involved it's bound to be carnage. Just remember, there'll be a lot of heavyweights there tonight, people with real pull. I know it's not in Solly's vocabulary, but try to encourage him to be as subtle as possible, would you? And remember, if you get any leads on those German agents, I'm the first to know… Right, let's get in there, shall we? I just hope Miss Chatterton isn't too offended by the entertainment. If you ask me, she's a little too schoolmarmish for this place.'

'You'd be surprised. Bunty's more broadminded than she looks.'

'Trust me, she'll need to be.'

Just then, Harley heard a familiar voice call out from behind him; one with a thick Gorbals accent.

'Hey, Blondie!'

Irvine strutted over with all the swagger of a guard dog on his home patch. The Scotsman had his lanky sidekick Woody in tow, plus another of the Grimaldi san toys – a stocky individual, with the hint of a punch-drunk vacancy in his eyes.

The Glaswegian cracked a monkey nut between his teeth as he sized up Rosen. 'So, hen, you've decided to bring your big brother with you this time, have you?' He nodded at Harley. 'And your boyfriend as well? Quite the party.'

Rosen took a step forward, holding up a hand the size of a dinner plate. 'D'you want to stand back a little there, pal? You're cramping the lady's style.'

'Come on, Sol.' Harley was a little concerned to see his friend had adopted the lazy grin that was usually the precursor to a little boisterous intervention. 'Let's get in there, shall we? We haven't got time for this old madam.'

'Oh no,' said Irvine, wagging his finger. 'I dinnae think so, pal. See, the management of this establishment employ me to keep riffraff like you out.'

'Is there a problem here?' asked Lil.

'Mrs Lee! I didnae see you there. Nae problem. Just dealing with a couple of troublemakers.'

'These are my guests, Irvine,' she said, with a show of haughty indignation. 'And would you mind not showing me the contents of your mouth while you're talking? It really is most distasteful.'

Irvine took a deep breath and then stuffed the bag of monkey nuts into his jacket pocket.

'I suppose they can go in.' He gave Harley and Rosen a long hard look. 'But I'm gonna have to search these two first.'

'Don't be ridiculous!' scoffed Lil. 'Since when did you start searching the clientele?'

'With respect, Mrs Lee, I'm responsible for the security at this wee club. We have a number of very important guests in there tonight. If I see fit to search these men, then searched they'll be.'

'Do I need to get Mr Dubois involved?'

Irvine rubbed his chin. 'Well, that's your prerogative, of course. But if you're for causing a stooshie, there's a chance they'll nae be getting in at all.'

'Let him have his bit of fun,' said Harley, eager to get on with the job in hand.

'Yeah,' added Rosen, still sporting his lopsided grin. 'With a face like that I don't s'pose he gets much opportunity for physical contact.'

Harley sniggered at this as he offered up his set of brass knuckles.

'I want those back, mind. They've got sentimental value.'

'You can have them back, alright, laughing boy – anytime,' said Irvine, moving in close to begin a rough pat-down.

He turned to Rosen.

'Alright, big yin. Your turn. Any weapons?'

'Only these.' Rosen held up his clenched fists.

'Oh, aye? And what's this then?' said Irvine, extracting a rubber blackjack from the ex-boxer's trousers.

'That's Corporal Dunlop. He's my lucky charm.'

'Well, you're gonna have to stay unlucky tonight. Alright then, in you go… Oh, hold on there a minute, Blondie,' said Irvine, noticing that Bunty was clutching her handbag tightly to her side. 'Let's have a wee look in that bag of yours, eh?'

'That's quite enough!' snapped Lil, a flash of anger in her tigress eyes. 'Step aside.'

But the Scot stood resolute for a while, picking out the remnants of nut from his molars.

'I'm warning you, Irvine. It will not be good for Mr Dubois's business if you fall out with me.'

Irvine gave Rosen another quick once-over then smiled, holding up his hands.

'Just trying to do my job, missus,' he said, stepping aside with a little sarcastic bow. 'In you go. Enjoy the show.'

* * *

'Well then, here it is,' said Lil. 'The Grimaldi Vaults. I'm told, by those in the know, that it's the closest we have over here to the *real thing*.'

It took a moment for their eyes to adjust to the dimmed lighting, but the immediate impression was of a fevered dream sequence. The sprawling subterranean space was a conglomerate of small, vaulted enclaves – each illuminated by an eerie glow – clustered about a central dance floor. The curved cellar walls were decorated with bold daubings – pastiches of Futurist design, all violent angles and vertiginous perspective. This Fitzrovian Hades was populated by a suitably demonic congregation, not the usual frowzy West End crowd – no greasy, blue-chinned wide-boys or strung-out, malnourished motts here; no, the Grimaldi Vaults attracted a far more exclusive breed of punter. Languishing on the outer edges, strewn across chaises longues and settees, lay glamorous couples, entangled in various stages of undress. Further in towards the elevated stage, the tables were populated by voyeurs, poseurs and thrill-seekers of every variety. Androgynous beauties draped themselves over corpulent, ruddy-faced City gents. Tuxedoed matrons, their faces powdered lily white, with luxuriant Pre-Raphaelite wigs tumbling down their backs, supped with giggling, elfin gamines. Rich businessmen in ostentatious drag mixed it with hot sisters in sailor suits. Butch girls with made-up bruised eyes and five-o'clock shadows; topless nuns brandishing whips; obese, middle-aged babies… such was the extra-ordinary clientele of the Grimaldi Vaults. And dotted among them, their identities protected behind black domino masks, were the aristos and the aldermen, the cabinet ministers and diplomats – the great and the good of the fair city of London, all out to enjoy the carnal delights of the underground scene.

Attending to the needs of these curious patrons were the Joeys: a waiting staff of a dozen or so ersatz Joseph Grimaldis, in full eighteenth-century clown costume, their garish greasepaint adding an additional macabre twist to the surreal ambience.

'Gosh!' said Bunty, placing a hand on Harley's arm, as if to steady herself against the shock.

'Look at that bar,' said Rosen. 'No pump handles. Don't tell me they've got no beer here, Lil.'

Lil laughed and pinched his cheek. 'Solomon Rosen. Don't ever change, will you? Right, kids, I've got people to see. I'd grab a table, if I were you, while you still can. You boys will want a good view of Astarte's act, believe me. Remember what I said now, George.'

'Does that mean she likes me?' asked Rosen, rubbing his cheek fondly as he watched Lil sashay into the throng.

'I've told you before, Sol,' said Harley, sparking up a Gold Flake and making a quick scan of the interior of the club. 'She's out of your league. You'd be tasting canvas in the first round.'

Harley spotted an empty table and began to lead them over to it, just as the club's band struck up a drunken, jazz-infused polka.

As they skirted the edge of the dance floor, Rosen was pulled into the clutches of an elegant six-foot blonde, resplendent in a shimmering, couture ballgown. This vision in satin began to whirl him around in a crazed tarantella. When the song had finished, she kissed him passionately, threw her head back in a bout of maniacal laughter and went off to capture her next victim.

'There you go,' he said, looking rather pleased with himself as he joined Harley and Bunty at the table. 'The old Yiddish Thunderbolt has still got it.' He sat down with a grin and helped himself to one of Harley's Gold Flakes.

'I'm proud of you, Sol. Who'd have thought you could be so broadminded.'

'What d'you mean?'

'You do know that was a fella, right?'

'What?' spluttered Rosen, pushing back his chair. 'You wait till I get my hands on—'

Harley grabbed his arm. 'Remember what we're here for.'

Rosen slumped back down in his chair and leant across the table. 'Listen, George – if you go blabbing about this around the manor…'

'My lips are sealed.' Harley glanced over at Bunty. 'You're quiet for once, Miss Chatterton. All a bit too much for you?'

'Don't be silly,' she said, searching for something in the crowd. 'As I've told you before, I've been to a good deal of extraordinary places in my travels.'

'Who are you looking for?'

'I'd have thought that would have been obvious – Ilse Blau, of course. After all, isn't that the reason we're all here?'

'She's not going to be out here yet, is she? The main attraction? It'd spoil the suspense if she was hobnobbing with the punters before her big number. No, we just take our time, sit back, and observe. Don't be too obvious about it. And remember, our main priority is that little kiddie's safety.'

'But you said it yourself – the death of that poor girl, Tallulah, the little missing orphan – the whole thing seems to revolve around Blau. Shouldn't we be trying to seek her out backstage?'

'Granted, she seems to tie a lot of loose ends together, but in the mix you've also got those German agents, and last, but by no means least, that shicer Morkens. I'm not going to mess up a chance of getting my hands on that lunatic by jumping the gun.'

'I hear you there, bruv,' said Rosen.

'We need to do this right,' continued Harley. 'Look around you. Tell me what you see that might be of interest to us.'

'Well,' she said, still looking a little uncomfortable. 'It's hard to say. This place is so, I don't know… *decadent*, I suppose is the word for it. How one is supposed to notice anything out of the ordinary in such surroundings is beyond me, really it is.'

Harley sat back and took a long, contemplative pull on his

cigarette. There was certainly something out of kilter with Miss Chatterton tonight. She seemed exceptionally jumpy, on edge. He watched her fingers drumming nervously on the tabletop. Perhaps it had been a mistake to invite her along?

'What about those two over there?' he said, nodding to two of the Joeys standing at the bar, engaged in conversation.

'The waiters? Well, it's a rather unconventional uniform, of course. But… Well, I'm not sure how you can tell them apart from the rest of the staff here.'

'If they're waiters, then they're lousy at their job. They've not responded to one call from the tables since I've been watching them. And a couple of the other blokes working the floor have been giving them odd looks, as though they don't recognise them. A couple to keep our eye on, I'd say.'

Just then, up on his dais, the drummer began an extended roll on the snare. To the audience's delight, the house lights dimmed slowly to black, with the exception of a single remaining spotlight that framed the emcee's painted Grimaldi features.

'Quiet please, ladies and gentlemen,' he purred into his microphone, bringing the excited murmuring to a hush. 'And now, the moment we have all been waiting for. For your delectation and delight, our patron, Simeon Dubois, has once again engaged Berlin's notorious Queen of Depravity to present you with another of her scenes of horror… decadence… and desire!'

Framed by the bright circle of light, the clown mouth now stretched into a lascivious grin, revealing gleaming teeth, stained here and there with crimson lipstick.

'I give you – Astarte and her troupe in… *Heliogabal!*'

The spotlight was snuffed out, leaving complete darkness. There followed a few drawn out seconds of expectant silence…

Then, as though summoned by some incantation, she appeared centre stage, bathed in an infernal red glow.

Ilse Blau. The Queen of Depravity. Channelling the crazed Roman Emperor Heliogabal – part temple prostitute, part sun god – writhing to a demonic adagio, the shocking vision of her brazen naked poses immediately drew gasps of surprise and admiration from the crowd.

35

'**B**LIMEY!' SAID HARLEY, watching the last of Astarte's dancers – now bloodied and limp with exhaustion – exit the stage. 'They ain't exactly the Tiller Girls, are they?'

He looked over at a dumbstruck Solly Rosen. 'You alright, mate?'

'I don't know what I've just watched there, George. But for Christ's sake, don't tell Marni about it, will you?'

Bunty crossed her arms, glaring disdainfully. 'Well, I, for one, didn't think it the least bit clever. How one could describe that obscene exhibition as art is beyond me. Pure pornography. The woman is obviously suffering from some kind of mental aberration. It's a wonder she hasn't been committed.'

'I'm not sure this lot would agree with you,' said Harley, above the tumultuous applause.

'That's hardly surprising, is it?' Bunty was looking flustered now, as she searched around in her handbag. 'I mean, just look at them. I've never seen such an unhealthy bunch of degenerates.' She produced a handkerchief and gave a violent blow to her nose. 'Now, if you two have finished rolling your tongues back into your mouths, can we finally get on with the job in hand? I'm assuming you've no objections to interviewing Blau now?'

'Right, you need to calm down a bit.'

But Harley's disgruntled assistant had already begun to make her way towards the stage.

'Bunty! That's not the way to do it,' he said, having caught up with her on the dance floor. 'Climbing up on stage to get to the back of house? You'll be seen straight away. I don't know what's got into to you tonight, but can you just think for a moment before you act?'

'I'm sorry, George.' She heaved a sigh, looking a little deflated. 'If I'm honest with you… well, I keep thinking about that poor girl Tallulah. How she ended up in that awful suitcase. It's affected me more than I'd imagined.'

'Listen,' he said, with a reassuring smile. 'You go home. Solly and I can handle this.'

'I'm sure you can; but I want to see this thing through. I'm convinced Blau is the key to it all.' She took a deep breath and pulled herself up straight. 'Let's "crack on with it", as you'd say.'

'Alright, then.' He nodded surreptitiously to a door next to the bar, partially concealed by a curtain. 'I watched a couple of Astarte's girls go in there earlier. That's our way in.'

A few minutes later, they were sitting at the bar with Rosen, biding their time, waiting for a suitable candidate to follow through to the back of house area.

'Why can't we just go through on our own?'

'Too suspicious, Sol,' said Harley. 'If we follow a member of staff through, then to any onlookers it looks like we're being escorted… Right, here we go. After these two here, with the trays. Remember – plenty of front. Look confident, as if you're meant to be there. If anyone asks, we're British representatives of United Artists; we've got a proposition for Miss Astarte.

That should open a few doors. I mean, all these characters want to be in the movies, don't they?'

But as they got off their stools, Rosen placed a hand on Harley's arm. 'Hold on, mate. Looks like we've got company.'

Harley glanced across the room to find himself being scrutinised by Irvine's menacing stare. The Scotsman spat a mouthful of nutshell onto the floor and nodded at him.

'Alright,' said Harley. 'Change of plan. We'll need a distraction.'

* * *

Blau knew the muffled pounding from the club below meant they were halfway through their ridiculous little African pastiche number – all kettle drums and rattling skulls on sticks. She usually thought the piece anodyne and tiresome, but tonight the drumming had acquired certain portentous overtones for her. She sat on the stairs to catch her breath, shivering a little as she pulled her dressing gown around her pale body.

Her immediate worry was that it looked like her suspicions about the two new waiters had been correct. She couldn't help noticing them as she'd left the stage, staring at her from the back of house. It would appear Mendel's warning had been on the money. That meant the escape plan needed to be implemented immediately. She'd retrieve the film from the child's room, throw a few things into an overnight bag, collect her money from Dubois, and then disappear into the night. Back to Paris in the short term – after all, there were still a few loyal friends there from the old days – and then, who knew? New York? Hollywood? Perhaps the time had come to launch the movie career of the Queen of Depravity? She'd have to tone it all down a bit, of course – those corn-fed Americans liked things a little more clean-cut. But if truth be told, she'd long ago lost the thrill she'd once felt in dropping her knickers in public. What was it that Brecht had called her? Germany's most honest performer? Maybe there was some mileage in the idea. She'd have to acquire the correct representation, of course; if there was one thing those Americans knew how to do, it was negotiate a deal. But she'd always gotten along with the Jews; that wouldn't be a problem. So, on with the plan.

If only she didn't feel so exhausted. It was the comedown from the adrenaline of the performance, of course – that and the cocaine wearing off. She'd normally be feeding the beast by now; bathing in the sycophantic praise of her adoring audience, while self-medicating to the edge of unconsciousness with whatever intoxicant was at hand. But not tonight. Tonight she needed to keep a relatively clear head if she wanted to avoid those Bavarian bully boys.

As she approached the top-floor accommodation, Blau slipped off her shoes and padded barefoot towards Poppy's room.

She placed her ear to the door…

Good, it sounded like the little girl was safely tucked up in bed for the night. She went up on her toes to retrieve the key from on top of the architrave – those idiot Joeys were so unimaginative – and let herself quietly into the darkened room.

Blau had expected to find Poppy curled up under the covers; had planned how, if the little girl became frightened by this late-night intrusion, she'd softly caress her worried brow. And, of course, she wasn't a monster – she wouldn't actually steal the poor thing's doll. No, she'd carefully undo the seam, retrieve the canister, and then stitch everything up again, all good as new. She had the needle and thread ready in her pocket. That's what she'd expected. But what she found made her stop in her tracks, a creeping nausea rising from her gut.

* * *

'What about this distraction?' asked Bunty.

'Hold on, love,' said Rosen. 'Give him a moment. I've seen that look in his eye before. He's concocting something.'

'As it happens, I do have a little idea.' Harley killed his cigarette in the ashtray. 'Now, I just need to find out where…'

He made a quick scan of the room, finally alighting on a group of young men gossiping around a table by the bar.

'There he is… Ah! Perfect timing,' said Harley, as a gypsy violin struck up a florid introduction to the song 'Dark Eyes'. 'Solly, you're going to take Miss Chatterton for a little dance.'

'I'm afraid I might not be quite up to this sort of thing, George,' said Bunty, looking disconcertingly at the throng of revellers shimmying on the dance floor.

'I wouldn't worry about that – you'll spend most of the time avoiding those gigantic feet of his.'

'Oi! I'll have you know my "Black Bottom" was the talk of the party last New Year's.'

'There's an image it's going to take a while to shake off,' said Harley. 'Off you go, you two. And make sure you take a couple of turns over by our Scottish friend. I think he's got a bit of a thing for you, Bunty, so it should keep his eyes off me for a while.'

'Hold on a minute! You're not intending to slip in and see Blau on your own, are you?'

'No, don't worry. I'm just going to arrange a bit of a distraction, so we can get through that door without Irvine clocking us.' Harley glanced back to the table of young men. 'Alright. Go on, now. But keep an eye out. Be ready to meet me back here when it all starts to kick off.'

'Ooh, vada this one,' said a youth in a striped blazer, holding a lorgnette up to his eyes to study the private detective as he approached the table. 'Such a butch mince, too.' He turned to the fey redhead sitting next to him. 'One of yours, Cyril, dear? She looks like a bit of rough trade, to me. Right up your street, I'd say.'

The young man looked up from his glass of champagne, a broad smile immediately replacing his default pose of affected ennui. 'I should say he is…' He stood up and flung his arms wide. 'George! How fantabulosa!'

'How are you, Tommy?'

'Tommy?' repeated the boy in the striped blazer, arching an immaculately plucked eyebrow.

The redhead leant in to whisper in Harley's ear. 'It's Cyril now. New start and all that.'

Having made a quick check of Cyril's drinking partners, Harley thought he could probably guess why; after all, though nowhere near the dizzying heights of the top echelons of the club's clientele, there was no doubt this small group of revellers was a good few rungs up the ladder from Cyril's old comrades. Harley looked at the bottle in the ice bucket and at the half-eaten plate of hors d'oeuvres. It was obvious this particular dilly boy had fallen on his feet – the Tommy Harkin he used to know would have been quite content with a mug of sweet tea and a plate of egg and chips. All the signs were that 'Cyril' moved in altogether different circles.

'Looks like you're on velvet,' said Harley. 'Nice to see someone doing well for a change. Listen, can I have a word? I need a favour.'

As the band segued into a spirited rendition of 'Limehouse Blues', Harley laid out his proposition to the young man, culminating in the offer of half a crown.

'Put your money away, George. I still owe you for saving my skin with those soldier boys that night. When would you like me to start the performance?'

Harley took a quick look at the dance floor. 'No time like the present.'

'Right you are,' said the former dilly boy, with an arch smile.

Whether Cyril had ever met the smart young man with the tousled hair who he now marched up to and passionately kissed on the mouth was neither here nor there. The main thing, as far as Harley was concerned, was that it produced exactly the required reaction from both the assaulted party and his female companion. A slap on the cheek; a thrown glass of wine; a push; a shove; a broken string of pearls; an upturned table… within a minute of that first stolen caress, Harley had the minor brawl he'd been hoping for. Now, all that was left was for Cyril to remember his lines and…

'Look out! He's got a knife!' came an excited shriek from within the melee.

Good boy, thought Harley, as he left the ensuing chaos and set off towards the bar.

* * *

A few moments later, Harley, Bunty and Rosen had successfully slipped into the back-of-house area undetected and were quietly making their way down a narrow corridor.

'Nicely done, Georgie boy,' said Rosen. 'I'm not sure even I could have started a ruck as quickly as that. Irvine and his boys fell for it, hook, line and sinker.'

'Yeah, well. We're not home and dry yet. We've got to find our little Fräulein first, without getting rumbled… Here we go.' Harley pointed to a small sign on the wall. 'Dressing rooms. Come on, this way.'

It didn't take them long to work out which dressing room belonged to the star of the show: even before they could read the small nameplate, they had already caught sight of the large page torn from a sketchpad which someone had pinned to the door – a charcoal sketch of the cabaret dancer striking a pose, naked except for one silk stocking and a monocle. On the floor by the door was a tray bearing a bottle of champagne and two glasses.

Harley placed his finger to his lips, then picked up the tray and knocked boldly on the door.

'Miss Astarte?' Without waiting for an answer, he thrust open the door. 'Sorry to surprise you, only we've just seen the show and—'

But it was Harley who was in for a surprise. Instead of discovering the artiste sitting at her dressing table, removing her stage make-up, she was squaring up to a rather perturbed-looking Simeon Dubois, pushing the needle-like tip of a foot-long hatpin to his throat.

'Where is she?!' she hollered, her gaudily made-up eyes wild with maniacal rage. 'Vot have you done wiz the child?!'

Dubois flinched as the steel point pushed into his flesh, producing a small bead of blood, which quickly swelled to trickle down onto his wing-collar. Without moving his head, the dandy risked a quick glance at Harley.

'I don't know who the devil you are,' he said, through gritted teeth, 'but I'd be obliged if you could rescue me from this madwoman.'

'Mad?!' screamed Blau, flecking his face with saliva. 'You've seen nothing yet! What have you done with her?!'

Harley indicated for Rosen to close the door behind them before taking a tentative step forward.

'Miss Astarte? My name's George Harley. I'm a friend of Lily Lee. You know Lil, right?'

'I have no time for your little English chit-chats, mister,' said Blau, without taking her eyes off Dubois. 'I'm making busy with this one. You see him? Quite the gentleman, ja?' She twisted the pin a little, making Dubois wince. 'Could you believe such a man would kidnap a small child? Keep her locked up? Offer her up to his rich friends, like a plaything?'

'Preposterous!' said Dubois. 'The woman's a drug addict. It's all fantasy, I tell you, the result of a bout of delirium tremens, or the like.'

'Actually, I do believe her, Mr Dubois,' said Harley. 'I take it you are Simeon Dubois?'

Harley risked another small step forward.

'You see, Astarte, that's the very reason we're here tonight – to discover the whereabouts of a little orphan girl, named Poppy. Is that who you're talking about, Ilse?'

At the mention of her real name, Blau turned to regard the newcomers for the first time, and as she caught sight of Bunty Chatterton her expression changed from rage to shock.

'*Mein Gott*! You?!'

Taking full advantage of the lapse in his attacker's concentration, Dubois struck out with the back of his hand. As the cabaret artiste collapsed onto the small sofa, Harley jumped in to intervene, yanking Dubois away before he could do any more damage.

The club owner stood glowering at him for a moment, before pulling a silk handkerchief from his pocket to dab at the small wound on his neck.

'Bunty?' said Harley. 'What's going on here? Have you two met before?'

'I haven't a clue how she recognised me, really I haven't,' said Bunty. 'Bit of a nuisance, really, but there we are…'

With a sigh of resignation, she reached into her handbag; and for the second time that week, Harley found himself staring into the barrel of a Walther PPK semi-automatic.

36

'I'M AFRAID I'M going to have to ask you to step away from her now, George,' said Bunty, training the gun on him as she moved towards the sofa. 'That's right, all the way back, over there… And you, Solomon,' she added, noticing the ex-boxer's clenched fists. 'Please don't go getting any ideas about overpowering the little woman. Believe me, I shan't hesitate to shoot. You too, Dubois, over there. That's right. Now, all three of you, keep your hands in full view – there we are, thank you so much.'

She took a quick glance at her watch.

'Expecting someone, Bunty?' asked Harley. 'Though, of course, that's probably not your real name, is it?'

'Good Lord, no,' she said. 'I mean, it's quite awful, isn't it? I got it from a podgy little thing we used to bully at school. Still, it did the trick, wouldn't you say? Struck just the right note to muster certain preconceptions?'

Behind her, Blau sat up, groaning as she held a hand to the side of her face.

'*Zicke!*' she hissed, spitting on the floor.

Regarding the German with a patronising smile, Bunty took a step closer and pressed the muzzle of the gun against her forehead.

'Please be quiet for the moment, Fräulein. There'll be plenty of opportunity for you to speak in a short while – in fact, I shall insist on it.'

'I wish now I'd let that jock search your soddin' handbag,' said Rosen, trying to defuse the situation a little. 'So, if you're not Bunty, who the bloody hell are you, lady?'

'Isn't it obvious?' said Blau, staring defiantly at her persecutor. 'The blonde hair, the blue eyes? She's quite the poster girl, wouldn't you say?'

This last remark earned the dancer another slap to the face.

'Understand this, Blau. I am here for one thing, and one thing only. Now, you can prolong the process with these little histrionics, but you know, of course, that the result will be simply more misery and pain.' Keeping her eyes on the three men, Bunty now leant in close to whisper in the cabaret artiste's ear. 'Believe me, you little slut, I'd consider it an act of duty to rid the world of such an example of degenerate scum.'

Just then the door of the dressing room burst open, causing Harley and Rosen to tense up, ready to spring.

It was a pair of Joey clowns. The two men stood, cautiously surveying the scene before them.

'About time too,' said Bunty. 'Well, don't just stand there – come in and get that door shut.'

As they slipped into the room, Harley gave the men a quick appraisal. They were the two he'd noticed earlier, acting suspiciously at the bar. Even in their Grimaldi costumes and greasepaint, it was obvious from the way they held themselves that they were professionals. The odds had just changed significantly.

'So,' said Bunty, addressing the clowns. 'How was your stroll in the park today?'

'The weather was fine, but it was busy,' said one of the men.

'Tomorrow we will take a boat out on the lake,' added the other.

'Good,' she said. 'All is well, then... So, down to business. In my bag you'll find silk scarves. Bind their hands please, tightly. Be careful – the big one is a violent criminal. And a Jew. Take no chances with him.'

Rosen bristled at this but eased back when the clowns produced two pistols of their own.

'This one is a former MI5 agent,' she said, nodding at Harley. 'Treat him accordingly.'

'So,' said Harley, as his arms were roughly pulled behind his back, 'I'm guessing from your little coded paroles about the park that you're Abwehr, right? I've got to hand it to you, lads – your accents are spot on.'

'The clowns may be Abwehr,' said Blau, with contempt. 'But this one? Schutzstaffel. It's written all over her pink little Aryan face... Of course, I recognised her straight away.' She cocked her head, with a mocking grin. 'She might not know it, but at one time she was the source of much amusement among the Berlin set. Her and that moronic Mitford girl, with their peachy complexions and blonde curls. *Die Englischen Schülerinnen*, we used to call them. Hitler's little fan club, gushing over him every lunchtime in the Osteria Bavaria. Getting all hot over that creep – and she calls me degenerate.'

Bunty's pistol-whip sent the dancer flying across the sofa. When she struggled back to a sitting position, her bottom lip was split and beginning to swell. She probed the wound with her tongue, taking a moment to calm her laboured breathing.

'You see, you might not believe this, Mr Harley,' she continued, defiantly. 'But there was a time I used to hang around with little Adolf... Well, actually, it would be more correct to say that he used to hang around with us.' She took a wary glance at Bunty's gun hand. 'Like a little stray dog with his tongue hanging out, sniffing at our arses.'

Blau's raucous laughter soon deteriorated into a prolonged bout of coughing. When she finally recovered, the spittle she delivered onto the floorboards was flecked with clots of blood.

'You appear to be unwell,' said Bunty sarcastically. 'I do hope it's something serious.'

The cabaret artiste spat again, wiped her mouth and carried on.

'Of course, they are still very interested in me, these National Socialists. Very interested, indeed. I have something they want, you see. Something their crazed little demigod is eager to make disappear.'

'Enough!' barked Bunty.

She yanked back Blau's head and forced the gun into her mouth. 'Where is it?'

This was too much for Rosen, and he began to push forward into the Joeys.

'Easy, Sol,' murmured Harley. 'It's alright.'

'It's not fucking alright!' seethed Rosen, barely able to contain his rage.

On the sofa, though gagged by the gun barrel, Blau's eyes still sparkled with defiant humour.

'What? You think I wouldn't do it?' hissed Bunty, pushing her face in close. 'Believe me, this is the day you die, Blau. The only choice you now have is how painless it will be. So, tell me, where is it…? No? Alright then. Enough fooling around.'

She turned to the clowns.

'Before we start her interrogation, let's see if a little demonstration of intent might work.' She pointed to Harley and Rosen. 'They've already heard too much. Deal with the Jew first.'

She plucked a cushion from the sofa. 'Here – use this to muffle the shot.'

As the clown guarding him went to catch the cushion,

Rosen seized the moment, delivering the man a thundering headbutt, sending him sprawling to the floor.

Now somehow miraculously free of his bonds, Harley made his own move. After vaulting across the room, all it took was a deft chin thrust and a parry, and the SS agent posing as Bunty Chatterton was left disarmed and groaning on the floor.

'No, Sol!' he yelled, noticing his friend about to tackle the second gun-wielding clown. 'He's one of ours!'

'What d'you mean, one of ours?'

'Well, if I'm not mistaken, that's Commander Snip Taylor you're just about to clobber. Right, Snip?'

The clown lowered his gun and gave a brief salute.

'Sorry about the restraint, Mr Rosen. I gave George a slipknot, but my colleague there wasn't aware of your friendly status… And he might still need a little convincing on that score, by the looks of things.'

With a low groan, Taylor's partner struggled to his feet, holding his bloodied nose.

'At ease, Bradshaw. Rosen wasn't to know our true identities.'

'No, of course not, Commander,' said Bradshaw, testing his jaw. He held out a hand to Rosen. 'No hard feelings, chum.'

'But how could you tell these two were on our side, George?' asked a perplexed Rosen, shaking the agent's hand. 'I mean, with that gunk on their faces they all look the same to me.'

'Morse code,' said Harley, keeping a close eye on Bunty, who was beginning to come round. 'When Snip was tying my hands, he tapped out a message on my wrist.'

'We've been undercover here for just over a week now,' explained Taylor.

'So, that explains it.'

'Explains what?'

'Oh, nothing. A copper at Vine Street was putting some pressure on me to steer clear of this place, that's all.'

'Yes, the Yard may well have been aware of our interest in the club,' continued Taylor. 'You see, the Firm had been in receipt of some decent intelligence, leading us to believe that a female German agent, of some importance, might be operating within the city. A subsequent intercepted communication made reference to the Grimaldi Vaults; so we decided to take a closer look. The backroom Johnnies soon discovered Miss Astarte's real name, and that we had reports on file of an Ilse Blau attending occult gatherings with Hitler, in the years before he rose to prominence.'

'Occult?' said a concerned Rosen, taking a sideways glance at Blau. 'She some kind of witch or something?'

'Not quite, Solomon,' said Taylor, with a smile. 'This was more of a mystery-cult setup. Quite a number of these outfits sprang up in Berlin after the war. This one was headed up by a chap called Fedor von Görlitz.'

'Von Görlitz?' Harley spun around to Blau. 'Do you know where that bastard is now, Ilse? The truth now! After all, I'd say you owed us one, wouldn't you?'

'Ah, I see you have had your own dealings with Fedor, Mr Harley.' She smiled, tentatively probing her swollen lip with her finger. 'If it's any consolation at all I also think this man is a bastard.'

Harley thought he saw her give Dubois a knowing look.

'But alas, no, I cannot tell you where he is. These days I would be considered an unacceptable associate for Herr von Görlitz. You see, he has rather thrown in his lot with her little gang.' She nodded at the incapacitated female agent. 'He's become some kind of special adviser to the Nazi high command on all things occult. Himmler's Rasputin, they call him.' She gave a little dispirited laugh. 'Fedor always did have a flair for self-preservation. Even if you did know where to find him, Mr Harley, I'm afraid Herr von Görlitz now enjoys the protection of the Schutzstaffel, and all the rest of those Bavarian bully boys.'

'What about your lot, Snip?' said Harley, pulling out a Gold Flake and sparking up. 'Has the Firm had any recent intel on Von Görlitz? You know he was involved with the Morkens murders, don't you?'

'Indeed. But I'm afraid he only comes up in this investigation as the leader of this secret society, back in the mid-twenties.'

'I applaud you on your research, Commander,' drawled Blau. 'But our cult was a little more than just a "secret society". Nothing so boring. We were practising Sex Magick – the exquisite transmogrifications of the flesh… You should try it some time.'

'Yes, quite,' said Commander Taylor, with a little embarrassed cough. 'But the point is, Harley, what with Fräulein Blau's some-what compromising performances here at the club, and certain high-profile dignitaries she may have access to… well, we rather got hold of the wrong end of the stick, I'm afraid. As it turns out, it appears you were the one harbouring the Nazi agent.'

'Yeah. I've been taken for a proper mug.' He pulled Bunty to her feet and gave her a rough pat down. 'Stand there, up against the wall. And don't move until you're told to. Bradshaw – keep an eye on her.'

'Righto.'

'How are you feeling?' said Harley, taking a seat next to Blau. 'We'll need to get some ice on that. Are your teeth alright?'

'Don't fuss so! I'm fine.' She batted his hand away. 'Get me something to smoke if you want to be of use. There, on the dressing table. And a clean handkerchief.'

While Harley was busy searching among her things, Blau took a little surreptitious dip into her silver pendant.

'*Danke*,' she said, spitting on the handkerchief and pressing it to her swollen lip.

'Is it true, then?' asked Harley, holding up a match to her cigarillo. 'About Hitler?'

'*Na, klar.* He was once a member of the Order. Though there aren't many of us left to attest to such a thing. He was only a neophyte, of course; never rose any further up the ranks. Actually, we always saw him as a bit of a loser.'

This last comment elicited a black look from the recovering agent Chatterton.

'And I'm guessing his history with this cult has got something to do with whatever they're so desperate to get their hands on, right?'

Blau regarded him for a while, drawing deeply on her smoke.

'Come on, now. You can trust us, Fräulein,' said Taylor, his smile not quite so reassuring as he intended, delivered, as it was, from behind his grotesque mask of make-up. 'After all, haven't we just saved your life?'

Blau sniffed dismissively. 'Trust, Commander? I am afraid, since your little party in Versailles, we Germans have had to learn a different meaning of this word.'

'Listen, Ilse,' said Harley. 'If you really do have something on Hitler, where else are you going to share it? I mean, you can't exactly go back home with it, can you?'

'You're a traitor to your country, Blau,' hissed Bunty from across the room.

Despite her injuries, Blau now sprang up from the sofa. 'Is that so? I'm a traitor, *ja*? And what are you, then, *meine kleine Englische Schulmädchen*?'

'I'd wouldn't get too close, Fräulein,' warned Taylor.

'Oh, she is quite alone now, Commander. Aren't you, *Liebling*? Quite powerless.' Blau blew a cloud of cigarillo smoke into Bunty's face. 'I think it is you who will be receiving the traitor's reward now, from these good gentlemen. And your little Austrian chum? Well, he isn't going to be too pleased with you, is he?'

She pushed her face in close, forcing Bunty to meet her

gaze. 'You do know what we used to call him in the Order, don't you? That little watercolour artist, stammering for words, with his eyes as big as saucers, and his ridiculous schoolgirl's distaste for red meat. No? *Die Jungfrau.* Oh, he was quite the figure of fun back then, my dear.'

She laughed and turned to Harley.

'So, if I tell you what it is they are seeking, you will help me, Mr Harley?'

'What do you need?'

Blau pointed a varnished nail at Dubois. 'First, I need this one to tell me where he has taken the little girl – the child you called Poppy.'

'Well, funnily enough,' said Harley, looking over at the club owner, 'that's exactly what I'd like to know, as well.'

'Now, look here,' protested Dubois. 'I'm not quite sure what you're insinuating, but I assure that I—'

'Alright, Dubois,' said Taylor. 'You'll get your turn to account for yourself. Please – go on, Fräulein.'

'Secondly, I'd like an assurance that, if I do decide to stay in this country, I will be offered protection from these National Socialist maniacs. And finally, I need to know that, if I hand it over, you will put the item that I have to good use.'

Harley looked at Taylor. 'Commander?'

'Well now, I am not officially authorised to sanction such conditions, you understand… but I'd say that all sounds most reasonable to me.'

'Good,' said Blau, smiling as she turned her attention back to Bunty. 'And so, my little Aryan friend, do you know what it is I hold? Have they told you what I have photographic evidence of? No…? Well, your little Chancellor won't last a day longer in office once these images are released to the world's press. He'll be the laughing stock of Europe.' She took a satisfied draw on her smoke and chuckled. 'When every-one sees his pale, skinny little arse. And his tiny, shrivelled *dick.* When they learn about all of those nasty, perverted little things he got up to. Well, then I am afraid that—'

If it hadn't had been for the cabaret artiste's animated gesticulations, the others might have noticed Bunty's hand creeping towards the discarded hat pin, resting on the arm of the sofa. As it was, by the time Harley caught sight of the improvised weapon, it was too late – the SS agent had already plunged its vicious point deep into Ilse Blau's pale-blue eye.

As Commander Taylor wrestled Bunty to the floor, the dancer emitted an odd, mewling sound, and thrust one trembling hand in the air.

'Bradshaw – the scarves!' said Taylor. 'Bind her feet for me.'

But as the commander rolled his captive over, he noticed the glassy, lifeless stare. He quickly searched for a pulse, then forced open her mouth and took a sniff.

'Damn it!' he said, standing up and rubbing his hands on his trousers.

'Sir?'

'Strong smell of almonds, Bradshaw.'

'Cyanide, sir?'

'Looks like it. Suicide capsule – standard Abwehr practice. How's Blau, Harley?'

Harley was cradling the injured dancer in his arms on the sofa. She was now racked with convulsions and drooling pink spittle.

'Not looking good,' he said. 'The point must have penetrated the brain… Hold on… She's trying to say something.' He lowered his head to make sense of the gurgling.

'*Puppe… Die Puppe…*' repeated the German, gagging between each word. '*Die Puppe… von der Kleinen.*'

'The little girl's doll,' said Taylor.

'Is that where you've hidden it?' asked Harley. 'In the doll?'

Then, with an almighty effort of will, Blau turned her face slowly towards Dubois, fixing him with a nightmarish stare, her ruined eyeball a deep purple against the ashen complexion, looking like some grotesque bauble stuck with its bejewelled spike.

'*He* knows…'

Gripped in a final grand seizure, Blau's body contorted violently, like some cruel parody of her erotic choreography. After a minute or so of this torturous thrashing, she finally relinquished the struggle and slumped back into Harley's arms.

'Save the girl…' she whispered, 'and you save Germany!'

'Ambulance, Bradshaw. Quick as you like,' said Taylor, kneeling down in front of the sofa.

'I reckon it's a little late for that, Snip,' said Harley, placing a gentle hand to the dead dancer's extraordinary face.

37

'I SAY, DO YOU really think it's necessary to keep those weapons drawn?' asked Simeon Dubois, lighting another of his fragrant Turkish cigarettes. 'I mean, I'm hardly likely to overpower the four of you, now am I?'

For the last twenty minutes, Harley and Commander Taylor had been attempting to extract the whereabouts of the kidnapped orphan Poppy from the club owner, but Dubois had continued to meet every turn of the interrogation with the insouciance of a pedigree Siamese cat.

'You know I'd dearly love to help you gentlemen,' he said, smoothing down an eyebrow. 'I mean, a missing little orphan girl? Why, one would have to be a brute not to be moved. But, you see, it's all just fantasy. A product of the poor creature's drug-addled brain.' He paused to nod distastefully at Blau's body, which lay on the sofa, covered by a Persian throw. 'In the last few weeks, she had become increasingly paranoid, you see. Such a waste of talent.'

Rosen jumped up from his chair and began to crack his knuckles.

'I've had just about enough of his old gammon, George. Why don't you leave me alone with him for a few minutes? I'll soon drag it out of him.'

'I'm afraid we can't do that, Solomon,' said Taylor. 'After all, we only have Blau's word for it that Mr Dubois is involved at all.'

'Her dying testament, though,' said Harley. 'What would she have to gain from lying?'

'Must we really go over this again?' said Dubois, in a patronising tone. 'The unfortunate woman wasn't in her right mind. I ask you – what possible need would I have to kidnap a little girl? And if Astarte were so convinced of my involvement in this nefarious business, well then, why on earth didn't she go to the authorities with her concerns? No, it's all too ridiculous... Tell me – apart from the final ramblings of our poor coryphée, there, what other evidence do you have to suggest that I might know the whereabouts of this missing child?'

'Well, George?' asked Taylor.

Harley gave a sigh and rubbed the back of his neck. 'None,' he said, deciding that Commander Taylor wouldn't make the most receptive audience to a discussion on his famous gut instinct.

'In that case, I suggest we hand the matter over to Scotland Yard; see what they can make of it. I'm afraid this is no longer MI5 business.'

'Come on, Snip!' said Harley, becoming animated. 'You heard what's on that film. That's gold dust, ain't it? Enough to topple that shicer Hitler from his pedestal for good.'

'As you well know, at the Firm we are neither politicians nor policemen. Bradshaw and I have a strict brief – to root out the female German spy and discover her primary mission. I believe that brief has now been fulfilled. As a bonus, we also have her two colleagues who were masquerading as waiters.'

'I don't believe this. Typical Security Service bullshit.'

'Steady now.'

'I'm sorry, but you must see it's to the nation's advantage to get hold of that film. Can't you take the initiative for once, go outside of the brief? And what about the kiddie, eh? Isn't her life worth anything? God knows what this lot have got planned for that poor little mite.'

'Commander Taylor,' said Dubois, finally dropping his supercilious smile. 'I really must insist that this fellow retracts these wild accusations.'

'Cheese it, Little Lord Fauntleroy!' barked Harley, much to Rosen's amusement.

'That'll do, George,' said Taylor. He thought for a moment and then pocketed his gun. 'Mr Dubois, I trust you wouldn't have any objections to answering a few questions from CID?'

'I suppose not. As long as we can finally settle this matter for good. Though, I think it's only fair to advise you that I have some very well-positioned friends in the Metropolitan Police Force.'

'What a surprise,' said Harley wearily.

'Perhaps, then,' continued Taylor, 'we might move to your office, to use the telephone?'

* * *

A few minutes later, as they gathered around Dubois's elegant mahogany desk, waiting for Commander Taylor to be put through to Scotland Yard, there came an urgent knock on the office door.

'Simeon?! Why the devil have you got this locked?' Even though it was coming from the other side of the panelled door, it was obvious from the slur in his aristocratic drawl that the Honourable Hugo Fitz Corbet was somewhat the worse for wear. 'Are you avoiding me? I know you're in there – I can hear you!'

'Not now, Hugo, there's a good chap. I'm a little busy at the moment.'

Harley thought he caught the briefest look of apprehension flash across Dubois's face.

'Not now? You're not addressing the bally footman, you know. If it's not too much to ask, I'd be grateful if you'd afford me a minute or two of your precious time.'

There was a dull thump as Fitz Corbet slumped against the office door.

'I've been trying to talk to you all night, Simmy,' he continued, a maudlin note entering his voice now. 'I was an ass talking to the Preceptor like that the other night; I can see that now. I understand what a privilege it will be to attend that ritual. You really must give me another chance.'

Dubois hurried across the room, struggling to retain his strained smile.

He quickly turned the key, clenched tight the doorknob, and cracked open the door a couple of inches.

'Oh, thank goodness!' squealed Fitz Corbet, pushing his sweaty face to the gap. 'I know it's tonight, Simeon; there's no use denying it. Just tell me where. Is it at the same place as before – that warehouse affair, by the river?'

'I really am rather busy just now,' said Dubois, through gritted teeth. 'Just let me attend to these gentlemen, and I shall be able to—'

The club owner gave a little involuntary yelp as Harley's hand clamped down on his shoulder and yanked him out of the way.

'Don't listen to your mate,' he said to Fitz Corbet, throwing open the door. 'We've got plenty of time. After all, this sounds important. Why don't you come in and tell us all about it, eh?'

The startled aristocrat backed up against the lobby wall.

'No, I don't think so,' he said, dabbing a handkerchief to his florid brow. 'Perhaps it would be better if I came back later.'

'Oh, but I insist,' said Harley, suddenly brandishing Bunty's commandeered gun. 'In you come.'

'Alright! For the love of God, don't shoot!'

'I won't, sunshine – as long as you tell me where this little gathering you're talking about is being held.'

'Commander, do something,' said an uncharacteristically ruffled-looking Dubois. 'That's the fifth Marquess of Clenham your man is threatening there.'

'Harley!' snapped Taylor. 'What the devil do you think you're doing?'

'Just trust me on this one. You wanted evidence that Dubois is involved? Well, here it comes.'

'Commander, did you say?' said Fitz Corbet, nervously. 'Who are these chaps, Simeon?'

'There's nothing to worry about, Hugo. You don't have to answer any of his questions.'

'Schtum, Dubois! Solly? Make sure we're not disturbed.'

'Got it,' said Rosen, quickly taking position by the door.

'Now, Lord Clenham, is it?'

'That's correct,' said Fitz Corbet, keeping a worried eye on the pistol pointing at his chest. 'Wh-what do you want from me?'

'Just some information. You mentioned someone called the Preceptor?'

'Did I? Oh, Lord…' Fitz Corbet caught the black look that Dubois was giving him. 'No. I think you must be mistaken.'

Harley grabbed a handful of shirt, yanking the quivering aristocrat towards him.

'Where exactly is this going, George?' asked Taylor.

'This Preceptor – that's Osbert Morkens, right?'

'Morkens? The child-killer?' said Taylor. 'But he's in Broadmoor, isn't he?'

'Escaped. It's a long story… Now, Lord Clenham. You see those two men there, dressed up as club clowns? They're government agents.'

'Government agents?'

'That's right. You see, you've got yourself mixed up in a right old mess, here. The best thing you could do now is to just tell us all you know.'

'Don't do anything foolish now,' said Dubois, sitting down calmly on the office chaise longue. 'They haven't got anything on us at all.'

'Bradshaw,' said Taylor, drawing his own pistol. 'Stand that man up and keep him quiet… Go on, George.'

'So, what's it to be, Hugo? You going to get yourself arrested? Have your name splashed all over the papers? Drag the family reputation through the mud? Or are you going to tell us all about this little cult ritual you're involved in?'

With rapidly blinking eyes, Fitz Corbet looked over at Dubois and then back at Harley.

'But you don't understand. This fellow, the Preceptor – he's… he's *dangerous*.'

The private detective leant in close to whisper in Fitz Corbet's ear. 'So am I, your Lordship. And do you know what they'd do to a posh boy like you in prison? Especially when they find out there's a kiddie involved. You wouldn't last a week, my old son.'

The marquess let out a little juddering squeal.

'It's called the Order of the Thelemic Knights of the Unicursal!' he blurted out. 'And the ritual is tonight, I know that much.'

'Where?'

'I'm not sure. But the last one was in a disused warehouse, south of the river, near Tower Bridge somewhere… I don't know the name of the street.'

'You know, Hugo,' murmured Dubois, shaking his head, 'you really are the most pathetic little coward.'

'Don't you worry about him,' said Harley. 'You're doing great. Take your time, we need the name of that street. Think carefully, now.'

'I don't know, honestly. I've only ever been driven there before.'

'Sol, see if you can find a map of London on that bookshelf over there... Do you think you'd remember if you heard it again?'

'Possibly,' said Fitz Corbet, nervously. 'But I really couldn't promise.'

Harley looked over to Dubois and noticed the dandy glance anxiously at his desktop.

'Have a butcher's on the desk there.'

'Bingo!' said Rosen. *Bacon's Pocket Map*. Right...' He unfolded the map and spread it across the desk. 'Near Tower Bridge, you said?'

'I believe so,' said Fitz Corbet. 'On the south side.'

'Tooley Street...? Shad Thames...? Butler's Wharf?'

'I can't think. I-I-I'm really not sure I'd remember it, you know.'

'...Pickle Herring Street?'

'That's it!' cried Harley.

'Well, looks right for a warehouse,' said Rosen, rubbing his square jaw. 'Runs right along the foreshore. But what makes you so certain that's the one, George?'

'Trust me, it'll be there... Alright. Things are warming up. You've done very well so far, Hugo.'

Fitz Corbet nodded enthusiastically.

'But we need to know one more thing – the missing child, the little girl that was kidnapped. What do you know about her?'

'Oh yes, she'll be there. She's part of the ceremony.'

'What do you mean, part of the ceremony?' asked Rosen. 'Will those perverts be fiddling with her?'

'Oh no. She must remain pure, you understand – for the ritual. You see, she's the host, as it were.'

Rosen looked confused. 'It's her party?'

'Good Lord, no,' said Fitz Corbet, with a nervous giggle. 'The *host*, as in the Eucharist. I believe it comes from the Latin, doesn't it, Simeon? *Hostia*?'

Finally losing his cool, Dubois pulled frustratedly at his Van Dyke beard. 'You asinine fool,' he murmured, giving the aristocrat a black look.

'Take this bastard away, Snip,' said Harley, thrusting Fitz Corbet across the room. 'Before I do something I might regret.'

'With pleasure,' said Taylor, frogmarching Fitz Corbet over to the desk.

'We need to gatecrash this little witches' Sabbath of theirs. What d'you say, Commander? You up for it?'

'I'm sorry, George.'

'What?! You heard what he just said, there's a kid's life at stake here.'

'I understand. But unfortunately, we have to operate under strict protocols. We shan't be able to join you on this one, I'm afraid. But I'll call it in, immediately. And hand these two over to CID. I suggest you take Solomon and proceed immediately to the location. Do a recce and wait for backup from the Yard. They should be there within the half hour. Do you have transport?'

'I've got the Norton outside.'

'And Solomon?'

'He can go in the sidecar.'

'Alright then... Now, I know you, Harley – no heroics, d'you hear? You're to wait for that backup.'

'Right you are, Commander.'

'Good luck.'

'Come on then, Sol,' said Harley making for the door. 'Let's go catch us a child-killer.'

* * *

'Did you notice,' said Harley, as they made their way back out into the empty cloakroom lobby, 'our friendly jock and his pals have disappeared?'

'Probably at the bar. They like a drink, don't they.'

'Or maybe they've gone off to join the congregation?'

'Hmm, could be... What you up to?' Rosen watched as Harley vaulted the small reception counter and begin to rummage in the shelves beneath it.

'Thought I might be needing this at Morkens' little party,' said the private detective, producing his brass knuckles from a box of confiscated items.

'I was thinking of something a bit more persuasive... But listen, George, about this gathering we're off to – I still don't really understand that bit about the Eucharist. It's a yok thing, ain't it?'

'The host is the consecrated bread they give at communion. It's supposed to be the body of Christ.'

'But what's that got to do with the missing kid?'

'Bloody hell, Sol! Don't you get it? Those shicers are planning some kind of ritual cannibalism. Remember how little Eddie Muller was so chubby when we eventually found him? It was because Morkens and his cronies had been fattening him up, like a Christmas goose.'

Rosen stood there, slack-jawed, as he processed this information.

'So, if we hadn't have rescued him... he'd have been eaten? And that's what they've got in store for little Poppy?! Well, that fucking settles it. Sod waiting for the backup. We're stopping off at the pub to collect a little backup of our own from my cellar.'

'I thought you said you were going to get rid of that gear?'

'And I have... mostly. But I kept a little bit back, see. Plenty enough to deal with a shicer like Morkens and his little coven of witches.'

38

HARLEY AND ROSEN emerged from the Joseph Grimaldi pub to discover a greasy veil of London smog had descended on the night.

'That's all we need,' said Harley, turning his collar up against the chill air. 'It's going to be slow-going in this soup.'

'Look over there.' Rosen pointed to a hazy figure standing beneath the pale halo of a streetlamp. 'Who's that mooching about next to your bike?'

They watched as the silhouette paced back and forth under the streetlamp, casting warped shadows in the mist.

'What d'you reckon?' said Harley, lowering his voice. 'A little welcoming party from one of Bunty's little Abwehr playmates?'

'Let's go and find out, shall we?' said Rosen, rubbing his hands together. 'I need something to warm me up a bit... Here, but what about that little brama, Bunty, eh? Sheez! She looked like butter wouldn't melt. Talk about leading a double life. Quite funny really, you being a sherlock and everything.'

'Yeah, hilarious, ain't it? Come on. We'll circle around the back of him.'

Even without the cover of smog, a surprise night-time attack from the formidable duo would have put even the most talented field agent at a disadvantage; as it was, after just a few stealthy moves through the thick mist, the stranger found himself clamped tightly in Rosen's iron grip.

'It's alright, Sol, you can let him go now,' said Harley, after getting a close look at their captive.

'What?' Rosen removed his hand from the man's mouth and span him around. 'Blimey! You're John Franklin's boy, ain't you? Sorry about that, chum. No hard feelings, eh?'

DS Franklin took a moment to catch his breath. 'I suppose anyone can make a mistake,' he said, probing tentatively at the back of his neck.

'Well, I must say, that was quick – how many bodies have we got, then?' asked Harley enthusiastically, the tip of his Gold Flake glowing cherry red in the fog. 'Are the Q cars here or are they meeting us at the river?'

'There are no Q cars, George. It's just me, I'm afraid.'

'But didn't Commander Taylor explain the situation? I was expecting a full crew, tooled up and ready to go.'

'Commander Taylor? I don't know what you're talking about. After you left the office this morning… well, to be honest, I felt bad that I hadn't done more to help with trying to track down that little deaf girl. You said you were going to be here tonight, so… well, here I am, to lend a hand.'

'That's very noble of you, Alec. Disobeying orders like that.'

'I, for one, am impressed,' added Rosen, adjusting the crumpled collar of Franklin's gabardine. 'A chip off the old block, I'd say.'

'We're actually all done here,' continued Harley. 'But we've got a lead on the little girl. Me and Sol are just off to follow it up now. We could use another pair of hands, if you're game.

The Yard's been informed. They'll be sending some backup, so it's all kosher.'

'Might be a few wrong 'uns, there, mind,' said Rosen.

'What kind of wrong 'uns?' asked Franklin, a little wary at the thought of working alongside one of Mori Adler's henchmen, regardless of the mission.

'Professor Osbert Morkens for starters,' said Harley, retrieving his leather helmet and goggles from the motorbike's sidecar. 'What d'you say? You up for it?'

'Morkens?' Franklin mopped away the damp fog from his face with a handkerchief. 'Well, I don't suppose I've got much choice, have I?'

''Atta boy.'

'And I'm guessing this little escapade involves clinging onto the back of that infernal machine as we make a mad dash through this disgusting smog?'

'That's about the size of it.'

Franklin gave a sigh as he inspected the streaks of grime left on his handkerchief from wiping his face. 'You know, I sometimes struggle to see the attraction of this bloody city.'

Once Rosen had squeezed himself into the sidecar, Harley kick-started the Norton, filling the small back street with the holler of its 500cc engine.

'Come on, Alec, stop dawdling!' he shouted. 'We need to make a quick stop-off at Solly's boozer first. I'll fill you in on the way.'

* * *

Having visited the Bag O'Nails – where the CID officer was kept busy talking while Solly stuffed the suspicious-looking knapsack into the footwell of the sidecar – Harley drove his two companions out of the West End and motored eastward, with the intention of crossing the river at Tower Bridge.

From the onset it proved difficult going. The reduced

visibility meant Harley had to restrict their speed and negotiate any road junction with extreme caution. As they waited at one set of traffic lights, a strange dancing light materialised ahead of them in the eerie fog, a will-o'-the-wisp, which appeared to be leading some bestial hulk through the gloom. But as it passed by, this apparition was revealed to be nothing more fantastical than a well-wrapped conductor walking ahead of his tram with a naphtha flare.

'If it carries on like this, we might have to ditch the bike and take the Tube,' shouted Harley, having stopped at a junction. 'I suppose one saving grace is that Morkens' little cabal will have been delayed as well.'

At Cheapside, much to their relief, the fog began to clear a little, allowing the increase to a relatively decent speed. However, as they began to cross the river, they were plunged once more into the thick, mustard-coloured smog.

Harley stopped the Norton on the south side of the bridge and pointed out a hazy row of riverside buildings.

'I know we can't see much from here, but it's got to be one of those warehouses there, don't you think?'

Rosen peered into the mist. 'It's hard to say.'

'What about that one?' said Franklin, pointing to a row of first-floor lights, each one encircled in the fog by a shimmering corona.

'Well, it's possible,' agreed Harley. 'I mean, no one's going to be working the docks at this time of night, are they? Alec – you armed?'

'Yes. I thought it would be best. But I sincerely hope you two aren't?'

Rosen shared a brief knowing glance with Harley. 'Don't you worry about us,' he said, holding up his fists. 'We'll be alright when the roughhouse starts.'

'So,' said Harley, 'are we all agreed that the kidnapped girl is the priority, and after that, the recapture of Morkens?'

Franklin looked a little concerned with this question. 'Well, yes… But didn't you say Commander Taylor was organising backup? Surely, we should just surveil the place and wait for assistance.'

'That depends on what we find. We've lost a lot of time, remember.'

'I'm with George,' said Rosen. 'I don't know about you, but I won't be standing around with my thumb up my arse while those bastards start tucking into that little kiddie like a Sunday joint. Come on then.' Rosen banged on the panel of the sidecar. 'Enough of the old gammon. Let's go catch us a rabbit.'

* * *

After parking the bike on the south side of the bridge, they made their way silently into Pickle Herring Street. Being so close to the river, the smog here was all-pervading, leaving its icy touch on the back of their necks and making their lungs raw with its caustic bite. Even the cobbles underfoot were slimy with its oily residue. In the dense, sepia pall, the riverside street – with its wall-mounted jibs, overhead walkways and shimmering gas lamps – had taken on the dramatic appearance of a German Expressionist film set.

'Quiet, isn't it?' said Franklin, in a hushed voice. 'Doesn't sound like the troops have arrived yet… Listen, George, we passed a police box back there. I suggest we make a cautious recce of the building, and if we get a positive sighting of Morkens, I'll go back to call it in. What do you think?'

'Sounds like a plan. Come on then. Follow me and keep tight to the wall.'

After leading them single file for a while, Harley raised a hand and pointed to a blurred rectangle of light which had suddenly appeared in the thick mist ahead of them. He hunkered down with a finger to his lips as they watched the opening grow wider. Though muffled by the smog, there was no mistaking whose voice they now heard growling out from the gloom.

'Woody, son? Where are ye?!'

'Over here,' came the muffled reply. 'Waiting for Mr Dubois, just like you said.'

'Simeon's nae coming. There's been a change of plan.'

Harley shrank back as a figure appeared just a few paces from where they were crouching, crossing the street to join the Scot at the open door.

'Stay here. Guard this door,' continued Irvine. 'The Preceptor wants me inside. Make sure you check the identity of any latecomers… here's the guest list. I'll send one of the others down to help. Keep your wits about you, now.'

Harley pulled Rosen and Franklin in close.

'Looks like we've got the right place. That Preceptor he's talking about? That's Morkens. Go and make that phone call, Alec. Solly and I will try to get an eyeball on the girl.'

'Alright. But promise me you'll wait for backup. They're probably only a few minutes away. Don't do anything stupid.'

'I promise we'll only go in before the troops arrive if it becomes absolutely necessary.'

'Solly?'

'Scout's honour,' said Rosen, giving a three-fingered salute.

'Alright then,' said Franklin. 'I'll be as quick as I can. Be careful.'

Harley watched the policeman disappearing into the gloom.

''Course, you do understand I already think it's absolutely necessary to gatecrash that little shindig, don't you?'

'Never doubted it for a moment, George. And I was never in the bleedin' Scouts neither, was I?'

'Just as long as we're singing from the same hymn sheet. As I see it, the authorities had their chance with Morkens the first time round. This is my party now. And I've got a bit of personal business to sort out with that shicer.'

'I know, mate,' said Rosen, grabbing his friend by the shoulder. 'Any way you want to play it is fine by me.'

Harley gave him an appreciative nod, then stepped in a little closer.

'Come on then, let's have a look at what you've got in that knapsack.'

While they were divvying up the weapons, a hundred yards or so up the road, DS Franklin was approaching the entrance to a short tunnel, at the end of which stood the police box he was heading for. What he didn't know, as he ploughed on through the fog, was that he was heading straight into the path of two of Irvine's cronies, sent to scan the riverside for any signs of unwanted guests. As he emerged from the tunnel, the distorting effect of the smog on the san toys' silhouettes gave the policeman the reassuring but false impression he'd stumbled across the backup sent by Scotland Yard.

'Hello, there!' he shouted, holding up his warrant card for identification. 'DS Franklin, Vine Street. Have you chaps been sent by Commander Taylor?'

39

HAVING DISPATCHED ROSEN to cover the riverside elevation, Harley decided to try to bypass the guard on the door by gaining entry to the premises directly opposite the warehouse – noting that the two buildings were linked via an enclosed walkway which spanned the street at first-floor level. This proved far easier than expected, and before long he was up the stairs and into a vacant storage area, redolent with the aromatic spices ingrained into the old timber of its floorboards. He took the opportunity to check over the weapon he'd chosen from Solly's cache.

He was no stranger to the model – the Webley Mk VI had been the standard-issue sidearm back in his trench-raiding days. Top-break, double-action, six rounds: a reliable bit of kit. Though usually averse to carrying a 'barker' on civvy street, Harley knew it would be suicidal to go up against the combination of Irvine's crew and the psychopathic Morkens with just a set of brass knuckles for protection. And if he was going to carry a firearm, what better than one which had saved his skin on numerous occasions during the war?

One last thing was needed before he went over the top. Doc Shandy's pick-me-up had long since worn off, and although he could feel the adrenaline beginning to raise his pulse, he knew his jag the previous night was bound to have had an effect on his stamina. There was no doubt he'd need to be at the top of his game over the next hour or so. He quickly searched out the Benzedrine from his field kit pouch and chewed down a couple of the bitter-tasting tablets.

Here we go then, Morkens... He hefted the Webley's reassuring weight. *Let's see what you've got, you shicer.*

Keeping low, so as not to be spotted through the latticed windows, Harley made his way along the enclosed walkway above the street and then down some wooden steps, at the bottom of which he found a door, secured with a heavy padlock.

He placed his ear to this door.

Inside he could hear the deep, rhythmic boom of a drum, throbbing beneath the dissonant fusion of strings and some harsh, medieval-sounding wind instrument. Every so often this unsettling music was accompanied by a burst of frenzied wailing.

The ceremony had evidently begun.

Removing the set of picks from his field kit, Harley set to work on the lock. But as he inserted the tension wrench into the opening, the shackle simply sprang open. He smiled – someone had obviously been careless when locking up. He replaced his tools, drew his weapon and teased open the door.

A gust of warm air brought with it the sickly perfume of incense. The warehouse was smaller than he'd expected, illuminated by flaming torches and large wrought-iron braziers, giving it a sinister, infernal quality. The walls were draped with large red-and-black hangings, embroidered with magical sigils and a unicursal hexagram he recognised as the emblem of the AOU – Fedor von Görlitz's secret occult society.

As he peered in through the doorway, a cavorting group of cult members passed close by – men and women, some draped in rough pelts, others naked apart from skilfully crafted animal masks with sinister, grinning features. This enraptured pack shrieked as they frolicked to the unearthly music; falling on each other; biting and groping; peeling off in pairs to retreat to the shadowy corners of the room. Harley was alarmed to see that one of the women, lost in the throes of some orgiastic ecstasy, had recently had her sternum branded with the AOU symbol, the hexagram showing as an angry red welt on her otherwise flawless skin.

He opened the door a little wider and slipped inside, hoping to go unnoticed among the frenzied revelry. After the cold night air, the room felt hot and stuffy. Concealing himself behind one of the large wall hangings, he ditched his hat and coat and made a quick scan of the room.

There! On the stage at the far end. Sat upon an ornate throne. The rangy, confident bearing; the ivory-pale skin – he was sure that was Professor Morkens, even if the face was hidden behind that goat mask of dark burgundy leather, the colour of congealed blood.

This is all too easy, thought Harley, searching out a gap in the crowd where he could get a clear shot at his nemesis. *A round in his leg to incapacitate him and then whistle for Solly. All too easy by far...*

And indeed, it was. For, just as he levelled the Webley at the stage, the figure rose up from the throne and clapped his hands, silencing the musicians.

'Well, well! What have we here?'

That voice. It was definitely Morkens. And the criminal lunatic was now pointing a twisted skeletal finger directly towards him.

'George! So pleased you could make it. Don't be shy now, do come forward and show yourself.'

Silently cursing his hesitation in firing, Harley stepped out from his hiding place and took a few tentative steps towards the stage, the revolver held out before him. His appearance provoked a wave of frenzied chattering among the bizarre congregation.

'How predictable you are,' said Morkens.

Harley made a quick assessment of his surroundings, noting a group of monkey-masked individuals dotted among the crowd. Unlike the rest of the congregation, these were fully clothed, sober and alert – here, then, was the professor's bodyguard. Irvine among them, no doubt.

'Predictable?' Harley found it hard to keep the emotion from his voice. After all, regardless of the circumstances, here he was, face-to-face with the monster responsible for Cynthia's murder – the mere squeeze of a trigger away from vengeance. From justice.

He steadied the gun with his left hand and took another step forward. 'How's that, then?'

'How's that?' the professor cocked his head, the goat mask exaggerating the gesture. 'Why, the way you've dutifully followed my little trail of breadcrumbs, of course. This has all been choreographed, dear boy. Every single step. Right up to choosing the correct entrance through which you'd make your appearance – unguarded, the lock not quite snapped shut. Almost too good to be true.'

The cult members broke into a little ripple of spontaneous applause as the professor stretched out his arms.

'This is all for you, George! You do hold such a dear place in our hearts, you see.'

Harley continued to move slowly towards the stage, keeping his gun trained on Morkens, as the throng of cult members parted around him. The smell of the incense was much stronger here, overpowering, adding to the overall claustrophobic atmosphere. It was a heady concoction, rich with rose and frankincense, and some other unidentifiable note lurking beneath, akin to the leathery tang of a ripe plum. There was something disconcerting about this smell, something that took him back to that infernal cellar in Morkens' farmhouse, with its gruesome specimen jars... and those *noxious candles*.

He noted with concern the thick smoke swirling from the brass censers on the stage. More of the professor's insidious narcotics, no doubt. No wonder the congregation were so enraptured. He shook his head and took a few deep breaths, trying to regain the keen edge to his concentration.

'That's enough of your old madam!' he yelled. 'If you have led me here, then more fool you.'

As Harley went to cock the hammer on the revolver, he was puzzled to discover his fingers had started to go numb. He glanced around him at the jeering crowd closing in on him, their grotesque masks strangely distorted now, as though reflected in the back of a spoon.

With a creeping sense of dread he rubbed at his eyes, attempting to clear his vision.

'Where's... where's the girl?!' he shouted, his voice sounding strangely distant.

'My dear boy, are you quite alright?' said Morkens, with a malicious chuckle. 'You're looking rather peaky.'

Now Harley felt hot hands begin to paw at him from behind as a ripple of derisive laughter swept through the crowd. He jerked around in an unsteady circle, wielding the gun and thrusting the cult members back with his free hand.

'Where's the girl, I said?!'

'Little Poppy?' The professor pointed to his left. 'Why, she's here of course...'

His brain now foggy with the narcotic incense, Harley had to concentrate hard to bring the stage back into focus. He looked to where Morkens was pointing. He saw now that what he'd taken to be sculptures on either side of the stage were, in fact, the naked bodies of a young man and woman, held in a deep trance-like state. They were bent backwards across a small platform, their limbs contorted in strange, mannequin-like angles, each bare torso providing an improvised table for a large, silver cloche.

'Aren't they fascinating? My living altars. I got the idea from a colourful little soiree I once attended in Berlin, thrown by a promiscuous Hungarian countess. As a matter of fact, Fräulein Blau was there, I seem to remember... By the way, I hear your assistant killed Blau this evening, then took her own life. I must say, George, you do seem to bring the most frightfully bad luck to anyone who gets close to you.'

With a sinister smile, Morkens walked over to the male altar and drew a long fingernail down his muscular abdomen.

'Ah! The beauty of youth. The irony is, of course, it's utterly wasted on them. These two are brother and sister. Exquisite specimens, don't you think? The children of a devout member of our congregation; an offering. Such dedication to the cause... So, you were asking after the little girl?'

Morkens held up a hand to silence the murmuring of the crowd and then, with a dramatic flourish, whipped off the lid of the large cloche resting on the youth's chest.

From the floor came gasps of appreciation and delight as he revealed the pitiable figure of a naked little Poppy, trussed up like a Sunday joint on the silver platter.

Desperate to get a closer look at the kidnapped girl, Harley began to jostle his way to the front of the stage, fighting off the clawing hands of the frenzied congregation, who'd been galvanised by the sight of their cannibalistic offering.

There! She was still moving, struggling against her bindings, her little eyes showing their whites in panicked terror.

Still a chance, then.

'You sick bastard!' he yelled, struggling to make himself

heard above the baying crowd. 'You cut her free, Morkens! Cut her free! I'm taking her with me!'

'Oh, I think not. Look at her. So pale, so plump. Quite irresistible, don't you think?' He pinched the little girl's flank. 'Yes, she's fattened up most admirably; such a scrawny little thing when she came to us. Oh no, she's not for you, dear boy.'

'Then...'

Harley faltered. Close to the brass censers, he was now exposed to the full effects of their noxious smoke, and he found the grotesque features of the child-killer's mask had begun to swim before his eyes. He concentrated with all his might to stop the room spinning, counting silently in his head, grasping hold of each precise second, so as not to unravel fully into the stupefying embrace of the drug.

'Then what, George?'

'Then... you... die,' he mumbled. But it was all he could do to keep the Webley held up before him, let alone aim it accurately.

'Not just yet, I think... Irvine!' Morkens had directed his instruction to the back of the room. 'Would you bring him here, please?'

Harley now turned drunkenly and watched as DS Alec Franklin was pushed forward through the jeering crowd, his hands tied behind his back and Irvine's cut-throat razor poised at his windpipe.

40

'IT'S QUITE SIMPLE. Relinquish your weapon immediately, or your friend there will have his throat cut.'

As he tried to focus on Franklin, Harley felt his grip on reality slipping away from him. The glint of the razor's blade in the guttering torchlight; the swirling kaleidoscope of leering, bestial faces; the deranged contortions of the cavorting congregation – all appeared as some grotesque tableau, flickering through the distorting lens of a mutoscope.

The comforting idea suddenly occurred to him that it might all be just some hellish opium trip, and at any moment he would awake, safely ensconced in his parlour back in Bell Street.

But when he saw the razor slice through Alec Franklin's earlobe, clothing Irvine's hand in a burgundy glove, he realised the horror surrounding him was all too real... and that the game was up.

'Stop!' he shouted, letting the revolver thud to the floor and raising his hands. 'Enough!'

'How wise,' said Morkens. 'That'll do for now, Irvine.'

The Scot relinquished his hold on Franklin, using the policeman's gaberdine to wipe the blood from his hand. The DS crumpled to his knees, clamping a hand to his bloody face.

'Pat him down and then bring him up here,' said Morkens to the two monkey-faced heavies who'd swept in through the crowd to seize Harley by the arms.

Having confiscated his gun and brass knuckles, they hauled him up the steps.

'Give me the pistol… You may let go of him now, he'll be quite powerless.'

The private detective stood before the child-killer, swaying a little, his head slumped on his chest.

'Behold, my brethren! George Harley!'

This was met with whoops of delight from the faithful.

'This man has the impudence to mock the gods of antiquity!'

A collective intake of breath. Gasps of disbelief.

'Mark you well the consequences of such hubris, for this man's fate will be a lesson for you all.'

As the crowd broke out in a clamour of admiration, Harley fought hard to keep his focus on the goat-faced figure before him, like a seasick man fixing on a point on the horizon. As he did so, he realised the initial overpowering effects of the incense had begun to fade somewhat; a puzzling development, seeing as he was closer than ever to those brass censers.

He took a brief glance at the audience – the masked congregation seemed to be acting as crazed as ever. So why was it he could feel his own faculties beginning to return? Was it his pen yen habit? If the professor's narcotic were opium-based, then maybe his tolerance to the drug might be helping.

No. Of course – it was the Benzedrine. The amphetamine had obviously started to kick in.

Emboldened by this thought, Harley surreptitiously broke through the foil on the tube of tablets in his jacket pocket.

Under the guise of a cough, he tossed two more into his mouth and quickly chewed them down.

His head was definitely clearing, and at close quarters he now noticed the professor's mask looked bulkier than those of the congregation, with thick straps clamping it under the chin.

He looked to the bodyguard at his side.

Yes! The monkey masks were constructed in a similar way. He thought back to Oona's note:

Remember – they gather where the pickled herrings are stored. And don't forget: a mask not only disguises!

Some kind of air-filtering mask, then, like the Hypo helmets they'd used in the trenches? Alright, that was something to work with. Maybe a glimmer of light at the end of the tunnel.

He turned to the baying crowd and yelled for silence.

'This shicer doesn't have any mystic powers!' He pointed to the brass censers. 'It's not magic; it's just chemistry. He's drugged you all! This bloke's just some crusty old university lecturer. Ancient gods and demons? He couldn't summon a fart!'

Moving quickly to the front of the stage, Morkens raised his hands to quell the jeers and catcalls this speech had provoked.

'Silence, my brethren!'

Harley, meanwhile, took the opportunity to shuffle a few steps away from his guards, keeping a close eye on the professor, who now walked over to the trussed-up Poppy and snatched up something placed beside her on the silver platter.

The doll!

Blau's dying words returned to him:

Die Puppe… Save the girl… and you save Germany.

It was a sobering call to arms, but his deliberations were interrupted by Morkens, who now mockingly thrust the toy into Harley's face.

'Whither is God?' he intoned, wiggling the doll as though it were speaking. 'We have killed him – you and I… So, how shall we comfort ourselves, hmm? Who will wipe God's blood off our hands? What festivals of atonement, what sacred games shall we have to invent?'

The professor tossed Piecrust to one side and thrust the barrel of the Webley under the private detective's chin, forcing his head up. 'Trust me, you deluded non-believer, as you watch this century unfold – if you live that long – you may regret hankering after such a godless world. I have brought you here, Harley, so that you might witness just how depraved, how gullible – how evil – your fellow man really is.'

Morkens beckoned to his audience, who dutifully applauded this account of their own shortcomings.

'Take our loyal company here tonight. Upstanding British citizens, the crème de la crème. And yet, look at them…'

He chuckled as he singled out an elderly dowager who, just at that moment, had lifted her mask to fellate one of her fellow guests at the side of the stage.

'At the promise of a little excitement, a brief moment of ecstatic release, a mystery unveiled – any such dangling bauble will do – well, you can see for yourself what they're reduced to. And these are educated people, George. The bourgeoisie, as you might term them. Just imagine what I could do with your beloved proletariat; those hordes of the disenfranchised which you and your kind hold so dear, who, in your new godless world, have lost the main check to their rapacious envy. They could be coerced into committing the most heinous of crimes. And there are so many of them, of course… Ah, but such work is for others, who will come after me. And they *will* come; you mark my words. *Après moi, le déluge!'*

The professor now strode over to the other side of the stage, where the second silver cloche rested upon the naked torso of the entranced young woman. He drew his fingernail slowly across the pale flesh between her breasts, before tapping the silver lid.

'Of course,' he said, 'there is another reason I brought you here tonight.'

Harley felt a nip of fear in his gut as it dawned on him what the serial killer might be about to reveal.

'You see, I'd also like you to experience more of that exotic emotion.' He was almost purring his words, obviously enjoying himself now. 'An emotion almost mythical to one such as myself.'

Harley kept his eye on the long fingers as they closed around the silver handle.

'Yes, I'd simply adore to further cloak you in that cumbrous mantle of *guilt…*'

The professor once more cocked that menacing goat head.

'…but not quite yet, I think.'

Was it relief or disappointment that Harley felt, as he watched that anaemic hand relinquish its hold on the silver lid?

Morkens now sprang across to the terrified Poppy, placing his spidery fingers on her pale skin. 'Understand that it is you, Harley, who must bear the responsibility for this child's sacrifice. You have been the inspiration for our ritual here today. And our brethren thank you for it.'

Sensing the approach of the ceremony's climax, the crowd made another surge forward, gathering in an excited, hushed throng in front of the stage.

'When I have snuffed out her brief, insignificant little life, our faithful brethren will partake of her body, making a sacrament of her uncorrupted flesh.'

'You pathetic animal!' said Harley, spitting out the words. 'You disgust me.'

'Disgust? Oh, how I pity you then. How frightened you must be.'

'Not of you, you sad bastard.'

'No, perhaps not,' said the professor, walking back to Harley to tip his chin up once more with the barrel of the gun. 'You're far too arrogant for that... But frightened, still. Frightened to turn your mind to that place of shadows within you, within us all.' Morkens moved closer in. 'That Stygian gloom, from whence all hungers spring. The hot foetid lair of all that writhes and squirms in that delicious slime. Of flesh torn... bloody torrents... silken, yeasty mucus... unctuous sin. Oh, my little Apollo, if you'd only allow yourself just one sip of the ecstasy of the depraved.'

He came closer still, his laboured breathing resonating loudly through the leather goat snout.

'Why don't you try it, George, hmm? Give in to temptation. Listen to the voice of our glorious Baron de Rais, whispering to you from the depths of your tortured soul. Do you hear him? *Venez nous rejoindre!* Partake in the sweetest of sacraments: the succulent flesh of this innocent. Trust me, you will never look back.'

Harley leant in to whisper in the professor's ear: 'Fuck off! You madman.'

'Oh my!'

Morkens chuckled as he walked to the edge of the stage to address his congregation. 'Such a wasted opportunity. I offer him a banquet of the senses, and at what expense? A mere trifle – one feeble, worthless life. After all, what good do they serve, the weak, the defenceless? Oh, that ultimate liberation. That delectable power. That validation of the will which comes with the final realisation that no self has value but your own.'

Morkens raised his arms to the crowd:

'Do as thou wilt, as a great god can, O Pan!'

And they answered in unison, chanting their shrill mantra:

'Io Pan! Io Pan! Io Pan!'

'Mannikin, maiden, Maenad, man! In the might of Pan!'

'Io Pan! Io Pan! Io Pan!'

Harley yelled out to Morkens before he could continue, deliberately garbling his words.

The professor walked back to him, leaning in close, so he could hear above the noise of the crowd.

'What was that, now?'

Seizing the moment, Harley yanked at the strap under Morkens' chin, wrenching the mask from his face. As he watched the professor stumble to keep his balance, a switch tripped in the private detective's brain. Once again, he was Corporal Harley of the Essex Regiment, 13th Battalion, brawling for his life in some godforsaken enemy trench.

He ducked low and deftly spun around to deliver the full weight of his right hook into the side of the monkey-faced heavy's neck, compromising the clavicle nerves, sending the man crashing to the deck. Knowing he only had a few seconds before the second san toy made his move, he dipped low again and bowled into Morkens, grabbing at the Webley as it flew out of his grasp, then leapt to the back of the stage and fired a round into the air.

The crowd were immediately silenced.

After frantically disentangling himself from his cloak, Morkens scrambled across the stage to seize the monkey mask from the unconscious heavy. Holding it up to his face, he rose shakily to his feet and gestured with his free hand to his congregation.

Harley looked to the crowd and was alarmed to discover Irvine and two of his henchmen levelling pistols at him. With his own gun trained on the professor, he quickly donned the leather goat mask, taking in deep breaths of the filtered air. He then began to back away slowly towards Poppy.

'My, my! How exhilarating,' said Morkens, still a little breathless but regaining his composure now he'd secured the straps of the purloined mask under his chin. 'And what exactly do you intend to do now, George?'

'Free this little girl and get her away from you bunch of lunatics.'

'Oh, I think not. I mean, Irvine and his men may not have had the advantage of your specialist training, but one of them should be able to hit the target, wouldn't you think? You won't get out alive, dear boy.'

'Then maybe I'll just put a bullet through that sick brain of yours, and be done with it,' said Harley, cocking the hammer on the Webley.

41

'I F YOU SHOOT me now, George, you'll miss the chance of seeing my little surprise.'

The professor edged back towards the living altar at the side of the stage and placed his hand on the silver cloche. His gleaming, jet-black eyes seemed somehow to have melded with the simian mask.

'Stand still!' barked Harley.

'But don't you want to see her one more time? It must torment your every waking hour, not to mention your nightmares. You poor boy.'

Harley watched in horror as Morkens' fingers drew closer to the polished handle.

'You'll be pleased to hear I've perfected the preservation technique. After all, I had all those darling little boys to practise on... Just one little glimpse? No?'

Harley's voice began to crack with emotion as he took a step forward. 'I swear to you, I'll put one in your gut, you shicer!'

Morkens raised his hands in submission.

'Ah, well. More's the pity. I think we might all have enjoyed the drama of such a moment. But calm yourself, now. You mustn't provoke my men. I'd hate to see you shot… No, really. You see, it's imperative to me you walk out of here alive, so that you can spend all those tormented years riddled with guilt.'

The professor gave a menacing chuckle.

'So, I have a little proposition for you – a most generous one, I think you'll agree. I'm going to allow you to walk out of here, unmolested. You may even take my little surprise with you, if you wish; so that you might become reacquainted with your loved one in the privacy of your own home.'

'Enough of this bollocks! You said it yourself – I've had the training, Morkens. If push comes to shove, I'll be taking out at least a couple of you lot before you get to me. And you, Professor, you will be first to go… I'm taking the kid now. I'm going to cut her free and walk her out of here. If we all behave ourselves, no one gets shot.'

'Oh, no. I can't let you do that. You see, we intend to eat that little girl, George; I thought I'd made that quite clear?'

The professor bent down so he was in Poppy's line of sight.

'We're going to gobble… her… all… up!'

The child's eyes widened in terror at the leering monkey mask, as an excited wave of muttering rippled through the crowd.

Harley stepped between them, his pistol raised.

'And I'm telling you, that ain't happening.'

'Oh dear. We appear to have arrived at somewhat of an impasse.'

'Not for long.'

Harley produced a police whistle from his jacket pocket and flipped up the goat mask.

Morkens chuckled again. 'And what on earth are you going to do with that?' He pointed to DS Franklin, lying inert on the floor in the midst of the crowd. 'I'm afraid your little policeman friend is well past coming to your rescue.'

Harley smiled and put the whistle to his lips.

The long, harsh note drew a silence to the room… soon broken by the professor's sarcastic handclap.

'Oh, well done. Bravo!'

'Shush!' said Harley, pointing to the back of the stage. 'Watch…'

All the monkey heads now turned to study the backdrop, from where a curious sound could be heard, something akin to heavy balls being rolled along a metal walkway.

'Well, George?'

But the private detective had taken advantage of this distraction to slip quietly across the stage towards the trussed-up Poppy.

'Irvine! See to him!'

Of course, Harley made such an easy target, with his back turned to them as he scooped up the little girl in his arms; but it was at that precise moment that the timer fuses in Solly's grenades reached their detonators.

A thunderous explosion ripped through the warehouse.

The two large loading bay doors tore through the backdrop, demolishing the brass censers, and scattering red-hot coals across the stage. The resulting panic of the crowd was added to by the sudden appearance of a gun-toting Solly Rosen, framed in a glimmering halo of mustard-coloured smog, roaring crazily as he sprayed a deafening flurry of bullets into the air from his Thompson gun.

The shock tactics paid off handsomely. Fearing they were under attack from a platoon of the British Army, Irvine and his men flung their weapons aside and joined the desperate rabble of cult members clambering for the exit.

The explosion – and the blast of fresh air it drew into the hall – was enough to stir the wounded DS Franklin back to full consciousness. He came to just as one of the heavies was barrelling towards him through the throng, working frantically at the strap of his monkey mask. Although still disorientated, Franklin had no trouble recognising the grizzled features of the Glaswegian Irvine as the mask came away.

He kicked out instinctively at the fleeing villain, sending him careering to floor. The hardman hit the deck with the full force of a fourteen-stone san toy running at full pelt, winding him badly and knocking him out of action. He lay there groaning, among a carpet of strewn monkey nuts.

Seeing his chance, the groggy Franklin forced himself to his hands and knees, clumsily searching for his handcuffs. When he looked up, he saw one of the congregation had stopped to attend to Irvine – a young woman with a striking figure, clearly visible through her transparent chiffon gown, her strawberry-blonde tresses a perfect match for the elaborate fox mask that covered her face.

Desperate to apprehend the mobster before he escaped, Franklin redoubled his efforts, stumbling through the crowd now, ricocheting off the fleeing cult members, some of whom seemed to have completely lost all sense of direction in their panicked state.

But when he got there, the fox-headed woman had disappeared.

The Scot lay fitting on his back, a new gaping maw opened up for him in his neck with his own cut-throat razor, which lay discarded on the floor by his head. Franklin watched in horror as the lifeblood pumped out of the villain in ever-diminishing spurts, the monkey nuts now floating slowly away from him in the ooze of a viscous burgundy puddle.

Back at the side of the stage, with little Poppy now swaddled in his jacket and lodged safely beneath the musicians' podium, Harley removed the goat mask and took a moment to clear his head with a long draught of the chilled night air flooding in from the river.

He realised there'd been a lull in the clattering gunfire. Fearing Rosen might have succumbed to some of Morkens' devilry, he retrieved the Webley from his waistband and spun around, preparing himself for the worst.

But Rosen was fine – there he stood at the front of the stage, Tommy gun in one hand, proudly surveying the results of his handiwork like the poster boy for a Howard Hawks movie.

It was Osbert Morkens who was in trouble.

Some of the hot coals from the toppled censer had landed on the train of his cloak. Within seconds the velvet had begun to smoulder violently, and now, as Harley looked on, the child-killer was beating frantically at the flames threatening to engulf him.

Harley looked around the hall. In such a state of confusion, who could ever testify to exactly what had gone on there? Franklin and Rosen were probably the only credible witnesses in the place. One shot, and Morkens would be snuffed out. One simple squeeze of the trigger.

He raised the Webley and took careful aim.

Then – and Harley could never decide if this was due to the residual effects of the incense or some kind of pen yen flashback – he found his vision beginning to mutate, the chaos of the warehouse swirling away to be replaced by a shimmering, scintillating pattern of brightly coloured geometric shapes. He closed his eyes and was immediately plunged back into that star-speckled universe.

And there she was.

Cynthia.

Beautiful. Serene.

And he could hear her voice. Gently pleading with him *not to do it*. Not to kill an unarmed man in cold blood. Not to succumb to the same evil morals as Morkens and his ilk.

Harley was wrenched from this vision by a hand placed

on his shoulder and another voice – equally mellifluous – purring in his ear:

'What are you waiting for, my little tin soldier?'

He opened his eyes to an elegant vixen mask, framed by cascading auburn hair.

'You finally have him, George. Shoot him… Kill him now!'

Harley turned back to the stage, his attention suddenly drawn to something lying at the professor's feet – the silver platter, its cloche dislodged slightly to reveal tresses of raven-black hair.

His hand began to shake, the trigger now slick with sweat.

Oona's cool hand was on his wrist, steadying the gun's aim.

'It's quite simple. Go on. You've done it before. Kill him. Kill the professor.'

He thought of that night at the sewage works. Whispers' watery eyes pleading at him from behind the thick pebble lenses… Of little Eddie Muller, standing terrified in his sailor suit… the bloody footprints on the carpet.

Harley lowered the pistol.

Up on stage, now fully ablaze, Morkens let out a wailing, savage scream.

Harley watched in wonder as the professor's leather mask fell away in smouldering pieces, exposing his tortured face, its blackened skin seething with blistering welts behind a flaring mantle of ravenous fire.

Then, for the briefest of moments, their eyes met; and even in the agonising throes of his immolation, Morkens' stare was something of pure evil, the chilling conduit to a nihilistic void.

Then the moment was over.

With a macabre rictus stretching his blistering lips, the professor's ruined head drew back in an involuntary spasm. He began to thrash across the stage in a hellish tarantella, engulfed in flames, his claw-like hands raking the air in agony as his muscles contracted in the searing heat of the blaze.

There could be little doubt that these were the last dying moments of the nefarious Nursery Butcher.

As the nauseating stench of burning flesh reached his nostrils, Harley finally awoke from his stunned trance.

'Solly!' he bellowed. 'Put the shicer out!'

But before Rosen could get to him, the professor let out one last harrowing cry, and then, finally consumed by the flames, collapsed to his knees and tumbled headlong through the open loading bay doors.

Harley scrambled up on stage and raced to the opening.

But Morkens was gone. Swallowed whole by the filthy yellow smog.

He turned back to find Oona. But she too had disappeared.

* * *

'Did you see him go in?' asked Harley, as Rosen joined him on the small gantry overlooking the river.

'Can't see anything in this muck. But I heard the splash as he went down.'

Harley leant over the rail, trying to peer into the water below. 'You sure?'

'Where else could he have gone? You saw it, he went up like a lucifer – which is about right for that dybbuk, ain't it?' Rosen spat over the side. 'The state he was in? The temperature of the water? Nah, that's the end of Professor Morkens. And good riddance, is what I say.'

'I've got to be sure. Go and get a torch.'

'We ain't got a soddin' torch, George. And it wouldn't help anyway – you can't see your hand in front of your face out here.'

'I should have plugged him while I had the chance.'

'It makes no difference, mate,' said Rosen, giving his friend's shoulder a gentle shake. 'Listen to me – it's over. He's gone. You saw him – his skin was hanging off him. He would have been dead before he hit the water. That fucker has finally got what he deserved… Hold on!' He pointed in the air at the distant clanging of police cars. 'That'll be the cavalry – late as usual.'

'Alright,' said Harley, with a resigned sigh. 'We'd better do a bit of housekeeping before the bogeys get here. Lose that Tommy gun in the drink and then go and get your little bag of goodies.'

'What, just dump it? These squirters don't come cheap, you know.'

'Listen, son. If you're still holding that Thompson gun when the Cossacks arrive, they'll throw away the key. Launch it, now! And any Mills bombs you've got left. Then go and grab the kid; she's hidden under the podium at the side of the stage. After that, check on Alec – he got roughed up and then had a taste of Irvine's cut-throat, but I saw him back on his feet just now. I'm hoping he missed your little Tony Camonte impression, otherwise we've got a bit of explaining to do.'

'Missed it? How could he have missed it?'

'They were burning drugged incense. I'll fill you in later. Now, come on, pronterino. There's something I've got to do.'

A few minutes later, Harley was crouching silently on the stage as an exhausted Franklin appeared, clutching a blood-soaked handkerchief to the side of his face.

'What happened to waiting for the backup to arrive, George? It's a wonder any of us survived… George?'

'Give him a moment,' said Rosen, approaching from behind, with Poppy clinging tightly to his neck. He nodded to the silver cloche by Harley's foot.

'Dear God!' said Franklin, spotting a tress of black hair. 'Is that…?'

'Schtum,' said Rosen, quietly, taking a step closer to Harley. 'Listen, mate. Don't you think you should leave that to us?'

Harley took a deep breath.

'It's not her.'

'Are you sure?' asked Franklin.

'What, this?' Harley turned and tossed the mannequin's head towards the policeman.

'Oi!' shouted a Rosen. 'You'll scare the kid.'

'Well, you shouldn't have brought her up here,' said Harley, testily. 'Go and hand her over to the bogeys. She needs to be somewhere safe and warm.'

'Good grief!' Franklin said solemnly, moving the discarded dummy's head with his foot.

'What's up, Detective Sergeant?' said Harley. 'Lost your sense of humour?'

'I don't really think it's something to joke about, George.'

'Maybe that's for me to decide, eh?'

'Don't listen to him, Alec,' said Rosen. 'He don't mean anything by it. He's upset.'

Harley scoffed at this inspired insight from his old friend and pulled out his packet of Gold Flake – just as a clutch of enthusiastic bobbies, led by two CID men, tumbled in through the entry doors to the hall.

'Here we go – Fred Karno's army,' he said, sparking up his cigarette. 'Better late than never, I s'pose... Right then, Alec. Off you go with your pals. That wound's going to need stitching.'

'D'you think?'

'Oh yeah,' said Rosen, with a sharp intake of breath. 'That's going to leave a lovely little souvenir, that is. You'll look like a proper tough.'

'And listen,' said Harley. 'Thanks for showing up tonight, mate. You didn't have to – it's appreciated.'

'Well, I'm not so sure I had much choice, given the circumstances.' Franklin smiled and held a hand to little Poppy's cheek. 'The main thing is we got this little one back safe and sound.' He gave a sigh and looked to the demolished doors of the loading bay. 'The problem's going to be trying to explain what happened here to the superintendent. What with Solly's little dramatic entrance.'

'I don't know what you're talking about,' said Harley. 'You were out cold for most of the event.'

'Didn't you say they were burning a load of dope, George?' added Rosen.

'Heaps of it. Strong stuff an' all. Messes with your memory, that kind of thing.'

Franklin smiled. 'Now you come to mention it, it is all becoming a little foggy.'

'There you go. Good boy.'

'Besides,' added Rosen, gently stroking the now-sleeping Poppy's hair. 'It's the missus you should be worrying about. What's she going to say when she sees that ear of yours, eh?'

'I'm sure she'll calm down when they give him another promotion,' said Harley. 'Off you go, Detective Sergeant. And tell them about Morkens going into the water. I want them to muster the river police for a search.'

'You don't really think he might still be alive, do you?'

'Not a chance,' said Rosen. 'He was lit up like Guy Fawkes when he went in. And he was no spring chicken, was he?'

'Well, I for one would like to see a body,' said Harley.

'It shouldn't be a problem,' said Franklin, tentatively pulling the handkerchief away from his ear. 'I'll get it organised... Right then, gents. It was, erm, interesting, shall we say?'

'Yeah, weren't it just?' said Harley, pulling on his cigarette with a wry smile. 'Abyssinia, Alec.'

As the policeman joined his colleagues at the entrance to the hall, Harley began to rummage through the mess left on the stage.

'Lost something?'

'Don't you remember?' Harley shook his head. 'It's probably all those clouts to the knowledge box you took in the ring.'

Harley signalled to one of the young bobbies helping to

round up the clusters of disoriented cult members.

'Constable? You got a moment?'

'Mr Harley, isn't it?' said the policeman, having joined them on the stage. 'DS Franklin said we were to offer you any assistance needed.'

'That's great, son, because we need some help searching for something. Something of great importance.'

'What are we looking for?'

'A child's doll.'

'Really?' The policeman holstered his truncheon and looked between Harley and Rosen, trying to work out if he was being made the butt of some elaborate joke. 'And it's important, is it, sir? Only, we've rather a lot on our hands here at the moment.'

'Is that right?' said an exasperated Rosen. 'And where were you lot half an hour ago when the real graft was being done? Back at the nick with your feet up, no doubt.'

'Alright, Sol, take it easy… Believe me, Constable, I wouldn't ask if it wasn't important. There's something hidden in this doll, see? Something that concerns our national security.'

'Really? Righto, sir,' said the bobby, unstrapping his helmet. 'A child's doll, you say? Where do we start?'

'Well, it was definitely up here on stage, that cowson Morkens had brought it along to tease the little girl with.'

'Well, there's a big hole in the boards over there, due to the explosion, no doubt. It could have fallen through. By the way, any idea what caused that explosion, Mr Harley?'

'Not a clue, son.' The private detective flashed his friend a conspiratorial look. 'Maybe the gas supply, eh? It was all a bit confusing in the heat of the moment. But listen, that doll's got to be around here somewhere. Find a way under the stage and make a start there. We'll have a go at this lot.'

'Right you are, sir. Don't you worry – if it's here, we'll find it.'

42

THE LONDON SKY was uncharacteristically clear above the river, with just a few tattered rags of cloud strung out above the main towers of the bridge. To the east, a blue-grey haze hung over the dark surface of the water, blurring the outlines of the narrow jetties and decaying wooden piles.

Harley watched as a seagull looped lazily above his head. He stood on the foreshore of Butler's Wharf, with an old pair of work trousers rolled up to the knees and his feet submerged in the greasy Thames mud, splashes of which were streaked across his bare arms and forehead. He'd been there since first light, having started further upriver, at St Olave's Wharf – directly below the location of the previous night's occult ceremony – sifting through the mud and shingle. 'Mudlarking', they called it; though, in this case, the private detective wasn't hunting for Roman coins or Georgian glassware; the particular treasure he had in mind was the burnt corpse of a serial killer and a waterlogged Kewpie doll. But he'd had no luck so far.

He decided it was time for a cigarette break, and was just

tapping out a Gold Flake when he heard someone call his name above the *putt-putt* of an approaching boat's engine.

'My God! Fellowes!' he shouted, recognising the figure standing in the prow of the River Police motor launch. 'This is a bit adventurous for you, isn't it? I thought they had you chained to that desk in Whitehall!'

'Yes, very droll, Harley,' responded the Secret Service man, with his usual deadpan demeanour. 'Found anything?'

Harley shook his head. 'Nix.'

'Well, you'd better leave it to these chaps now.' Fellowes indicated the three navy divers, busy kitting up in the stern of the boat. 'You've brought a change of footwear, I trust…? Well then, get out of those wet boots and I'll meet you up on the bridge there. I have a flask in my bag.'

Five minutes later, Harley was leaning on the balustrade of Tower Bridge, nursing a steaming cup of coffee.

'That hits the spot.'

'It has a little cognac in it,' said Fellowes. 'I thought you might need warming up. Have you had any sleep at all? It must have been a late affair at that infernal warehouse.'

'I got my head down for a couple of hours. But I couldn't really sleep, not after what happened. I wanted to get down here as soon as it was light.'

He nodded down to the motor launch, where they were bolting on one of the diver's helmets. 'Do you think they'll find anything?'

'Oh, the chances are pretty slim, wouldn't you say? I'm no expert, but I'd imagine both a child's doll and a dead body would both be swept out to the estuary on the current. I'm assuming corpses float?'

'They sink at first, until the putrefaction process creates enough gas to bring them up again. On the front, you'd sometimes see them bobbing around in the flooded shell craters, like rubber ducks.'

'Well, there you are then. You obviously know far more about it than I do.'

Harley finished his coffee and handed the cup back.

'Thanks… Listen, Fellowes, I've got something I want to ask you: that ceremony last night – did MI5 have an agent there, working undercover?'

Fellowes chuckled as he screwed the lid back on the Thermos flask. 'Come now, Harley. Are you forgetting that you no longer work for the Firm? And even if you were still on active duty, you know damn well that I'd only divulge such information to those immediately involved in the operation.'

'So, you're saying there was an operation?'

'I'm saying nothing of the sort. I'm saying that to pose such a question is a pointless exercise. Why do you ask?'

Harley thought of those Theda Bara curves beneath the chiffon robe. He sighed and rubbed the back of his neck. 'Oh, it doesn't matter. I'll work it out some other way.'

He took another look at the river, then picked up his knapsack.

'Right, the Navy boys seem to have everything in hand down there, so I think I'll make a move and catch up on my shuteye. Make sure you let me know if they turn anything up.'

'One moment, Harley. This cabaret artiste – Ilse Blau. In your opinion, was she a credible source? Do you think there really are compromising images of Hitler on that roll of film?'

'I'm sure you've had a debrief with Taylor. Blau told us that the little girl's doll could save Germany. Those were her dying words. Why would she lie?'

'Well then, having seen the latest intelligence from Berlin, let's hope, for all our sakes, that little doll comes to light.'

Down on the motor launch the suited diver gave a thumbs-up with his gloved hand, then climbed down the last few rungs of the ladder to disappear into the inky swell of the Thames.

After enjoying a few uncharacteristically ruminative pints with Solly Rosen at the Bag O'Nails, Harley arrived back home at Bell Street at around nine o'clock that night. He'd already teased open the soggy newspaper wrapping of his fish supper, and as he mounted the steps to his front door he popped another hot chip into his mouth.

Needs more vinegar, he thought, wiping the grease from his fingers on his trousers as he searched for his key.

'Not me – the chips,' he mumbled, in case the fates were listening. Then immediately wondered whether he'd actually muttered it out loud.

By Christ, he was tired! The kind of tired that, if you were away from your bed, it felt like some kind of bone disease, but if you had the downy in your sights you could almost relish it – like the ache before a sneeze.

He kicked the door closed behind him and tossed his hat onto the newel post.

Moloch, his shabby tomcat, came plodding heavily down the stairs, his one chartreuse-coloured eye fixed determinedly on the packet of fish and chips in Harley's hand.

'Alright, you old cove. I'll save you a bit, I promise.'

Then the old black cat did something he hardly ever did. He stopped halfway down the stairs and delivered a long, hoarse meow. It was almost if the old tom was trying to tell him something.

When Harley walked into the kitchen, he got an idea of what that something might have been.

Oona.

There she was, sitting at the kitchen table, with a Mona Lisa smile and a bottle of champagne in an ice bucket – which she must have brought with her, because he certainly didn't possess such an item. He didn't ask her how she'd got in. Or what she was doing there. Or any of the other questions he'd previously asked himself about her. It might have been because he was so tired, but it just didn't seem important at that moment.

They popped open the champagne, which at first invigorated him, and then got him drunker than it should have done for a card-carrying lush. They talked for ages. Or rather, she talked, and Harley listened, entranced by her stories and her seemingly all-encompassing knowledge of a whole host of subjects. As they progressed to whisky, she regaled him with the histories of the philosophers, ancient civilisations and the lost wonders of antiquity. Fuelled by the alcohol, her wild eyes flared with passion, and Harley found himself inexplicably aroused by the alluring blush he noticed creeping up the alabaster contours of her slender neck.

Then – he wasn't sure just how much longer – he became aware of her teasing him for his struggles to stay awake and, a few minutes later, she was pulling him up the stairs, shedding her scarlet, Spanish-heeled shoes with abandon as she went.

Oona gasped with joy on spotting the large cast-iron, claw-foot tub and insisted on drawing a steaming bath for them both, adding to the water a few drops from an ornate crystal perfume bottle she had in her handbag.

She stripped in seconds, standing naked before him on the chequered tile floor without the merest hint of modesty. She then turned her attention to his clothes, pulling at the buttons greedily as he stood there like some virgin schoolboy, dumbfounded at the perfection of her body. He couldn't quite get his head around it. She was like some Greek sculpture come to life. Unearthly. The flawless skin; the taut, upturned breasts; the slender muscled limbs; the subtle curve of her abdomen leading to the small flash of fiery hair between her thighs. Somehow her naked body seemed to defy the normal restrictions of flesh and bone. To his drunken mind it was like some magician's trick, and for a few dizzying, intoxicated seconds, he was reminded of the summoning of Helen of Troy in *Doctor Faustus.*

But then, somehow, they were squeezed into the bath, with Oona raising suds in the hair on his chest, her hand gliding under the water like a fish, teasing with her fingers now instead of words.

And then it was his turn to lead her, up one more flight of stairs, to his bedroom; to slip between the cool sheets, where he discovered, remarkably, that he was no longer tired at all.

* * *

Harley awoke in the morning to find Oona already up, busily dressing in front of the wardrobe mirror. He was relieved he hadn't woken himself with a shout – something which had become a regular occurrence since he'd glimpsed Morkens in the back of that cab at Piccadilly Circus.

'Going so soon?'

'It's half nine, George. I've things to do.'

Her reply was businesslike, without emotion.

'No time for a spot of breakfast?' he said, trying to read her mood.

'Not this time.'

She gave him a brief smile. Which went some way towards reassuring him.

'But listen,' she said, as though suddenly realising she should make an effort, 'I had great fun last night. We really should do it again.'

'Don't rush off like this.' Harley patted the bed. 'Come here a minute. I want to talk to you.'

Oona gave a little disgruntled sigh, then put the hairbrush down on the dressing table and perched herself on the side of the bed.

'What is it, my little tin soldier?' She combed her fingers through his hair, leading him to close his eyes and give a little purr. 'Missing me already? I don't want you getting all infatuated, now. That would be most tedious.'

'Infatuated? Behave!' He propped himself up on the pillows. 'It's nothing like that… I just… well, I hardly know anything about you.'

'Am I to be interrogated, Corporal Harley?'

Harley narrowed his eyes at her – he still wasn't wholly comfortable with being called that. It reminded him too much of Cynthia.

'Come on, George – I haven't got all day. What is it you wish to know?'

'Well… your name, for starters.'

'My name? Well, I know a lot of people don't like their own names, but I rather like mine, actually. If you must know, I was named after the Irish faerie queen. Although, I believe she's Oonagh with a GH at the end. Apparently, she was the most beautiful of all the faeries, beguiling anyone she met… But she had her dark side as well: every seven years she had to pay a tithe to the underworld, which she would honour with one of her mortal lovers. So, be warned.'

Harley laughed and reached across for his packet of Gold Flake.

'That all makes absolute sense,' he said, striking the lucifer match with his thumbnail and holding the flame to his cigarette. 'But I actually meant your surname.' He pulled heavily on the smoke, savouring the first hit of the day. 'I mean, we've… you know…' He rubbed the back of his neck, searching for the right phrase. 'With everything that's happened… well, I don't even know your full name.'

Oona stood up now, cocking her head with a frown.

'Are you teasing me? You know, I don't always get sarcasm. It one of my little quirks. Goes over my head.'

'I swear I'm not teasing you. I genuinely don't know your surname. How could I?'

She sat back down on the side of the bed, closer to him this time, clasping his hand gently in hers.

'Oh dear! I assumed you knew… Why, my surname is Morkens, of course. I'm his daughter, George.'

43

HORACE DEWHURST WATCHED with quiet satisfaction as, with a seemingly effortless twist of his oar, the lighterman teased the low barge into position, allowing the river's current to draw it alongside the small island of boats, which floated like a cluster of black water beetles near the shore of Gallions Reach. He closed his eyes for a moment and listened to the soothing *flop flop* of the water's play, as the meagre warmth of the morning sun caressed his face.

Dewhurst was pleased the weather had cleared – having had his lungs ravaged by German gas during the war, he always suffered so with the London Particulars; after all, having just started a new job, he could ill afford to take any time off due to sickness.

He savoured the thought for a moment: a new job – after almost two years of unemployment. All those futile hours spent at the Labour Exchange; the sleepless nights calculating how to stretch what remained of their savings; the endless days spent pounding the pavement or frittered away on park benches and in library reading rooms – anywhere to get away from that look of Norma's, with its unspoken accusation. Two years of feeling worthless, impotent. And now, finally, a job.

Of course, Norma hadn't been impressed.

'Whatever has it come to, Horace? Nightwatchman at a brickyard? And to think where you would have been by now if you'd have stayed at Fuller & Twigg's.'

But, of course, he hadn't stayed at Fuller & Twigg's – how could he have done? He'd been as keen to volunteer as the next man; eager to do his duty. And now, with his disability, he couldn't possibly face the daily commute to the City. Even during a rare 'quiet period', as he called it, when he might be free for a day or two from the debilitating cough, he just didn't have the stamina anymore. Ah well, there was no sense in dwelling on the gloomy side.

Come on, old son, up you get. There's a hot supper and a soft bed waiting for you at home.

As Dewhurst eased himself up from the bench – with a little more trouble than he would have liked – something lolling around at the water's edge caught his eye. As the object tilted with the swell, his heart tripped a little in his chest.

Was that a face?

Feeling a little flurry of trepidation, he looked for someone to share the discovery with. But it was early, the only other soul about was the lighterman, and he was too far across the water to be of any assistance.

So, Dewhurst allowed his morbid curiosity to draw him to the narrow flight of steps, and, taking care not to slip on the ragged green fringes of algae, he climbed down to the foreshore. Having negotiated the rotting timbers and slime-covered rocks, he soon made it to the water's edge. And there, as he fought to catch his breath, he let out a little exclamation of relief – it had been a trick of the light all along! Of course, close up, it was easy to see how the scale had been all wrong.

Yes, it had been a face he'd seen, but not the bloodless face of a drowned child – oh dear me, no – but the ceramic face of a doll.

Chuckling at his foolish imagination, Dewhurst bent down to retrieve Piecrust from the murky water. Well, now. She was a queer little thing, there was no doubting that. But her features were all intact, and with a decent wash, and Norma's deft application of a needle and thread here and there... He gently wrung the water from the cloth body and wiped the mud from the painted cheek... yes, she should scrub up just right. Valerie was visiting with little Molly at the weekend – they could both do with a bit of cheering up, bless 'em.

With the morning sun on his back and the feeling that things might finally be taking a turn for the better, Horace Dewhurst thrust the doll into his coat pocket and made his way back up the steps to head off home to his supper and his bed.

* * *

'Why on earth have you brought this dirty old thing into the house, Horace? Horace! Did you hear what I said? What is this?'

Horace snapped to from his doze by the fire to find his wife holding the shabby doll at arm's length.

'I found it, dear. On my way back this morning. It'd been washed up, on the riverbank.'

'Yes, I can well believe it, riddled with germs and vermin, I dare say. But what in God's name possessed you to bring it back home with you?'

'Well, I thought little Molly might like it. It looks of good quality to me, probably cost a pretty penny new. A good wash, and maybe you could—'

'So, it's come to this, has it? Have you no pride left, man? Isn't it enough that we've been reduced to living in this godforsaken place? Must you really go sifting through other people's cast-offs, like some vagrant on the streets?'

'Oh, come now, my dear. I think you're being a little… a little…'

Roused by his wife's rebuke, Horace now succumbed to a violent fit of coughing. But Norma Dewhurst was not a naturally compassionate woman, and any sympathy for her husband's condition had long since been exhausted by all the distasteful hawking of phlegm, the broken nights' sleep and the endless laundry of soiled handkerchiefs.

'If you think for one minute that you're going to be giving this mangy old thing to our grandchild, Horace Dewhurst, then you've got another thing coming.'

To demonstrate the finality of this pronouncement, Norma tossed little Piecrust into the fire, wiped the invisible germs from her hands, and strode purposefully out of the parlour.

At first the doll's damp clothing merely smouldered, issuing little plumes of grey smoke. But soon the flames caught, and as they reached the tightly packed roll of celluloid hidden within, they flared with explosive violence. Horace wiped the last of the spittle from his chin and slumped back in his armchair. As he watched the little childlike figure be consumed by the blaze – its ceramic face, now charred and shattered, staring out from among the ferocious yellowy-green flames – he was overcome with an intense weariness, and a menacing premonition that things might not be taking a turn for the better, after all.

GLOSSARY OF SLANG

I have endeavoured to use authentic slang in *The Devil's Banquet*. As well as referring to contemporary fiction of the period, the following dictionaries of slang proved invaluable:

Captain Francis Grose, *A Classical Dictionary of the Vulgar Tongue* (London, 1931)
Eric Partridge, *A Dictionary of the Underworld* (London, 1949)
Jonathon Green, *The Cassell Dictionary of Slang* (London, 1998)

Abbreviations

backsl. Backslang: a type of slang where the written word is pronounced backwards (e.g. 'yob' for 'boy').
Pol. Polari: theatrical cant first used by actors, circus folk and fairground showmen. Later taken up by the gay subculture.
Rom. Romany: the language of the Romany people (Gypsies). An Indo-European language related to Hindustani.

rhy.sl Rhyming slang: a variety of slang where a word is
replaced by a phrase (usually clipped) which rhymes with
it (e.g. barnet = barnet fair = hair).

Yid. Yiddish: the historical language of Ashkenazi Jews,
based on German dialect with added words from Hebrew,
Polish, French and English.

Abyssinia Goodbye ['I'll be seeing you!']

amscray Scram [backsl.]

bogey CID detective ['Old Bogey' = the Devil]

brama A pretty woman [British Raj; *Brahma* is the supreme
God of Hindu mythology]

cackle Empty chatter, gossip [the sound made by a hen]

chazzer Pig [Yid. *chazir,* pig]

cheese it! Shut up! Stop it! [a corruption of 'cease it!']

chiv A knife, a razor [Rom. *chiv, chive,* knife]

chiv-man A criminal apt to use a knife or razor as a weapon
[see *chiv*]

clobber Clothes [ety. unknown.]

Corporal Dunlop A short rubber truncheon [Dunlop is a
rubber-tire manufacturer]

cowson A general insult, similar to 'son of a bitch'.

derby kell, derby kelly Stomach [rhy. sl. *derby kelly* = belly]

dilly boy A teenage male prostitute [abbreviation of
Piccadilly, which was well-known for its prostitution]

dinarly Money [Pol. Spanish *dinero,* money, Italian *denaro,*
money]

dreamstick An opium pipe

gammon Chatter, nonsense, cheating patter [perhaps from
tying up a ham]

gelt Money [Yid. *gelt,* money]

giddyaps Horses, horse-racing ['giddy-up!']

gonif A thief [Yid. *gannabh,* thief]

hampton The penis [rhy.sl *Hampton Wick* = prick]

ikey-mo A Jew [derogatory; from Isaac + Moses]

jane A prostitute [rhy.sl *jane shore* = whore; Jane Shore – mistress of Edward IV]

judy A woman, a girl [from Punch and Judy]

lavender, lavender boy A male homosexual [possibly from the lavender water they used]

London Particular Thick, acrid London fog, caused by air pollution

lumbered Arrested

madam, a load of old Nonsense, rubbish; flattery [possibly from shopkeepers' patter: 'Of course it will, madam']

manor A police district; a policeman's beat; a wide-boy's or criminal's patch [from 'Lord of the manor']

meshuggener Crazy, a crazy person [Yid.]

milky Cowardly, scared [allusion to its white colour]

mott A woman, girlfriend, prostitute [possibly from Old Dutch *mot*, whore]

Mr Peaslin A euphemism for the penis [the initial letter p of penis + Standard English in]

nanti Not, nothing, none [Pol. Italian *niente*, nothing]

nark A police informer [Rom. *nak*, nose]

nix Nothing [from German *nichts*, nothing]

nymph of the pave A prostitute

on velvet To be well off, living in clover

Piccadilly daisy A prostitute [Piccadilly was well-known for its prostitution]

ponce A pimp, a man 'living off immoral earnings' [possibly from French *Alphonse*, or possibly *pont* or *pontonnière*, a prostitute who works from the arches of a bridge]

pound-noteish Pompous, affected [seen as characteristics of the rich]

pronterino Quickly

put the squeak in To inform on

riah Hair [backsl. or possibly Pol. From Spanish *raya*, a parting in the hair]

rosie Tea [rhy.sl *rosie lee* = tea; Gypsy Rose Lee – American stripper]

san toys Villains, criminals, gangsters [rhy. sl. *san toys* = the boys; San Toy was the brand name of a small cigar]

schmundie The vagina [Yid.]

schmutter Clothes [Yid. *shmatte*, rags]

schtuk Trouble, bother [despite its appearance not a Yiddish word; possibly *stuck* adapted to a Yiddish model]

schtum Quiet, silent [Yid. *shtum*, dumb, voiceless]

sherlock A private detective [Sherlock Holmes]

shicer A lowlife, good-for-nothing [Yid. *scheisse*, shit]

spieler An illegal gambling club [German *spielen*, to play]

take stoppo To make a getaway

thrupennies The breasts [rhy. sl. *threepenny bits* = tits]

trade A prostitute's clients

vada To look at [Pol. Venetian *vardia*, a look]

vig, vigorish Interest on a loan, or debt [possibly Yid. *vyigrysh*, profit, winnings]

wheesht! Be quiet! [chiefly Scottish & Irish, natural exclamation]

wide Sharp-witted, shrewd; also (of clothing) flash, ostentatious [wide awake]

wide-boy Petty criminal, wheeler-dealer, minor villain [see *wide*]

yok A gentile, a non-Jew [backsl./Yid. *goy*, a gentile; from the Hebrew *goy*, a nation]

zhooshy Showy, ostentatious [Pol.]

ACKNOWLEDGEMENTS

I'd like to thank my agent, James Wills, at Watson, Little Ltd, for all his superb mentoring and expert advice, and his assistant, Megan McCreanor, for her attentive support. Thanks also go to my editor, Fenton Coulthurst, for his enthusiastic contributions; to Rufus Purdy for his early championing of the series; and, of course, to the fantastic team at Titan Books – especially Charlotte Kelly (UK) and Katharine Carroll (US), who have worked tirelessly behind the scenes on this book's promotion.

Special thanks go to Karin Goodwin for correcting the German dialogue in the novel.

Finally, I'd like to thank my wife, Susie, for her unwavering support, as well as all the family members, friends, and colleagues who have encouraged me over the years in my efforts to become a novelist.

Abyssinia!

ABOUT THE AUTHOR

Phil Lecomber was born in Slade Green, on the outskirts of South East London. Most of his working life has been spent in and around the capital in a variety of occupations. He has worked as a musician in the city's clubs, pubs and dives; as a steel-fixer helping to build the towering edifices of the Square mile (and also working on some of the city's iconic landmarks, such as Tower Bridge); as a designer of stained-glass windows; and – for the last quarter of a century – as the director of a small company in Mayfair which specialises in the electronic security of some of the world's finest works of art.

For more fantastic fiction, author events,
exclusive excerpts, competitions, limited editions and more

VISIT OUR WEBSITE
titanbooks.com

LIKE US ON FACEBOOK
facebook.com/titanbooks

FOLLOW US ON TWITTER AND INSTAGRAM
@TitanBooks

EMAIL US
readerfeedback@titanemail.com